Nikki kept her eyes lowered as she hurried along the aisles of the Louisa Lake Shop and Go looking for marshmallows. With her chin on her chest, she rounded the bottom of aisle three and ran into a cart coming the other way. Reaching behind to prevent a fall backward, she stuck her fist into a pyramid of canned soup and stumbled back as cans of chicken noodle crashed to the linoleum floor.

An arm yanked her out of the path of toppling missiles. She tumbled into her rescuer's firm torso.

"You okay?" His voice was one day away from laryngitis.

"Yeah, thanks." From under her five-dollar baseball cap and through seven-hundred-dollar sunglasses, Nikki sneaked a quick peek and righted herself. He wore jeans, a dark blue T-shirt, and a small metal amulet on a leather rope around his neck, his look reminding her of a middle-aged cowboy from a Ralph Lauren ad. Too handsome for Louisa Lake.

"Let's kick them out of the way," he said. "Like this." He used his foot to push the cans to the side of the aisle and she copied him. What else could she do? She couldn't race out the door without calling attention to herself.

Even though he was probably a customer like she was, suspicion snaked through her. If he'd been following her since Seattle, she hadn't noticed. But any solitary man raised her radar today, especially after the media's reaction to her announcement. The Goldy story had taken the front page of all publications, and the world was frantic for news of her whereabouts. Fifty thousand dollars was out there for anyone who snapped a shot of the newly retired rock legend.

Praise for *NECESSARY DETOUR*

"From the opening glitz-and-danger concert scene, this story rocked my world! Nikki's insatiable curiosity and prying antics had me laughing, while her deep need for love and stability made her story richly human. Only a man as daring and thick-skinned as sexy Pete could handle such a tough woman let alone penetrate her guarded heart. And while danger lurks around every corner for this burned-out rock-star and this hunk in wolf's clothing, their near-fatal attraction was what kept me wide awake."

~Christine M. Fairchild, author

Necessary Detour

by

Kim Hornsby

Rock On!

Kimberly

Necessary Detour

Cover Art by *Kim Mendoza*

The Wild Rose Press, Inc.
PO Box 708
Adams Basin, NY 14410-0708
Visit us at www.thewildrosepress.com

Publishing History
First Crimson Rose Edition, 2013
Print ISBN 978-1-61217-723-6
Digital ISBN 978-1-61217-724-3

Published in the United States of America

Dedication

To my father, Gord Hornsby,
who was a fine writer of letters to the editor,
newsletter articles, and emails.
This one's for you, Dad.

Chapter 1

Goldy Crossland ran on stage to the thunderous screaming of the Los Angeles crowd. The explosion of applause inside the Staple Center was the tangible evidence of their love for her—love that had fueled her drive over the years to get to this point. Soon she would desert them.

"Necessary Detour," she mouthed to the band, not waiting for her ex-husband, Burn's, reaction to the song choice. It hadn't been played since she vowed to never give it credit again. Written about a female stalker they'd called Yellow, the hit had been dropped from their repertoire when the stalker slit her wrists at a Goldy concert and bled to death.

Tonight, for personal reasons, Goldy wanted it to be the final song. A new crazed fan, code-named Shakespeare by the FBI, had threatened to kill her at the end of the concert, and, if he was successful, she was damned well going to have the last word.

The opening chords filled the cavernous arena and, recognizing the long lost song, the crowd cheered to barely tolerable decibels.

"You think you got me.
You think we're done.
You think it's over.
You haven't won."

Burn's guitar screamed with the intensity of a

locomotive as Goldy scanned the crowd, not knowing if she was staring into the face of the demon. Tonight she dared any one of them to take her on. The FBI had insisted on a bulletproof skin under her costume, and she could only hope that if it came to that, the material would save her life. Knowing that a quick bullet to the chest wasn't Shakespeare's style, she stood at the edge of the stage.

A dozen FBI agents peppered the audience searching for anyone who might have written six months' worth of heinous letters that threatened to torture his prey with unimaginable creativity. Trickling acid along her face then watching her melt was more like Shakespeare. To capture, torture, then relish in the hours, possibly days, that it took him to claim her life. That was his "fondest wish." He'd been code-named Shakespeare because he quoted the bard, but there was nothing poetic about his twisted mind.

Getting closer to the end of the song, Goldy moved to stage left where a stray bullet wouldn't hit anyone else. With only two lines left, she pulled the microphone away from her lips to make a powerful run to the end. A sharp, burning pain pierced her hand and dominoed along her arm to her shoulder, hitting her torso like a jackhammer. The pain was formidable. *Electricity. I've been electrocuted.* When her brain got the message, the hand flew open and the microphone dropped with a thud to the stage floor. *Pretend nothing is wrong. Finish the song.*

Goldy ran over to Burn's microphone, acutely aware of the one lying behind her, like the pariah it was. Agent Gateman took two steps and stopped at the edge of the stage, seconds from shutting everything down. She shook her head emphatically, calling one last shot.

Her left arm hung limp as she reached for Burn's microphone with the right. What if this was the plan? Toy with her, knowing she would persist? Then finish the kill with Burn's microphone. Leaving it on the stand, she moved in. Hearing the approaching notes, she took a deep breath to make the final run to the end. This time she was careful to keep her lips off the metal.

"It's a Necessary Detour
This detour's...Necessary!"

She punched the air with her good arm, stepped wide and threw her head back—her trademark pose that punctuated the final moment of every Goldy concert.

The applause was deafening. She'd survived the final song, despite what Shakespeare said. *"I shall end it all with your final note, my love."*

The six band members who made up the group Goldy laid their instruments down and applauded with the audience in their adoration of the international rock legend.

What they didn't know was that this was not only the last song of the tour, but the final tour in a twenty year career. The final everything. No more CD's, touring, concerts. No more Goldy.

"Goodnight, everyone!" she shouted above the din. "I—HAVE—LOVED—YOU!" Gold confetti rained over the masses as she spun a sparkly Frisbee that promised a family vacation to Hawaii.

Applause filled the arena's rafters. "Goldy! Goldy! Goldy!" Searing pain in her left arm reminded her that she'd just been electrocuted. She needed to get offstage. Taking a final bow with her partner and ex-husband, she hugged him with one arm and turned to her audience. The mass of people in front of her had been her reason for almost everything she'd done in the last twenty years. A wave to them, a bow to her band, and then Goldy left the party while she was still having fun.

Paramedics waited just out of sight, their dark blue uniforms a comfort to her worry. But it was her bodyguard, Dwayne, who lunged to catch her multi-million dollar backside before it hit the floor in a faint.

****

Faces were fuzzy, then clear, like focusing a camera. Why was she lying on the floor in the backstage area of the Staple Center? Quinn was positioned at her left elbow, her tears dropping onto her mother's sparkly costume.

"Mom! Mom! Wake up." The girl's voice gained volume with every second. No seventeen-year-old kid should have to endure as much as Quinn had in the last year.

"I'm okay, sweetie." Goldy tried to sit, but one of the paramedics motioned for her to wait.

"Just let me finish checking your stats. Almost done, Ms. Burnside."

The crowd parted and the real Burnside burst through to kneel at her feet. "Nikki!" He used her real name. "What the fuck?" Burn was eloquent in any situation.

He looked in worse shape than her, but that was no surprise. He'd always needed more coddling than anyone. "I got a shock from the microphone," she said, "but I'm fine." She'd hold to the story that it was simply an accident and Burn would believe it. "I'm still on the floor to let the paramedics do their job, nothing more."

Burn had been an unintentionally horrible husband—negligent and unfaithful but never malicious. And everything they'd been through in their marriage had been necessary to achieve this end result which she wouldn't have traded for the world. Her career and her beloved Quinn meant everything.

"Give her room." One of the paramedics waved his arms to part the crowd, while the other put away equipment.

"Thanks for your concern," she said. Being Goldy had been a sweet ride for a very long time and seeing their worried faces, she was reminded of how much her staff counted on her. For years, she'd signed their pay checks, put food on their tables, financed college for their kids, and knowing all that was going to end for them wasn't a pleasant thought. But it was a necessary detour.

"Enough." She waved away the paramedics and looked to the two bodyguards who rarely left her side. "Help me stand. I have an important announcement to make."

Chapter 2

Nikki kept her eyes lowered as she hurried along the aisles of the Louisa Lake Shop and Go looking for marshmallows. With her chin on her chest, she rounded the bottom of aisle three and ran into a cart coming the other way. Reaching behind to prevent a fall backward, she stuck her fist into a pyramid of canned soup and stumbled back as cans of chicken noodle crashed to the linoleum floor.

An arm yanked her out of the path of toppling missiles. She tumbled into her rescuer's firm torso.

"You okay?" His voice was one day away from laryngitis.

"Yeah, thanks." From under her five-dollar baseball cap and through seven-hundred-dollar sunglasses, Nikki sneaked a quick peek and righted herself. He wore jeans, a dark blue T-shirt, and a small metal amulet on a leather rope around his neck, his look reminding her of a middle-aged cowboy from a Ralph Lauren ad. Too handsome for Louisa Lake.

"Let's kick them out of the way," he said. "Like this." He used his foot to push the cans to the side of the aisle and she copied him. What else could she do? She couldn't race out the door without calling attention to herself.

Even though he was probably a customer like she was, suspicion snaked through her. If he'd been following her since Seattle, she hadn't noticed. But any solitary man raised her radar today, especially after the media's reaction to her announcement. The Goldy story had taken the front page of all publications, and the world was frantic for news of her whereabouts. Fifty thousand dollars was out there for anyone who snapped a shot of the newly retired rock legend.

A teenage boy in a Shop and Go green T-shirt jumped in to clear the aisle and re-stack the cans. "Don't worry about it, ma'am. People do this all the time."

She was careful to avoid his eyes. "Really?"

"Yup. I'll clean it up." He gathered soup like he was next in line for a promotion and Nikki smiled at his eagerness. The cowboy had disappeared. She needed to leave the store before anyone else saw her.

Rounding the aisle, she hurried to the checkout with her bags of marshmallows.

"Find everything you need today?" The super-pierced checkout girl didn't look up.

"Yes, thanks." From the corner of her eye, Nikki noticed someone move in to line behind her. The cowboy was unloading his groceries onto the conveyer belt—bread, milk, hamburger and buns, bacon, cereal, a pile of frozen dinners, and several cans of chicken noodle soup.

Nikki slid the divider back to him, their hands almost touching.

"Thanks." The husky voice again. "For some reason I'm craving chicken noodle soup." His voice held a smirk. Damn. She nodded almost imperceptibly. He wouldn't be paparazzi. They mostly stayed in L.A. and had an aura of desperation and a predatory look in their eyes. Not that she'd looked into his eyes, but he didn't fit the bill in any way, shape or form. Whoever he was, his groceries indicated he was staying in the area for at least a few meals and not eating fast food out of a rental car in a celebrity stakeout.

"Two dollars and thirty-two cents." The checkout girl put the marshmallows in a small plastic bag.

Nikki's fingers went for her Amex card until she remembered how easy it would be to trace. The cowboy cleared his throat, and Nikki glanced back before thinking. A grin teased the sides of his mouth as he pretended to be interested in the rack of magazines.

He knew who she was. Shit. Did he?

She had to get out of there. She shoved some cash to the checker. "Thanks." Not waiting for the receipt, Nikki grabbed the bag and rushed through the doors. She'd outrun him to the car. If he chased her, he was bad news. Photographers had ditched groceries before to get a shot of Goldy. It was still possible he was simply someone who recognized her. Or that he was only a man flirting in the grocery store.

Was it only a matter of time until they discovered Goldy was hiding in northeastern Washington State? She hoped not. And she hoped to hell she was wrong about this guy. The last thing she wanted was to return to L.A., and to the fallout of what she'd created in the last few days.

Hurrying to her black, nondescript SUV, Nikki switched the grocery bag to her other hand and was reminded of her diagnosis four nights earlier. "Use the hand, but carefully," the doctor said. "And hope the nerves weren't damaged." The blisters were healing nicely after two days in the Los Angeles hospital but the FBI still hadn't solved the mystery of her stalker. Los Angeles didn't feel safe anymore, and Louisa Lake was as close to a home as anything, especially now that she'd given Burn the Beverly Hills house in the settlement.

She closed the car door and waited for Quinn to exit the hardware store. Why had she risked stopping in town? Quinn wanted a can of paint to redo her bedroom at the lakehouse and needed a fishing license, and Nikki relented.

While waiting, she realized they'd forgotten marshmallows in their frenzied grocery run that morning. Toasting marshmallows to golden brown, squishy perfection over the fire pit was tradition at Louisa Lake, and Nikki was determined to proceed as normal this week for her daughter's sake. Just because the previous twenty-four hours had been a whirlwind of subterfuge, didn't mean they couldn't assume a low level of normalcy now that they were almost in the clear. Before the soup fiasco. Ugh. The only better way to call attention to the fact that Goldy was in the Shop and Go would have been an announcement over the intercom and a spotlight.

Jamming the key into the ignition, she watched Quinn stroll across the parking lot swinging the can of paint, oblivious to the emergency at hand. She'd probably chosen shocking pink or lime green, given Quinn's excitement about an entire week with her mother before starting university. Her mood had sunflowers and popsicles written all over it. She'd been singing along to the radio all the way from Seattle, harboring most of the excitement for the twosome, even though Nikki was making a valiant show of enthusiasm.

"Get in, sweetie." Nikki threw open the passenger door. "We might have one behind us."

"Fuck." Quinn slammed the door.

"No F-word or we'll have to start the swear jar." Nikki's voice was light and singsongy in spite of her worry about the cowboy.

Luckily Quinn was used to avoiding the press. She'd grown up comparing it to a game of dodge ball, the Burnside Family always "it." Today, the game had higher stakes.

If Nikki's cover was blown this early, she didn't know what she'd do. There was no plan B. Besides, she wasn't just avoiding the media. Shakespeare was still out there, and Quinn had no knowledge of a stalker. She only thought there was the usual advantage to avoiding the media bloodsuckers, both geographically and strategically.

Louisa Lake was twenty-three miles long with a two-mile expanse at its widest. From the air, it looked like a scraggly feather with numerous small bays and inlets on one side.

In the past, the Burnsides had often arrived by float plane to avoid the town. The property's appeal had been the lake's remote location and ultimately the inaccessibility of the land where they built the house. One side of the lake was not reachable by road and half of the remainder was barely accessible on old logging roads. That left a small patch dotted with cabins and houses at the feather's base. The town.

Navigating along the road that hugged the twinkling shoreline, Nikki thought about how she'd run out of the Shop and Go. "I might've been too paranoid, honey, but Gateman asked that we lay low."

"Shhh, Mom. This is my favorite part." Quinn sang to a Beyoncé song, her voice slightly off-key—a fact that made Nikki both relieved and wistful.

Louisa Lake was surprisingly quiet on that late August morning as Nikki closed the distance between herself and the lake house. Her small dog, Elvis Pugley, hung his mug out the back window, ears flapping in the wind.

"The smells flying past his nose have to be promising good times," Nikki laughed.

Quinn looked back and giggled. "Good times that involve chipmunks and lots of barking."

Turning onto an old logging road that followed the shore, they sang along to the radio.

The bumpy surface narrowed at the two-mile mark and branched off in several directions, the farthest road leading to both her place and one other property that shared the small bay. Now that the owner of that house was elderly and incapacitated, the road was rarely used.

Once inside the locked gate, they navigated another quarter mile of bumpy terrain until the dark green metal roof of Birch House was visible through the trees. Birch House. When she and Burn built it seven years ago, he'd named it for the trees that surrounded the property. Nikki simply called it home.

"Here's your castle, Goldy," Quinn teased.

"Indeed it is." As the car slid to a halt, Nikki mentally shed what still remained of the Goldy persona like last year's snakeskin. She wasn't a rock star here. She was simply Nikki Crossland. Back to where she started. The thought of her divorce brought the feelings of triumph and loss. She'd have to get used to this, as well as all the other changes meteoring toward her.

Exiting the car, Nikki reacquainted herself with one of her most cherished scents—the northern Cascade forest. The fresh, tangy scent of the Douglas firs that towered above them made her almost dizzy with euphoria. The sight of hemlocks with their curled tops was heaven, as was all the fauna that struggled to thrive beneath the dense canopy of green.

In the last eighteen months Nikki had endured the exhaust of Tokyo, Paris, London, and every major city between Auckland and Madrid on her world tour. Now she was home. This time of year at the end of summer, the birch trees had a sticky-sweet smell, bringing to mind memories of campfires and fishing on another lake in Oregon thirty years before, with her grandparents. The forest was in her blood.

"Smells like home, Mom." Quinn spun around, her arms flung out.

Nikki closed her eyes. "God, I love this place."

"Don't swear."

Fishing the house keys from her purse, Nikki grabbed a loosely packed duffle bag from the back seat. Having traveled with several thousand tons of equipment for the past twenty years, she'd gone easy this trip. One bag for toiletries, favorite jeans, a few novels.

"They won't find you here." Quinn scanned the forest, and then followed her mother up the back stairs.

"They never have."

The door stuck, swollen from humidity and a year of disuse. Having to shoulder it open was nothing new. Nikki punched a sequence of numbers into their alarm system, while Elvis shot inside from his quick sweep of the driveway. Rescued from an animal shelter only ten months earlier, Elvis had never been to Louisa Lake. "Looks like he approves." Nikki laughed as he raced down the hall.

She dropped her keys on the hall table and followed Quinn into the front room—which was more than just timber beams and down-filled couches. Burn had designed the house with an award-winning architect, insisting on alcoves, window seats, interesting angles. Disproving that he was merely a pretty face who played guitar like Jimi Hendrix, Burn had discovered a talent for design. Now it belonged only to Nikki—just one of the things Burn gave up for his freedom.

"Don't ever sell this house." Quinn threw open the front doors leading outside to the deck that overlooked Half Moon Bay.

The water sparkled in the noontime sun, like diamonds jiggling on the surface of a mirror. After their wild escape from Los Angeles, and, with only three hours sleep, Nikki's body began to relax enough to allow the exhaustion to set in. Both she and Quinn stood mesmerized by the stillness of the lake. It was so quiet she could hear the tiny birds rustling in the bushes at the beach. She envied their simple task.

Encircling Quinn with motherly arms, she kissed her daughter's floral-scented hair and pulled her in close. Ah, Louisa Lake. The world stopped here. The two stayed this way until the sound of a car broke through the silence. Nikki froze. If they could hear a vehicle this clearly, it was beyond the locked gate.

"Goddammit." Nikki turned and ran into the house with Quinn. "Elvis, come." She shut the doors, fastened the locks, and hurried to the back bedroom, cursing the fact that their Escalade was not in the garage.

Quinn peeked through the print curtains of the guest room. Seeing her opportunity, Nikki took a moment to check for her handgun in a zippered pocket of her purse. The car had to be Harold or one of the Dickersons but still. The blot of blue got bigger as it advanced.

"Pickup truck. Chevy," Nikki said.

"Not a rental." Quinn sounded hopeful.

Tinted windows made it impossible to see how many people were inside the truck or if the driver looked like he might quote Shakespeare.

"Keep going, keep going," Nikki muttered. The truck drove on to the Dickerson place.

"That's good." Quinn let the curtain fall back into place.

"They could be turning around." Nikki held her breath and remembered what the FBI had said about Shakespeare…

"When we find this guy, he'll probably be someone who hasn't got enough money for a plane ticket to follow you anywhere. They usually are." The agent's words had been reassuring enough for Nikki to insist on leaving Los Angeles without security people. She'd always considered herself highly intuitive and had a good feeling about being at the lake. If that ever changed, she told herself she would leave. But for the first time since they'd left L.A., Nikki questioned the practicality of that decision.

"Quinn, get the binoculars, will you? He might be parked." *And walking through the woods.* They moved to the kitchen for the best view of the Dickerson's house.

With binoculars pressed against her face, Quinn

looked out the kitchen window to scan the road then the log house across the bay. "Nothing."

Elvis listened and growled, his two bottom teeth sticking out from his under bite. "Elvis, I wish your size matched your attitude." Nikki patted his head.

"The truck is in the driveway, and I think Dickerson's back door is open." Quinn was an expert with binoculars, having been raised with suspicion.

"Someone must have the key to the gate and house." *Either that or they had just picked two locks.* The Dickerson's back door slammed shut. Someone was inside that log house. "Must be a fix-it guy." She squeezed her daughter's hand. "All clear. Nothing we can do."

Soon the fridge was plugged in, taps run, windows thrown open, and food put away. While taking stock of supplies in the pantry, a truck's noise startled Nikki. She bounded into the guest room to watch the blue Chevy pass Birch House without slowing, the open window showing the silhouette of a man at the wheel. It drove out of sight. Gone.

Taking the stairs two at a time, Nikki headed for her bedroom. "I'm putting on my bathing suit," she called to Quinn. A silver-framed photo of Nikki and Burn smiled from her bedside table. Taking it in her hands, she remembered they'd been casually hugging, like the friends they'd become, when Quinn yelled, "Say cheese!" In some ways, Burn had never fit in here, more suited to the Los Angeles rock scene with his need for attention.

She slid the photo in the drawer, face down. This was her bedroom now, and her ex-husband had no reason to be here.

Quinn opened and closed drawers in her room across the hall.

"Whatcha doin', girly?" Nikki asked. God she loved this kid. Quinn was the one person in her world who truly loved her, flaws and all. And no one knew better how flawed Nikki was, especially in the mother department.

"Just looking at my stuff." Quinn's bedroom at Birch House was a girl's museum of collectibles. She had years of feathers, birch-bark drawings, photos, pretty rocks, a hat made from the cattails at the end of the bay, a bird's nest, a wall full of photos. The only thing missing at the lake had been friends, because of their need for privacy.

"Ready, Mom?" Quinn glided into the master bedroom wearing a checkered bikini made from a square of material the size of a tissue. "You like?" She struck a pose in front of Nikki's French mirror.

"I like, as long as you don't wear that in public." Goldy's typical work costumes—shiny bundles of asset-covering fabric—put her in a shaky position to criticize Quinn, but she didn't want her daughter dressing provocatively.

"It's just for here, Mom."

"Then I like it." This was Quinn's week and Nikki's mission to make it light-hearted and fun was driven by the fact that her daughter deserved to leave for college without worry pulling at her heart. Without knowledge of Shakespeare or what was about to change all their lives.

In the last months, twenty-six letters had arrived from Shakespeare, all similar. Recently they'd been arriving more frequently. The last one said very little.

My Dear Goldy,

Soon I will come to get you, to free you from this life of excess and indecision.

You'll be frightened at first but I'll make sure you don't suffer too much.

When I'm finished, I'll have you sing for me one last time. Something romantic, sweet and final. Of course you will tremble, beg. That will be delightful. When you hit the last note I will free your soul of my serenade, I will cut your tongue out, leaving you to never sing again. I'm sorry, my love but it is necessary. The drugs will ease your pain. You see? I do love you.

"She speaks, yet she says nothing. What of that?"

We'll be each other's last memory before we leave for the next life, the one where we are together.

This bud of love by summer's ripening breath,

May prove a beauteous flower when next we meet...

Images of a deranged man with long, thinning gray hair and a scraggly beard always came to mind, dressed in dirty breeches, sitting beside a collection of medieval torture instruments, penning letters. Although they hadn't identified him yet, Gateman was sure Shakespeare was in the L.A. area. A stationary stalker, they called the ones who didn't physically follow their prey.

Nikki hoped the FBI was right. This lunatic made her skin crawl with descriptions of the heinous acts he'd perform on her. The image of him wanting to cut her tongue out and inject windshield washing fluid into her veins was something she couldn't shake, no matter how hard she'd tried and his latest words had fallen on her like acid rain, the poison only slightly diluted by the

FBI's involvement.

Although Gateman thought the electrocution attempt was a message from Shakespeare, Goldy wasn't so sure. It hadn't been a strong enough current to cause any lasting damage. If someone had planned it, they either didn't know what they were doing, or hadn't meant to kill her. She'd suffered a few blisters but there'd been no amnesia, nerve damage, or heart problems. Or funeral.

****

Bedtime came early that night for both. Even though the maintenance man continued to hammer over at Dickerson's, Nikki began to relax. Putting on an old T-shirt of Burn's, she threw back the fluffy duvet and slipped into bed. The coolness of the cotton sheets was a long-awaited heaven except that she was without any prospects of filling the empty spot beside her with anyone but a feisty little pug mix.

"Is it lonely without Dad?" Quinn leaned against the door jamb.

"A little." Nikki patted the bed for her to sit. "I'll get used to it." She didn't want to say that it had been lonelier with a cheating husband lying next to her.

"I feel terrible for you because Dad has a girlfriend and you're all alone, Mom." Quinn stretched out on the duvet.

"It's kind of nice to be alone, for a change." She stroked her daughter's arm. How did she end up with such a gorgeous kid? She'd been terrified to be a mother when she found out she was pregnant at twenty-one. "I'm not entirely alone. I've got you this week and Elvis for years and years to come."

"I want you to find someone for yourself. Someone

to love." Quinn curled around Elvis's small body while Nikki played with her daughter's long auburn hair.

"I'm sure I will someday." She moved a lock behind Quinn's ear, fighting to keep tears from pooling.

"I just want you to make an effort." Quinn sighed. "Even though you're here at Birch House, don't miss Dad."

"I already put his picture away." Nikki pointed to the drawer on her bedside table.

Quinn smiled at her mother, kissed her cheek, and left for her own bedroom. "Don't spend all night watching that guy on the ladder next door," she teased.

"Sweet dreams, darling girl," Nikki smiled. The man was probably just a fix-it guy from town. Reporters wouldn't come this far. They were back in L.A., perplexed about her sudden retirement. It wouldn't occur to anyone yet that the choice to re-invent herself had been made for Nikki eight weeks earlier, when a tiny life inside her took root and began to grow from a stranger's seed.

Chapter 3

He was frustrated. Why hadn't Goldy stayed in Los Angeles where celebrities belonged? It would be so much easier. This remote location changed everything. All the careful planning was a joke now that Goldy was hiding out at Louisa Lake. Hell, he'd have to be on his toes with this one.

Lugging the stepladder back to the garage, he tried to put it away without making a sound. The lights were out at Goldy's, which meant any noise he made would probably be heard by the two women lying in bed over there. Fuck. The thought of Goldy in bed, only footsteps away from where he stood made his blood quicken. Her long blonde hair, that body, her smile. He'd fantasized about kissing that smile. At the last Goldy concert, he'd fantasized about more than that. Him and thousands of other men in the audience.

If he marched over there right now, let himself in to her house and slipped upstairs to her bedroom, what would she do? The reality was that she'd be terrified. He had to stay away from her. Things were about to go down, and he needed to keep a clear head.

****

As she made her morning cup of tea, Nikki noticed that the Chevy truck was still parked beside the garage at the Dickersons. The maintenance man had stayed the night. His hammering went on until well after ten.

Maybe the Dickerson family was getting ready to put the place up for sale. She hoped they didn't sell it to anyone who actually wanted to use the property. Having an absentee neighbor had been handy when they visited the lake.

Edna's son, Andy, the DA in Seattle, was in charge of the house now and Nikki punched in his cell number. When she got voice mail, she simply left a message. "It's Nikki Crossland. Can you call me back on this number? I have some questions about your lake house and who's over there." Andy had been trustworthy in the past about the secrecy of the Burnsides showing up at the lake, each year.

Later that day, Andy Dickerson left a short message saying he had a guy over there. "Just ignore him," he said.

Even though the "guy" was gone, Nikki contacted Sheriff Harold Gaines of the Louisa Lake Police Department, one of the only people she knew in town. "Are the Dickerson's selling?" Harold had once told her that he knew all the gossip on the lake.

"Not that I know of."

"I just wondered because there was a maintenance man out here."

"Probably just that." It sounded like she'd interrupted his lunch. He was a big guy, with a doting wife and retirement staring him in the face. Nikki imagined him with a tray of food in front of him.

"Can you let me know if you hear anything? And Harold, as always, it's a secret I'm here, so I'd appreciate you keeping it under that sheriff hat."

"Roger that."

****

Labor Day was over, and the lake was once again engulfed in the September hush. Without Quinn, Birch House seemed in desperate need of everything. It would take days to adjust to the deafening silence. They'd had such fun together, just what Nikki envisioned. Their toe nails were Petal Pink, they'd trimmed each other's hair, written a little song about themselves, suffered together through sunburns, finished the book *Little Women*, invented three new recipes to put in the Birch House Cookbook, water skied, and walked the loop with Elvis each day. They had even created an account for Nikki on Dating.com that she secretly had no intention of using.

When Quinn slung her duffle bag into the trunk of the car and slammed it shut, Nikki had watched through tears. "It's a five-hour drive to the coast," Quinn said. "I know. I'll be busy writing the movie soundtrack." Her daughter had always taken a back seat to Goldy's career and that thought brought a new wave of tears to Nikki's eyes. "I love you, my sweet Quinny." Her lips lingered on her daughter's forehead as she took in the familiar scent. "You are my golden child."

It wasn't only Quinn she missed. Walking around the house after her daughter's departure, memories of Burn ghosted her. She missed his jokes, his good-heartedness. Everybody loved Burn. Especially women. It had taken Nikki years to turn her love for him into something manageable, eventually finding a place in their lives for his behavior. She hoped the next few months wouldn't be filled with loneliness, especially over Burn, who probably hadn't thought twice about her since she'd announced her retirement.

With thoughts aimed at the deck hammock, Nikki

took a novel outside. But before she could deposit herself in the swinging bed, something moved over at the Dickersons' house and she scooted behind the branches of a leafy rhododendron at the deck's edge. A man stood perfectly still at the side door of the log cabin, staring into the forest.

She grabbed the binoculars from the patio table and crept across the grass, to the cover of a dense clump of trees. The fix-it man now stood where the dock met the beach, his arms folded across his chest, staring across the bay. He looked younger than she'd imagined. Maybe in his late thirties, but from this distance it was hard to tell.

He moved to the shadows of the large cedars along the beach. She couldn't see his face, wearing what looked like a Mariner baseball cap with sunglasses. An arm lifted to adjust his cap then he turned and, staring directly at her hiding spot, tipped his hat to her.

She buckled back into the bushes. "Oh, God." Maybe he was only adjusting his hat. Dropping to the grass, Nikki lay in a ball wondering if it was too late to go undetected. Had he seen her peering through the trees? She covered her head with her arms and backed farther into the dense brush.

"Oh God, oh god, oh god. Don't see me!" Nikki whispered. Elvis barked behind her. "Shhh! Elvis! No barkies," she hissed.

Jumping circles around her, Elvis begged to play, now that she was on his level.

"No, Elvis. Mommy is sleeping." Nikki lifted her head from her arms and tried to steal another look across the water.

He was gone.

Was he gone?

Yes.

Did he see her? Maybe not.

Did he?

If so, would he have seen the binoculars from that distance?

Probably not. He didn't have binoculars. Where was the sun? In his eyes?

No.

In her eyes! And illuminating her side of the bay.

Shit. Damn. Shit damn.

Running toward the house, Nikki gasped when she caught her reflection in the glass door. Oh no. She was wearing a red sundress! Red was the worst color for standing out in the forest. She yanked it off, stripping down to her blue bikini. If he looked again, he'd wonder if his eyesight was playing tricks on him. Maybe he'd think he saw a red bird. She winced at the likelihood of a hundred and fifteen pound red bird.

Her instincts told her to get to the kitchen. She ducked behind the counter and plopped on the floor to think. "Who was that guy?" she asked Elvis, who hunkered with her. The dog threw his little nose in the air and raced out the open patio door, barking his way across the deck and around the side of the house.

"Elvis!" she hissed.

"Hey, little guy," a strange voice said, overtop of Elvis's barks. "Where's your Mom?"

Oh God! He was at the side of the house. Nikki looked out the kitchen window where she separated two blind panels and tried to look around the corner, without success.

Where was her pepper spray? She had to exercise

caution. The whispery voice said something else but the only clear word was "binoculars."

Nikki groaned as she grabbed her robe from a bar stool, put the pepper spray in her pocket, and followed the sound of Elvis's barks around the side of the house.

****

Was this the right decision, coming over like this? It was risky, but god dammit, Goldy Burnside, world famous rock star and probably the only celebrity he'd ever had a crush on, was next door. From what he knew, it was just him and Goldy on the whole east side of the lake right now.

He'd done his research. The title of the house was in the name Nicole Ann Crossland. And that was Goldy. She'd never been here in September before but here she was, probably counting on privacy. Having her close by made his plan easier in some ways.

When Goldy rounded the corner of the house, his breath caught in his throat. This was better than a slow-mo beer commercial. She was drop-dead gorgeous. Of course she was. In the grocery store she'd been wearing a sweat suit, a hat, and sunglasses—covered up and incognito. Today she looked more like the rock star. Shit. How was he going to do this? He really didn't want to feel tongue-tied. What was his name? Oh yea, Pete Bayer, this time.

Her smile was all show. It originated and stayed in the mouth. He didn't blame her. His smile was probably goofy, complete with drool.

"Wait a minute." She laughed. "You're the Soup Guy."

He acted surprised. "Ah, technically you're the Soup Lady."

She wagged a finger at him.

Their common ground was a hundred cans of chicken noodle soup.

"Thanks for your help that day," she said.

"No problem." When her little dog sniffed his feet, he leaned down to scratch its ears. What had he read about this dog? Adopted recently. Goldy and the dog did promotion for the Humane Society.

"Have you eaten all your soup yet?" Nikki grinned brazenly at him.

"I realized it's the one thing I can't eat." He shrugged. "It's a boring childhood story that involves puking." Pete was gratified when she laughed. "I'm renting the Dickerson place." He pointed to the log house.

She nodded like she'd just added two and two. "I didn't notice anyone over there."

Ha! That was cute because she'd been watching him just now. He played along. "Good because I've been hammering. Kind of noisy."

"S'okay. I'm Nikki by the way."

Her gaze made him nervous. "Pete Bayer." Meaning to shake her hand, it turned into more of a joining of hands. He let go and she folded her arms across her chest and tilted her head. He'd held on too long. Shit. She could now tell he was falling all over himself. Probably used to that.

The dog barked at something in the bushes.

"Do you live here full time?" He'd pretend he didn't know she was Goldy, try to find out when she was leaving. That's what he'd come over for. That, and to let her know he could see her spying on him. And that had to stop. Immediately.

"This is just a visit." she said. A look of suspicion crossed her pretty face, like she'd put up crime scene yellow tape. Probably it was normal for a superstar to question everyone's intentions. He'd crossed a boundary.

"You hit some nice weather." Try to draw this out. He looked at the sky and waited for her to say she was leaving soon. When he looked back, she was still staring at him. She was good at this. He was too. Usually. "I'm going to be busy working, but if you need help with anything..." Pete took a step back and almost fell over a tree root poking up through the dirt.

"What kind of work do you do?" Goldy stepped forward to close the distance. Now she was in charge. Interesting.

"Computer software." It sounded believable.

"Well, I'm sure you won't find Elvis and I distracting." She shrugged. "Or helpful." They both laughed.

"It's technical stuff." He wished he'd told her he did something more interesting. More macho. Crocodile wrestler or stuntman.

"Nice to meet you." She turned to go.

He'd been dismissed. "You too." Okay, she wasn't going to reveal her plans to a stranger, but he considered continuing the conversation just to watch how her lips slid across her teeth when she talked. She was so damned pretty.

She walked to the front of the house without looking back, her silk robe blowing out behind her. Did she know how dangerous that was to turn her back on a complete stranger?

Pete mentally kicked himself for not getting more

information. It would be difficult with her so close but not impossible.

****

Nikki's face was hot and her heart pounded against her rib cage. If that man wasn't paparazzi or a stalker, who was he? Maybe he was a renter, working on computer software like he said.

She'd been shocked to see her neighbor was the cowboy from the grocery store. The very attractive cowboy from the grocery store. He had a large scar across his chin, suggestive of stitches, maybe a childhood injury and when he smiled, the scar turned white. He still sounded like he'd swallowed barbed wire.

Just in case she was wrong and this Pete guy was taking photos through the trees, Nikki had to stay sharp. It would put her at a slight advantage to have him dumbstruck over meeting Goldy. Most reporters and photographers had a glazed look in their eyes when face to face with her for the first time, and Pete Bayer was no exception. She understood the celebrity thing. He'd be used to seeing her on TV, hearing her referred to as a rock goddess. Hopefully he'd report that she'd been gracious and approachable. They often were unnecessarily cruel.

If he was writing a book about her or a magazine piece, then his visit wouldn't have been simple curiosity. Meeting her would add credibility to his story. He'd say he'd lived next door, knew her well enough to say hello, and was perfectly qualified to write the dirt about the star's withdrawal from the world. She hoped she was wrong.

Placing a call to her security people, she came up

empty on the name Pete Bayer. "Sorry, Ms. Burnside. I'll keep working on it. Maybe I should send someone out there."

It was standard for them to offer security, but if she consented to having a bodyguard at Louisa Lake, then the whole purpose of this retreat was shot down. Another person at the house to watch her every move would be horribly intrusive. She might as well be back in L.A.

"No thanks, Steve. I'm safe here, as long as you haven't traced my call."

He didn't laugh. "Don't worry about us."

****

Nausea moved into Nikki's body in full force. She'd felt slightly woozy for the last few weeks, but not this bad. After eating a few bites of dry toast, she climbed the stairs to the loft that overlooked the great room and sat down at her piano.

Most of Goldy's hits had been written at that baby grand, and Nikki cherished it, not only because it had made her a lot of money, but because it made music. With eleven platinum CD's and twice as many hits spun from them, it had served her well. Many of her fourteen Grammy awards owed their existence to her time at that piano.

With her hands drifting lovingly over the keys, Nikki remembered the lyric she'd written months before. Now the song needed music. The first melody that trickled off the keyboard was wrong for the sentiment of the song. Too sweet, too mushy. She added some minor notes, more staccato. The music would have to be forceful, warlike in its message.

"Danielle, you took me for a fool,

Danielle, I sympathized with you,
And now, you have him back with you,
Is this what you wanted me to do?"

She recalled writing these words in the Goldy deluxe touring bus in the middle of the night, driving from Chicago to St. Louis. Nestled in her chair, she plucked away on the guitar, as they headed toward their next concert.

By then, Burn was sleeping in a single bunk, probably dreaming of the busty woman who'd been all over him at the after party earlier. He was snoring and Nikki realized that problem would soon be some other woman's, not hers. Strumming the Les Paul on her lap, she thought about all the women who'd pretended friendship with her over the years, then turned around and slept with her husband.

"Danielle, I sat and held your hand
While you were working on your plan
To get your claws back in my man
By now you know I'm not your biggest fan
Danielle, I only asked you why,
The truth was harder now to hide
My pain is not exceeded by
Your ability to lie…"

Burn had been cheating for years and Nikki had been the ultimate good sport for everyone's sake— Quinn, the band, her fans, even Burn. It was only when she realized that she was still young enough to find love in someone else, she gave up. The marriage ended within the week and the relief was like coming around a corner on a turbulent river to find a calm peaceful pool.

Nikki was thinking of giving *Danielle* to Burn's latest protégée, Rebecca Raven, who'd asked for a

Goldy song for her next CD. This lyric begged to be a hit, she could already tell. Burn would know it was about him. They always were. Perhaps Rebecca would too, when it came time for him to bed her. If he hadn't already.

Feeling satisfied with the song for now, she moved downstairs to the hammock. A warm breeze blew in off the water. It was frivolous and wonderful to lie around like this. When the house phone rang, she almost flipped over onto the deck's floor.

It was Harold, the sheriff in town. "What's up?" she asked.

"I just wanted to tell you that Andy Dickerson rented the house. It's not for sale FYI.

She offered a tidbit for more information. "I saw him."

"Some guy from the city. Andy said he took it for the month so you'll see him around, if you're staying."

"Who is he?"

"Dunno. Hey, I read that you're MIA. Big story. If you're out there alone at Birch House, I better do a daily check on you."

Nikki froze. Harold was the epitome of a nosey neighbor, and she didn't want him coming to call.

He grunted like his back was hurting him. "Thing is, I can't really be driving out there, can I, with the time it takes to get there and everything else I got going on in town?"

"No. I'm fine, but thank you, Harold." What was he getting at?

By the time Nikki convinced him he didn't need to visit on a daily basis and that phoning would suffice, she realized someone had probably asked him to do this. Probably Quinn. No one else knew she was at Louisa Lake. No one.

"The man at Dickerson's looked about forty, forty-five." She tried to sound casual, even throwing in a yawn like it was no big deal, instead of someone who had nothing better to do with her time than peer at men through the bushes.

Harold was maddeningly ignorant. "I dunno. Call me tomorrow to report in... and Nikki." He paused, while he took a bite of something. "Let me know if you need anything."

I need to know who this guy is, Harold!

"Wait, I just remembered something about the renter," he said.

"Yes?"

"About the man renting Dickerson's house?"

"Yes? What?"

"Andy said not to worry about checking on him. He's not very friendly, apparently. He's writing a book or something and wants privacy."

Chapter 4

Dusk moved in across the lake like a sheer veil as Nikki stood on the deck wondering how she'd last for months in the bush. Already she was worried about how much she talked to herself. If Pete Bayer was writing a book she had to avoid him. Let him write the damned thing and then sue him if it was inaccurate. She'd done it before.

A thumping noise, followed by an ungodly screech, broke the evening's silence. Car tires slid across the gravel road and Nikki's heart jumped to her throat. That order of sounds meant one thing. A vehicle had hit an animal. The yelping was from a dog.

"Elvis!" She bolted around the house.

Pete Bayer, only sixty feet away, was crouched over a lump on the road.

"It's your dog," he called, not taking his eyes off the body.

Nikki sprinted to them. Elvis was still howling and that meant he was not dead. She knelt beside Pete and put her hand on Elvis's ribs. "S'okay, boy. Please don't die on me, Elvis." He wasn't flattened. There was no visible blood or open wounds.

"I think he rolled under the truck." Pete ran a hand over Elvis' small form.

Nikki's heart thumped against her chest wall. "The tires didn't run over him, right?"

"They didn't," Pete whispered.

Nikki leaned in and stroked the dog's head, tears dripping onto his fur. "Elvis. Don't die on me, little boy." A pink tongue emerged to lick her hand and Nikki stifled a sob. Pete had a flashlight on his keychain, and ran it over Elvis. His tummy was scraped but there were no gaping wounds. Not on the side they could see.

"Looks like road rash." Pete sat back on his haunches and looked at Nikki.

Her hands drifted over the dog's abdomen, checking for tender spots. Nothing. Was he simply dazed? "I can't tell if it's serious." Her strangled voice surprised her. She couldn't lose Elvis. If her dog was dying, she wanted to hold him. She slid her hand under his head and crouched lower to cradle him. "You are all I've got right now." She lifted the dog's shoulder to peek underneath. "He's not whining. That's got to be a good sign."

"Could be." Pete didn't sound convinced.

"Maybe it just knocked the wind out of him." She kissed Elvis' neck and buried her face in his fur. "Mommy loves you, Elvis."

Pete's hand rested against Nikki's back and she wondered how long it had been there. The warmth was comforting. "I'm so sorry, Nikki. I didn't see him." His voice was still raw, like a growl.

Nikki turned and saw pain in his eyes. "I know."

Elvis lifted his head, sniffed, and uttered a noise, like a snort. Nikki's heart dropped to the pit of her stomach. "No Elvis, don't leave me." The little dog's head lifted further and he snorted again and sniffed the air.

"Sniffing is good," Pete said, leaning in.

Elvis's snort turned into a half bark as he tried to focus on the bushes behind Pete. He squirmed, and Pete reached across Nikki to hold him down. "Take it easy, boy."

Elvis's ears were in full alert. He tried to get his legs under him so they moved him to stand. Pete's light enabled them to do a full check for wounds. Nothing big, just some rash burns on his leg and tummy. A chipmunk chattered close by and Elvis cocked his head.

"See if he can walk," Pete suggested.

Nikki let go of Elvis and watched him wobble a few steps. When he ambled off into the underbrush, she wiped the remaining tears that had stuck on her jaw line. "Elvis. Come here. I can't believe he just walked away. I'd say you definitely didn't run over him with that three ton truck if he can move like that."

"Thank God." Pete's hand went to his heart. "I'm so sorry. I didn't see him until it was too late." He turned to face her. "Maybe we should take him to the vet, if they have one in town." Pete watched Elvis emerge from the darkness nearby. "At least get an x-ray." Elvis was happily scouring the ground for smells, his hopping around another good sign.

"I don't think he's broken anything." She'd risk the town and vet if she thought Elvis needed medical attention but he looked perfectly normal as he zigzagged around the bushes. "I'll keep my eye on him tonight. But thanks for suggesting it."

He stood and reached for her hand to help her up. Without thinking she put her hand in his. It wasn't the first time he'd helped her and she remembered the feel of his firm torso against her shoulder at the Stop and

Go. Maybe it was the worried look on his face or the touch but seeing the compassion on his face, Nikki stretched up with the intention of giving Pete a reassuring kiss on the cheek. But at the last moment, he turned his head and her kiss landed on the side of his mouth.

Before she could pull away, he whispered against her mouth, "Did you mean to do this?" His lips found hers square on and lingered as he kissed her lightly. Softly.

She jerked back. "Actually, no." Unable to meet his eyes, she considered slapping him but it was too late. "I meant to kiss your cheek to reassure you there's no hard feelings." When Pete cleared his throat, she detected a suppressed chuckle. "And you shouldn't have made it more." She turned to go.

He took a step in front to block her and held up his hands in surrender. "I actually thought you were trying to kiss me. And then I just wanted to reassure you too, but you seemed to force the issue, like *you* wanted to kiss *me*. So I let you." He was making fun of her.

"I did not!" She flashed him a look. "That is not true and you know it. Come on, Elvis." The little dog trotted around now as if he'd never rolled under Pete's truck.

"I apologize," Pete said. "But now that we're kissing buddies," he continued, "I'm wondering if you're going to stay here at the lake for another few days?"

What? "We are not any kind of buddies. I don't even know who...I don't know you." True, she'd participated in the kiss but for only the tiniest of moments. And he knew. Her face felt hot as she scooped her dog up and turned to the neighbor. "And, I'm not available for anymore of that kissing, if that's what you mean."

This time he didn't hold back a chuckle. "Sounds like you're sticking around then. Maybe we can have coffee tomorrow or the next day. You could get to know me."

"No, we definitely can't and furthermore, you have a lot of nerve after hitting my dog and then trying to kiss me to suggest such a thing." Nikki shot him a look and left him standing at the side of his truck as she stomped into the house and set the alarm that would alert her to creepy neighbors skulking around.

****

Night had descended on Louisa Lake when Nikki pulled a lounge chair to the beach and plunked down. Elvis had fallen asleep on his kitchen bed, exhausted from his ordeal. Touching her lips where Pete's had been, she took a deep breath and let it out slowly. *Now I really hope he isn't writing a book about me.*

Stupid. She'd only leaned in to give him a cheek kiss to say thanks. But what was a cheek kiss anyhow? Was she some silly maiden, honoring a suitor with a brush of her lips? Pete Bayer was a good-looking man who smelled like a Caribbean vacation, but she wasn't free to go around kissing him. She didn't know anything about him. If that memory didn't get squelched, she'd have to leave the lake just to get the kiss out of her mind.

Bats circled overhead, hunting for flying insects. A loon called to its mate and she waited for the answer. Loons mated for life. Such an honorable act. That had been her intention. And now she was divorced from one man, pregnant by another man, kissing another, with no firm plans beyond the next few months.

The baby would be born in April. Her heart twinged at the thought of the fetus's fragility and she mentally shook away the statistics of miscarrying at her age. Regardless of what happened, she'd never regret leaving the spotlight of the music business. Her retirement hadn't been all about the pregnancy but knowing she'd conceived was the impetus.

The sexual encounter eight weeks earlier had been so brief in the grand scheme of her life. A minuscule portion of time, now etched in her mind forever because of what it produced. Nothing would ever soften the memory and she wished the moment itself had been beautiful for the child's sake and hers.

Goldy had been booked at the Dolphin Amphitheatre in Miami for two shows. When she heard that a certain sexy movie star was in town filming, something ignited in her mind. He was recently divorced from his wife and because she was now officially divorced and had drooled over him in his latest spy thriller, Nikki made the decision to stand at the edge of the dating cliff and jump off.

"See if he wants to come to my show on Friday," she'd said to her assistant, Merilee. "Offer one ticket."

Merilee looked excited to be in on this momentous occasion. "What if he wants two?"

He didn't.

After the show, he waited for her in the green room. Nikki ran off stage from her last encore and Merilee handed her a fresh towel.

Sweaty, and still buzzing from the performance, Nikki patted her face and steeled herself for the possibility of something wonderful. She sauntered into the green room flanked by her bodyguards.

His eyes sparkled at the sight of her. "Nice to meet you, Goldy." He stood and lifted her hand to kiss it, just like the characters he played on the big screen.

Oh my God, he's gorgeous! "Did you enjoy the show?" She knew the answer.

After showering, she changed into jeans and a simple T-shirt and stepped through the bathroom door looking more like a farm girl than a rock icon. His face froze. Hadn't he ever seen a photo of what she looked like out of costume?

"Where's your leather and chains?" His British accent would've been an aphrodisiac in itself, if he hadn't sounded disappointed.

"They're too hard to get out of...quickly..." *Oh God. How cheesy was that?*

He grinned, appeased for the moment.

They shared a glass of champagne, then, just before they left the Amphitheater, Nikki pulled on a pair of black leather stiletto boots, darkened her eye makeup, teased her hair and they walked out with his hand on the small of her back.

Dining on the hotel suite's balcony, with the ocean in front and the lights of Miami spread out to the north, they eventually found conversation. Usually ravenous after a concert, Nikki was only able to push the savory dinner around her plate. The possibility of sex hovered between them like a party gift not yet opened.

"You are beautiful without the rock star package, you know that?" He grinned over his wine glass.

"Thank you." Nikki reminded herself that she could handle this man even though Goldy was the huge flirt. As the rocker, Goldy had a plethora of provocative witticisms that Nikki had no idea she even knew. As Goldy, flirting had always been easy when words didn't need to be backed up with action. But tonight, Nikki was willing to try.

By the time dessert was served, Nikki's flirting muscle had loosened and flexed. "Tell me about your new movie. Are you dangling from high wires, dodging bullets, and fashioning guns from tin cans?"

"Of course. What would be the fun in anything else?" He was a beautiful male specimen, even though he was slightly reserved conversationally. Stiff. Nikki sensed his words were well-rehearsed material. Talking about his new movie relaxed him though and, in watching him talk, she found herself aching to touch him. Most women in the world who'd ever gone to the movies probably had the same idea—that the man in front of her had the most perfect face she'd ever seen. Studying it with the tips of her fingers would be heaven. The wine was making her heady. She hardly noticed that he hadn't asked anything about her. Until this.

"I always wondered what the life of a rock star would be like."

"It's a wild ride." This was not a question, but a good start. "Do you sing?" she asked.

He laughed. "Not unless I'm being tortured."

Nikki laughed, even though she'd heard this answer countless times. Giving herself a two-minute time limit to explain the life of a rock star, she chose words like "hectic," "thrilling," "pervasive," and "fantasy." It was her standard answer, crafted especially to avoid boring anyone with a short attention span. Her dinner companion did not last long and lost interest after the first minute.

"Does your husband approve of you entertaining men in your hotel suite?" he interrupted like he was trying to get the party started.

"I'm not married anymore." Nikki wrinkled her brow. She'd told Merilee to explain that fact, discreetly. "We haven't announced it yet." She peeked at him from under her eyelashes and tipped her head coyly, knowing exactly how that looked in photographs. She hoped Nikki did it as well as Goldy.

Setting down his fork, he wiped his gorgeous mouth with a linen napkin and looked directly at her. "So, here we are, having a lovely supper together. I'm wondering what comes next."

Although it sounded like a borrowed line from a movie, Nikki could have jumped him right then and there. "I'm sure you understand discretion in your personal life," she said.

"I do." He raised his glass. "To impeccable timing."

She joined the toast. She gulped her wine, thinking they were right where they should be in his process.

With the promise of a night of passion laid out in front of them, they found themselves at the railing kissing, his tongue slipping into her open mouth. He tasted like wine. Expensive wine that she paid for. Feeling more desperate than she wanted, Nikki reminded herself to go slow. They had all night. She pulled back to look at him and took a deep breath.

His hand wove into the back of her long hair and gathering a handful, he pulled her to him. She rubbed against his hips. Nothing yet. Nikki reached up to cup his beautiful face in her hands, simply examining his cheekbones, his jaw line, his jade-colored eyes. She was close enough to see his contact lenses. As she stretched to kiss him again, he cupped her breasts. She moaned and, as though this was his signal, he slipped his tanned hands under her shirt and undid her bra.

Oh yea. This was going to be good. He pulled her T shirt over her head and threw her lacey bra over the edge of the balcony. They watched it fall thirty-five stories. "Poor sucker below who won't realize its worth," he joked.

Seeing her stripped to the waist, his enthusiasm picked up and he bent to take a nipple in his mouth. She pressed his blonde head into her chest and leaned back as he moved from one breast to the other. They crossed the floor hurriedly to the bedroom and, standing beside the bed, Nikki reached down to feel his readiness.

He pulled her hand away. "Not yet, love. It'll be over too quickly. First, let me satisfy you," he whispered against her hair.

Pulling off her boots, jeans, and panties, he slid the boots back on, grinning as he did so. He pushed her back on the bed and she lay naked, except for boots, on the crisp, white coverlet of the hotel bed. "Oh yes, you are lovely, aren't you?"

"A condom?" she whispered.

"Right here." He pulled a package out of his pocket and tore the wrapper off with his teeth, smiling rakishly with one eyebrow raised. She couldn't help thinking it was probably something he'd practiced in the mirror.

Nikki looked down to see the level of his arousal but it was difficult to gauge with him fully clothed. "Let's take your pants off and you can make me feel lovelier."

"Patience, darling." He lowered himself on top of her and dove on her neck again. A move that held more drama than emotion.

Reaching down, Nikki unzipped him and managed to pull his pants a few inches down his long thighs. He wore skimpy bikinis and she hooked her thumb around an edge. So far she hadn't felt a reason to get the briefs off but she couldn't be certain.

As she tugged, his hand slid between their hips and undid her thumb. In one motion he raised his briefs to their starting position. Nikki unbuttoned his shirt. Skin on skin was her ultimate goal.

"No, not yet," he whispered.

He was holding on to his clothes like a life preserver in a storm.

Running her hands up under his shirt, Nikki wondered why. From what she felt, he had the finely chiseled body she'd seen on screen and so far was doing very little with it. He was mostly gyrating around on top of her, fully clothed and kissing her neck. When he moved his hips back and forth on her pelvis he seemed to be concentrating on something. Whatever it was, it wasn't her pleasure.

She waited, slightly annoyed that he was so out of touch with her lack of interest. She tried to pull his shirt off but he reached up and grabbed it. "Oh, no, you don't," he said, like she was a naughty schoolgirl.

Did he have shameful scars? A third nipple? It was dark in the bedroom. And besides, what would it matter? She was naked, and they were halfway to having sex, for God's sake.

Before she realized what was happening, he bit her

bottom lip then thrust his tongue down her throat. His hand slid between them and with some fumbling against her thighs, Nikki felt something slightly inflated try to slip into the V of her pubic area. The image of a softened breadstick came to mind and Nikki froze, wondering what was happening. He barely had enough there to make the plunge, which ended up being more of a slip and slide. Two little shoves later, he collapsed in a heap on her, panting. Or was he pretending to pant? She wasn't sure.

Her face froze, her brow furrowed. The act was unlike anything she'd ever experienced before, not that she'd had many lovers. Listening to him breathe too lightly to have climaxed, Nikki was hesitant to ask if he was done. With two hundred pounds of muscle, motionless on top of her, she wasn't sure what was going on. His heart wasn't pounding against her chest. He wasn't trying to regain a normal breathing rate.

"Is there anything I can do?" she whispered, stroking his back with one hand and reaching down with the other to wedge her hand in to assess the situation.

"What? No." He grabbed her hand quickly. "That was great." He lifted himself off her and stood. His bikini briefs were in their preferred position with little to fill them. He quickly slid his pants up and zipped.

Nikki gathered the covers around her, not wanting the sight of her multi-million dollar body accessible to a fully-clothed sex partner, sex being the questionable word. Besides some fiddling that she hadn't recognized as the sex act, she was pretty sure they hadn't consummated their tryst. True she'd only been with one man in the last twenty years but Burn liked videos and she'd watched plenty of actors pretending to have sex, people who probably fucked a lot in their private lives and knew how to do it.

He sat on the side of the bed and slipped into his Ferragamos. Lucky for him his socks hadn't come off during sex and it was easier to put himself back together.

"Are you leaving?"

"Yes, I'm sorry, love, I have an engagement, but thank you for dinner and ...everything." He glanced in the direction of Nikki's sheet-covered crotch and playfully pinched her leg.

"An engagement at midnight?"

"Yes." He looked incredulous that she doubted him. "Look, you are gorgeous. I have wanted to shag Goldy since I was a teenager, and I thank you for fulfilling this fantasy."

Since he was a teenager? How old did he think she was? Nikki knew for a fact that he was older than her. She slid back to lean against the pillows, the sheet still tightly gathered around her bodice. He hadn't even unbuttoned his shirt and here he was insulting her.

"When you were a teenager, I was singing in elementary school recitals."

He chuckled. "Let's not get testy, Goldy." The way he emphasized her name made her angrier. "We both know what this was."

It was now clear that he'd come here tonight to fuck Goldy. Not get to know Nikki and then make love to her. She should have just done him in the dressing room, in full Goldy regalia. Why had she thought he might be interested in Nikki?

"Wait." She'd try to save this. "We were having a

nice time. Can't you stay and …..snuggle? Maybe talk a bit?" She gave him her irresistible sex-kitten look.

"I'm not much of a snuggler, love." He looked at her almost pitifully, unveiling an expression she'd hardly ever seen in her privileged life. "Let's just remember it as fun and leave it at that, shall we?"

He turned to go and Nikki sprang off the bed with the sheet. She still wore the black leather, thigh high boots, for God's sake.

Nikki followed him out of the bedroom, tripping on her king-sized cover up. All the things she wanted to say were stuck in her throat as she watched him grab his expensive leather jacket from the couch and throw it over his shoulder, like he was exiting a movie scene. Nikki stood in the bedroom doorway, shoulders slumped. "I expected more…"

He sighed and turned to face her. "Look, Goldy—you of all people should know how to do this. You invited me here to fuck you, right?" He didn't seem so conversationally stilted now. "Well, we fucked."

She nodded. "But I wanted…more."

He threw out his hands. His coat swung from his right hand. This move was definitely choreographed. "Well, whose fault is that?"

Hers. She'd wasted this chance, this moment to be with one other man after a lifetime with Burn. After working him into a lather, she'd tried to secure his affection as Nikki when all he wanted was Goldy.

At the very least, it was embarrassing. He'd seen her naked. Sucked on her tits. Holding back angry words was not going to be possible now. She needed to hurt his feelings.

"I know how touchy men are about this sort of

thing and I do understand if you're embarrassed and want to go, but I just think we could keep trying…" she stopped when she saw the look on his face.

Now she had his attention. "Sort of thing? What sort of thing?"

Nikki pulled the arrow back and let it fly. "Erectile dysfunction." Her lips twitched under the strain of a smile.

"You're joking, right?" He spun around and glancing at the blackness outside, ran his hand through his hair.

"I can imagine it's difficult when you're faced with your fantasy woman but…"

He turned and lowered his voice to a whisper. "Look. I functioned. I came. We fucked."

Nikki took great delight in seeing his restraint. "I didn't. I barely got started. And you say you actually climaxed?" Nikki tried to look confused.

He stared at her for a few very long seconds, trying to hold in his temper. "There's no need to get all pissy about it."

That silenced her. Her balloon had lost all its air. He was right. It was a fuck, or an almost fuck and there was no need to get pissy, especially seeing that's what she wanted in the first place.

She'd had a few minutes of passion and, just because it hadn't been good and he'd planned a quick getaway, didn't give her the right to judge him and then get mad that it wasn't what she'd expected. She'd brought him here on the premise that she would be Goldy and they'd do the nasty deed. This was all she got.

He'd expected more too, she realized. Until that

moment, she hadn't noticed that he'd only called her Goldy.

His footsteps tapped across the hall tile. "You owe me a bra!" she called just before the outer door slammed.

Chapter 5

Louisa Lake sunshine beckoned from outside the bedroom window. Judging from the angle of the rays, she'd slept in. Elvis snored through his flattened nose while Nikki eased out of bed and dressed in her favorite jean shorts and a soft blue T-shirt.

Her flip flops clapped noisily on the wooden stairs as the little dog shot from behind and beat her to the kitchen. Nausea lingered somewhere between reality and anticipation as she made some tea. With a steaming mug in hand, she sat at her laptop to check the online gossip columns.

"No Goldy in Them Thar Hollywood Hills," "Goldy Fever," "Panning for Goldy." The word plays were predictable and almost infinite. Goldy's whereabouts was anyone's guess, although several articles speculated she was at a penthouse in Nassau. She smiled to hear that her decoy's efforts were successful. Days earlier, a bellboy had seen Goldy sneaking into the private elevator at the Atlantis Resort. Sightings of the rock star were coming in from all over America and even Europe, but Nassau ranked number one for Goldy sightings. With reason.

The Goldy decoy was paid to sneak up to the penthouse, order room service discreetly three times a day, and wait for further instructions. "At least I'm not paying her for nothing." Elvis wagged his curly tail and

Nikki laughed as he danced around the kitchen. "I'm told she looks a lot like me in the blonde wig."

She grabbed her cell phone and informed her security company to go ahead with plan B—flying the decoy to a private island in the Keys with two bodyguards and a staff of four. "Tell her to pack up."

Staring out the kitchen window to her garage, she considered simply taking the car out for a drive. The walls were closing in around her even with her daily boat rides. The thought of the press's possible presence in Louisa Lake seemed to lose all credibility on a glorious day at the lake. Shakespeare didn't seem so horrid in the sunshine either. The FBI was confident he'd be in California. She hadn't heard anything for a while. Who knew if he was obsessed with other celebrities? He might have a whole ring of famous people he was threatening.

On impulse, Nikki called Agent Gateman at the FBI for the latest report. "Anything new?"

"Nothing." He sounded almost cheerful. "I'll make an educated guess that he's probably less motivated after the announcement of your retirement. But we haven't closed the file."

Next, Nikki called her publicist, Phyllis.

"All is well. Things are dying down already," she said. Phyllis didn't believe the strange neighbor was anyone threatening. "Maybe he's a biographer, but someone's bound to write your story eventually, darlin'." Nikki cherished Phyllis's casual take on catastrophes and always felt better after a conversation with her.

A disguise would take care of any lingering fears and allow Nikki the freedom to enjoy her trip to town.

After all, costumes had always allowed Nikki to attend normal events like the movies, restaurants, taking Quinn to the fair. The curly brown wig was still in the duffle bag in her bedroom. The fat suit too.

Elvis's reaction to the wig was comical and Nikki laughed out loud. "It's Mommy, silly boy." She'd been transformed into a different woman. One baggy dress later, Nikki grabbed sunglasses and headed to town before noon, before any residual September tourists hit the town for supplies. A car ride would do as much for her attitude today as summoning a personal bodyguard from her L.A. roster.

Anyone watching the road into town would have seen a lady in a black car pull into Barney's Gas Station shortly after nine o'clock and slide to a stop at pump number four. The other bays were empty. Nikki contemplated using her debit card to avoid having to go inside the store with cash. No, no cards, just in case they were traced. She paid in the convenience store and hurried outside to fill her tank.

It was a postcard-perfect day in Louisa Lake and Nikki closed her eyes to let the heat of the morning bathe her face while she pumped her own gas. This was yet another simple pleasure she hadn't done in awhile. Hearing a car pull up to the next island, Nikki first turned her back then looked over and saw the familiar blue Chevy truck. Dammit. When Pete stepped out, her first thought was that he might be following her.

He kept his back to her and Nikki was able to stare. Jeans fit him well. He had broad shoulders, nicely muscled arms. He whistled a tune from the radio, watching the highway as he pumped his gas. This was the man who'd kissed her, his lips softer than his rough look suggested.

Fifty dollars, sixty dollars, and finally Nikki's pump stopped. She caught herself humming Pete's song and stopped immediately, returning the gas nozzle to its holder. Under his scruffy hair at the back of his neck, he wore the leather string that held the small amulet.

Jumping into the driver's seat, Nikki realized she'd left her keys inside the store, at the cash desk. The spaced-out, red-eyed cashier was busy setting up a display, so Nikki grabbed some magazines, gum, and a few other items. Stepping up to the desk, she absently knocked a box of condoms off a display. Setting the boxes to the side, she paid and left.

Her front window was partway down, but she felt blissfully unrecognizable as she pulled away from the gas pumps.

Pete looked up. "Morning, Nikki," he called and tipped an imaginary hat.

What? Pete had said her name plain as day, even though she wore big sunglasses and a frizzy brown wig. How did he know? He wouldn't recognize the car. She'd given Quinn the Escalade and was now driving the car they kept at the lake for when they flew in by helicopter or float plane. Glancing in the rear view mirror, she saw the problem. Elvis hung out the back window, panting and smiling at everything out there in the big wide world. He must've stepped on the window button and, of course, Pete recognized her dog.

"Elvis!" she wailed. The man who kissed her had just seen her in a silly wig trying to ignore him. What would he think about her wandering around town in this ridiculous getup?

Resisting the urge to bang her head against the

steering wheel, she headed out of town. She was useless at sneaking around. Pete was everywhere she went and Elvis seemed to be on his side. Pete wasn't a photographer. That much she knew. If he was, she'd have seen photos by now all over the internet. Those long lenses of the paparazzi could zero in on very distant objects and Nikki had been outside enough to give him plenty of fifty-thousand-dollar shots.

"Let's stay ahead of this guy, Elvis." From the passenger seat, the little pooch hung on every word. She checked her rearview mirror and saw no one. "I am screwed if Pete is writing a book on me and I let him kiss me."

A hefty wind blew off the lake, rustling the trees and sending an abandoned piece of white paper somersaulting across her driveway. Nikki clicked the garage door closed, grabbed the paper, and looking skyward, saw clouds moving in to change the beauty of the day.

She walked to the side of the house to rescue anything that might blow away and, stopping to watch the dance of the birches' leaves flickering in the wind, she caught a glimpse of something at the Dickerson place. It was just a flash of color in the front window Looking closer, she saw nothing.

The wind picked up and waves blew across the bay. The papery sounds of the flickering leaves almost drowned out Elvis's barking and when she turned to see what he'd found, her heart jumped. The blue pickup truck was parked in her driveway. Pete stood to the side of it, his eyes on her. Realizing this was the second time she'd been caught spying, her face blazed with embarrassment, until she considered that he might think she was simply looking out at the bay.

She toddled toward him. "We meet again." Her attempt to be casual sounded forced and Nikki was painfully aware of how unusual she looked in the padded suit.

Pete held up a small plastic bag. "The guy at the gas station thought these were yours." His voice sounded like sandpaper on lava rocks.

Seeing the Trojan logo through the thin bag, she froze. This was either creepy or amusing. "I'm not missing anything." Nikki's vision drifted to the scar on Pete's chin, then to his eyes. A chill travelled up her spine when their eyes locked.

"He said he charged you." Pete looked genuinely confused and handed her the bag. "I told him we were neighbors." His hands were callused. Not necessarily a writer's hands. Or a software engineer.

"I went to town in a fat suit because I like anonymity." What could she say? Even though now would be the time to peel off the suit and shed the pretense, she had only underwear beneath. Instead she chucked the bag at the trash can in an overhead throw. Landing on the grass in front of the can, the bag became a perfect retrieve for Elvis, the non-retriever, and he took off for his prey.

"Your secret is safe with me." The hint of a smirk passed over Pete's lips.

Elvis dropped the condom box on her toes and sat down obediently, waiting for Nikki to throw the box. "These aren't mine." What else could she say?

Elvis's excitement was irresistible. "He's not usually a fetcher." Picking up the box, she chucked it toward the garbage can again, only to have Elvis take off joyfully.

"Your costume is…charming."

She was just about to ask him if he was writing about her, but stopped before the words left her lips. "Privacy is important to me." She returned his stare but it was hard to look mean in a costume.

"Obviously." The wind blew his hair around his face. He needed a haircut. "Bad weather coming in."

"Delivery Man *and* Weather Man." She smiled at him and was surprised when he blushed. This sudden show of vulnerability touched something in her. Pete had a crush on Goldy. Must've been a good kiss after all. "Maybe it won't last." Was she talking about the weather?

Pete looked over to the trees which were jostling in the wind. "I thought you were leaving the lake." He stepped back, put one hand in a pocket of his jeans, and grabbed the truck's silver door handle with the other hand.

Nikki bought herself a moment by throwing the box for Elvis again. Pete was awfully eager to know her schedule. "I don't know." He almost sounded like he wanted her to leave.

"You here by yourself? It's kind of remote location for one person." He opened the truck door.

"I have friends coming soon." She looked at her watch like they might be pulling in at any moment. "And of course I have my watchdog." They both laughed at Elvis who, by now, had torn the box apart and was scattering condoms across the yard.

"How is he doing after getting rolled by my truck?" He dropped his hand from the truck door handle.

"He's a survivor."

"His barking is good protection. Even just for notification."

Elvis looked at Pete and wagged his tail, abandoning the condoms for sniffs around Pete's jeans. Elvis jumped up to Pete's knees. "He doesn't usually like strangers," she said.

"Especially people who hit him with their truck, I bet." Tiny lines fanned out from his turquoise eyes when he smiled, and Nikki imagined he didn't wear colored contact lenses like celebrities. As he reached down to pet her dog, he chuckled. "I had bacon for breakfast, in town. He probably smells that."

"Ah, he does like bacon." So Pete was already in town when she saw him at the gas station.

"Let me know if you need anything, seeing you're here by yourself and all." He jumped inside the truck and backed away, leaving Nikki to wonder what he had that she might need. He'd write an article if she was feeling unpublicized? She couldn't let her guard down yet.

****

He'd gone too far. It wasn't helpful to get sidetracked, but Nikki was so damned cute. She'd gone from a hot rock star to the pretty lady next door. And she was entirely someone else in that costume. Pete laughed out loud at the thought of her in that wig. He was sure she didn't have friends coming over like she said, but understood that she didn't want him to think she was alone. That probably worked out better for him. Her being cautious and all. Especially because he'd kissed her.

He had thought she'd leave the lake if he came on too strong, but she was still here with no hint of going.

And asking the sheriff about Goldy at the lake hadn't flushed her out. Shit. He'd embarrassed himself by kissing her and didn't get the end result he wanted. He'd have to stay away now. No more flirting with Goldy. Soon she'd leave and he'd become someone else.

Scanning the perimeter, he noted that something was different but couldn't put his finger on what it was. Everything looked the same. He left the grocery bags in the truck, and silently crept to the side door of the house. With his ear to the door, he listened.

A faint murmur of voices came from inside. There'd been no sign of a vehicle on the property. Stealing along the side of the house, he peeked over the window ledge knowing he'd left the drapes open on this side. And there they were. Standing in the middle of the kitchen. Waiting for him. Three bodies looking drastically out of place in the rustic log house.

When he barged through the door, they looked like cornered rabbits and he knew at that moment it would be easy. Easier than the others.

****

Nikki positioned herself with a ham and cheese sandwich at her elbow and watched the scene in the film she was both looking forward to and dreading. The music she wrote for this part of the movie would determine the film's entire score. It was the pivotal moment in the story and she hoped to draw a melody from it, a hook to haunt the entire film. The audience would walk out of the theatre humming it and when it played at the Academy Awards, the poignancy of the music would insure tears. Nikki had to make it memorable.

She studied the scene on her computer, playing the piano as it progressed. Nothing came that reflected the emotion needed. She had to put herself in the main character's place, to feel the horror of the woman who'd been asked to give her child to another woman to save her town's decimation. The childless wife of the Nazi commander had made a deal with her husband to spare the people of the town if the prisoner woman gave them her baby. She had to.

Thinking about Quinn, Nikki remembered how sweet she'd been as a baby. One of the hardest things she'd ever done in her life was to leave her child in a nanny's care for days on end, in order to fulfill her obligations as Goldy. Poor Quinny had had such a rotten mother. No wonder her child had experimented with drugs at the age of fifteen, gone to rehab at sixteen, and had her own sponsor at AA at the age of seventeen. Thank God she'd been sober and drug-free for the last nineteen months.

Nikki found herself sympathizing with the anguish of the heroine. From deep within, the pain of the mother's choice gripped her heart and twisted it until notes poured out of her and filled the room with emotion. As she played, she found something lingering on the edge of her mind. She repeated it and continued, playing the eight bars over and over then built on it, filling in notes where necessary. Working it over, adding notes, slowing it down, repeating passages. Finally she hit the record button to lay down a rough track of what she hoped would be the base of the melody. After years of writing, Nikki no longer questioned how she found the music. Notes arrived from somewhere she couldn't explain and, as they surfaced, she played them.

Finished for now, she laid her head down on the cool, polished surface of the Steinway, her tears pooling where they fell beside her face. In her half-slump, Nikki's hand went to her belly. She wanted this baby with everything she had in her heart. These tears had nothing to do with the music she'd just written, they were filled with the knowledge that her child would be the heart of who she was and nothing would take that away from her. Not this time. Burn had given her one child and they'd agreed that was it. Goldy's focus on work had been necessary to too many people back then for her to have "a brood of kids running around," he'd said.

Nikki walked down the grassy lawn to the dock, watching the moon's ascension from the mountain tops across the lake. Without conscious thought, she stripped down to nothing and dove into the blackness of the bay. Daily temperatures were still summery warm and the water's contrasting coolness was blissful.

Her legs kicked silently below the surface to take her out to the deeper water. Glancing back at the pile of clothes on the end of the dock, it looked like her body had mysteriously disintegrated to leave only a pair of shorts, a shirt and underwear. Her hands cut the surface as she swam to the center of the bay, slightly drunk on the haunting tune that lingered in her head. Rolling onto her back, she stared at the stars, her breasts bobbing on the dark surface of the lake. They were tender now. Soon, other changes would present themselves and she'd feel more confident about the longevity of the pregnancy.

She moved closer to shore. Her bare body felt

unencumbered, rolling from front to back and around several times. Her breasts hit the cooler air on the surface and a sexual thrill shot through her body. She recalled making love with Burn near the dock. Never again. Her sex life would now only involve fantasies about men who might possibly love her, not ever knowing she was Goldy.

"You were a singer?" they'd say. "I didn't know." Her fantasy man never had black hair past his shoulders, no tattoos, never wore leather and chains or heavy eye makeup. Funny thing was, without all that, Burn was actually a sweet-looking man—beautifully boyish, just out of the shower. It was his curse that he worried constantly that everyone didn't love him enough.

Swimming to the shallows, Nikki pondered the conundrum of Pete Bayer. Physically he was so different from Burn, more likely to know how to swing an axe, drive a racing car, rock climb, and survive in the wilderness. Pete was probably the type to sleep in the nude, enjoying the coolness of sheets on his skin, not the type to keep his clothes on during sex like her movie-star crush. Judging from the way Pete kissed her, she guessed he'd be aggressive in bed. He had those sleepy-looking blue eyes, that gravelly voice, the strong torso, and those arms that caught her before she fell at the grocery store.

She grabbed her clothes from the dock and walked through the water toward the beach. The shirt slipped over her head easily and fell past her shoulders and down to her hips. Walking bare-assed out of the water in the dark, Nikki headed for the towel on the lounge chair but stopped when a muffled yell came from the house across the bay. Her initial thought was that Pete had climaxed during sex but realized she'd only been fantasizing about him. She wrapped the towel around her waist.

Elvis's yipping from the cottage drowned out every sound now that he'd spotted Nikki. When she opened the door, another noise called from across the bay. This time it was not a man's voice. It was softer, higher, like a whoop. She hadn't thought that Pete Bayer might be entertaining a woman.

Moving to the dock's edge, she sat facing the Dickersons' house. Spying was what other people had done to her for two decades, and she chided herself for this cartoonish, snoopy version of herself. Still, she waited to listen. Just in case. But nothing else punctuated the night air. No laughing, no yelling, no screams of sexual satisfaction.

Too cold to stay longer, she returned to the house, set the security alarm and trudged up the stairs to bed, feeling rejected and old. People were probably having sex next door while she was swimming naked by herself.

Chapter 6

Skimming across the water at full throttle, the feeling of speed was both scary and exhilarating for Nikki. She'd been staring at the insides of her eyelids a lot lately. Napping, sometimes twice a day, had become the norm but soon the second trimester would allow her more energy. She'd have to break the news of her pregnancy to Quinn before the obvious look of pregnancy arrived. But what words would soften the news of her mother getting knocked up on a one-night stand? Anything said, sounded cheap.

Rounding the bottom of the lake, Nikki cruised lazily back up the opposite side, only fifty feet from shore. The privilege of staring at everyone else's empty cottages was new to her. She usually hid from prying eyes on shore. But this was September and few people remained. Hardly anyone had a place on the side with no roads. And except for the town at the south end, no one visited the northern part of the lake in the winter. When the snow flew, the trails and old logging roads would be impassable.

When she was level with Half Moon Bay, Nikki turned the boat and headed for home. Skimming the surface at a low speed, the boat stopped, waves washing up the sides from the sudden halt.

Elvis fell from his perch on the chair and Nikki lunged to make sure he hadn't hurt himself. Once satisfied her dog was fine, she said a silent prayer to the goddess of motors and turned the key with no success.

Damn. She knew nothing about boats. She'd wait and try again.

Elvis watched her. "S'okay, Elvis. Mommy meant to take a break in the middle of Louisa Lake." She plunked down in the captain's chair and exhaled loudly. Elvis wagged his tail and flew to his perch at the bow. One, two, three...Nikki counted to twenty and looked around. No other boats in sight. When she turned the key again, the silence baffled her.

She opened the engine compartment. Maybe there was an obvious problem, like a dead rat or a fish or something blocking the thingy that helps the boat start.

But she saw nothing unusual even though everything in an engine compartment was grossly unusual to her. She tried the key one more time with no success, and, as she checked her pockets, Nikki remembered her cell phone was back on the kitchen counter. Dammit all. The boat was closer to Dickerson's property facing the backside of her neighbor's peninsula, which was so overgrown with shrubs and blackberry bushes that a stranded boat would be invisible from the house.

Then she noticed the stern line still attached to the cleat, trailing into the water. It had probably been flapping behind the boat for twenty minutes before the propeller caught it. She looked over the side. The rope was pulled tighter than a drum—definitely wound around the propeller. She hit the button to raise the propeller but it wouldn't budge. There wasn't a knife, scissors or anything sharp on board to cut the rope.

"Elvis, can you gnaw through this if I send you

over?" He tilted his head at mommy's ridiculous words. Dammit. She'd have to go in and investigate. The phrase "up a creek without a paddle" came to mind. Remembering a paddle in the floor hatch, she pulled it out and checked the distance to the closest shore. The only way to avoid paddling was if someone came out to tow her. Ten minutes earlier, Nikki had been happy to be the only boat on the lake. Now she cursed her isolation.

Wait a minute…She looked to the mouth of the bay and saw something on the point. Someone was out on the point at Dickerson's. Abandoning dignity, Nikki jumped up on the bow and waved frantically. "Pete!" He could phone the marina and have someone come to get her. Or, if he was resourceful, he could paddle her canoe out to bring a knife. Nikki made half circles in the air with her arms then held the binoculars to her eyes.

No one remained. Hopefully he was phoning the marina to report Nikki's predicament. After fifteen minutes, she was confused and started paddling again, wondering when help would come. Her arms ached, back burned, and Elvis had fallen asleep in the shade of the boat's bimini cover.

Fifty minutes later, the wind came up and making headway became challenging. If she didn't paddle, the boat would be carried into the most isolated part of the whole lake. She shuddered to think how she'd get back to civilization if that happened.

By the time she crossed the mouth of the bay it had been ninety minutes since the breakdown. Her dock was now in full view and when she pulled out of the wind, she took a break. A flash of color at the

Dickerson's window made her blood boil.

Although her first instinct was to yell "What the fuck?" she kept her swear words on the quiet side of her lips. Was he over there laughing that Goldy had to maneuver her boat two miles across the lake? She picked up the paddle and continued, eager to be out of his view. If Pete was a reporter, he'd have driven to the marina to rent a boat and squirreled away the favor she owed him for another time.

With Elvis perched in the bow, Nikki awkwardly closed the distance between the bay's mouth and her dock. "Oh, Elvis, wasn't that fun?" The little dog, who'd assumed the job of a piggish masthead, wagged his tail. "And such good exercise." *For a pregnant woman.* She'd long since tied her T-shirt around her forehead to minimize the sweaty drips into her eyes and now pulled it off to appear more collected than she felt.

Forty feet from the dock, she jumped into the water, both to cool off and to ease the strain on her back. With the bowline in her hand, she towed the floating monstrosity the final few feet, her own beast of burden.

Once the boat was tied up, Nikki stomped across the grass to her house, her middle finger raised in case Pete was looking. She had a good mind to call over to Dickerson's and ask if he had any Tylenol or ask him to rush her to the nearest hospital for muscle cramps.

Instead, she fixed a mug of strong tea, slathered a blueberry muffin in butter and when that found the insides of her stomach, she planted herself in front of the piano. She'd fix the boat later when she could stand the sight of it.

Fury dictated her music as she played with the

emotions of someone who'd been forced to paddle a burdensome boat for almost two hours when a solution stood staring selfishly at her from the trees. There was a desperation that had been lacking in earlier musical efforts. By the time Nikki completed the musical passage, she was mentally exhausted from the effort of being so angry. At Pete.

****

The next morning, crippling stiffness set in and Nikki could barely drag herself out of bed. Stepping into the shower, she let the hot water rain over her aching arms to loosen her shoulder muscles. Even her abdominal muscles were screaming. Apparently being in top physical condition didn't count for paddling a motorboat against the wind for ninety minutes.

She imagined the baby as a tiny roller derby queen. Despite twenty vigorous shows and an electrocution, it had grown inside her these last months. Soon it would be noticeable. To her at least.

Her level of anger had died down to a tolerable level and after tea and soda crackers, she decided to pay Pete a visit. If he said anything about watching her struggle the day before, she'd be tempted to vent her anger. But for now she'd saunter over there like her muscles weren't shrieking at her and he wasn't a jerk.

Nikki pulled out her baking sheets and gathered the ingredients for her grandmother's buns—flour, sugar, salt, raisins, milk. The sweet hot cross confection was about the only thing Nikki knew how to bake and she was determined to deliver the mouth-watering buns to Pete Bayer with an equally sweet smile.

She packaged them warm and added a jar of Quinn's homemade blackberry jam to the basket.

Donning a skintight tank top and short shorts, Nikki set out to make him suffer. This was a man who'd kissed her, shown interest, then abandoned her in a time of need.

Along the way, she thought of what to say. *Oh, it's nothing. I love to bake and of course I can't eat everything myself and keep this knockout body. By the way, were you too busy to help me with the boat yesterday or were you designing software? Or maybe writing a scathing expose about me?*

At the last bend in the dirt road, she heard a rustling noise in the bushes ahead and stopped short. A hundred feet in front, was a young boy. From the looks of him he was probably nine or ten. He stood with his back to her, slashing the bushes with a long stick, oblivious.

Pete Bayer was a father? The high voice from the other night must have been the child, not a girlfriend in a state of sexual pleasure. As she stood watching the boy slay imaginary dragons at the side of the house, thoughts raced through Nikki's head, falling into her path like sparks from fireworks. Pete's excuse for not helping her might have had something to do with the boy.

She backed up a few steps. He couldn't paddle out when there was a child to supervise. He had responsibilities as a father. This put a whole new slant on the situation.

When the boy whirled around to thrust his sword, he caught sight of Nikki and froze, eyes wide.

"Hi," Nikki called, waving her fingers at him. He instantly dropped the stick, ran toward the house and disappeared inside, probably telling his father there was a lady with a basket, standing in their driveway. She waited motionless for so long that a chipmunk scooted past her on its way across the road. Still, no one came out to welcome her.

Maybe the boy was alone? She spun around to see the truck was gone. Perhaps the boy was not allowed outside with his father off the property.

When the curtains rustled at the window, she held her breath. He'd be alone in there. She didn't want to frighten the kid any more than she already had. An eerie feeling warned her to walk away and she did, knowing she was being watched.

****

Pete glanced at the top monitor like he did a hundred times a day and saw the back of Nikki walking down the road. She was crossing the bridge on her way home. He hadn't heard a knock, but he'd just taken a one minute shower.

He took a deep breath and watched the screen. Nikki disappeared out of camera range. Maybe she'd come over for that cup of coffee and thought no one was home. He'd hidden his truck in the garage. Good. He never should have introduced himself to her in the first place. Or kissed her. He thought she'd be gone by now.

But there she was, walking down the road, swinging a basket, like Little Red Riding Hood. Probably coming over to snoop, maybe wondering why he hadn't come out to help her yesterday. He'd tried, but no one answered the phone at the Louisa Lake Marina. He'd even phoned Sandy's Bait Shop and left an anonymous message that someone was stranded in the north end. But he couldn't leave the property even if he'd had a boat. Which he didn't. He'd finally phoned the sheriff and the old guy chuckled and said he'd send someone out in the police boat. Pete seriously doubted there was a police boat. He felt bad—she'd had to bring the boat in herself—but he couldn't let himself get wrapped up in a neighbor's problems.

When he'd agreed to renting this house, the owner said the neighbor wouldn't be there. "She comes one to two weeks a year, always in the summer." But here she was, for God knows how long. Aside from the obvious perk of seeing Goldy in a bikini on a daily basis, living next door had drawbacks, especially when he had a crush about as big as the lake. Something in her eyes told Pete that she might be feeling it too. He knew attraction when he saw it. He'd spent his life reading people. On the few occasions he'd spoken to Nikki, she seemed to be trying too hard, almost nervous to be around him. He had to walk away from this. This plan was already fucked in so many ways. He hoped it would all be over before she saw he had a wife at the house.

****

With a blank sheet of watercolor paper in front of her, Nikki stared at Birch House from her easel at the end of the dock. Finally she had the time to do something as normal as paint a picture. Assuming she had enough talent to do this, she mixed a color for the morning sky and put brush to paper.

The sweet high soprano of a child's voice drifted on the morning air across the bay. It was the boy. She smiled at the innocence of a young child composing his own sound track to his life. She didn't look over. Instead, she filled the top quarter of the page with a

69

dusty blue and wondered if Pete was a good father. September meant school to most kids unless you are the child of a rock star and aren't even safe at a private girls' school. The boy obviously wasn't in the school system or he'd be gone during the day. Maybe Pete homeschooled him. Maybe school started in October.

Her strokes increased in intensity, and Nikki found herself painting in time to the boy's singing. Lots of high action drama was indicated by the staccato of his song. Nikki chuckled, trying to remember if she'd done that sort of thing when she was young. Or had Quinny? Had her precious daughter ever been young and carefree like this?

Between colors, she noticed the child's small frame dash through the trees to the side of the house. He was easy to spot in a white T-shirt. Then, the boy's fantasy was interrupted by a woman's voice. "...Get in...thinking?"

Nikki couldn't make out all the words. The meaning was clear though. An arm waved from the side porch, like a mother who has asked ten times for her son to come in for lunch.

If this was the boy's mother, Pete must be married. If so, what was he doing acting all handsome and flirty with her? And he'd initiated a kiss. What was that all about? She dropped the brush and covered her mouth with her hand.

Recalling her indignation at the kiss, she was somewhat relieved. She'd told Pete he'd taken advantage of the situation. It was a more than a cheap shot to kiss her and think he could get away with it. She felt used now. Something needed to be done to show him she would not be played like this. She'd offer the buns and jam again, this time with a different approach, this time as an offering to the woman. If she was his wife, it would hold an underlying meaning that Nikki was sorry about being stuck with a husband who kisses other women. This visit would put her and Pete on a new track—one that didn't include flirting.

"It's the right thing to do," Nikki said to Elvis, who looked thrilled at the prospect of a walk. Having traded her tracksuit for tan capris and a filmy blouse, Nikki headed down the driveway for the Bayer house with her expectations only an inch off the ground. Her goal was to knock on the door no matter what she saw or heard. She knew an adult was home this time.

Elvis sniffed his way along the road, prancing off into the forest to emerge every few minutes to check on Nikki's whereabouts. Rounding the corner after the bridge, she saw someone ahead. Pete Bayer stood on the deck of the house, leaning against the railing, staring at her, waiting for her.

"Hi." The husky word caught in his throat, making it sound more like a whisper. Today he looked entirely different as a married man.

"Hello." A breeze had been blowing all morning off the lake and Nikki was glad she'd tied her hair back in a ponytail. Pete's uneven hair was just long enough to blow around his face, like fire licking the sides of a log. She came to a halt twenty feet off the deck, trying to look androgynously innocent.

He descended the four stairs and closed the distance. "What's up?"

The amulet at his neck bounced when he talked. Did the symbol have anything to do with a society who kissed women who weren't your wife? "I baked and thought you might like some buns." She held up the basket.

When he flashed his endearing smirk at her, she had to remind herself that this was the man who knew his wedding ring was only one house away when he'd flirted. And this was the same man who'd watched her struggle with the boat. He wasn't her friend.

"That's very nice of you." He didn't look grateful.

Was he being facetious? Reaching for the basket, their fingers touched and his hand lingered longer than necessary, showing her that on his left hand, fourth finger, was a definite gold wedding band. Had he worn it before?

"My daughter and I make this jam and it's pretty good, if I do say so myself." Nikki waited for him to mention his son, or wife...or sister. "My daughter, Quinn," she added to prompt him. "She makes the jam."

In the five seconds they stood facing each other, she got the distinct impression Pete Bayer knew exactly what was going on. She did too. Nikki was being nosey and Pete was hiding something. She needed to put an end to the nonsense. "I thought your son and wife might like the buns." She stuck her chin in the air and waited.

"Thanks," he said, holding back an obvious grin.

It was a struggle to not break down and say, "Hey, what planet are you from? I just acknowledged that you have a son." Anyone else would've said something about the son and wife, or asked what kind of jam it was or if she wanted to come in for a cup of coffee. That's what normal people did, she'd heard. But this guy just stood there, rattling the keys in his hand.

Elvis broke through the trees and charged toward

them, barking at Pete. Unfazed, Pete bent down to let the dog sniff his hand, even though Elvis looked like he might take a few fingers from him. "It's just me, boy."

"Elvis, stop."

"It's okay," he said. "I like dogs."

Elvis stopped barking and let Pete scratch him behind his ears.

"No, it's not okay." She didn't want Elvis fraternizing with this guy.

"He's just protecting you when he barks." Pete stood and they stared awkwardly at each other. "Thanks for the buns and jam."

"Yes, well…" Nikki stumbled for something, anything. "We…I hope…"

Pete cut her off. "I have to get something from the truck." He walked her down the road like a goddamned magpie or whatever those birds were who led predators away from the nest.

She took the hint, thinking that Pete had to have enough social skills to know this was rude. Was being rude the lesser of two evils? If so, what was the other one—revealing he had a wife?

"Goodbye." Nikki walked away, chin higher than usual, trying to pretend she hadn't been rebuffed for the second time.

"Come on, boy," she whispered under her breath. "He's a major weirdo. He's probably going inside to tell his wife that the nosey neighbor was spying again." She mentally snipped the thin thread that connected the two houses, and once inside her house, she set the security alarm to the highest setting.

Chapter 7

Connie hadn't been particularly impressed at the thought of having a rock star next door when Pete told her.

"I'm telling you this in case you see her. Don't talk to her, if you can help it," he'd advised. There was no reason for those two to meet. "And Tony, you stay away from the windows. She's not dangerous, but neither of you need to make a friend."

When he and the kid first met, Tony was resentful of Pete, but that was normal. The boy had big problems and was just trying to protect his mom. Too bad he was so strong-willed. Being a buddy didn't interest Pete, but everything would go a lot easier if Tony didn't oppose everything Pete said.

Tony ran over to see what was in the basket and hadn't been disappointed it was food. After all, he was an eleven-year-old-boy.

"I love these," he said.

"They're hot cross buns from the neighbor, but let me eat half of one first, to make sure they're yummy."

Connie shot him a look of concern as Pete popped a hunk into his mouth and dipped another piece into the jam jar.

"Hey, give me those." Tony grabbed at the basket while Pete held it high enough to make a game of it.

"Say please."

Tony laughed. "You're not so tough. You like jam too."

Pete didn't have time to wonder what Tony thought of him. He had to avoid these bonding moments with the kid. If the boy got in the way and jeopardized everything, he'd have to be removed from the situation. Pete was so close now. Screwing it up would be idiotic. After this one, he'd be done. He had to be. His number would be up soon. Luck had followed him over the years, but he couldn't ask much more from fate. Soon he'd walk away and never look back. A free man.

****

The movie score was almost complete, and Nikki rewarded herself with a moment of solitude on the dock. Twirling her tanned legs in the water, she called Quinn for her daily check-in. Her daughter had been attending regular AA meetings with Julie, her sponsor, and all was well with her boyfriend and at school.

"The guy next door is a little weird, turns out," she said to Quinn.

"Why? What?"

"Mr. Fixit has a child over there and probably a wife, but they never come outside." She went into more detail but didn't mention the kiss.

"They sound creepy, Mom. Don't try to befriend them, okay? They could be hiding something or someone over there in that old house."

Nikki laughed at Quinn. "Okay. That was my last attempt to be neighborly." She wouldn't call them creepy but agreed to stop snooping. Why would a family rent an old log house at the end of summer and never go outside?

Earlier Nikki had found a site online that sold

amulet necklaces and had located the symbol she'd seen around Pete's neck. "I bought you a necklace online."

"Thanks!" Quinn loved jewelry—like her mother.

"It's an amulet that provides protection. The Yoruba luck symbol from Nairobi is known for its protective properties," she said. "It's one of the oldest amulets on the African continent."

"Nice. What do I need protection from?" Quinn asked innocently.

"I don't know, sweetie. Bad marks?" They laughed.

"Just wear it to appease your mother, will you?" It was impossible to not continually worry about Quinn's safety, but she was trying to let her daughter lead a normal life, just like Quinn was trying to not worry about her mother alone at the lake. A thought jumped into Nikki's head to make her blood quicken. "Quinn, please tell me that Pete Bayer is not someone hired by you or Merilee or anyone else on my staff."

"Not that I know. Besides, Merilee doesn't know where you are."

"That's right," she said. No one knew but Quinn. Merilee wouldn't go behind Nikki's back to hire a security guard. She was loyal, like Elvis. And Security Steve had assured her that Pete wasn't on his payroll. She'd already searched the name Pete Bayer online and came up empty. Nothing. She had another call coming in. "Have a wonderful day, my sweet girl, and call me if you need me." This had always been their sign-off.

"Mrs. Crossland? It's P.I. Services in Seattle."

Nikki had been waiting for this call. "Did you find anything?"

"No, I'm sorry. I've been unable to come up with

anything for the name Pete Bayer with that description and the license plate number isn't registered."

"What do you mean that plate isn't registered?"

"The number doesn't exist."

"He's got a plate and it's not made out of cardboard."

"It probably means it's an old plate. I'm guessing his name is an alias." He said it so casually that Nikki wondered if a lot of people went around telling neighbors fake names and making their own license plates. If so, she had a lot to learn about how normal people functioned in the real world. No one knew who this guy was. It was like he didn't exist. At least not under that name.

Hanging up, she saw the Dickerson's side door open. The woman and boy made circles around the garbage can area, hunting for something on the ground until a whoop sounded from them like a cry of victory. Whatever they'd been looking for must have been found. Nikki saw the mother try to hug the boy as he jumped up and down.

Nikki stood at the end of the dock watching until the boy stopped jumping. The mother glanced over to see her staring at them. "Hi!" Nikki called before she could stop herself.

Without a wave or hello, they ran inside the house and slammed the door to leave Nikki frozen in confusion. That was the second time the boy ran away from her. And now the wife did it too. She'd baked them buns, for crying out loud.

The pickup truck sped back to the house, stirring up dust from several weeks of sunshine. Keeping one eye on the house, she sat down on the dock again and dipped her feet in the water. Pete flew out of the truck and bounded into the house. He'd only been gone a few minutes, no time for groceries.

The lake was getting colder. She watched the watery ripples fan out from her immersed legs. The tune she hummed was the melody from the movie. Singing it over and over she let it unravel as she continued on to a new part she hadn't known was needed. Excited, she ran into the house to record the newest addition to the melody. She played and wrote, rewinding the movie over and over again to get the music to fit the track perfectly.

Nikki lost track of time until a knock on the door broke her concentration. Looking through the peephole, she saw Pete Bayer. Her heart flipped at the sight of him, and, taking a deep breath, she disarmed the system and swung open the door. She waited for him to speak. After all, he'd been rude the last time she attempted conversation.

"Returning your basket." He twirled it between them. "Thank you."

She took the basket from him, making sure their fingers didn't touch. "You're welcome."

He lingered.

She waited.

"My wife said she saw you and didn't wave.

Hearing him say the word "wife," her heart sank fully to the bottom of where it hovered. She'd been hoping they were something less until this confirmation.

He waited.

"I scared them." *Why did you kiss me if you're married?*

"They were looking for Connie's wedding ring that fell off. She's lost weight and it's too big now."

This seemed like far too much information, but Nikki nodded. "Looked like they found it."

He nodded.

"Wedding rings are important," she said, folding her arms across her chest, to reveal the absence of one.

He started to say something then stopped.

"Did your wife like the buns?" She emphasized the word "wife."

"Yes, thanks and so did…the boy. The jam was a big hit too." She and Pete Bayer were pathetically struggling for conversation, and Nikki was embarrassed for them. Still she waited for him to say more, almost enjoying his squirminess.

"Anyways…I'd better be going," he said.

"Maybe your wife would like the recipe for the buns." Nikki stared hard into Pete's face.

"No, she doesn't cook. She would've come but she's helping Tony with homework."

Nikki nodded, seriously doubting the wife would've walked down the road for a neighborly visit. Maybe she knew Pete kissed her and was purposely avoiding the temptress next door. That would be a shame when it was her husband she should be avoiding.

"I'd better get back to work." He nodded.

The conversation pained her with its need for honesty, and she couldn't wait to put the door between her and Pete. Still, she said nothing.

"Bye." He turned on his heel and with the athleticism of someone who'd played sports all his life, descended the back porch stairs and walked away.

"Let me know if your son wants to go for a boat

ride." The words were out of her mouth before she could censor them. "I go every day."

Pete was thirty feet from the porch when he turned around and walked backward. "Thanks, but he's not much for the water." He turned and disappeared down the road, leaving Nikki wondering about the family—a wife who doesn't leave the house, a boy who wasn't fond of water, and a father who rents them a cabin on a lake in the wilderness and kisses other women.

****

All hell had broken loose in Los Angeles. According to Quinn, Burn was accusing Nikki of hiding in Birch House, avoiding her duty, and leaving him with a colossal press mess.

"Dad's not handling the negative publicity very well," Quinn said, during their morning phone call.

The tone of Quinn's voice made Nikki want to shield her daughter from Burn's belly-aching and throttle her ex-husband. Of course he wasn't doing well. She'd recommended he go somewhere to lie low until the media frenzy died down. He'd refused. Burn was an alarmist, and it had been his decision to stay in L.A.

"I'll call and see what I can do." Nikki sat in a front deck chair in a pair of shorts and T-shirt with her bare feet on the railing. She dialed Burn's cell phone. "What's going on, Burn?"

"Hi, baby. How ya doin'?" He didn't sound upset.

"Fine. I hear you're being hounded." Concern did not leak through into her voice.

"Yeah. It's bad here. The fucking press is everywhere."

"I heard that you phoned Quinn to tell her." *You're*

complaining to our child, you dumb ass!

"They won't leave me alone."

Someone spoke in the background. Then in true Burn form, he said, "Can I call you back? I'm in the middle of something."

He couldn't be running from the press as they spoke. "Okay."

"Ten minutes."

Thirty minutes later, she gave up waiting, knowing that Burn was not immediately in need of her help. She called Phyllis to see how things were going. Phyllis rarely initiated a call to Nikki, which was golden in a publicist.

"How are we looking in the press?" She'd avoided the entertainment news online for the last few days.

"Not bad, not bad at all. Burn, a little worse than you, seeing he's openly dating. They're speculating that he might have played around while he was married to you."

Nikki almost laughed, to think about how much Burn had played around.

Phyllis continued. "I'm going to let them speculate. Burn fired me last week, and now I'm only working for you."

"You're kidding."

"Nope."

"Well, I hope he's got a good substitute. He might be groveling soon."

"The press is saying that he drove you away with his affairs. You're still America's rock sweetheart."

Nikki frowned. "I really don't want Burn to look bad, Phyllis. For Quinny's sake." She felt the need to mention her daughter, whom Phyllis loved. "Can we make a statement or something? Maybe say that Burn and I had a wonderful marriage and, like every couple in the world, we had our challenges."

"How about 'Goldy would like to remind her fans that she and Burn are still dear friends and that their marriage had trials like any other, but that they loved each other deeply. Their divorce was private and shall remain so, and it hurts Goldy to have her marriage judged and dissected in the press.' Something like that?"

"Yes, just like that. Thanks, Phyllis."

But when the press heard the statement from Goldy, instead of being appeased, they grew more desperate. "Goldy Speaks from Seclusion" and "The Search for Goldy" were the immediate reactions. The Goldy web site broke all records for hits that day and soon no one was convinced that the woman in Nassau was Goldy.

Nikki had no intention of continuing with this dialogue. It was never enough. She could give interviews and they'd still want more of her. Regardless, she spent the whole day on the phone to staff—Phyllis, Merilee, her manager Grant, security staff, even Burn.

Then things took a turn for the worse when the press involved Quinn. Reporters camped out on the lawn of the apartment building where Quinn and Julie lived, watching and waiting to get a statement.

Action had to be taken. Nikki called Steve and he notified the local police as well as sending a bodyguard from L.A. whose job was to stay by Quinn's side until this blew over. Even though Quinn ranted about the injustice of having someone hover over her while her mother went without, Nikki insisted. "No bargaining on this one, kiddo," she said.

"Steve is sending Dwayne." He'd been one of Quinn's favorite guards on tour, always happy, a reformed alcoholic who took Quinn's abstinence seriously. She hoped Quinn would appreciate his familiar face instead of working to avoid him.

Dwayne's report the first night indicated that the press were local, no pestering paparazzi that he could see, and everything seemed to be under control. No one was breaking the law, at least. "We're just sitting here at Pepe's pizza, having dinner, Ms. Burnside. I'm watching Quinn and her friend Julie eat while reporters watch them through the window."

"Keep my baby safe, Dwayne." Nikki clicked the cell phone shut and headed for the dock. A light shone from behind a front curtain at the Dickerson house. As she stood studying the house, the idea that the Bayer family might have been hired to watch her seemed silly now.

****

A blanket of low clouds hung over the lake, threatening rain. It was perfect timing to make a pot of chili. Nikki had been craving savory foods lately and wanted to honor what her body craved and ultimately what her baby needed.

The bodyguard was doing his job in Seattle but also driving a college girl crazy with his presence. Not much had been written about Goldy in the last few days, and there'd been no new letters from Shakespeare in nearly four weeks. Nikki considered the possibility of letting Dwayne return to Los Angeles. He had a messy custody battle with his ex-wife on the court dockets soon.

Rain bounced off the deck as Nikki snuggled into the couch with a novel. She'd just gotten settled when her cell phone rang.

"Nicole Crossland?" Gateman always asked.

"Yes."

"This is Agent Ted Gateman of the Federal Bureau of Investigation."

"Hi, Ted."

"How are things where you are?"

This helped verify her identity. "Louisa Lake, Ted. I'm at my house at Louisa Lake." She gave him her social security number. "Now what's going on?"

"We got another letter."

A jolt shot through her like she'd been slapped in the face with a wet towel. "Was it a goodbye letter?"

"Not exactly."

"You'd better send it on." She glanced fearfully at the computer monitor.

"My better judgment tells me to ignore your request to see all letters."

Her hand went immediately to her belly, and her face muscles clenched. "Why do you think I shouldn't see this one?"

"You're alone out there."

"Ted, I feel safer here than in Los Angeles."

"The letter mentions Quinn in Seattle."

The blood drained from Nikki's face.

"Not a threat to her. It just mentions her name. And remember it's common knowledge she's at school in Seattle."

"Oh, God."

"We sent an agent to Quinn. She's with her right now."

"Quinn has a bodyguard, too."

"Do you have a bodyguard, Nikki?"

"No. Did he mention my location?"

"No."

"You know how isolated I am, and this state-of-the-art security system tells me when every chipmunk runs across my deck."

Gateman hesitated. "You have your dog, right?"

Nikki would've laughed if it had been funny. "He's a small pug mix, you know that." She looked down at Elvis who was wagging his tail like everyone's friend.

"The letter was mailed from Los Angeles."

"What did he say about Quinn?"

"Not much, and the letter sounds like he's still in L.A."

"Send it, Ted. By email. I need to call Quinn. Hang on." With the house phone, she punched in Quinn's number. Hearing her daughter's voice on the other end allowed Nikki to exhale. "Sweetie, I got a weird letter from a stalker and just as a precaution, we've sent over a federal agent to check on you."

"She's here now. I'm fine. Jarrod and I are just getting ready to go to class."

"Just ignore her, like Dwayne." Quinn would be trying to think of an argument, so Nikki preempted any protests she might make. "Indulge me, okay?"

"Mom?"

"Yes."

"Are you safe?"

"I'm fine out here. You know that." Just then the security system buzzed to indicate someone was on the property. "I'll call you later, sweet girl." Nikki hung up just as someone wrapped on the back door. Ted was still on the other phone. "There's someone at my door, Ted. Hang on, I'll read the letter in a minute."

"Nikki, don't open the door without…"

After looking at the video monitor, she disarmed the system and opened the door to a woman in a yellow rain slicker and a boy cowering behind her. Both were dripping wet. "Come in," Nikki said.

The woman pushed her son inside and, grabbing the edge of the half-open door, slammed it shut behind her. "I'm Connie Bayer and this is my son, Tony." She stood with her arm around the boy. "I'm sorry to disturb you, but there's a squirrel in our house and while Pete is trying to take care of it, I was hoping we could wait here."

The boy glanced from his mother to Nikki and back again, his brows knit together.

"Of course, come in." Nikki couldn't imagine how big and dangerous the squirrel must be to make them this frightened, but after she locked and bolted the door, she took their coats, armed the security system, and walked down the hall with her guests. The email jumped out at her from the computer screen across the room.

The boy followed his mother to the great room, where the fire crackled in the hearth. His eyes were glued to her.

"I'm Nikki." She smiled at Connie Bayer, like this was a perfectly normal social call. "I was just going to make a cup of tea. Would you like to join me?" Her voice sounded anxious, but her distracted guests didn't seem to notice.

"That would be nice." The mother nodded and smiled reassuringly at the boy.

Remembering Agent Gateman, she told Ted she had company and would call him back.

"Tell me who your company is."

"My neighbors, Connie Bayer and her son, Tony," she whispered as she walked into the open kitchen area to start the kettle.

"Call me in twenty minutes. And Nikki, be careful."

She promised, then hung up and filled the kettle with water.

"This is such a pretty house," Connie commented from the far side of the great room.

"Thank you. My husband and..." She caught her slip. "I mean, my ex-husband and I built it years ago. Our daughter was ten at the time." She smiled at them from the kitchen. "How old are you, Tony?" Before the boy answered, he checked with his mother.

"Eleven." Connie smiled at Nikki as if to say children are funny sometimes. "He just turned eleven," she clarified, forcing a pinched smile.

Not wanting to make Connie and Tony concoct a story they weren't prepared for, Nikki opted to forget the squirrel and pretend it was perfectly normal to have them run down the road in the pouring rain to avoid a rodent. It was a remote possibility that Connie Bayer was terrified of small wildlife and had transferred that phobia to her son, but something told her that wasn't the case. Something strange was going on and she had to stay out of it.

Chapter 8

"Are you enjoying Louisa Lake?" Nikki took three mugs from the cupboard and retrieved a packet of hot chocolate from the pantry.

"Yes," Connie answered. "Tony." She motioned with a nod for the boy to get away from the window.

Nikki pretended not to see. "It's rainy today, but we've had a nice September, haven't we?"

"Lovely."

"I hear your husband is a writer?"

Connie looked uncomfortable. "Computer manuals."

"Oh, not novels and memoirs?" She laughed lightly.

"No."

Nikki wanted to believe her. "Where were you before this?" The conversation sounded like a job interview as Nikki waited for the kettle to boil.

"New York." Connie shifted uneasily.

"Oh, I lived in New York for a while," Nikki said, but her guest didn't seem to care, or hear. Nikki got the distinct impression they were hiding at her house. She poured the hot water into the teapot and carried the tea tray to the table.

"It's a pretty house, isn't it, Tony?" Connie said. Tony strained to look out the window from his perch on the couch.

She tried again. "Isn't this a nice house, Tony?"

"Mom, should we check on…the squirrel and see if…Dad is ok." He spoke in jerky spasms as he took the hot chocolate from Nikki.

"He'll let us know." Connie smiled at Nikki, but a moment passed between them when both women understood there was no squirrel. Nikki wasn't sure if the secrecy was for the boy or for her, but she nodded almost imperceptibly at Connie.

Connie Bayer was in her late thirties, shorter than Nikki and bursting out of her black jeans and sweater. She had a brown curly hairdo, suggestive of a bad appointment with a far-sighted hairdresser and, without makeup, her high cheekbones and large, deep-set eyes gave her a haunted look.

Staring at her teacup, with hands clenched in her lap, Connie looked pained. Maybe she didn't like tea. "It's a beautiful house, isn't it, Tony?" She had a slight accent that Nikki couldn't place.

"Mom, you already asked me that." Tony got up and ran his hand over the books' edges, almost lovingly. "You have a lot of books."

"My daughter and I like to read. How 'bout you?" Nikki leaned against the corner of the couch, hesitant to sit down.

"Yeah." His lanky frame didn't remind Nikki of Pete Bayer at all. Even if this was a second marriage, something didn't quite fit.

"If you see one you like, you're welcome to borrow it."

"No, thanks." Tony spoke too quickly.

Connie lifted the tea mug to her lips slowly.

Nikki sat down. "Are you spending October on the

lake?'

Connie set the mug back on the table, without a sip. "I don't think so, but we'll see."

"Pete'll tell us," Tony blurted.

Connie looked at her son disapprovingly, and he turned to face the books, hiding his embarrassment at either calling his father Pete, or talking overtop of his mother.

"It's all right," Nikki whispered to Connie, not sure why she said this, but the look in Connie's eyes conveyed a trust. "Don't worry about me." On closer inspection she noticed that Connie's hair was a wig—just another question mark on a page of unanswered strangeness. The edge of the wig was visible through a curl at the back.

Nikki tried to fill the gaps with chit chat while Connie kept the tea cup at her lips, looking like she was trying to keep her mouth busy in case words started to pop out.

"Nice town." "Touristy lake." "Days getting shorter." Nikki's words were stilted.

"Yes." "Hmm." "They are," Connie answered.

She was about to ask Connie if they'd like to go boating some sunny day, when the boy yelled, "There's the police!"

Nikki's first thought was that Gateman had sent the police, but when she looked out the window, the sheriff's car sped past Birch House, coming from the direction of Dickerson's.

"There's Pete…I mean, Dad." Tony craned his neck.

Connie's face went white and she turned to Tony with wide eyes. "Tony, get away from the window!"

"Looks like the police got the squirrel," Nikki said. What was going on? The sheriff had been summoned to the log house. All Nikki could think of was that Pete had done something to frighten Connie and Tony, and she'd called the police.

"Was Pete in the cruiser, Connie?"

Connie looked flustered but chose that moment to return to her seat on the couch to quietly add sugar to her cup of tea.

"Did they take Pete away? Connie, you must know this looks strange." Nikki followed and looked into her guest's eyes. She dropped her voice to a whisper, for Tony's sake. "Tell me what's going on."

A loud knock sounded at the back door. If Pete was in the squad car, who was knocking on her door? Tony rushed to his mother and shrank in to her side.

The video monitor revealed Pete at her back door. She disarmed the system and opened the door slowly. He stood on the threshold dripping wet, wearing only a clinging shirt and jeans, no coat, no shoes. "What's going on?" she asked tentatively.

"Are Connie and Tony here?" He spoke quickly.

"Yes." Why didn't he know that? "Are you coming in?"

Pete's cheeks were high with color. He shook his head. "I shouldn't. I'm really wet. I just came to get …my family."

"Step in so I can close the door. Why were the police here?" Nikki heard herself asking the million dollar question.

Pete looked at her strangely for a few seconds. "I didn't see them."

Daring him to continue to lie to her, she squinted

and held her gaze. "Really?"

"Probably a routine call." He shrugged. "I heard they cruise around checking on people in the off season." He stepped in and closed the door. "Connie!" he called.

"We're here, Pete." Her voice was wobbly.

Pete's hair hung in strings and his shirt clung to his form, giving Nikki more of a view of his physique than she wanted. She gulped and retrieved a fluffy beach towel for him. After throwing him the towel she returned to the family room. "Looks like the coast is clear."

Connie and Tony didn't move. Just looked at each other.

"Maybe your husband would like something hot to drink."

"No." Connie said this so quickly that Nikki stopped in her tracks.

"I can wait for them," Pete called from the back door, annoyance leaking into his words.

Tony watched his mother.

After a long pause, Connie set her mug on the coffee table and stood to leave. "Time to go, Tony."

The disappointment in the boy's face prompted Nikki to tell him to wander over anytime. "Come to dinner tomorrow, if you like. All of you. I can make a pot of spaghetti." The invitation was in the air before Nikki thought about it. It might be a good opportunity to dispel any theories she was tossing around about Pete being an abusive husband who'd just had a warning from the police.

"I don't think tomorrow works." Connie patted her synthetic hair.

"I love spaghetti!" Tony was at the window again and Connie waved him back.

"Maybe the next night?" Nikki shrugged.

"I'll check with Pete, but I don't think we can."

Nikki leaned in to whisper, "You could come without him."

Connie took her mug to the sink where she rinsed it and set it on the counter. Her delicate hands were so graceful. They were hands that would never provide protection against a man as big as Pete.

At the back door, Connie glanced at her husband holding out her rain slicker. "We've been invited to dinner tomorrow, Pete, but I told Nikki I didn't think we could." She didn't make eye contact with her husband.

"Sorry." Pete's look of annoyance was barely masked. Why was *he* mad?

Nikki threw him Burn's bush coat. "Return it later." She didn't give him a chance to refuse. "How's your writing going?"

Pete didn't miss a beat. "Good." He looked at Connie. "Ready?" He opened the door and stepped out before his wife, which Nikki thought strange until she saw him scanning the forest.

Nikki wanted to offer help, but for what? And she wasn't even sure they needed it. She and Connie had only exchanged a look that verified something was going on.

"Connie." Nikki touched the woman's sleeve as she passed. "You can always come here."

Pete stood on the deck with the boy. Hearing Nikki whisper, he spun around.

"Thank you, Nikki, the tea was just what I

needed." And with that, the Bayers set off down the road through the rain without looking back. Pete's arm around Connie's shoulders looked stiff and assertive.

Nikki had to remind herself to not judge their relationship based on what she saw. Pete and Connie could be perfectly happy even though they seemed different in every way. The only thing Nikki was sure of was that there was no squirrel in their house. Something had chased those two out fast enough that running to Nikki's place was a better choice than staying in the house with Pete.

Nikki was reminded of a documentary she'd once watched on killer whales. The cameraman had filmed a seal jumping into the research boat to escape the attack from its predator, the whale. The seal's fear of humans was less than its fear of the whale and weighing that out, had chosen the boat. In this instance, Connie and Tony were the seals.

With her back to the wall and Elvis beside her, she read Shakespeare's latest letter:

My Dearest One,

Why have you forsaken me? I am in waiting for your return. Or are you close and teasing me? Have you followed Quinn to Seattle, my love?

Wherever you are, you must return and we must finish this. You will succumb. Your blood will run freely over my trembling body.

The courses of true love never did run smooth.

Your Beloved

It was short, not as graphic as usual, and his words indicated that he was going to wait for her return to L.A. His question of her whereabouts was a good sign. Just as Nikki closed her laptop, her cell phone rang.

Caller ID indicated a name she knew to be Agent Gateman.

"Nicole Crossland?" he asked.

"I got the letter, Ted, and it's not as bad as all the others. Isn't that a good sign?"

"Nikki, listen carefully. In the last hour, a man was apprehended on your property, and the local police have taken him into town for questioning. I'm sending someone to Louisa Lake."

"Oh, God!" Nikki hadn't locked the door or set the security alarm behind the Bayers. Running to the back door, she bolted it and punched in the numbers to the security system.

"It doesn't mean we got Shakespeare," the agent continued, "but a Caucasian male was coming through the trees from a parked rental car, big guy, 40ish, with a gun."

"He was here at Louisa Lake, just now?"

"Affirmative."

"And Harold caught him?" It didn't seem possible. Harold was all doughy and smiles, close to retirement.

"Yes."

Was that what the last hour was all about? Had Connie and Tony been threatened somehow with someone who was coming through the trees? "I saw the police car pass my house." Nikki was frozen to her spot, imagining what could have just happened. The only way Harold Gaines could take down a man running through the woods was if the stalker was in worse shape. "Did Harold shoot him?"

"No shots fired."

Agent Gateman took another call, and Nikki waited. Pete must've been the brawn in that operation.

What the hell?

"I recommend you get a bodyguard, Nikki, until we verify the identity of the perpetrator. I'll get in touch, within the hour. And don't open your door to anyone until you talk to me."

When the call came from Gateman twenty minutes later, Nikki and Elvis were sitting in the great room, waiting to hear the rest of the story, her handgun on the table in front of her. Nikki hadn't expected what came next.

"Nicole Crossland?"

"Hi, Ted. What's going on?" She imagined the FBI team searching a stinking North Hollywood hovel, sifting through incriminating evidence, thumbing through photos of her and copies of the horrific letters Shakespeare had written her.

"This is Agent Gate—"

"What's happening?"

"Do you know a Dwayne Capleoni?"

She froze. "Yes, he's my daughter's bodyguard in Seattle."

"He's not in Seattle. He's the man in the Louisa Lake jail right now, waiting to be questioned on charges of armed trespassing."

****

Fuck. Living beside Goldy was not as safe as Pete had originally hoped. When the signal alerted him to a visitor on the road, he ran to the bedroom where all visible points of approach were being monitored. A black sedan drove slowly along the dirt track. He hit "zoom" on the keyboard and saw it was one man driving, alone.

Connie was making peanut butter cookies—Tony's

favorite. "Connie, someone's on the road, approaching the gate," Pete shouted above the video game noise. The road in was long enough that it would take at least three minutes to make it to the gate and several more to run through the woods. Pete could find this guy in five minutes. "Get under the bed. Both of you. Now! Lock the door behind me." Running through the kitchen, Pete fingered the gun in his holster and bolted outside into the pouring rain.

He cut through the forest to where he'd intersect the intruder on the road. One minute later, he was close to Nikki's house in the trees and caught sight of Connie and Tony in yellow rain slickers knocking on her back door.

Shit. Didn't Connie know it was dangerous for her to run around outside like that? Her stupidity was going to get her killed. And Tony. No matter what he told her to do, she found her own plan. He'd have to chew her out after this one.

When Pete saw the perp exit his car at the gate and sneak through the brush, he anticipated his path. The man did not have a weapon in either hand. Pete slipped behind a big tree. As the man plodded through the woods, Pete readied himself. Just as the perpetrator passed, Pete crept out silently. Undetected, he closed the distance between them in two strides and grabbed the man in a choke hold. Good resistance made it a challenge but the forest creeper didn't have a chance. He brought the intruder to the ground and dug the gun into the man's side. His victim stopped squirming.

"This is private property," Pete said quietly. "Hands behind your head."

"Don't shoot. I'm just looking for my friend's

house."

"Who's your friend?" Pete found a gun holster and a nice Glock inside it.

"Female, long blonde hair, named Nikki."

He was after Goldy. Pete should've known. This man was not looking for them. Wearing a fancy pair of cowboy boots and a satin bomber jacket, he could've been a Goldy roadie but Pete wasn't taking chances. "Then why are you sneaking through the trees, buddy?" Pete cuffed him.

"I was going to surprise Nikki."

"With a gun? Ha! Why would someone's friend have a gun if they're on a social call?" Pete pulled the guy to his feet and pushed him in the direction of the log house.

"I have the gun in case I see a bear."

Pete laughed. "And I was born yesterday, pal. You'd have surprised her all right with that Glock." He'd run a check on him just in case, verify he wasn't looking for Connie.

"Are you taking me to Nikki?" The man slowed down at the turnoff to Birch House.

"Indirectly. First to that house, then to the sheriff in town, then you might see your friend Nikki at the hearing." He couldn't march this scum to Nikki's door to see if she knew him. Connie and Tony were there.

"You're making a big mistake. I know Nikki. She'll tell you."

"Shut up and march." Pete pushed him forward.

After handcuffing him to a post in the log house kitchen, he stuffed one of Tony's dirty socks in the guy's mouth and grabbed his wallet from his back pocket. Nothing showed on the background check except that he was from Los Angeles and had never been arrested. Pete called the sheriff.

"Harold Gaines here."

"This is Pete Bayer at the Dickerson house. I just found someone roaming around the woods out here with a Glock who says he's on a social call looking for someone named Nikki."

"Well, well, well...we better talk to him." Harold sounded amused.

"Probably should."

"I got a deputy on that side of the lake. I'll radio him to come get our visitor."

"I'm holding him at Dickerson's."

Forcing the intruder outside to the driveway, Pete motioned for him to sit on the wet ground. He didn't want him in the log house any longer than necessary, looking around, dripping on the floor. "Looks like you can tell the sheriff your story and see if he believes you."

The squad car pulled up minutes later, and Pete handed the guy over. Let the police do their job. He had enough to worry about and didn't exactly want the local cops sniffing around inside the Dickerson's house. This was bad enough.

As the squad car passed Birch House, Pete hoped that Connie and Tony weren't standing at the back door in full view for the deputy.

The clouds above the lake grew heavy, and sheets of rain pelted the ground like heavy bullet fire. God damned trespasser putting him through all this. Pete sprinted toward Nikki's house. He imagined Goldy had endured her share of deranged fans over the years. This guy was probably one of those. But a gun? And why hadn't Connie and Tony hid under the bed like they'd been told? Now Pete was mad. He had rules, and if they weren't going to follow them, what was he doing with these two?

He waited in Nikki's back room, listening to the muffled conversation down the hall, dripping on Nikki's floor. The coats that hung on hooks indicated one adult man's, two smaller jackets, and a sweatshirt he assumed was Nikki's. Who owned the man's jacket? Her ex? Somehow a plaid quilted jacket didn't suit the rock legend, Burn Burnside.

This was bullshit, all this drama. It proved they had to cut ties with their next-door neighbor. She was a magnet for attention, and this remote location wasn't secure anymore.

Thinking about his sailboat, he considered the possibility of taking Connie and Tony there. A live-aboard, in the middle of the ocean had to be better than being next door to a goddamned rock star.

Chapter 9

"Dwayne Capleoni!" Nikki stared at the phone in disbelief. Hadn't he been with her in every city on tour last year? He wasn't some stalker, writing and mailing letters from L.A. He was the best bodyguard she'd had. "I think you must be mistaken, Ted. Dwayne works for me on security. He's a good guy."

"He was apprehended on your property with a gun. The town sheriff is holding him until our agent arrives."

Why was he running through the woods at the lake and not with Quinn in Seattle? Another thought struck like a lightning bolt. If Dwayne was Shakespeare, was her daughter safe? Or even alive? "Who's with Quinn?" Nikki's heart was in her mouth.

"I'm waiting for a call to confirm that the agent has arrived."

Nikki dialed Quinn's cell number from the house phone, keeping Agent Gateman on the line. It went to voice mail. "Call me, as soon as you hear this, sweetie." Nikki returned to Agent Gateman who was talking on another line.

"Keep me posted," he said to someone. "Okay Nikki, we followed Quinn and her boyfriend, a Jarrod Creeley, walking to class ten minutes ago and are now waiting outside her classroom door. Can you verify that's the boyfriend?"

"Yes." Nikki described her daughter's boyfriend

from what Quinn had told her. "I can't figure out why Dwayne came to the lake. Quinn isn't supposed to tell anyone where I am." Nikki paced the room with the phone to her ear. "I won't feel better until I hear from her."

"Remember, Nikki, we haven't found evidence that this guy is Shakespeare."

It was hard for Nikki to believe Dwayne could be the deranged stalker when she'd had so many dealings with the guard in the last year. He'd always seemed friendly, harmless. Nikki swept through her address book to find the phone number for Steve. He'd hired Dwayne.

Gateman continued. "According to the sheriff, Capleoni says he was told to check on you and had authority. I'm waiting for verification on that."

"On whose authority?" she said. "I hired him to guard my daughter, and I'm the only one who can change his job." She plunked down on the couch and unsuccessfully tried to picture the nice man she knew as Dwayne, writing scathing letters about torturing her.

The stalkers she'd known over the years always had a deranged look, and Dwayne didn't fit the bill. Yellow, the girl who killed herself, had appeared desperate and breathless, more possessed as the obsession grew over the year she followed the band. She had alternated between threatening to kill Goldy and professing her love—something that turned vulgar and evil in time. Unfortunately, the FBI couldn't find her. She'd been tricky, staying out of sight in the last few months. Until the final night. The stadium had long emptied but one audience member remained seated in the top corner of the last row. Security found her slumped in her seat, dead, pumped full of sleeping pills, drained of blood. If the pills hadn't kill her, the blood loss would.

Three hours after his capture, Dwayne's story checked out. He'd been convinced by Quinn to drive to the lake to check on her mother. Hearing the confirmation from Quinn, Nikki was furious that her daughter would do that. And that Dwayne would agree to such a scheme.

"I didn't just want to get him out of my hair, Mom. I'm worried about you." Quinn was in tears over the confusion and embarrassment she'd caused. "Mom, why did you call the FBI on Dwayne?" She was still blissfully ignorant of Shakespeare.

"Harold summoned them according to protocol."

"I think it's unsafe for you to be out there on your own. Please, Mom, get a bodyguard."

A bodyguard would ruin everything. "No, sweetie. We've been through this. Don't start with me."

"Why me and not you? It makes no sense." Quinn's voice had risen to a squeak that Nikki recognized from childhood. If she didn't redirect the conversation, it might not end well.

"You are amongst people. I'm living in a secluded, wilderness cabin. It's different. Anyhow, I'm planning on coming to Seattle soon and I might get a bodyguard for that."

"Dwayne?"

"Probably not. I'm sending him home, but you have to let me know if the press bothers you again. And in the future, don't ever go over my head to change the plan."

"I'm sorry." Quinn's voice was tiny and full of

regret.

****

After the FBI cleared Dwayne, Nikki told Steve to send him home without stopping at Quinn's. He'd insisted that his run through the woods was simply to verify Nikki was fine and then report back to Quinn without detection. Steve wanted to fire him, but Nikki vetoed that idea. Although Dwayne had made a serious mistake by disobeying orders, she could only imagine how persuasive Quinn had been in getting him to drive five hours to the lake for one glimpse of her mother. Nikki didn't want to add to his problems by having him fired.

"Just put him on a time-out or something. I mean it."

Steve sighed. "If that's what you want."

"He's a good guy." Even though he'd joined the tour late, Dwayne had been one of her favorites, always there when she needed him and never complaining about late nights, early mornings. She'd heard on tour that Dwayne had his share of personal problems and Nikki liked to take care of her family of people. "Just swear him to secrecy, will you. I don't want my location known."

****

The next day the sun rose in full force, and it was once again summer. While making breakfast, Nikki glanced out the kitchen window and saw Pete walking along the road toward her house. Her heart did a little dance at the sight of him. His body moved like a panther, with every muscle firing perfectly with minimum effort. The morning sun hit him from behind, giving him an ethereal look. God, he was handsome.

Nikki's face flushed as she waited for his knock. When she didn't hear one, she ran to the kitchen. When he disappeared around the bend in the road, disappointment hit her like a two-by-four.

Nikki opened the back door. Burn's old plaid jacket hung from the doorknob, and a note was taped to the edge of the window.

"Can't do dinner. Connie." Before hanging the coat on the hook, Nikki absently held it to her face and breathed deeply. It smelled like Pete. Realizing what she'd done, and how his scent made her feel, she held the coat at arm's length. "No, no, no," she admonished herself, but Elvis heard and cowered at her feet, thinking he'd done something wrong. "Not you, big guy. Me. I gotta stop this crush I have on the crazy, married neighbor." She tossed the coat into the dirty laundry hamper. It was best that the Bayers turned down her offer.

It was a perfect October day. The lake was too cold for swimming now. Yesterday's rain had left a glistening on everything, bringing out the deepest green from the surrounding foliage. Little birds chirped as they flew from tree to bush and darted to the sandy beach in search of food.

Standing on the deck with a cup of tea, Nikki watched her boat bob alongside the dock as if nodding a good morning. Elvis's ears rose and fell with the movement of the birds in front of him, his interest only heightened if they flew too close to his post on the grass.

Nikki brought her keyboard out to the deck's table. Planting herself in front, she played randomly, drifting and flowing through a lilting melody, her fingers dancing across the keys. It was a pretty tune, and as she began to hum, she closed her eyes. It felt so good to make music, to take the tune into her heart and free it. She loved being able to put notes together, decide on a tempo, redirect the melody, change the tone of the piece to suit her mood. The gift of just being able to do this was something she never took for granted. Other people found their passion in running, gardening, but Nikki's voice gave her such pleasure, it didn't seem fair to all the women over the years who'd told her they wished they could sing. Singing had always been Nikki's release and her joy. The fact that she sounded as good as she did and had been able to sustain a career doing what she loved, was the true gift. Nikki never wanted to forget that.

She'd loved the piano since she was a child, though she'd eventually become famous for playing the electric guitar. Years after debuting as the guitar-playing singer with the band Goldy, she started to resent that instrument for its inability to make her as happy as the piano. But the guitar suited her rock image better in the beginning, allowing her emergence from behind the confines of the piano. Strutting and dancing eventually became more important than the guitar, and in the last few years, she'd only picked it up for a song or two in her show.

Nikki watched Half Moon Bay as she played the little keyboard. A group of ducks headed to the cattails at the bottom of the bay. She switched tunes, launching into a song she'd written months before but had forgotten about.

"Have you ever been alone?

Have you ever been afraid?

When no one left would talk to you,
Because of what you had to do,
Have you ever been alone?"

She'd written the song in Houston, knowing that soon she would announce her retirement and quit the life she'd known. When it was time to board the bus to Dallas, she made everyone wait while she finished the song. It had never been recorded.

When she saw Pete across the bay, sitting on his front steps, Nikki softened her voice, wondering if he knew she was Goldy. Probably.

"They avoid your eyes,
They avoid your path,
They can't be part of what you do
And in their way they're damning you
They avoid your eyes.
And baby, you'll have to get me through,
Cause maybe, they'll need to know the truth
And you know, I cannot run and hide.
Someday, in the years ahead, they'll see my side."

He was still listening, his head resting in his hands. He wouldn't hear the words, only a fuzzy melody from that distance.

"Have you ever felt alone?
Have you ever felt afraid?
When no one else would talk to you,
Because of what you had to do.
Have you ever felt alone?"

She looked up, and Pete was gone. It was wrong to sing with hopes of impressing him, but her feelings for Pete were strangely exciting and as long as she avoided him, Nikki figured it was harmless.

"He doesn't like my music, Elvis." Getting up from the keyboard, she called Harold Gaines for her daily check-in while Elvis frantically raced around looking for his favorite squeaky toy. After leaving a message on the sheriff's voicemail, Nikki picked up Elvis's well-chewed plastic alligator and threw it across the room.

Next, she phoned Phyllis to ask what the world was saying about her. According to Phyllis's report, the media fire had been freshly fanned by the fact that Burn was openly dating Rebecca Raven, barely old enough to go clubbing with him. Phyllis didn't have the luxury of ignoring Burn since he'd rehired her as his publicist. "He's gone public with the teenager." Hollywood's most talented publicist did not waste words. "Someone else will take the spotlight soon. We just need someone to get a DUI or enter rehab…"

"Watch it," Nikki warned. Quinn was only eighteen months out of rehab.

"Oh, sorry, hon, but you know what I mean. If someone else has a disaster, you'll be old news."

"Yes, Phyllis." Nikki's weary tone matched her energy level. "Okay, we'll ride it out. If only Burn would attach his name to a cause or start dating someone who did charitable work for the homeless, he'd look so much better in the press." She smirked at the thought.

Over the years, Goldy had been asked to support many causes and did her share of charity work. Eventually she'd formed a foundation, hired trustworthy people to run it, and donated part of all her proceeds to the charities it supported. This became Nikki's sole reason to make such shameful truckloads of money over the last decade. One day, Quinn hoped to run it when her education was complete and she had some experience under her belt.

"If the Foundation rebuilds a school damaged by the recent hurricane," Phyllis said, "and we put Burn's name on it, his public likeability would increase."

Nikki agreed. But the idea of him taking time to work on something like this would have to be delivered to him on a silver platter. She'd do the initial ground work, as usual, then, once they needed photos, Nikki would slide Burn in behind the helm. She'd email the Foundation team.

Happy to be involved in a project again, Nikki hummed around the house all day until her mood was broken by a call from Agent Gateman.

"Sorry, Nikki, but we got a letter today."

Her eyes flew to the computer screen beside her. "Send it." Nikki needed to read it to determine her level of fear. In the time it took to tap a key, the letter was in front of her, cryptic as usual.

My beauteous flower, Goldy,

I am getting weary waiting for you and may have to act sooner than later.

My love is changing daily with disuse.

I tell myself that "Love is a familiar. Love is a devil. There is no evil angel but Love."

However I feel my love for you is evolving into something more sweetly evil, if that's possible. Why a remote lake?

I wait for your return but cannot love without a promise.

Give me a sign.

Tell me you know me.

I am nearer than you think.

Signed,
The one you call "Shakespeare"

Oh, God. He knew she was at a lake. He hadn't identified the lake though. The words were not hideous. No descriptions of torture. It was almost a love letter. "Postmark?"

"L.A., two days ago," Gateman said.

"I think he might be backing off. What do you guys think?"

"Possible."

"I'm thinking he doesn't know exactly where I am."

"Hard to say, but I think it's time to tell you that I haven't wanted to take any chances with this guy."

"Meaning?"

"Meaning that I have a man watching you."

"What? Where?" Nikki hadn't seen anyone suspicious.

"You'll never see our agent, I assure you."

Being a rock star and mega-celebrity, she was used to people watching her but still felt disappointment at the news. "Is he watching me now?"

"No one's looking in the windows or anything."

"His name isn't Pete Bayer is it?"

"The guy next door? No."

She detected a pause. "How do you know the name of the guy next door?"

"The arrest of Dwayne Capleoni. Nikki, we only want you to be safe." Gateman paused. "We had to clear Pete Bayer."

What did that mean? Nikki couldn't get any more information from Gateman but knew he wouldn't let her flail unprotected in the wilderness. Was Pete Bayer the agent? If so, what was he doing kissing her? Regardless of all the unanswered questions, it didn't feel intrusive to know someone was close. But if Pete was the agent, why would he bring his wife and child on the job and then act so strangely? No. That didn't fit at all.

****

Harold Gaines called early the next morning to warn Nikki that there were suspicious-looking characters lurking around town, asking questions about Goldy. Nikki groaned at the possibility of who they might be.

"What do you want me to do?" Harold snapped his gum.

"Oh geez, Harold…let me think…how many?"

"Two."

"Asking where I live?"

"Yup."

She wasn't sure someone in town wouldn't sell her privacy for a hundred dollar bill or a five-year subscription to People magazine but knew it wouldn't be Harold. She imagined the sheriff sitting in his chair, staring out the window just waiting to run someone out of his town.

"Where are they now?"

"Sandy's."

What were they doing at Sandy's Bait Shop? The crusty owner of the marina store would never spill the beans even if she knew Nikki was in town, which she didn't. The old shopkeeper hardly ever spoke to anyone, unless it was about fishing. In seven years, Nikki had only ever had one small conversation about lures, and it had been painful to draw any words out of

111

her. "Any suggestions, Harold?"

"Well, the way I see it, we need to send those leeches back to Hollywood and let you get on with your privacy."

Nikki agreed.

"So, I could head over there, see what they know already and try to steer them away from the lake. Maybe I could suggest I heard you had a place down Spokane way."

"It's worth a try." Moving on to another location seemed like a possibility even though she'd hoped for a few more weeks, at the very least. There really was no way to hide away without being found if the searcher was good enough.

"Will do," Harold said.

Out the window, Pete Bayer slammed the door of his pickup and walked toward the log house with a black briefcase under his arm. He bounded up the steps, looked around the grounds as he made a complete circle and then disappeared inside. He always seemed to do that spin. He was either a very cautious software designer/writer or the FBI agent. The latter made more sense.

Grabbing the binoculars, Nikki ran upstairs to the bedroom window to do her own check on the surroundings. The way the sun was hitting the log house, she was able to see a woman at the sink doing dishes. Was it Connie? Yes, but she now had a blonde ponytail, not the curly brown hair Nikki had seen before. Her real hair was long, blonde, and very similar to Goldy's platinum hair color. Connie wore the blue sweater and as she stood at the sink, Nikki saw her lips moving like she was singing or talking to someone.

Connie's head sank forward and she laughed, doubled over on the sink edge in her hilarity. Tony moved into view and appeared to be laughing too. His small arms hugged his mother from the side. Looking closer, Nikki realized they weren't laughing at all. The mother and son were crying. Sobbing.

Pete moved in beside them, but they didn't notice him. Strange that he didn't kiss Connie's cheek, put his arm around her waist, or try to comfort her. Instead, he gently pushed her away from the window and reached to shut the curtains.

Nikki sank to her unmade bed, binoculars on her lap. She shouldn't be spying on the family next door. One thing was clear. Pete and Connie were not FBI agents watching over her. They had their own agenda, and it wasn't pretty over there. What misery would make a mother sob like that in front of her child, knowing how it would affect him to see her that way? The weight in Nikki's heart sat like a boulder on her chest, but what could she do?

It was none of her business.

Chapter 10

The phone rang, and Nikki's first thought was that it might be Connie Bayer to say she needed help.

"Hello," she said tentatively.

"Harold here."

"What have you got?"

"They're photographers from L.A. and got a tip that you were here on Louisa."

"Oh, God." It was all over.

"Sandy tried to tell them she didn't know you, but they're convinced you're here." He cleared his throat nervously and used a cop voice that Nikki didn't recognize. "I'm going to follow them around a bit. See if I can get them to leave, but they're not breaking the law yet."

"No, and they won't. Photographers from L.A. are very clear on boundaries and laws," Nikki said.

"Well, if they come down your driveway, they're on private property then, aren't they, and I'd have to run them off." He paused. "But you don't want them knowin' which house is yours."

"No."

"It looks like they're at the marina now. Oh, fudge."

"What?"

"They're renting a boat. I guess I can't do much about that."

"No, you can't, Harold." He couldn't follow them in a boat and wait for them to do something illegal. She'd have to think of something fast before two photographers were at her dock looking for Goldy. She needed a plan. The fat suit was close by. She spun around searching for an answer, her mind racing. If they got here and thought the woman at the house wasn't her, she might be safe. She would put on her suit and the bucket hat wig, except that Us Magazine had published a photo of her recently in that very wig. Maybe she could run next door to borrow Connie Bayer's curly brown wig.

An idea came to her.

Connie or Pete could pretend they lived at Birch House. They owed her one after the squirrel incident. At the very least, she had fifteen minutes before the boat arrived in her bay, and that was if they knew where they were going. Nikki would need all of those minutes to explain to Pete or Connie how to get rid of the press, and why.

She flew out the back door and ran down the lane to the Dickerson's house. If an FBI agent was watching her, he'd be confused right now. Flip flops made the run challenging and the possibility of twisting her ankle occurred late, as she took the bottom step sideways and fell on the stairs.

She grabbed her foot in pain, but it was the yelling from inside the house that stopped her. Tony's voice sounded very unlike the sweet boy she'd seen at her house.

"You aren't my dad, you can't tell me what to do!" His voice was higher than usual and full of strained emotion. "You don't even care about me and my mom."

Nikki pulled herself up to grab the deck railing and tried to put some weight on her foot. The pain was subsiding slightly, which was a good sign.

"Tony. It's all right. I'm fine. Look, I'm done crying now." Connie's muffled voice was calm, but the words clear. Nikki stood frozen, waiting to hear if she could possibly ask these people to involve themselves in her predicament when they were struggling themselves. Or would the Bayers welcome the interruption?

"Tony, I care about your mother," Pete said, like Tony had left the room.

There was a silence, and as Nikki crossed the deck to the house, a beeping sounded from inside.

Without warning, the door flew open to reveal Pete Bayer pointing a nine-millimeter handgun at Nikki.

She instinctively threw her hands in front of her, waiting to be shot. "It's me. It's only me." When Nikki didn't hear or feel anything, she opened one eye to see Pete had lowered the gun to his side.

"Don't shoot. Please."

"Shit, Nikki. What are you doing sneaking up like that?" Pete put the safety on and tucked the gun into the back of his jeans. Maybe he was FBI, after all.

Connie and Tony were nowhere to be seen.

Nikki sank to the deck, her head in her hands, and let out the breath she'd been holding. "Who did you think I was?" Her heart raced. She looked at him, standing there in the doorway.

At least the expression on his face was appropriate. Not horrified, like hers, but close. Pete opened his mouth to speak then Nikki heard a noise. At first, it sounded like a bumblebee humming its way closer. A motor. The rental boat was out there, cruising along the shoreline, minutes from her house. She stood up.

"What's wrong?" Pete asked.

"Besides you pointing a gun at me?" She proceeded. "I need to ask a favor. There are reporters coming, and I don't want them to know I'm here. Would you pretend that you live at my place?" She looked at him pleadingly then thought of something. "No! Wait! Say you rented the house for a month and don't know who owns it."

Pete looked confused, but she continued.

"That boat you hear right now…" She paused. "…is on its way to my dock." She spoke quickly and gestured to the mouth of the bay. "You don't have to help me, but…" Her voice warbled. "You kind of owe me."

Pete looked like he was considering the possibility.

"If you just pretend you don't know who they're looking for…" Pete had his own problems. "It would be a huge favor. I could even stay here with Connie." Was he worried about his wife?

The sound of the boat got louder, and if Pete wanted to look like he wasn't running from next door, he had to get going. "Payment for almost shooting me." She gestured to where he'd tucked the gun.

"Anything else?" Pete looked ready to head over.

The small aluminum boat snaked its way toward the bay's head. "Don't use your gun on them."

Pete turned toward the log house. "Connie!"

She appeared at the side of the door.

"Lock the door with you, Tony, and Nikki inside and set the alarm, like I showed you." He looked at

Nikki. "You are going to owe me big-time for this. Now get inside and don't show your faces."

When she nodded, Pete took off running to Birch House.

Nikki's ankle was sore, but she took a few steps into the kitchen.

"Hi. Sorry." Nikki looked apologetically at Connie and noticed her puffy eyes. "Bad time to come by for a visit?"

Connie broke away, locked the door, set the alarm, and blew her nose. "I'm fine. What happened to your leg?"

"Twisted my ankle running over here." Nikki rolled her eyes. "I need Pete to get rid of some people for me, so he's gone to my place."

"Yeah, I heard." She wiped her nose with a tissue.

Nikki crossed to the window that afforded the best view of her dock. "I want to hear what he's saying if I can, but first, I want to make sure you and Tony are not in any danger." There wasn't time to soft-pedal what she feared. Nikki looked at Connie, who was now gazing out the kitchen window. "Your husband just pulled a gun on me."

Connie didn't flinch.

"…and I'm concerned for you and Tony if he's waving a gun around."

"I'm sorry about that." She turned to look at Nikki. "He's very protective." She laughed a cold, weary chuckle. "I'm okay."

"Connie, if Pete is hitting you or holding you here against your will…"

"He isn't."

Something occurred to Nikki and her eyes

widened. "Where's Tony?"

"He's lying down on his bed. Really, Nikki, you are sweet and thank you for caring, but we are fine. Aren't we, Tony?" She raised her voice for the last part.

"What?" The boy sounded like he was busy.

Aside from the tear streaks on her cheeks, Connie's face looked normal. No black eyes or red marks. There was nothing she could do to help if Connie didn't admit she needed it.

The motorboat crossed the head of the bay and swerved toward the Birch House dock. Nikki pulled the curtains apart and opened the window to listen. Connie stayed well back. The man in the bow was dressed in a Louisa Lake sweatshirt, probably just purchased at the store where he got his information. He stood up in the boat, his camera raised, taking photos of the house.

Nikki whispered, "And if Tony is in any danger—I heard them fighting."

"He's fine. He's very...fond...of Pete."

Nikki sensed she wasn't going to get anything more, so she quickly took Connie's finely boned hand and said, "I'm going to give you a code word to use if you're in trouble. You can say it in front of Pete and it'll mean you need my help." The boat slowed down as it approached the dock.

Connie smiled and shook her head. "Not necessary."

"Just in case." Nikki looked back to the dock. The reporters would descend on the Goldy story like hungry tigers. "Say something like...like...Goldilocks. Use the word 'Goldilocks' if you want me to know you're in danger." Nikki's eyes bored a hole in Connie's face as she said this next part. "I have friends in very high

119

places that will help you, if you need."

Connie nodded and half smiled. "I appreciate the gesture." She patted Nikki's hand, her warmth lingering after she'd moved away.

The sound of the motor cut out, and Nikki saw Pete sauntering along the dock to meet the photographers.

"Pete will get rid of them for you." Connie whispered, as if the intruders might hear her. "He's very persuasive."

Nikki strained to hear the conversation next door but it was too far away. Pete stood with his arms folded across his chest, and when the men tried to tie up to the dock, he shook his head and casually pushed them off with his foot, causing them to nearly capsize.

Murmurs did not translate into actual words and Nikki turned to see if Connie could hear any better.

Connie stared at the men on the dock for a moment. "I suppose he's telling them he's your renter, like you asked him. I wouldn't worry."

"Connie. Tell me this much." Nikki had to know. "Pete is not writing a book about me, is he?"

With that, Connie stifled a grin and covered her mouth. "No, no, he's not."

Nikki believed her. "And he hasn't been assigned by the FBI to watch me?"

"No."

Pete was crouched at the end of the dock, shaking his head. He gestured to Birch House.

She turned to Connie. If she took the chance and confided in this woman, would she then be able to draw a confidence out of Connie? "These guys in the boat are the press. I'm well known and they want a photo of me. That's what that is all about."

Connie nodded, but her thoughts seemed far away.

Pete pointed his finger at the photographers and Nikki hoped he wasn't getting ready to pull the gun on them. She could see the bulge in the waistband of his jeans, even from across the bay. The reporters were trying to park alongside the dock, their bow rope in the hand of the smaller man. Pete stood, rubbed his face and shook his head again.

Connie whispered. "They'll be gone soon, and they won't be back."

"What makes you so sure?"

"I can guess what he's saying." Her voice sounded cold.

As Pete pushed them off, they gripped the side of the boat to prevent tipping and started the little motor. It didn't look like angry words had been exchanged, but when the press motored away at top speed, Nikki's curiosity piqued at what was said. Would they be back?

She took a deep breath and closed the window. She could only hope they were not just temporarily gone until they rounded up re-enforcements.

"Thank you, Connie. Remember 'Goldilocks.'"

Nikki hurried out the door. Her ankle hurt, but at least she could put weight on it. Hobbling closer to her house, she heard Elvis barking from inside. When she met Pete on the road, he only slowed his pace and passed her, seemingly in a hurry to get home.

"They're gone?" Nikki asked.

He spun around to walk backward. "Yes."

"Thanks. What did you tell them?" She followed him.

"What you told me to."

"That's it?"

"Pretty much."

"Really?" She wasn't convinced.

"Really."

Didn't he want to know who those guys were? Nikki was all but running to keep up with him.

"You have no idea how huge that was for me." They approached the deck of the log house. "Uh, let me make you dinner tonight to show my thanks." Nikki meant the whole family.

He turned around with a tender look on his face that frightened her. Then the moment was gone. The look that replaced it was almost exasperation. "What time?"

"Seven?"

"Seven, it is," he called back as he disappeared inside the house, shaking his head.

If he was FBI hired to watch Nikki, why would he have pulled a gun on her? No, Pete was preoccupied with something in that house. Connie said he wasn't writing about Nikki or watching her. Hopefully she'd get a feeling for what was happening over there at dinner that night.

****

Pete knew why he'd said yes to Nikki. Being around her was like medicine to his fractured soul. She set something off in him. Knowing he was almost free of this life, he was softening now, melting. The thaw was leaving his weak underside exposed and the concept of Nikki was slowly trickling in, whether he wanted it or not.

The night before, he and Tony had been flipping channels, looking for something to watch, when Goldy's face flashed on the screen. Pete grabbed the remote from Tony. "Wait a minute."

"What about the military channel, Pete?" The kid didn't recognize the woman on the screen.

"Yea, just a minute, sport." Goldy was on TV, in full costume, makeup and regalia.

Connie walked into the room and Pete considered changing the channel, embarrassed to be caught. "That's Goldy, right?" she asked.

"Yup." Pete gulped at the sight of the rock star in that little costume, parading around with her backup dancers. She wore a gold headdress and a very small dress that covered only the illegal parts, with high-heeled black boots that hugged most of her legs. How could she dance in those things?

Connie plunked down next to Tony. "Wow. She is really something, isn't she?" Connie looked as starstruck as Pete felt.

He didn't dare comment. Her guitar player, now her ex-husband, had the whole black leather thing going. He looked like the type who'd run off with a teenage girl and not think twice. As the camera panned in to his fingers for the guitar solo, Goldy was barely visible, grinding on him from behind, with one arm around his shoulders. When Burn's solo ended, Goldy locked lips with him and the crowd cheered.

"Whoops! Maybe we should change the channel?" Connie glanced from the remote to Tony.

Then Goldy broke from Burn, and as she backed up, the guitarist advanced playfully, like he wouldn't let her leave. She turned, the dancers rushed in and swooped her up above them, carrying her around the stage.

"A love like this

Comes just one time
A love so strong
You gotta hang on
Hang on
Hang on forever,
Forever, forever, forever…"

Pete knew the song. It had been a huge hit two years before, all over the radio, and if he remembered correctly her world tour had been called the Forever Tour. Had she written the song about her husband? Because his love definitely did not last forever. The song ended and Goldy struck a pose. Words flashed on the screen.

"Goldy in Tokyo—The Forever Tour"

Connie broke the spell. "Tony, do you recognize that singer?"

He looked at his mother like she was crazy. "No."

"That's our neighbor Nikki." Connie smiled at the Tony's open-mouthed, pop-eyed reaction.

Chapter 11

Nikki didn't even have spaghetti in the cupboard and she'd asked the Bayers for a spaghetti dinner. She'd have to use what she had—manicotti. It was too late to go to town for groceries. She'd already blown the authenticity of the meal by using sauce from a jar. This wasn't a good time to experiment with homemade sauce. Nikki had stowed the jar in the recycling bin to hide the fact Ragu had done most of the work for her. The manicotti was slightly overcooked, as Nikki tried to stuff the cheese mixture into the tubes, cursing her ineptitude in the kitchen.

"Dammed. Why can't I cook?" she asked Elvis, who waited for something to drop to the floor. "It's my own fault after twenty years with personal chefs who I ignored until it was time to eat."

The manicotti flopped around with her efforts. "Dammit, again," she said. "I don't have anchovies for the Caesar salad. What was I thinking, Elvis?" The little pug stood by her feet with his red and white checked neck scarf, looking like an Italian waiter. At least to Nikki, he did.

It was only 6:10. Good. She was ahead of schedule.

The table was set, the manicotti in the oven to bake. She'd go change out of her shorts. Salad could be made at the last minute. Elvis almost tripped her in his haste to get ahead on the stairs. "Slow down, Elvis. It's just the Bayers." Pete would wear jeans and his amulet necklace. The Yoruba Luck Ring. Connie would wear black jeans and her blue sweater, like always. Every time Nikki saw her, she wore the same thing. Except for the wig. It was off in private, and on when she left the house.

Pulling off her jeans, Nikki jumped into the shower and tried to imagine the conversation they'd have over dinner. "Have you done any fishing here? The ice cream is good at the Double Scoop town. Did you know I'm a famous rock star?"

Nikki dried herself and pulled on a sparkly top, but her reflection looked overdressed for a dinner with neighbors and she switched to jeans and a black V-neck sweater. After slipping into a pair of black velvet mules, she dried and straightened her hair. Hot rollers usually did the trick but Nikki didn't want to give the evening that kind of attention. Nothing more than what was necessary.

At the last minute, she applied a little eye liner, mascara and clear lip gloss. For reasons she didn't want to admit, she was trying to look pretty. Understated, but still pretty. This might be the last time she saw the Bayers if she left tomorrow, which was now a definite possibility.

She'd been thinking all day about going. The photographers today probably got some shots of the house and although they were gone now, it was only a matter of time before they returned. After the Bayers went back to the log house, she'd pack her bag.

Nikki had made a list of possible locations that weren't too far from Quinn. Vancouver, Canada, or one of the islands off the Washington coast would be a good choice if only she knew of a house. Tomorrow, she'd check online to see if anything looked private enough.

Quinn had called earlier to thank her mother for the Yoruba amulet and, in conversation, asked why she was so excited at the prospect of having dinner guests. "They're just the weird people next door, Mom."

"I'm not really excited. I just haven't seen anyone in so long," Nikki protested.

"If you're this thrilled about cooking for strange neighbors, I'd say you better come to Seattle to see me."

"I will, sweetie. Now that I'm pretty sure Pete isn't writing a book about me or watching me for the FBI, I just feel relieved."

"You better be careful, Mrs. Nosey Parker." Quinn had no idea about Pete pulling a gun on her mother earlier.

Seven o'clock came and went.

Seven ten came and went, and Nikki began to wonder if they were actually coming. The Caesar salad was ready, and she turned off the oven to keep the manicotti and garlic bread from overcooking. She changed the music from The Red Hot Chili Peppers to U2 and when she was folding napkins at the table, a faint knock sounded on the back door. Nikki startled and ran to disarm the security system.

On the monitor, Connie stood with a bouquet of wildflowers in her hands, the kind that grew around the lake. Nikki was touched by the gesture and threw open the door.

Connie held the bouquet out, blocking her own face in the porch light. "For you."

"How nice. Thank you." Nikki peeked around the

flowers to see Connie's smile.

With a Nintendo in hand, Tony gave her a strange grin as he passed. She could tell a fan when she saw one, and he'd probably just found out she was Goldy. She preferred the Bayers not know, or at least not say anything, but that seemed like an unreal request.

"I'm glad you could come."

Connie wore black jeans, but instead of the blue sweater, she wore a black blouse with a large crucifix around her neck. Nikki was strangely pleased that her neighbor was treating the evening with a sense of sociability. The wig was back on. Why? She considered snatching it off Connie's head and saying, "Can I relieve you of this pretense too?"

"Nice house," Pete said under his breath as they walked down the hall.

"Thank you. I was telling your wife the other day that my ex-husband and I built it, and then we stuffed it with everything we love."

Coming into the great room, Pete stopped when he saw their reflections in the front windows. Connie blanched to see his reaction.

Nikki was used to trusting the security system in the yard, but, seeing Pete's face, she was reminded that they weren't entirely safe from spying eyes. She crossed the room and lowered the blinds to envelope them in the safety and privacy of the room.

"Dinner is almost ready. Would anyone like a drink?" Earlier, she'd retrieved a bottle of wine from the closet stash but all three Bayers requested Sprites.

Tony scanned Nikki's book shelves, announcing with pleasure when he saw one he liked. "Lord of the Rings. Awesome," he said. "And Eragon."

Nikki nodded and handed the boy his Sprite. "They're my daughter's books."

"Tony loves to read." Pete nodded.

"If you see one you like, feel free to borrow it," Nikki said.

"This is such a lovely place, almost like a lodge, isn't it, Pete," Connie said, before Tony could answer.

Choosing the seat on the couch next to his wife, he nodded, looking around the room.

Nikki retreated to the kitchen and took the manicotti out of the oven. She couldn't believe she was actually entertaining people. Even though Birch House was built as the haven for the three Burnsides, it was strangely interesting to have guests inside the walls. When she and Burn had finished building the house, they'd moved in all the wonderful things they'd missed from years of living out of hotel suites—comfy furniture, board games, framed photographs, what other families took for granted when they aren't living amongst a stranger's choice of furnishings for years on end.

Nikki grabbed the pita chips and dip from the granite countertop. "Are you thinking of buying something on the lake?" she asked.

"Maybe." Pete glanced at his wife blankly.

"It's peaceful," Connie agreed.

The conversation continued awkwardly, until tension heightened when Nikki asked, "Where were you before this?"

All three guests answered in unison. "Tacoma."

Nikki laughed, unable to help herself. It sounded so ready.

Connie laughed with her.

"What type of work do you do, Nikki?" Pete looked genuinely interested, his eyes searching her face.

"I'm writing the score to a movie, right now. I'm a musician." Nikki waited for a reaction, but no one commented and she continued. "That's why I appreciate the peacefulness here at the lake."

Connie reached for a cracker. "The photographers today were trying to take pictures of you?"

"Yes. Thanks for helping." She almost burst out laughing again, thinking how comical it was for the four of them to have this stilted conversation without revealing any personal information. Just doling out small bits of nothing that led nowhere. "How's the computer work going?" Nikki persisted.

Pete was ready with his answer. "Good."

"Writing a book, I heard."

His expression didn't change. "Actually, more like a software manual."

Pete didn't ask where she got the information, and Nikki found that odd. Connie and Tony meandered over to a shelf that held framed pictures of her with Aerosmith, Bon Jovi, Fleetwood Mac, and several presidents. Just then the stove timer went off, and Pete jumped out of his chair.

"That's just the stove, Pete," she said. "Excuse me." As she passed him, Nikki whispered, "I hope you didn't bring your gun to my dinner party."

He looked defensive. "I have that to protect my family."

Nikki shot him a look that said she wasn't buying it and left to put dinner on the table.

Pete directed Connie to sit facing the shrouded

window across from him. "And Tony, you sit here." He definitely called the shots. And they listened.

Nikki placed the manicotti, salad, and garlic bread in front of her guests and sat at the end. "Elvis, go lie down in your bed." The little dog backed up and found his cushion on the floor.

"This looks delicious, Nikki." Pete sounded like a regular person, not guarded and jumpy, but a grateful dinner guest.

"Well, I have to admit I'm a beginner cook, so I'm hoping it tastes good." Nikki passed Connie the basket of garlic bread.

"Mom is a great cook." Tony took a mouthful of manicotti.

"Yes, she is," Pete concurred, and Nikki felt a tiny stab of jealousy, as she caught him smiling at his wife.

"Thank you, boys." Connie turned to Nikki. "You have to love eating to be a good cook."

"Then there's hope for me." Nikki laughed as she thought about her voracious appetite of late.

After the initial pleasantries were out in the open, the conversation was limited. Uncomfortable. Counting the minutes until the end of dinner, Nikki realized she should never have asked them to come. And they shouldn't have accepted. Why had they? The four people around the table were an odd group. Interaction was painfully forced. It wasn't until dessert, when Nikki asked how Pete and Connie met, that bad turned to worse.

Connie glanced to her husband and Pete took the lead.

"Mutual friends introduced us." Pete took another mouthful of cheesecake.

This was obviously the short version. Four words hardly summed up a courtship. They'd left out the part that Connie had a small son or that they'd had a big wedding in Tacoma or fell in love immediately or dated for a year. Or whatever. There were no details. Nikki wouldn't let it go. After all, they'd come to dinner. They must have known there'd be conversation. "Did you live in Tacoma and work in software design when you met?"

"No, actually, we lived in Bellevue after we married and that's when I worked for Microsoft." Pete didn't look up. "And you? Did you always write movie scores?"

"Kind of," Nikki said, wondering what kind of game they were playing. "Did you marry in Bellevue?"

"Yup," Pete said. "Have you ever performed?"

She shot him a look to shut up. "A bit."

When dessert was over, they moved to the great room and, while pouring tea, Nikki tried to catch Connie's eye, but she was avoiding contact more than usual. Tony leafed through Quinn's copy of a book about dragons.

"That's a wonderful series," Nikki said to Tony. "Have you always liked books?"

"Yeah. They say." He didn't look up.

"Me too. I think my favorite story when I was a little girl was either Cinderella or Goldilocks," Nikki smiled at Connie.

Connie's head snapped up, and she gave Nikki a look that was slightly reproachful.

Pete caught Connie's gaze and stared, hard.

Had she told him the code word? "Did you have a favorite fairytale, Connie?" Nikki said.

"No, I didn't." She looked defiantly at Nikki. "I'm not much for fairytales."

"You must have had a favorite as a little girl?" Nikki asked.

Pete followed the conversation closely, his eyes narrowing.

"Snow White." Connie stared at the floor.

"Mom, you like those romance stories." Tony teased her in his quiet way, and Connie blushed.

"Yes, I do like those, sweetie." She ruffled his hair in abject fondness.

"Me too," Nikki agreed. "Romance makes the world go round." Without thinking, Nikki glanced at Pete.

"Time to go," Pete announced.

Nikki wasn't surprised. They'd already stayed too long.

****

Goldy was hiding at Louisa Lake in northern Washington. Obstacles presented themselves everywhere. But knowing her location had changed everything. Having Goldy alone in a wilderness cabin for days on end would be perfect. Much could be accomplished if things went well. Preparations were needed. Soon all labor would be rewarded. Revenge would be sweet.

Out the window, the morning smog was thick. Los Angeles was oppressive. The heat, the crowds of people, the traffic. It was too much for someone not used to city life amongst the masses. A Goldy poster on the wall had faded in the afternoon sun. Was there need for another poster with vivid colors or would it all be over soon? The plan to leave L.A. was like having a vacation itinerary in hand, even though the time spent in Washington wouldn't be anything like a vacation. It would be more like fulfilling a dream. Retribution. Quinn would be broken gently to the point of giving information. The problem wasn't Quinn. It was the bitch, Goldy.

A phone rang across the room. Someone else picked it up. Answering the phone was not for someone who was leaving soon, in search of Goldy's hiding place. In search of justice.

****

Nikki opened the deck door to let the cool morning air of dawn drift in. When the kettle whistled, she made a cup of tea, pulled on her gum boots, wrapped a blanket around her shoulders, and headed down to the dock in her pajamas. The mist drifted and caressed the surface of the water as Nikki studied its patterns, inspired to sing.

Elvis had long since disappeared into the bushes after something. She reminded herself that the house across the bay had three sleeping people. She compromised by humming softly to herself.

Last night's dinner party had been a strange evening and sleep hadn't found her until sometime after one o'clock. Her voice felt tired, raspier than usual, reminding her of Pete's scratchy voice. She'd wanted to ask him if he had chronic throat problems, but it was such a personal question. Besides, all answers given last night had been lies.

Nikki sat on the dock and kept her singing low, taking the melody only as high as she could this early in the morning, then dropping to the bottom notes to add some mysterious minors for effect. The blanket of fog was slowly dissipating to reveal the flat dark surface of the lake, like the surface of a black mirror.

She dangled her toes in the water. It was too cold for swimming, but adequate for toe dangling. Taking a deep breath, she sang quietly. A pure sweet note, escaped her lips, lifting higher, then lower, running along the surface of the water and up, up, up to the mountains across the lake. Closing her eyes, Nikki let the music overtake her as she found new combinations of minor notes to match the mysterious mist hovering over the lake.

When she opened her eyes, ripples indicated a fish had jumped. The watery circles grew bigger and just as she hit a quiet little high note, a river otter surfaced ten feet off her swirling feet. Just beyond the drop off. Startled, she stopped singing.

Her eyes locked with the otter's and then it dove below the surface, the tip of its long tail the last thing to leave for the lake's bottom. The otter was gone, knowing when to leave a party early. Did she? Certainly she'd left show biz while she was still having fun, but what about staying at the lake when things were less than secure? She needed to leave. Reporters were most likely on their way. Grateful to have had a month at her beloved lake house, that had to be enough for now. She might get back before the snow fell.

Pete Bayer came out the side door and walked to his truck. She might have called a hello but didn't. For one thing she was wearing a blanket over cow-patterned pajamas and felt silly, suddenly. And if she left today or tomorrow, there was no point in being friendly with the Bayers anymore. It had been a strange dinner party, accomplishing absolutely nothing. Why had she even invited them?

The family was weird. First you had a flirty father, who seemed to be overly protective and jumpy around his wife and son, then you had a wife who was hiding the fact that her husband was a controlling bully, and lastly you had a shy, sad boy being subjected to all this. Nikki's last conscious thought before she'd succumbed to sleep last night had been that Connie needed help in some form or another.

Nikki walked back to the house and threw the blanket on the couch just as her cell phone rang.

"Hi, Phyllis. What's up?"

"Have you seen?" Phyllis didn't mince words. "You have been found. Apparently you are hiding out on an undisclosed lake in eastern Washington State."

"Oh, no."

"Oh, yes, and there's more." She paused but Nikki waited. "You have run off with a studly man."

"Who is it this time?"

"You tell me. I just emailed you the photo taken of him at your house."

Nikki frantically opened her emails. Before she saw the photo, she knew exactly what the studly man looked like. For one thing, he'd be wearing jeans with a dark green shirt and the wind would be blowing wisps of hair around his handsome face.

Typing in "Goldy Gossip," Nikki chose a site and opened a photo of Pete Bayer standing at the end of her dock. Her first thought was that he took a good picture. Phyllis was right. The camera had captured him smiling. Nikki knew it was a patronizing smile, but she doubted that was obvious to anyone who didn't know him. Although the photo was grainy, the world could see that this was one good looking man at "Goldy's Love Shack." He looked like someone the famous rock star might be interested in, after the rocker look of Burn. "Poor Pete," Nikki groaned.

"Do you know him?"

"Yes, I know him." Had he seen it?

"What do you want to do?" Phyllis was all business.

"Let me think." Even though there was no proof this was Goldy's house, Nikki knew most people would believe it to be true, and wonder if she'd shacked up with this man. "Firstly, I want to apologize to that man's wife who lives next door." Nikki tried to enlarge the photo. "Then, I want to issue a statement saying that he lives beside a property I own, and he was only trying to see what the photographers wanted, because I'm not in residence. Finally, I want to say that Goldy apologizes for any fallout from the speculation brought to this man's family, because of this photo."

She hung up. Had Burn seen the picture? What would he think of Pete as his replacement? Someone had probably sent it to him by now. She should have been mortified, but it was difficult to hold back a smile. There was no doubt in Nikki's mind that she had a huge crush on her neighbor. She was also sure of one other thing. Even though Goldy was a master at flirting, Nikki had never flirted with a married man with intention, and would not start now, no matter how innocent it seemed, no matter how many holes popped up in Connie and Pete's story of being a married couple.

And now that the photo was out there for the world to see, Shakespeare would be privy to it. Would he

137

know where she was now?

Quinn would see it too.

Next, she phoned Quinn to explain that a photo of Pete Bayer would be all over the tabloids later that day. Then she called Gateman to explain that the man next door had done her a favor by getting rid of the photographers. She wasn't comfortable owing Pete a favor.

Chapter 12

Elvis trotted happily down the road to the log house as Nikki rehearsed what she would say to the Bayers. It was a gross imposition and an insult to Connie to have that picture of Pete all over the news. As a married couple, there was a strong likelihood that Pete and Connie had friends or relatives who'd phone to question the news that Pete had taken up with a rock singer—people who were bound to recognize him. Nikki realized she should have told him to wear a hat or sunglasses, knowing that they'd get a shot of him. And, until Goldy's statement was picked up in an hour, she owed the Bayers an apology.

As she walked across the bridge of land to Dickerson's, Nikki could smell the skunk cabbages rotting at the end of the bay. Autumn was in full bloom and she pulled her cashmere cardigan tighter across her chest. Elvis took off into the trees, challenged by a squirrel that was chattering from high in the trees. Nikki let him go. The sunshine had ducked behind a great cumulous cloud above her and Nikki wished she'd worn a coat.

"You can't go into town and that's that!" Pete Bayer's voice was muffled, but his words were clear enough, from where Nikki stood near the door. "If you want something I'll get it, but you..." and he emphasized the last word, "cannot leave the property.

And Tony, don't even think of stealing the keys again! Are you stupid? I told you how it is. Do you want to end up dead?"

"Pete!" Connie sounded frightened.

"I have rules and both of you better damned well follow them or that's what's going to happen."

Nikki stood paralyzed, twenty feet from the log house's door, sickened by the tone Pete used with his wife and son. Did Tony want to end up dead? Who was going to kill them? Pete?

It all became clear now. Connie and Tony were being held captive at the Dickerson's house, and Pete had just said he'd kill them if they didn't follow his rules. Had he kidnapped them? Nikki's heart jumped against her chest as adrenaline set in. She had to get to a telephone to call Harold, and if he didn't take this seriously, she'd bring in the bigger guns, literally.

As she turned to run, she heard the door open behind her.

"Nikki?" Pete said.

Thinking he might have the gun pointed at her, Nikki turned slowly, hands in full view.

"What's going on?" Pete seemed surprised to see her, his gaze softening, as he walked toward her. No gun.

She let her arms fall to her sides. Did he know she'd heard him yelling at his family? She'd have to improvise. "Hi, is Connie home?" *Of course she was home. She wasn't allowed to leave the property.*

Pete glanced back at the house. "I think she's in the shower."

"Can I talk to her?"

"Not if she's in the shower." He laughed without

smiling.

"I'll wait." Nikki's heart beat against her chest, as they exchanged a strange look.

Pete hopped up onto the deck and disappeared inside.

Nikki stood in the driveway. Pete Bayer had gone from being a tyrant, to being a congenial neighbor in twenty seconds. Nikki knew damned well Connie wouldn't have had time to get in the shower after their argument, unless she jumped in fully clothed.

Something was terribly wrong with this family, if it was a family, and Nikki had to do something. Tony was only eleven years old. She walked across the deck and opened the door to the house. "Connie?" Her voice sounded as scared as she felt. The alarm buzzed to warn of her intrusion.

Pete and Tony emerged from the living room with Connie close behind. "Are you looking for me?" she said. Connie didn't look like her life had just been threatened.

"Yes." Nikki had to think fast. "I'm on my way into town and wanted to know if you need anything." She tried to sound casual.

Connie smoothed her blue sweater over her jeans. "Oh, thanks, I don't think so." She glanced at Pete and he shook his head. Connie didn't appear upset about not being allowed out of the house. Had Nikki heard correctly? The situation in front of her was confusing, but she wasn't ready to walk away from the Bayers just yet.

"Or..." Nikki paused. "Why not come with me to town, and we'll see if someone at the beauty salon can do our nails." She tried to look like this was the offer of the century and it would take a huge stick-in-the-mud to turn down the adventure.

Tony stared at his mother strangely, like they'd been caught with their hands in the cookie jar.

"You can come too, Tony, and we'll get ice cream." Nikki would run them to the bus station, give them cash and they could take off from there, as long as they had somewhere to go.

Connie glanced at her husband, who was staring at Nikki, then she glanced at Tony and back to Nikki. "Thanks for the offer, but I'm just getting ready to make some cannoli." She smiled sweetly.

Was she kidding? Cannoli? Nikki was giving her the opportunity to go to town. To be free of the man who'd just threatened her son, if nothing else. "Cannoli can wait. Come on, Connie."

"Maybe some other time." Connie was the epitome of calmness, which confused Nikki all the more.

They stared at Nikki like she'd suggested something out of the question. She'd drop her attempt to rescue them for now and pretend she hadn't heard Pete moments before, telling his wife she couldn't go into town and he'd kill Tony if he took the keys again. What else could she do?

"Honey, go get your nails done." He nodded at Connie. "Tony and I can manage."

Nikki got the impression this was some sort of test for Connie.

"No, thanks." Connie answered too quickly. "I was just in town yesterday, and I really want to get at those cannoli."

Connie hadn't been in town the day before, unless it was the middle of the night. They had to drive by her back door to leave the property and Nikki would have heard. What kind of game was she playing?

Use the code word. Nikki cursed her choice in words. How could Connie use "Goldilocks" in a sentence right now?

"Well, I'm also going to the library if you want any books. Romance fiction? Fairytales? Suspense?" Nikki smiled widely. *Goldilocks?* Any semblance of that stupid name would do.

All was silent, and it was obvious that they were waiting for Nikki to leave. That or they were only several sentences away from spilling the truth. "If you think of anything you need, call me. I'll give you my cell number," Nikki said, heading toward a piece of paper and pen on the counter.

"I've got it," Pete blurted, before Nikki took a step.

"How could you have my cell number?" Nikki spun around.

He looked at Connie. "Do we have it?"

She shook her head. "No, I don't think so."

"In that case," Pete said, "write it down." He handed Nikki the pen and paper.

Tony watched this exchange like a spectator at a tennis match, his gaze going from one person to the next. It was strange that he found this more interesting than the video game he'd been playing.

On her way out the door, Nikki shot Pete a look as if to say "I'm watching you," and he looked genuinely shocked. Good.

Walking back to Birch House, Nikki contemplated what she should do. Call the FBI again? Dammit. She'd forgotten the reason she'd come over—the photo of her supposed boyfriend on the news today. Funny, but in the photo he didn't look like a psychopath with a dual personality. He looked like a studly man who might be the lover of a world famous rock star. But, she admitted that she'd been a poor judge of character before.

****

"They're strange?" Harold asked when she phoned him.

"Yes. Extremely! He won't let her go into town, he has a gun, and I'm sure he said he'd kill them if they left the house. Something is going on over there, Harold, and I can't get Connie to admit it."

"Well, there's no law against being a sonofabitch."

"There is if he's threatening them, and it's more than that. They might not even be married. The wife and son are scared of him. He's not nice around them but is sweet around me. Please, Harold, I think she's in danger." Nikki didn't want to go over Harold's head on this, but she would if she had to, and if she did, people would act. "Can you check them out?"

"I'll look into it, but Nikki," Harold said, "just leave them alone." He sighed. "Most marriages have their problems."

Harold didn't sound like the situation warranted his attention, and Nikki hung up, frustrated. Would a sixty-two year old sheriff in a sleepy little tourist town, know how to investigate someone? Nikki wasn't sure.

Next she phoned Gateman to see what he knew about this guy next door. He'd been elusive when she'd mentioned his name, but why?

"Nikki, you need to leave the lake. That aside, my job is to investigate the stalker, and I'm sure the next door neighbor is not him."

"He sounds like just the sort of person the FBI

should investigate, Ted!" Nikki couldn't convince Gateman to report Pete Bayer and according to Ted, whoever they had planted to watch Nikki wasn't about to include protecting Connie Bayer. "No can do." Gateman sounded almost annoyed. "Ignore the neighbors and please reconsider going to a place where we can protect you better."

Later, Nikki phoned Harold to see what he'd found and got the impression he hadn't even thought about it since they'd talked.

"Hello, Nikki. What's up? Oh, I looked into your family next door."

"What have you got?"

"They're perfectly legit, nice folks." His voice was patronizing, like her request to investigate them had been silly child's play. "They're from Tacoma then Bellevue; he worked for Microsoft. The kid is from a first marriage, just what you told me."

"Does he have a license to carry the gun?"

"Everything checks out, Nikki."

Harold found the information her private investigator couldn't? "Then what should I do about her situation? I can't let him forbid her to go to town."

"You can and you will, Nikki. It's none of your business. You know marriage is hard."

Nikki wished he'd stop saying that.

"Just stay out of it." Harold yawned.

God dammit. She hung up the phone and questioned her level of involvement in the Bayers' life. What if something happened and she could've helped? Everyone advised that she mind her own business, but she knew what needed to be done. She had to get Connie alone. Trouble was that Pete never left them, unless he was walking around outside or going out to his truck. And then there was the matter of the gun that Nikki had to consider. He'd almost used it on her. If she helped Connie and Tony escape to a safe house at an undisclosed location, she had to believe he'd use the gun to get them back. He would suspect Nikki's involvement, and then she couldn't return to the lake until Pete left. She'd have to continue on to her own type of safe house. But, if she didn't try to help Connie, she'd never be able to live with herself, especially if Connie was murdered by her husband, and Nikki hadn't tried to intervene.

****

Phyllis issued the statement to the press about the male neighbor's reputation being compromised and Goldy not being in residence. The decoy was still ordering room service at the Atlantis Resort and doing a damned fine job of pretending to be an elusive rock star. Nikki hoped that would end the speculation that Goldy was canoodling with a hunk on a lake in the Pacific Northwest.

Still, she couldn't figure out why the visiting photographers hadn't identified the lake. They hadn't said the words "Louisa Lake." Maybe too afraid. The Goldy camp had recently won a lawsuit against a tabloid for printing defaming photos of herself and Quinn during what looked like an argument, in the privacy of their own home. Some slimeball was up a tree taking pictures of them and used the caption "Perfect Mother? You Decide." The worst photo showed Nikki with a monstrous look on her face and Quinn cringing. What they didn't print was that Nikki was re-enacting a scene from a movie, and a few seconds later, the punch line would make Quinn laugh hysterically.

Twenty-five million dollars later, the press was more careful and the Humane Society was thanking Goldy for her generous donation. Unfortunately, Nikki knew there would always be a percentage of the population who thought she was a bad mother after seeing that photo. And without having the world policing her parenting skills, she had enough to worry about. All Quinn's life Nikki had questioned her own proficiency as a parent, never allowing herself more than an "adequate mother" label. Most of her childhood, Quinn had been handed off to a nanny so Nikki could run onstage or get to a photo shoot, rehearsal, TV appearance. Nikki's absence in the daily stream of her child's life had been heartbreakingly difficult, sharing motherhood with paid workers. But she was Goldy and, as Burn reminded her constantly, hundreds of people counted on her to pay their wages, not to mention the thousands who counted on her to entertain them. Having now made it through the first trimester with this baby, Nikki was determined with all the fierce of a mother lion, to give her second child what Quinn never knew—her undivided time.

****

The next day, Nikki hadn't left the lake and saw an opportunity to speak to Connie alone, when Pete started up the truck. He'd done this before but always returned within five minutes. Taking advantage of the small window of opportunity, she was ready when the Chevy flew by her house.

Nikki raced to the Dickerson house and knocked frantically. Unable to wait, she tried the door, expecting to let herself in. It was locked. "Connie! It's Nikki. Can I talk to you?" The lock clicked.

"Pete isn't here." Connie looked through a crack, the door still bolted.

"I know. I want to talk to you."

Connie undid the bolt and, as Nikki stepped in, she realized that Connie was not wearing her wig and might have hesitated because of that.

"Is Pete gone long?" Nikki asked.

Connie shook her head. "Just a few minutes."

"Hi." Tony appeared from his bedroom.

Nikki wanted to say this without Tony, but she only had a minute. "Connie, I know you are in some sort of trouble. You and Tony need to get away from Pete. I found you a safe house in Spokane. They've agreed to hide you and help get you back on your feet. I can drive you there." Nikki wanted Connie to consent to a getaway plan before Pete showed up. At the very least, Nikki wanted her to agree it was the best thing.

Connie's face softened. "Oh, Nikki, you are the sweetest person."

"Let me help you." Nikki took Connie's small hand in hers and to her surprise, Connie smiled. At first it was just barely a grin, beginning at the corners of her mouth, and then it spread to a wide smile.

"Mom, what does she mean?" Tony was beside his mother now, looking at her.

"I'll tell you later, honey." She turned back to Nikki. "You have this wrong. Pete is no danger to us."

"But I've seen him…" Nikki didn't want to say this in front of Tony but she had to. "I've seen him….bully you and intimidate you."

"Not really. He's looking after us." She smiled

warmly.

The sound of a truck drove up to the house. "Connie, don't be foolish. You have your son to think of."

Connie shook her head.

"Don't be too scared to leave him. I'll help you." Nikki's voice rose in intensity.

"You can't help me." Connie's voice was quiet, a whisper.

"I can take you to a safe house." Nikki was frantic.

Outside, Pete's truck door slammed.

Connie dropped Nikki's hand and backed away. "This is safe." She turned around, grabbed the first thing on the counter which happened to be a stick of butter, and as the door opened, spoke. "Let me know if you need more. I have another pound in the fridge." She handed Nikki the butter.

Pete slammed the side door.

"Nikki came by." Connie smiled at her husband. "She came over to borrow some butter."

"Nikki again?" Pete walked into view. "More buns?" He didn't sound friendly this time.

"No." Nikki turned back to face Connie, waving the stick of butter. "Thanks, you're a lifesaver."

Pete opened the door and, on her way out, Nikki spun around and with a look meant just for Connie, said, "Let me know if I can be a lifesaver for you."

****

When Pete returned to the house, something wasn't right. He drew his gun and listened through the door. Two people talking and one wasn't Tony. Two women. Probably Nikki with Connie. The door was unlocked. Shit.

He burst in, gun drawn, only to see the back of Nikki. How'd she get past him? She sure was giving that FBI agent stationed at the road a run for his money. Pete tucked his gun into the back of his pants. Something was up with these two women. When Nikki left, Connie assured Pete it was nothing. "She thinks you're strange and came over to see if I'm safe."

Strange?

Having the FBI close had come in handy with the reporters. Although Pete couldn't threaten them, the FBI sure could and did. The guys in the rental boat must've feared for their lives. They'd kept the Goldy location a secret for several days. Until it leaked. How boring was it for the FBI agents in the van to sit all day long and watch the main road? Were the squirrels moving their video cameras too?

This location was losing its appeal. Connie would be safer somewhere else. He'd suggested they leave for his sailboat, but it hadn't cleared with the powers that be. Stay put, they'd said. He might have to take matters into his own hands and ask for forgiveness later. Nikki was getting too snoopy.

The picture of him on the dock came close to blowing everything out of the water. Being called Goldy's new man was an interesting concept, he had to admit, but a picture of him on the internet was not good for business. Connie had had a big laugh over it, and he had to admit it was nice to hear her laugh, finally.

He'd taken some shit for leaving Connie and Tony to go over to Goldy's house but that had blown over. The department didn't consider this case high risk. Still, he wanted to go out in style. Clean record. Everything according to protocol. But if things didn't die down with this high-profile neighbor, they'd have to leave.

As a precaution, Pete had Connie and Tony pack and be ready to bolt at any moment.

****

Patience was a virtue and was needed to achieve the end result. A few more weeks would ensure success. Too many people were watching her. Going to Seattle would leave a hole in Los Angeles that might be noticed. Questioning Quinn would get results. That kid was weak. But the target was Goldy, not the daughter. Focus on the bitch. The airport loudspeaker announced the flight to Seattle and people crowded around the ticket taker like they might not get a seat if they didn't push and shove. Crowds did crazy things to people. Made them desperate. L.A. did crazy things to people especially when faced with the possibility of fame.

Soon the press would surround Goldy's lake house. Only then, under cover of the crowd, would the plan work. Soon.

Chapter 13

Just as Phyllis predicted, another celebrity's misfortune took the spotlight when a young actress fell off a sailboat and disappeared during a midnight cruise.

With an equal measure of caution and hope, Nikki held off on an escape plan, knowing she and Elvis could be in the car and gone within fifteen minutes. A bag packed with essentials stayed at the back door. Ready to bolt.

Night temperatures had sunk to the forties, which changed the water temperature drastically. Swimming was over for the season and Nikki missed being in the water. But, today, the sun had come out and she slid the cedar-strip canoe into the water. Jumping in at the last moment, she managed to keep her running shoes dry. Elvis waited in the bow and she set a course for the bay mouth, executing a perfect J stroke to keep the canoe straight. Stroke, turn, lift, stroke, turn, lift. A loon called from across the lake—the only noise, aside from the quiet droplets that dripped from her paddle. Stroke, turn, lift.

It was blissfully quiet as Nikki sliced through the dark water. No wind. No noise. Elvis caught a scent and stood up in the boat. "Sit down, Elvis." He jumped up on the caned seat and Nikki braced with her paddle. "Elvis, no. Sit down."

The little dog's head swiveled. Something was out

there, behind the canoe, and Nikki turned slightly to see what it was. As she did so, the river otter broke through the surface ten feet from the boat, and Elvis flew off the seat to perch at the edge of the canoe, barking. "Elvis, no. Sit down." Nikki shifted her weight to compensate for Elvis. She dropped on her knees to lower her center of gravity.

Her paddle lay braced across the gunwales for stability. They weren't going to tip, but it wasn't until that moment that she noticed she'd forgotten life jackets. The little dog barked maniacally and as the otter dove and came up on the other side of the canoe, Nikki attempted to keep the boat steady. As she leaned toward Elvis to try to grab his collar, the boat rocked sideways. She compensated just in time but water had trickled into the boat. "Shit!" She let go of Elvis and flung the paddle off port side to brace them.

The otter dived under the boat, and Elvis jumped to the other side. Nikki stayed low and whipped her paddle around to the far side. Just as the otter surfaced Elvis gave a big shove, at the same time that Nikki leaned, and he flew out of the boat.

The canoe tipped and Nikki fell into the frigid dark water.

Pulled down by the weight of her layers of clothing, she kicked herself to the surface. The shock of the cold water robbed her of breath and as she came up, the pointed bow smacked her head. She heard herself cry out with pain. The extra weight of her wet clothing made it hard to stay on the surface. She kicked and flapped her arms to keep her head above water. *God dammit, Elvis!*

She and Quinn had once taken a course on canoe

safety and staying with the boat was the rule. Nikki kicked off her shoes and tried to yank her heavy fleece jacket over her head but instead, sank five feet under. Her jeans dragged her down too but they'd be much more difficult to remove. She groped her way to the surface for a breath and trying to think beyond the numbing coldness, she asked herself, what was the most immediate problem—her weighty clothes or grabbing onto the boat?

In the distance Elvis swam toward the shore. The bow had sunk inches below the surface and as Nikki grabbed the stern, it went under too. Nikki knew that if she got it upside down, she could dive under the thing and go into the air pocket she could hang onto the yoke to keep from sinking. But when she did, the canoe didn't have an air pocket big enough for her head and it rolled over, refusing to offer the harbor she needed.

Without something to grab, she needed to get her clothes off. Nikki wasn't sure how long she'd survive in this temperature but her arms were starting to numb and the shore was at least two hundred feet away.

Trying to keep her mouth above the water, she undid her jeans and, lying on her back, was able to inch them off but it took a lot of energy. Nikki attempted to pull the fleece over her head again but her arms refused to work. The canoe was almost completely underwater now. Stupid old canoe probably had holes in the buoyancy pockets.

Nikki gasped for breath then went under to try the fleece again. Already her frigid legs were slowing down but had enough left to kick her to the surface. If her arms stopped working, she'd be a goner.

The fleece came off and she was able to gain a few

feet swimming toward the closest shore point. The water was colder without clothes, and Nikki noticed her motor reflexes slowing down.

In a short few minutes, an annoying situation had become something much, much more. She was now fighting for her life. *Don't let this be the end.* Nikki looked to shore and didn't know how she'd swim to the nearest point. It seemed impossible for someone with legs and arms that were numb with the cold.

"Help," she yelled. She fought to keep her head on the surface, rolling on her back. Was this how she was going to die—alone in the water, pregnant at thirty-nine years old? She could almost see Quinn's face when the autopsy stated that her mother had been pregnant.

Nikki was so tired. As she sank below the surface again, the numbing coldness crept up her legs and arms to invade her body's core. Her arms barely moved now, even though her mind told them to flap and fight. She couldn't feel her legs.

So cold.

It was surprising how possible it would be to give in and simply sink to the bottom. Like falling asleep. The frigid water was calming her, lulling her. She wanted to sleep. Dying like this wouldn't be so bad. But, as her head sank, Nikki remembered the life growing inside her belly. There was someone else dying besides herself. Deep inside her was the promise of a person, the beginnings of a baby who had come this far with her, defying all odds of being born. This was an innocent life, totally dependant on Nikki's ability to keep them both alive. No free will. Before she consciously realized it, she was kicking again.

Like being wakened from a dream, Nikki now had

clarity. She needed to fight to get herself back to the surface and to the shore after that. By rocking her body, Nikki was able to kick herself up, up, higher, follow her bubbles…. to the sunlit surface. This child was her gift, her reward at this stage of life. *Kick, move your arms, Nikki.*

Kick.

Kick.

She saw her arms float, ghost-like in front of her face and tried to push the water underneath, as she wiggled her body upward. No use, the arms were gone. She was losing the battle in spite of her efforts.

No!

Blackness crept to the edges of Nikki's vision. Breaking the surface, she gasped for air, and, as she endeavored to pike her body back and forth to hold her surface position, she tipped her head back and with everything she had left, screamed "Help!"

The surface disappeared as she sank again. The fight was almost over. Her vision went black and she sank. Down. Down…*I'm so sorry, little baby, and Quinn…*

She felt a yank at the back of her head. Something grabbed her hair. *Women aren't supposed to wear a ponytail when jogging, because rapists grab that.* Was it Shakespeare? Water rushed by her face and Nikki broke through to the surface. A gasp. It was her. A force flipped her on her back and she let it take over.

Her body was useless. Blurriness clouded her vision but light and color crept in. She was moving. Breathing air. She wasn't underneath anymore. The force pulled and yanked at her. Who was it? Connie? She could see Connie's bare feet kicking beside her shoulders. Blue sky above. Nikki had tried to rescue Connie and now Connie was rescuing her. She tried to say something, but her mouth didn't work and it sounded like a muffled groan.

Her head bumped something hard, in the same spot where the canoe had hit her earlier, and then Connie grabbed hold of Nikki's bra straps and lifted. Up and away. Nikki's head hit the swim step. S'okay. Connie was strong. Stronger than she looked. Then Connie's big arms had her around the waist, pulling her backward and laying her down on the soft padding at the stern of a boat. Red and white cushioned pads. Nikki saw the word "Sea Ray." She was on her own boat. *Thank you, Connie.*

But they weren't women's arms. They were hairy, and muscular. Of course. Burn was strong enough to lift her. "Thank you, Burn." Her voice was weak, but the tiny words escaped her lips to linger just in front of her mouth.

Burn loved the boat and he'd loved her. Burn had loved Nikki as well as Goldy. He'd made her into what she became. "Thank you," she said again in the tiny, faraway voice.

A blanket appeared and she was gathered into Burn's strong arms. But where were his tattoos? When the red blanket fell away from between their faces, Nikki couldn't focus. He'd pulled her in too close, trying to warm her with his body. Unable to move her arms and legs, she was entirely at his mercy. She'd been pulled onto his lap and hugged tightly into him. He seemed bigger, stronger now. The divorce had changed him.

Something pressed against her cheek, like a zipper

pull and it hurt. Lifting her head slightly, she tried to see what it was. The shape was familiar. It was a metal amulet, suspended on a piece of leather.

"Hang in there," the gravely voice said.

Only one person had a voice like stucco. Nikki let him pull her limp body in to his heat. Then the shivering began.

"This'll help," he said, rubbing her arms and back.

She pressed into Pete and realized he was bare-chested against her skin. He'd been in the water too.

"Nikki, come back, girl. Stay with me."

Accepting his body heat with gratitude, she pressed against him, letting him stroke her hair.

"Where's Elvis?" Nikki chattered.

"He's on shore." Pete's voice was whispery.

"My baby." It wasn't a question.

"Elvis is fine. I'll get you back to shore in a minute. Just wrap your arms around my back. It'll help." Sinking deeper into him, her thoughts cleared.

"So cold," she said, teeth clacking uncontrollably.

"I know. Is it getting better?"

Nikki could hardly speak through her shivers. "I think so."

A minute passed until he shifted her to the chair. "I'm going to take us back to shore. Get you in a warm shower." He tucked the blanket around her. "Hot tea and a shower are on the way."

He started the motor and they took off for Birch House. How had Pete gone through the house security system to get the boat key? And the blanket was hers, from the couch.

Elvis barked frantically from shore and, looking through a hole in the top of the blanket, she saw that

Pete had a puckered scar on his lower back. It looked old, but nasty. Too low for kidney surgery. It was a rip from something intrusive, not a scalpel.

Pulling alongside the dock, Pete tied off quickly then scooped Nikki into his arms. She greedily pressed herself into his warm chest. Kicking open the door, he took her to the guest bathroom. Nikki dropped the blanket just before Pete stepped into the stream of hot water and stood with her under the nozzle's stream. His face was stoic and the thin line of his mouth suggested focused and determined. He hadn't set her down yet, and she wasn't sure she could stand up if he did.

The involuntary clacking of her teeth made it hard to speak.

"Can you stand up?"

She nodded. "Maybe."

He set her gently on the shower floor, holding her under the elbows. The enormity of the last thirty minutes struck her like a flash of lightning. She stared up at him and together they shared a frightened look of what had almost happened. Then he leaned down and kissed her on the lips. Just a tentative touch at first, as if he wasn't sure Nikki was the right person. But when she didn't move away, it deepened. He tightened his grip, kissed her hungrily then moved to her cheeks, her eyes.

"Nikki."

Breaking away, she whispered, "No."

He breathed heavily against her wet hair. "I almost lost you. Oh, God, I shouldn't have done that." He stepped out of the shower, grabbed a towel from the rack then closed the sliding door.

Silence.

Nikki could see his dark form through the frosted glass. He'd be regretting the kiss. "My canoe capsized." She broke the silence.

"I saw."

"Did you hear me yell?"

The curtain flew open and Pete stood in dripping jeans.

"Why did you go canoeing in fucking October?" He gestured toward the lake. "What's the matter with you, Nikki?"

She managed a few words. "I didn't intend to go in the water."

"Where was your life jacket?"

What right did he have to be this furious? "I forgot it," she managed. Realizing that she wore only panties and a bra, Nikki closed the curtain. But he flung it aside and stared at her. "I don't believe that!"

His expression made her shy back against the shower wall, and Nikki remembered that this man might be a wife beater, a kidnapper, or at the very least, a controlling bully. He looked mad enough to hit her. She'd never seen a bruise on Connie's face, but anyone who used a gun to threaten his family might know how and where to hit without leaving a mark.

He spoke with more reserve. "You stay in here until you're thawed out, then make yourself a cup of something hot to drink."

The steamy water rained over her shoulders.

He sighed. "God, Nikki. Just tell me you weren't trying to kill yourself." He looked defeated, frightened, and something else she didn't recognize.

No one's husband should look at another woman like that. "I wasn't trying to kill myself."

The door slammed, and he was gone.

She slumped against the shower wall and let the heat penetrate her skin. Goddamned fucker, giving her a look like that. Goddamned fucker who saved her life. She'd be dead by now if Pete Bayer hadn't seen her drowning in the middle of the bay. She owed her life to that goddamned fucker. Her life and her baby's. Tears broke through, and she sobbed as the hot water pelted her back and legs.

****

Ten minutes later, bundled in a blanket and sitting in front of the fireplace, she let the heat soak through to her bones as she considered the logistics of what just happened. How did Pete know where the boat key was? She glanced to the hook by the door where she usually kept it. He must have noticed when they'd been over for dinner. Thank goodness he knew how to drive a boat. And that Pete knew how to swim and was strong enough to lift her out of the water and a million other things. How did he get in the locked house?

And the kiss. Her nerves ignited at the memory. Did he kiss Connie like that? Oh, God, Connie. What had she done? Guilt smothered any excitement Nikki might have enjoyed. How could she forget that Pete was married? How could he have kissed her like that? Her attraction to a married man, someone she knew to be a cheater, was shameful.

And then she realized why it had happened. Not because she was trying to steal a man away but because she'd always been a sucker for the bad boy. Burn had been off limits when she met him at seventeen. Her grandparents, who raised Nikki when her parents died in a plane crash, had firmly objected to her involvement with a man in his late twenties—a guitar-playing, long-haired rocker. She'd wanted him with every molecule in her body. And now she'd lost her bad-boy husband. Did this attraction have anything to do with Burn? Was she seeking a bad boy's interest so she could reject him like Burn rejected her? She winced, hoping she was wrong.

The fire crackled and when an ember popped out onto the hearth, she shoveled it back into the fireplace. Closing the screen, she sat back with her tea and let her head fall back against the cushion. Thoughts of her participation in that kiss would have to stay buried. She and Pete could not be alone together again. Connie was probably going to avoid her anyhow, now that Nikki said she blamed her for putting her son in peril by staying with this man.

Were Connie and Pete even married or just shacking up together? They always hesitated to say "my husband" and "my wife" and were strangely elusive about the marriage thing. Nikki had to admit she didn't know exactly what was going on over at that house or who contributed to all the strife, but the fact that Pete had a gun in a house with an eleven-year-old boy wasn't impressive, especially when it was out of its holster so much.

She sipped her cup of tea, feeling the warmth seep back to her body's core. Touching her tummy under the blanket, she felt her recent weight gain, a roundness only noticeable when she sat down. Without realizing it, Pete had saved two lives today. A sob escaped from her throat, a volcano of emotions rising to the surface. Before she could decide how to control this jumble of feelings, heavy steps sounded on the deck. Swiveling in the chair, she saw Pete Bayer opening the door.

Wrapping the blanket tightly around her, she watched him walk into the house like he had a right to do that. He wore dry jeans and a long-sleeved shirt.

"Feeling better?" He hung up the keys then glanced at Nikki.

She hugged the blanket to her. "Yes. Thank you."

Pete stood at the door, arms folded across his chest, his expression steely. "That was a stupid thing you did."

"I know. Thank you."

"You've thanked me enough." Pete backed up a few steps. "The canoe sank to the bottom of the bay so I hope I can count on you not doing that again."

She wanted to explain. "Elvis saw an otter and capsized me."

"You were damned lucky I saw you." Pete looked like he was the victim.

"I'd be lying at the bottom right now, if it weren't for you." She shuddered.

There was no going back to how it had been between them. Life had moved on. Pete saved her life. They kissed. Intimate moments had been shared, parts of each other given up.

"I had no right to kiss you." He looked at the floor.

She nodded.

"I apologize. I want to forget it happened." Pete looked pained at the memory.

He was taking it back. Sorry for the kiss. That was how it should be. But still, something inside Nikki dropped a long way to the bottom of her heart. The apology negated anything good, still left. She deserved the blow. "Me too."

Pete opened the door and started out. "I'm just glad you're alive."

She was too. Without him...If Pete Bayer wasn't the FBI agent assigned to her, then where was the agent when she was drowning, and why didn't he come get her instead of the handsome neighbor?

Chapter 14

Walking away from Nikki's house, Pete knew he had to forget that kiss. What bothered him more than kissing Nikki was that it looked like he was taking advantage of her weakened state after saving her life. He wasn't taking payment and hoped she knew that.

Without even remembering he'd been afraid of water for the last year, he'd actually jumped in the lake. If there was anything amusing in this situation, that was it. He didn't even remember that he couldn't go near water these days. Goddamned useless FBI agent stationed at the head of the road. What was the point of having those twits there if they didn't even know what was going on with her? By the time he was running to the dock with the boat key, the agent was probably trying to open the gate to get to the house. Useless rookie.

Pete had pulled away from the dock, not willing to wait for the numbskull to take his goddamned shoes off. When he got to where she'd sunk, he jumped in and dove under. Didn't think about it. Funny thing. But going out in the boat, just now to get the canoe, he'd started to hyperventilate again and had to come in.

Getting trapped in the storm drain last year had taken its toll on him. If Hansen hadn't dived down to pull him out, he'd never have made it. The memory of those few seconds of being plastered to the wall by the force of the current was his nightmare now.

But he hadn't thought about any of that when he ran over to Nikki's. He'd disarmed the security in one sweep, grabbed the key and taken her boat, hoping to get there in time to save her life. Good old adrenaline.

Being afraid of the water was ridiculous. As ridiculous as having a crush on Goldy. If he couldn't get past the nightmares and fear, what was he going to do about his retirement plan on a sailboat? He needed to swim, to voluntarily walk into water without his heart racing, to submerge and swim. Dive under. Laugh when he came up.

****

Nikki was being extra cautious since the near-drowning scare. She'd convinced herself to stay put for a few days. There'd be no running off to a rental house for a few days anyhow. The press's interest in her was tapering again, this time thanks to a high-profile celebrity who played an all-American dad on TV and was busted for committing adultery with a porn star. It would be awhile before this story died, seeing the porn star was naming names and other celebrities were being exposed.

Since her canoeing accident, she'd been talking to her baby. "I love you, little one. I really do love you so much." Knowing she carried another life in her belly, Nikki had fought beyond the edge in that cold water to hang on and ultimately save both their lives. They'd saved each other's lives that day.

Approaching the fourth month of pregnancy, her belly was rounding and it was time for a doctor to check on the baby's progress. Although she was not a candidate for a high-risk pregnancy, being pregnant at thirty-nine was a red flag seeing the medical community thought she was past prime child-bearing years. There was an obstetrician in Louisa Lake, and if Nikki wore her disguise, slipping into town might be possible.

Giving a fake name to the nurse she drove in for the last appointment of the day. Elvis had to remain at Birch House in case his celebrity status had risen without her knowledge. Taking a chance at being recognized wasn't smart. This doctor appointment was too important.

Dr. Robertson looked at her suspiciously, and when she asked Nikki to remove her sunglasses, she was surprised. "I'm a big fan," she said as she took Nikki's blood pressure. Luckily, the doctor seemed trustworthy and promised to keep her patient's whereabouts a secret. More importantly, she assured Nikki that there was a strong heartbeat. A quick ultrasound confirmed the fetus's health, and Nikki was so enamored with the sight of her baby, she almost walked out of the doctor office with her itchy wig in her hand. The waiting room was empty at that time of day and Nikki fit the wig back on her head and left the building with the ultrasound photo of her baby in her hand. Two hours later, she was back at the house, peeling off the wig and telling Elvis he was going to be a big brother.

****

The next morning, Phyllis called before seven a.m. "I'm sorry to wake you, Nikki, but this is what you pay me for."

"It's all right, Phyllis. What's up?" Nikki struggled to open her eyes. It would be bad news. Phyllis never called this early with good news unless it was the awards season, which it was not.

"It's Burn. He's fine, but the news this morning is going to report that a model is saying he fathered a son three years ago."

Nikki groaned and sat up in bed. "Not good." Elvis looked at her with his little head tilted. "I wonder if it is his." He'd been named in paternity suits before.

"I don't know. He'll probably have to do a test."

Nikki swung her legs out the side of the bed, her toes touching the cold floor. Elvis jumped off the bed and crouched, beckoning her to play.

"What do you think?"

"She's a big name lingerie model. She doesn't need money."

"Have you talked to Burn?" Nikki asked.

"He fired me."

"Again? Please call him, Phyllis, give him the details. Tell him I suggested he rehire you and tell him to call our lawyer." Nikki rubbed her forehead, anticipating a headache.

"It might have more credibility if you call him, Nikki."

"Yes." Quinn would be upset to learn she might have a half brother. At the very least, Quinn might be disappointed in her father.

Her baby would also be Quinn's half sibling, so what was the difference in the two situations? When Nikki conceived, she and Burn were divorced, but any way you looked at it, both of Quinn's parents had had sex with someone and produced a baby. *Poor Quinny with parents like us.*

An hour later the phone rang and Quinn's voice greeted her. Nikki wasn't surprised. "Hi, kiddo, I was just thinking about you."

"Did you see that Dad's in the news today?" Nikki asked.

"No. What for?"

"Paternity claim." It was a shame that at such a young age Quinn was only too familiar with women claiming a piece of her father through blood lineage.

"Shitfuck. Not again."

This was her daughter's favorite swear word. "Honey." Nikki tried to sound like swearing was more important than her father's fidelity.

"But you know how unfair it is to Dad." Quinn had no idea the women who claimed paternity had actually slept with him.

"I know, sweetie. Be warned it might be big news today. Or not." They hung up. Why couldn't Burn just keep his prick in his pants? And now, Nikki was no better when it came to having their daughter contend with indiscretions and babies.

Nikki gave Elvis a long look and he wagged his tail. "I have to tell her I'm pregnant now, don't I?"

****

The long drive to Seattle gave Nikki time to rehearse what she'd say to her daughter. But when she picked up Quinn at the apartment building and they headed to the Four Seasons Hotel, Nikki wasn't ready to reveal that she was pregnant from a liaison with a stranger. Any words used still made it sound cheap.

After the two polished off a barbeque chicken pizza in front of an old Katherine Hepburn movie in their suite, Nikki saw her chance.

"She was such a forerunner in the women's movement," Quinn said, turning off the TV. "Not caring what other people thought of her."

"I agree." Nikki took a deep breath and tackled the second subject of the night. "Quinn, Honey, you are taking the news about Dad's predicament well." She took a run at the next sentence. "...and because of that, I want to tell you something else."

Quinn looked up from texting her boyfriend.

Inch into it. "It's actually kind of ironic." Nikki took another run. "Your dad's situation prompted me to tell you this before I let any more time lapse."

Quinn laughed and looked at her mother, now sitting forward on her chair, head tilted. "What? You're pregnant?" Quinn joked.

Nikki paused and stared at her daughter meaningfully.

"Did you hear me?" Quinn chuckled. "I made a joke.'

The pause gave Quinn time to think.

"What?!" Quinn's smile was replaced with a look of disbelief, then horror. "You're kidding, right?"

Nikki shook her head.

"Oh, my God, Mom. Are you pregnant?"

"I am."

"Mom! You're too old!"

"Apparently not." She braced herself for the part that would follow. "I know the idea seems strange to you. To me too, sweetie. But I'm having a baby." She patted her belly. She had to let Quinn know that bursting her bubble wouldn't be nice if that was the direction she was headed. "And, after a lot of thinking, I'm happy."

"You're having a baby?" Quinn stared at her mother's belly with a sour look on her face.

"At first I was embarrassed and in shock, but now I'm excited. I'm having a baby in five months." She let the news sink in.

Quinn walked to the window of the living room and looked out at Seattle's downtown. "That's what this retirement is all about?"

"Not completely. I was going to retire anyhow in the next year. You knew that."

"I thought your retirement might have been for me."

Nikki crossed the room and hugged her, cradling Quinn's head on her shoulder. "I love you, Quinny Girl, and if you'd asked me to retire, I would have. Part of this is to be close to you here in Seattle, I'll admit. While you go to school. I do want to be available for you. So, yes, it is for you too. And remember I took those months off after rehab?" Nikki needed her to know that she'd tried to be a good mother, in her own way. "You are the light of my life, Quinn, and always will be my darling girl." She pulled away to look at her daughter's sweet face. "But you are seventeen, and I don't honestly think you want me in your face all the time, do you?"

"No." Quinn smirked.

"So maybe it's a good thing I'm able to give you some space now. Soon I'll have someone who needs to be diapered thirty-seven times a day."

Quinn pulled back. "Does Dad know?"

"No, sweetie." She'd assumed it was Burn's. "As if that isn't strange enough news, I have more." Nikki pulled Quinn to sit on the hotel room couch with her. "The baby is not Dad's. It happened during a brief love affair with someone else, after Dad and I divorced."

Surprise flooded over her daughter's face, but Nikki persevered. She'd rehearsed this speech on the drive. "I never cheated on Dad while we were married. Never. After we'd been divorced a month, I wanted a little attention and accepted a date with a man who turned out to be not my type. I made a mistake."

Nikki didn't want Quinn to know the details but enough to understand. "...see, I'd felt unloved by Dad in that way for a long time and I needed something. I'm ashamed to say that, but it's the truth. It's human nature to need love and I'm no different, Quinny."

"Oh, Momsy, it's okay," she sighed and hung her head in thought. "I want you to feel loved." Long pause. Quinn met her mother's eyes, her expression soft. "A baby. It's hard to imagine." Quinn almost smiled. "I'll help you raise her."

****

Two days later, Nikki was back at the lake, with Quinn's permission to be pregnant. She shuffled down the stairs, put the kettle on, made herself toast and looked across the bay to see if anyone was wandering around at Dickerson's. On her brief respite, she'd almost forgotten about the Bayers. Almost. When she arrived home, the night before, it had been late. Aside from the FBI's disguised delivery truck at the road, there'd been no activity.

Leaves were turning gold and crimson now and fall had moved in to Louisa Lake. Wandering out to the dock with her tea, Nikki let the cool wind blow her hair around and thought of the media blitz about Burn and the model. The woman insisted the boy was theirs. Although she wanted to believe their lives were separate now, she couldn't help but be annoyed with

Burn. At least her pregnancy happened after the divorce. Having told Quinn about the baby, Nikki's shoulders had become lighter.

Nikki zipped her jacket closed and remembered Pete rescuing her from the lake days before. Their kiss in the shower seemed months away now. They hadn't gotten far into it. She was grateful for that even though it would probably be years before she was intimate with anyone again. Who'd want a pregnant woman? Or a new mother? She sighed and looked over to Dickerson's. No truck.

The log house looked different. It looked uninhabited. The curtains were wide open, but it was more than that. It looked like no one had been there for days.

She'd been gone thirty-six hours, more than enough time for the Bayers to move out. The thought made her feel strange, like something unfinished would never be resolved. The Dickerson's front door key was hidden in a kitchen drawer.

Leaving Elvis in the house barking, she walked down the dirt road with the silver key on a Louisa Lake Marina keychain. Her step was quick, her purpose clear. She was going to knock and if there was no answer she would let herself in to see if, in fact, the Bayers had left.

After several knocks, she laid her ear on the heavy wooden door. Nothing. The key stuck slightly and she had to jiggle it to make it work. "Hello," she called, before stepping into the house. "Anyone home? It's Nikki."

Breakfast sat on the kitchen table in a state of incompletion. Three bowls of cereal and a box of cheerios in the center of the table made it look like the breakfasters had been suddenly interrupted. Two bowls held floating cheerios, and the larger bowl was empty.

Tony's video games were scattered on the table of the main room, his sweatshirt slung across the chair's back, and a game of monopoly remained in a stage of play on the table. If they hadn't gone for good, where were they? The Bayers never left the property.

Nikki's heart pumped faster. She stepped carefully into the closest bedroom where Pete's baseball cap hung on the bedpost, along with his rain jacket. The open closet was empty, but the strangest thing about the room was the electronic equipment on every surface, including the bed. Something beeped softly. One of the monitors displayed several views of the outside of the house—the back door, the bay, the side door, the road leading in to the property, the gate. There were computers, screens, wires, cameras and enough surveillance equipment to raise the hairs on the back of her neck.

How could someone sleep on this bed, with all that equipment? He and Connie probably slept in the other room. This one showed no sign of a woman's presence.

Walking by the bathroom, she saw towels on the floor and a state of messiness that the rest of the house lacked. She flipped on the light and stepped back, horrified. There was blood everywhere—the counters, the sink, the floor. Towels blotched in red lay on the floor. A large pool of blood dripped off the counter to the linoleum. The shower curtain was closed and Nikki stood frozen to her spot at the door.

Chapter 15

Nikki gagged and clutched her belly.

Oh, God. She had to get out of the house, run home, and phone Harold. Her heart pounded in her chest. Someone official would have to open that curtain.

Could Pete be Shakespeare? Oh God.

She backed up slowly, like she was in a slow motion dream.

There was no trail of blood outside the bathroom door. Nikki spun around, noting the fastest way out of the house and turned to make a run for it. But just then, a small scraping noise came from the second bedroom.

Her mind raced with possibilities. If Connie and Tony were in there still alive, hiding, she needed to open that door. Forcing herself to grab the knob, she turned it slowly and pushed.

The curtains were drawn, the room dark. Bracing herself, Nikki flipped on the overhead light. This was the larger bedroom with a king-sized bed and two night tables on either side.

At first glance, it looked normal. No blood. No half-dead body scraping its way across the floor. But, something inside the room had made a noise. Nikki held her breath and went to the closet, ready for the worst. Slowly, she slid back the paneled doors. The closet was empty except for two pillows on the top

175

shelf and a small open suitcase on the floor. There were no bodies or body parts lying in blood pools on the linoleum floor.

The scratching noise sounded again and she spun around to see a hamster in a cage on the dresser. She heaved a sigh of relief.

Elsewhere, Tony's books were piled on the closest nightstand and a romance novel sat on the far table. It looked like Connie and Tony shared this room. Moisturizer cream was open on the dresser beside the hamster cage and Tony's Spiderman slippers under the bed's edge. The unmade bed revealed two very distinct bodies, one short and one shorter. Connie didn't sleep with Pete.

Then she remembered the blood. Someone was critically injured. Or dead.

There was nothing but dust under the bed and, satisfied for now, Nikki exited the bedroom and quickly headed for the kitchen door. The sound of a car made her jump. Through the window she saw the blue truck coming down the road to the house. When it stopped and slid in to its parking spot beside the deck, Pete opened the driver door. She panicked. He was back from whatever he just did. The possibility that Pete killed Connie and Tony and had just disposed of the bodies was her first thought. She wasn't sure he wouldn't try to kill her too. She had to get out of there.

Oh God. Oh God.

Adrenaline kicked in and she bolted for the back of the house. A car door slammed outside as she slipped out the back door, silently.

With her heart hammering in her chest, she considered the possibilities if Pete saw her. He'd probably run faster than a pregnant woman. She had to have a smart plan if she wanted to escape this man.

As soon as she knew he was inside the log house she'd get herself across the bridge then run through the cover of the trees to Birch House. He'd probably see her on one of those monitors but hopefully she'd be in her car by then, on her way to the FBI at the road.

Creeping around to the house's corner, Nikki waited to hear footsteps on the deck. Nothing. She held her breath.

"Come on, Tony." Pete said.

Tony was alive?

The house door opened. She'd forgotten to lock it. Pete would know someone had been inside.

Footsteps ran across the deck.

"Back to the truck, get inside, quick, and lock it." Pete's voice was short. "And get down until I come get you."

This was the voice Pete used when he thought his family was in danger. He'd guessed someone was in the house. She had to go now. Fast.

Tony would be on the floor of the truck, waiting. Where was Connie? In the shower, dead? Nikki dashed to the far side of Pete's truck. A terrified little boy was in there. She couldn't run without him. She silently cracked open the door.

"Tony?" she whispered. "It's Nikki. Come with me. We'll make a run for it."

"Nikki?"

Connie's voice! Nikki opened the door wider and peeked inside. "Connie?"

"Get in, there's an intruder in our house," Connie hissed. They were crammed on the backseat floor, down as far as they could go.

"No, that was me. I was checking on you guys and saw all the blood."

"What?"

"Whose blood was that?"

"That was you in our house?" Connie got up, one hand still on Tony's back.

"Yea. Whose blood was in the bathroom?"

Tony lifted up a bandaged hand as he and Connie sat up.

The sounds of putting two and two together were deafening.

"Tony cut himself and we had to go to town for stitches." Connie looked behind her, just as Pete flew around the side of the house.

He stopped short when he saw the open driver door and drew his gun, aiming at Nikki's head.

"Don't shoot me. I was in your house, snooping."

"It was only Nikki." Connie shouted, climbing out of the truck.

"Put your hands in the air, Nikki," he yelled. His husky voice worked better when he yelled.

In a matter of half a minute, she'd been reduced from valuable witness at a murder trial, to a snoopy neighbor and her priority had switched from escaping a killer, to not being labeled as crazy. "It's just me, Pete."

Pete lowered the gun and motioned Connie and Tony inside. "Why did you break into our house?" He stood only a few feet from her, his eyes distrustful.

"Well." She was trying to buy time, sorting out what to tell him. "As a matter of fact, I was hoping you would ask me why I was in the house." What could she say? She smelled blood? The truth was usually a good idea. She'd tell a portion of that. "I've been away and I thought you might have moved out so I came over. When no one answered the door, I thought the house was empty. If you'd been home, you'd have answered, especially because Connie and Tony never leave the house..." She paused and stared at him, like they were the weird ones.

Pete didn't flinch and Nikki continued. "I let myself in with my own key. The Dickersons like me to check on their place when they're not here." She hoped that would suffice but saw from Pete's expression it wasn't nearly good enough. His gaze bore into her and she lifted her chin higher. "When I saw blood in the bathroom, I didn't know what to think. It looked like a crime scene."

He stared at her, his gaze softening slightly.

"I heard a vehicle and ran out the back door, thinking I might be next." She challenged him to find fault with the truth.

Pete took a deep breath and shook his head like this was the final straw. He tucked his gun into the back of his jeans.

"You can imagine how it looked," she said.

"God dammit, Nikki, you are a lot of work as a neighbor." He sighed. "Come inside, you can see for yourself. Connie and Tony are fine." They walked to the door and he held it open. "Connie? Can we offer Nikki a cup of tea now that we've scared her half to death?"

Connie came out of the bathroom with a scrub brush and a pail of water. "What?"

"I'm going to make Nikki a cup of tea. Where do we keep the tea bags?" Pete opened the kitchen cupboards. "She thought something terrible happened to you when she saw the blood." He looked over to Nikki. "Sit down, you don't look good."

Connie stood next to the bathroom door. She looked worse than Nikki felt. "Tea is above the stove in that jar." Connie's voice was robotic, her face drained of color. "I'll be out in a minute." She returned to the bathroom and Pete put the kettle on.

Nikki didn't know what to say. *I'm sorry I snooped. What's with all the equipment in your bedroom?* Instead, she got the pressing question out of the way. "Tell me the truth. Are you FBI?"

"God, no. Those guys are imbeciles." He looked like he was almost smiling. Pete put a tea bag in a mug. "I thought you'd left the lake, Nikki." He sounded almost relieved she hadn't.

Connie emerged from the bathroom, white as a sheet. She leaned against the door jamb and covered her mouth with her free hand, as though she might vomit. Pete went to her. "What's wrong?"

She shook her head. "I can't." She started to sob.

"Can't what, Connie?" He took hold of her shoulders and stared into her eyes.

"I just can't, Pete. I can't clean up the blood." She sobbed louder and, dropping the mop on the floor, sank into Pete's waiting arms.

He rubbed her back soothingly and pulled her into him. "I'll do it. Don't go in there." Pete held her tenderly as she cried into his chest. "You don't have to look at it."

Nikki rose from the kitchen table quietly. It felt wrong to be an outside witness to this display of tenderness between them. Walking to the stove, she turned off the kettle and let herself out the door of the log house. She was in way too deep with the Bayers.

****

A motorboat's buzz broke through the afternoon silence. As it got louder, Nikki speculated that someone must be lost if they'd found their way near Half Moon Bay. Nikki rose from the couch and, gazing out the front window, saw one man in a rented aluminum boat aiming straight for her dock.

Even with the binoculars, she didn't recognize him. Not Harold. Ten feet out he threw the anchor over the side. He seemed to be contemplating what to do as he bobbed in the waves he'd created. He didn't look like much of a boater. Photographers and reporters usually came in groups of two and he was alone.

When he wasn't looking, she lowered the front blinds then picked up the binoculars again. From the kitchen window she watched him take a black case from the floor of the boat, open it and extract something. Her heart sank as she realized what was in the case: a long lens camera.

She was not alone, anymore.

This was it—the moment she'd been dreading, and waiting for.

"God dammit all to hell," she whispered, just as the phone rang.

"It's Phyllis. They've found you, and if you don't want to talk to them, you better get out of there fast."

"Too late. One is pointing his camera at my house this very minute." She sank into the chair. "If they knew where I was, why did they wait this long?"

"I don't know but, according to what I'm reading right now, you were in Louisa Lake a few days ago at the doctor. Reporters are headed to the lake to take pictures of a possibly pregnant Goldy."

"Oh, no!" There was nothing Phyllis could do aside from issuing statements to throw them off the trail. "Tell them I'm out of the country, just in case it works."

When she looked outside again, Nikki was horrified to see two more boats anchoring and another one approaching. "Oh, my God, Phyllis, there's four boats in my bay." True, they were only press, not killers, but they were invading her life and she didn't want to give in to them. Was the FBI still around?

The fourth boat pulled up alongside the others. They'd probably rented boats at the marina after hearing the road was near impossible without four wheel drive.

Glancing at the computer screen, she stopped in her tracks to see a photo of her in the brown wig getting into her SUV in town. Taken at the medical clinic, it showed her with an ultrasound picture in her hand. The caption read "Gold Found!"

The wig was useless now.

Could she still make a run for it? Putting Elvis in his traveling bag with his head sticking out, she slipped on her runners and grabbed the car keys hanging at the back door.

A quick peek through the window before she opened the door revealed red and blue in the forest across the road. She squinted to see two men crouching in amongst the forest undergrowth. Was it the FBI agents? Her heart lifted, until she saw their cameras pointed at the very back door she'd almost walked through. She was trapped.

"Dammit! Shit! Dammit!" Nikki stomped her feet and Elvis jumped out of the tote bag to escape her swearing tirade. "Sorry, Elvis," she called. "Mommy's happy now," she said in a high, light voice.

Her house was surrounded.

What were the options? The only way out was to let them photograph her. They'd get a shot as she ran to her car, like a criminal. She could wear a coat over her head, jump in her car and race down the old roads, hoping to out run them. They'd follow her to Seattle probably, all the way to Quinn's.

And they'd win after all she'd done to keep the press at bay. She'd bought herself seven weeks. The idea of surrender sat heavily on her chest as she glanced over to the computer screen. "Gold Found." Someone had circled her wig and written "Real hair? I think not," and circled her tummy with the words "Baby bump? I think so."

"God dammit."

Someone in town had taken a photo of her that had been blown up to a grainy depiction. Even the ultrasound in her hand had been zoomed in on to invasive proportions. Who would do that in town? She hardly knew anyone besides Harold. Then a thought came to mind. She'd call Harold and see if he could escort her out of this mess. Maybe he could get the press to back off enough for her to get to her car, without being photographed.

Harold didn't pick up his phone so she left a message for him to call her at the house. Her vivid imagination had Harold tied up, surrounded by press in his little office, everyone waiting for Goldy to call.

Gateman hadn't responded either, so now it was a

matter of waiting. She'd do her hair and makeup just in case she was photographed. As she stared at the heating curlers in her bathroom, Nikki considered a float plane. Just getting to the plane, she'd be photographed. Besides, it was dusk and she doubted that float planes flew in the dark. A quick glance revealed that several more men had arrived on foot and were now scattered in groups at the side of her road. Good God, did they not have anything else to report this week?

At least there were no cars or news vans. Nikki was glad Pete had been locking the gate lately. The press vehicles were probably half a mile back at the gate, which could be good if she sped by them in her car. They wouldn't make it back in time to follow her. Then she remembered that she'd have to get out of her car to unlock the gate. If she could just find Harold, she could ask him if the reporters could be taken to jail for trespassing.

Nikki stared at the phone, willing it to ring, as she put curlers in her hair. On a whim, she tried to call the Dickerson house and got a recording that it was disconnected. That made sense. What was she going to say to the Bayers anyhow? "Oh, just so you know…those boats and the people lurking in the woods are after me." They knew.

Finally, Gateman called back to say their agents were standing by to help her leave. Just say the word.

When her hair and makeup were photo-ready, Nikki changed into her jeans and sat on the bed thinking about her escape. Should she wait another hour for darkness to set in? It was cold at night now. Maybe the reporters would go back to town to sleep or just give up. She could make a run for it then. And hope she wasn't tailed. Shit.

The upstairs bathroom afforded her a view to a portion of the road she couldn't see from anywhere else, and when she peeked out, what she saw was not good news. The road had filled up with reporters carrying flashlights. The colors through the trees made it look like someone was having a cocktail party on her dirt road. Except the party-goers all had cameras, very expensive cameras with long lenses, in case Goldy should come out her back door.

Some jerk was looking at his camera using the flame from a lighter. An open flame in the woods. This was getting out of hand now. She wished they'd just let it go. But they would never do that. This was their livelihood and many of them had small mouths to feed back home. Beyond the need to make money, Nikki understood the thrill of the chase and the feeling of victory when they got a good shot of her.

She leaned against the side of the window frame, feeling like the prisoner she'd made herself. With one protective hand on her tummy, she imagined sneaking through the trees in the dark to the main road. Harold could pick her up and put her in the jail for the night. No one would look for her there. But even if she got out the deck door without detection, how would she see to run through the trees? If they saw someone making a run for it with a flashlight, they'd chase her. She'd walk out the door in another hour, if they didn't leave, give them their picture and hope no one followed her God-knows-where.

She turned from the window and there he was, standing in her doorway.

Nikki yelped and jumped back against the wall.

Chapter 16

Elvis barked once.

"How did you get in here?" Nikki held her breath.

"It wasn't so hard." He looked smug. "I'm assuming these guys are after you."

"They are." Under different circumstances, having Pete Bayer standing in the doorway to her bedroom would have been a fantasy come true. But, not only was he off limits, but the house was surrounded by press.

"Tell me they didn't get a picture of you walking in to my house." She tried to sound upset, but in reality she was strangely pleased to see him and not just because he was a familiar face.

"No picture." As he stepped toward her, the strange look on his face made her question his motive. He lowered himself into the armchair.

"Why are you here?" She sat on the bed opposite him, and waited.

Leaning forward, with his hands clasped in front, he looked earnestly into her eyes. "I have a plan."

"Why would you have a plan?"

"If you want to escape this mob, I can help. I'm good at this." He paused. "There are a lot of them out there, and I'm assuming, if you wanted to talk to them, you'd have done it by now." He raised his eyebrows.

Nikki nodded.

"Let's get you out of here then." He almost grinned

and she wasn't sure she wanted to trust anyone who saw this as a game. Then she remembered that she'd been on her way to leave anyhow. "Let's hear your plan."

****

It was pitch dark outside and, although only a few boats bobbed around in the bay, the crowd assembled on the road had increased. Probably the marina had run out of rental boats. Nikki had been pacing and swearing for hours.

Harold had called when Pete was at Birch House and Nikki asked him to get his sorry butt out there to tell the throngs that Goldy had left days ago. Pete grabbed the phone from her and instructed Harold to move the people back to the gate and look authorative when explaining the consequences for trespassers. "Wear your gun," he'd said. "Let them see it. Be firm." He also suggested Harold grab the FBI agent at the road to help. "Oh, and bring a few deputies."

Pete gave Harold orders like someone used to being in charge of covert operations and Nikki was surprised that Harold agreed.

"If the press is determined to spend the night in the trees, let's not make our move until they're tired and cold." Pete was now running the show. "Wish I had a snow machine," he whispered to himself.

Nikki had given Elvis a doggy downer pill she used for plane rides that put him in a no-bark state, and after putting him in the dog travel case, Pete took him early to the log house so Nikki wouldn't have to carry him later.

The night was conveniently black without a moon to light the forest. At exactly 1:24, Nikki snuck silently out a side window and rounded the house. Harold would lock up the place in the morning but for now, he was busy standing on a fallen cedar just up the road addressing the crowd of thirty or more press. Exactly as Pete told him to do.

Nikki could hear snippets of what was being said.

"Remember...being lenient...private property..." Nikki imagined him waving his arms, gesturing wildly. "If everyone... get along fine."

She stole her way to the trees at the beach, then alongside the bay. The men waiting in the boats were making enough noise that she didn't have to worry when she stumbled over a tree root and caught herself on one hand before going down. She'd wrenched her wrist but would worry about it later.

"Good evening, gentlemen, or should I say good morning?" Harold's son, Travis, was on the dock shining a flashlight directly at the faces of the photographers in the boats. "Nice night for fishing." He chuckled to himself. It was cold and Nikki doubted the photographers had worn appropriate clothing.

She couldn't stay to watch Travis's planned distraction. Creeping slowly along the bay's shoreline, she found herself near the little bridge to the Bayers' house and advanced through the blackness to hide on the far side of the road. There she crouched by a clump of bushes, nursing her sore wrist.

"Fancy meeting you here."

"Pete?" she whispered.

"You ready? This'll help." Pete fit something on her head that felt like a baseball cap, then pulled goggles over her eyes. She could see in the dark. Trees emerged, along with Pete's face which was only inches from hers as he adjusted the goggles. He wore them too. Connie and Tony stood behind Pete, also wearing goggles.

Computer programmer, my ass.

Clumps of conversations murmured behind them from the boats. Would the reporters realize anything was different about the house in the morning?

"Follow me, single file," he whispered, carrying the tote that held Elvis. "Remember silence is key, not speed. No talking."

"Are we all going?" Nikki couldn't imagine why Connie and Tony were coming along.

"No talking." Pete put his finger to her lips. "I mean it, Nikki, be quiet."

Shouldn't a young boy like Tony be asleep? Because of the no-talking rule, Nikki saved her questions for later, but, as she walked, they stacked up in her mind like thrown horseshoes on a post.

****

Pete smiled to himself to hear how noisy the reporters were. He had a silent electric boat waiting on the far side of Dickerson's property.

Once in it, he pushed off the rocks, and Nikki took the driver's seat and got the thing going. Harold had guaranteed it would be "charged and quiet as a whisper" and it was. The boat would shave twenty minutes off their arrival time to the town's marina where a deputy had parked Pete's truck hours earlier. If someone was on to their plan, those twenty minutes could be the difference between escaping and not. Nikki needed to avoid the press for convenience' sake but his stakes were much higher.

He looked to the end of the lake where the lights of

the marina shone brightly then back to the passengers. Tony snuggled in to his mother's arms. Poor kid was tired. Even if they hadn't planned it, they'd have left when the press showed up, anyhow. Their safety had been compromised and plan B was now in action. Considering the high-rise apartment Connie and Tony had hidden in before Louisa Lake, the escape was actually plan C. Connie's fear of heights and claustrophobia had put a quick end to Plan A. When the prosecutor jumped in to suggest his cabin on Louisa, it seemed like a good idea at the time. Then Nikki moved in next door. To Pete, the job sounded easy after a year of doing flights. "Last one before retirement." They'd said at the Department. "Nothing too big to ruin your perfect record." No one foresaw trouble. There'd been no threats. Probably just routine. Murdering Connie before she testified would only serve one lowly person in this case, and that man was in jail.

Pete hadn't gotten approval for going to the sailboat, but his reputation in the Justice Department allowed him more lenience than some marshals and when it came time for forgiveness, he figured he'd get it.

It hadn't been easy the last month, with Nikki next door. He'd been off his game, and now the press she attracted was just plain annoying. Who'd have known that in the month they were at the log house, Goldy would decide to retire from a twenty-year career and spend autumn at Louisa Lake. When he'd secured the Dickerson's cabin, his report indicated that she used the house maybe twice a year and never in September.

The second problem was that she was not the reclusive neighbor he'd hoped. She was nosey as hell and couldn't seem to keep on her own side of the property. She watched them through binoculars, she faked canoeing to spy, she baked as an excuse to come over and she let herself in their house when they weren't home.

He couldn't leave her at Louisa Lake alone, with all she knew. Shit, she'd probably guessed what was going on by now. She'd probably even played with all his surveillance equipment that day she broke into the house. Even in a low-risk case, he wasn't going to take any chances. Especially when inside that rock-star body was the mind of a snoopy old grandma. He needed to keep her close to monitor who she spoke to, just until they called for Connie to testify. Then he'd let Nikki go.

The lights of the marina were visible now and Nikki adjusted their direction to make a straight line to safety. Tonight they'd drive to the sailboat in Shelton. Even though he hadn't put up the sails yet, it had a motor, it was his, he had a key, and had already spent a few nights on it. He loved that thing. They'd hide out for a week or two and wait for the call. He'd have to think of a way to break the news to Nikki that her life was in his hands until that call.

****

Pete's blue truck was parked at the back of the marina lot. Connie and Tony jumped into the back seat which confused Nikki more. They were all going off in the truck? Earlier, she hadn't thought past the immediacy of getting away from her house. Pete had sounded so confident, she'd just left the details to him.

"I'd like to go to the nearest rental car place," she said.

Silence.

"I'm not sure about Louisa Lake, but I'm sure there's one close."

He chuckled.

"I'm assuming that's the plan. You three can go back to your house after you drop me off."

Pete looked in his rearview mirror and sped up.

"Look, I appreciate you helping me escape, but now I need to rent a car and say goodbye."

"At two a.m., Nikki?" Pete stared ahead at the dark highway that was illuminated only by their headlights. "This is pretty much the middle of nowhere. I'll tell you our plan in a few minutes. Let me make sure we're not being followed, first." The truck climbed to sixty mph.

"You're pretty good at this for a software designer, Pete." Nikki wasn't smiling.

In the back seat, Connie told her son to turn off the video game he'd pulled from a pocket. "It's late and you need to sleep," she said.

Why would they put Tony through this? "I didn't expect all three of you to come with me on this." No one spoke. They increased their speed to sixty-five. Tony sighed in the backseat.

"Oh-oh." Pete stepped on the gas and they shot up to seventy mph.

Nikki turned around and sure enough, there was a car gaining on them.

"Hang on, everyone." There was a corner turn ahead and Nikki was in the death seat in the front of the truck. She grabbed her seat belt to make sure it was firmly fastened.

"Are you crazy? They're just reporters!"

"We're fine. This truck will take it." Pete slowed to

sixty and, keeping to the right side of the road, hugged the corner. As soon as they were out of sight from the vehicle, he jammed on the brakes, swerved right, down a road and turned off the truck's lights.

The car sped by them, tires squealing around the curve and continued south. Pete sat watching for a few minutes until headlights illuminated the far lane, heading back toward Louisa Lake. When the same car zoomed by, Pete took off south again. "Lost 'em." Pete's grin was visible by the dashboard's light.

"This isn't a game, Pete. Don't risk our lives." Nikki's words were clipped.

"Nobody's life is at risk, Nikki." Pete spoke softly then snapped his gum.

She felt on the floor for the dog tote. How would she escape if it was some creepy kidnapping plan? The gas gauge said half full and she considered that an escape might be possible at the next gas station.

He cleared his throat. "I suggest everyone get some sleep." Pete looked content to just leave it at that.

Nikki was anything but content. "If we're going near Seattle, you can drop me off there."

"No can do." He looked at her. "Sorry."

"Look, Pete."

"Look, Nikki. I got you out of there, everyone is safe, and now we're going to my sailboat just to catch some sleep tonight. We're all tired. Tomorrow we can talk about Seattle."

"I don't want to go sailing with you." The anger in her voice broke through the words. "I have family in Seattle. You can drop me off there. You can leave me anywhere, and I'll catch a taxi to my daughter's house."

Pete was silent.

"Why are Connie and Tony here?"

Pete looked as awake as anyone she could imagine at two o'clock in the morning.

He glanced over at her. "I just helped Goldy escape from the press, and I'd like a little gratitude here."

Ha! Pete knew exactly who she was. Of course he'd known. That's why he kissed her. A sense of disappointment invaded, and she tried to ignore it as she gently pulled a groggy Elvis up to her lap. Settling him in to her lap, she then looked into the back of the truck and noticed a tarp secured over a bundle.

"I'd like to be dropped off in Seattle or as close as you are going. No offense, but I don't care to holiday with you Bayers, thank you very much." Nikki looked straight ahead.

"No offense taken."

With that settled, she leaned her head against the headrest, her eyes heavy. Pete had the driving under control. She'd close her eyes, just for a little bit.

****

When Nikki woke up, the truck was still speeding down a highway in the dead of night. Pete was still chewing gum, driving with one hand, looking wide awake.

"Where are we?" She checked her watch.

"Heading west to the Olympic Peninsula. We just went over the Tacoma bridge."

It was six thirty. She'd been asleep for hours! "I wanted to be dropped off in Seattle." She'd missed her opportunity to go to Quinn's.

"You looked sleepy."

"Pete." She stared at him. Had they planned all along to take her with them, against her will? It was looking more like a kidnapping, as the miles drifted past them on that lonely stretch of early morning highway. Tony and his mother were curled into each other, asleep. "Why?" she whispered at him.

"It's a long story."

She imagined the worst. This man could be Shakespeare, and Connie and Tony might be his victims too. "Are you kidnapping me? Just tell me you're not a deranged stalker." Nikki's heart was in her mouth as she waited.

"I'm not a stalker, Nikki." He looked over at her. "Although in the past I have enjoyed your concerts. But you are here because you got caught up in our problem. The good news is that you're not the main attraction this time."

"What is going on?"

"I know you deserve some answers," he said, "and I sure as hell didn't expect you'd get involved in this, but right now I'm just trying to figure out what to tell you."

"Are you running from the law?" This was the burning question, now that he'd told her he wasn't the stalker. "Because if you two are bank robbers, or something like that, you can just let me out at the next gas station."

"Nothing like that."

"Are you bad guys?" Her voice was weary.

"Nope. We're the good guys." Pete popped his gum.

"That's not reassuring, because even the bad guys think they're the good guys."

"Well, we are the actual good guys. I brought you this far because, for one thing, you'd be recognized wherever I let you out and your problem would start all over again. I'm actually doing you a favor." He smiled at her again and reached over to pet Elvis who was starting to come around. "And for another thing, we need to keep you with us for safety purposes. In thirty minutes, we'll be at the boat and we can get some sleep. Then I'll help you go wherever you want. If you choose to leave us, then I can't tell you who we are."

Nikki looked at Connie's sleeping form in the back seat. "Are you two married?" she whispered.

"No," Connie said, before Pete could stop her.

"Connie." Pete groaned.

"Well, Pete, you have to admit we make a strange couple. I'm sure Nikki thinks so too."

"If we tell you more, you'll have to stay with us for the next few days. You'll know too much for me to let you go." Their headlights pierced the dark road as she processed what she knew already and what she guessed.

"Knowing your identity puts *you* in jeopardy, or me?" she asked.

"Everyone, especially Connie," Pete answered.

She hadn't thought Connie would be the wild card in this.

"Connie has the most to lose if you know who we are."

"Tell her, Pete," Connie pleaded.

He cleared his throat like he might speak, but popped his gum and steered the truck onto a small road, reducing the speed. "We're almost there. Wake up Tony."

"If you don't tell me what's going on and I leave, I'll never know who you guys are."

Pete lowered his scratchy voice. "It's not a bad

deal."

Connie jumped in. "I guess you're right." She sounded exhausted, and Nikki knew it had nothing to do with the fact they'd been up all night.

If she walked away now, she'd spend her whole life wondering who the Bayers were, but if she stayed with them for a few days and they took her into their confidence, she might be putting herself and her baby at risk. "So if I stay with you, you'll answer all my questions? Explain everything?"

"I'll explain enough," Pete said. "But don't stay out of curiosity."

"How many days?"

"Maybe a week to ten days."

She thought back to all her questions about the Bayers. Nikki had invested enough emotion in Connie. It would be hard to walk away. Pete was not married to Connie, but she couldn't think about that. "Is my life in danger by staying?" This was the deciding factor.

"I can't guarantee your safety one hundred percent," Pete said. "But if I didn't think this was safe, we sure as hell wouldn't be doing it." He chuckled without smiling. "You're safer with me, than most anywhere else in the world. I can guarantee that."

Nikki believed it to be true. Sounded like he was some high-tech bodyguard. She'd go to the boat slip with them tonight and make a decision in the morning. Maybe she'd be safer with the Bayers right now than at Quinn's. She wasn't sure. "I'm pregnant." The words sounded strange when spoken out loud. Especially because Pete had kissed her passionately only a week ago. This announcement ought to put an end to all flirting with Pete whether he was married or not. "I don't want to put my baby's life in jeopardy if there are bad guys after you."

Pete didn't look sideways, didn't say anything, and the only sound inside the truck's cab was Tony's waking groan.

Chapter 17

The little dinghy pulled up alongside the forty-foot sailboat, and Pete reached out to grab the ladder at the stern. Could her dog's bladder hold it on the sailboat until they saw a beach again? He'd relieved himself on the shore just now and was known to go for long stretches in hotel rooms, but she didn't want to make the little guy suffer.

"Have you ever had a dog on this boat?' She handed Elvis to Pete as he climbed aboard with the dog tucked into his arm like a football.

"I've never had anyone on this boat, but there's a first time for everything." Pete set Elvis down on the deck and helped everyone else on board.

Tony hadn't fully woken and after getting him up the ladder, Pete picked him up in his arms and carried him down below. "There's a big bed in the bow for you two, Connie. I'll put him there."

As Pete got the generator going, switched on the lights, and pulled off deck covers, Connie settled her sleepy son into bed. Nikki waited up top as Elvis sniffed around.

Even in the darkness, Nikki could see it was a beautiful boat. The yachts she'd known from Cannes and the Italian Riviera always belonged to someone she barely knew. This one belonged to Pete. He pulled the canvas covers off the seating area.

"I don't know much about sailboats, but this one is pretty." Nikki helped fold the covers and tuck them inside a hatch. The teak railings and highly polished wooden trim showed that someone had loved this sailboat over the years.

"Yeah, she is." Pete said.

"I saw the name was painted over."

"Yup. I haven't named her yet.

The way he ran his hand over the captain's wheel, almost lovingly, Nikki guessed it would be named after a woman he loved. Either present or past.

"The former owner called her Ishmael and that didn't suit me."

Peeking into the cabin, Nikki saw Tony burrowed into the bed in the V of the bow. The only visible bed. A dining area had benches on either side. The way she felt she could sleep on the table if necessary. Or out on deck. It was a cold night, but clear.

Pete walked to the bow to store the last of the canvas covers, Elvis shadowing him. "Have to get you a life jacket, little guy." He reached to pet Elvis. "What do you think of my boat? Pretty fancy, eh?"

Elvis wagged his tail when Pete scratched his ears.

Now that she knew he wasn't Connie's husband, Nikki was confused. Who was he? Not FBI, but he sure knew a lot about running away in the middle of the night.

"Just don't fall in the water, Elvis," he said. "I don't know if I'd go in after you like I did with your mom." He chuckled and watched the little dog sniff the air. "Hey, boy, you let me know if you hear or smell anyone out there, okay?" When they joined Nikki back in the cockpit, she was wiping down the outside seating with a towel.

"We can do all that in the morning." Pete sounded as wide awake as Nikki felt. The excitement of being on the water like this had postponed her exhaustion. If it had been summer and still warm, Nikki would be tempted to stay the week with the Bayers. Boat life might be an interesting distraction right now. As long as Pete wasn't her stalker, this was as safe as she'd been in the last year. That alone gave Nikki peace of mind. "I'm going to sit here on deck for awhile, if that's all right." Dawn was beginning to lighten the sky in the east.

Pete brought couch cushions from below and they fit them into the frames behind the wheel as Elvis sniffed every inch of the boat. He didn't appear ready to bed down either. The briny ocean scent was heavenly to Nikki, who hadn't been around the sea in awhile.

Pete disappeared below again and emerged with two warm coats and a blanket. "Here."

She gathered the man's parka around her and curled up with the blanket.

"You're a good sport, for a pampered rock star." Pete put on the other coat and seated himself opposite Nikki.

"I'm not that pampered." She didn't want him to know how pampered she really was. "Besides, I practically grew up in a cabin in Oregon. Before becoming a rock star. And I've been running from the press all my adult life." They smiled at each other.

"You must be tired of running." Connie came through the cabin door, gathering a blanket around her.

"I'm hoping to put an end to it soon." She tucked her chin into the neck of the coat. It smelled like Pete.

"I'm retired now."

"I'm going to get a beer. Want one, either of you?" Pete looked at the women, who shook their heads and he went below.

"How far along are you, Nikki?" Connie asked.

"Almost four months." She smiled apologetically although she didn't know what she was apologizing for. "Thanks for rescuing me tonight." Did Connie and Tony have a choice when Pete offered to help the neighbor lady escape?

"We had to leave too." Connie took off her shoes and tucked her feet in, under the blanket.

"Why?"

Connie looked sheepishly at Nikki. "I can't tell you." She leaned forward and glanced inside the cabin. "I shouldn't say anything but…" She looked again. "Pete is…guarding me," she whispered. "I'm waiting for something and he's keeping me safe." She covered her mouth with her hand and shook her head like she'd said too much.

Nikki tried to process the new information. Connie was the wild card and needed a bodyguard. Was Connie a celebrity too?

Pete's form filled the cabin's doorway. He'd brought with him a small telescope in one hand and a Corona in the other. She wanted a beer so badly that the sight of it made her mouth water. She'd just have to make a date with a beer in about six months, or maybe even later than that—after breast-feeding was done. "You must be tired, Pete."

"Oh, Pete doesn't sleep." Connie glanced over at her.

"I do so." He gave Connie a reproachful look. The

dynamics between them seemed so much more relaxed, more normal. Like brother and sister. He set the tripod between him and Nikki, and began to fiddle with the focus.

"How can you not sleep?" Nikki was envious, especially because she'd been sleeping so much in the last few weeks.

"I sleep," he said, looking through the eye piece. "I just don't need much."

"Two hours a night, if that." Connie stared at Nikki like she'd finally found someone to share this secret with. Apparently, Pete's insomnia was not classified information.

"Here's Venus, if anyone wants a look." He moved away from the telescope.

Nikki leaned to look through the lens. "Wow." She looked up at Pete who was close enough that she could feel his breath on her cheek.

"It's really beautiful, isn't it?"

"Amazing." Their knees touched and they moved apart quickly.

"I'm tired." Connie stood. "Sorry, everyone, but I'll see you in the morning." She stumbled slightly.

With lightning speed, Pete jumped up and grabbed her under the elbows without spilling his beer. "Both arms out, Connie. Like this." He over-exaggerated a wide stance. "You'll get your sea legs soon."

"Thanks Pete," she giggled, looking back at Nikki. "I'll be the first overboard, I'm sure."

"I'll jump in to get you if you are." Nikki smiled.

"No talk like that on my boat. No one is allowed overboard, even if I have to tie you to the mast." Pete pointed to the bow.

Pete was cute. Especially now that she knew he wasn't the bully, tyrant, or terrible husband. Instead he was Connie's protector, bodyguard, the one in charge of making sure she stayed out of sight, whether she liked the silence and boredom, or not. That was why he wouldn't let her go to town, exit the house, go near the window. But had he threatened to kill them or said that they'd get killed if they didn't listen to him? She took a deep breath of night air and gathered Pete's coat around her. Being on the ocean was so different from anything else.

When Pete picked up his beer to take a swig, she gazed brazenly at him. "I'm beginning to figure out who you are, Pete Bayer."

"Oh, yeah?" He smiled and nodded.

"Well, to start, I know you aren't married." She amended her statement. "…to Connie, anyhow."

Pete was silent.

"And I'm thinking that you were at Louisa Lake with Connie and Tony because it's a remote location. Good place to hide."

"Hmm." He was maddeningly noncommittal.

"…and, why would you be travelling with a mother and son you don't know well, keeping them in the house, away from the windows, and using a gun on neighbors who come calling?"

Pete sipped his beer.

"At first I thought you were a reporter, following me."

"Ah."

"Or a biographer. And now I know that's not the case. And you're not my latest stalker."

Damned poker face.

"I suppose you're a bodyguard, a security person or something like that." Nikki tilted her head, scrutinizing him through squinted eyes.

He leaned over the telescope for a look.

"For a long time, I suspected you were a horrible husband, bullying your family."

He looked insulted. "Really?"

"I worried you might be planning to do away with Connie, and when I saw the blood in the bathroom and the shower curtain closed..." She couldn't continue, just thinking about the emotions that ran through her at the sight of all the blood.

"Oh, my God, Nikki." He looked up, horrified.

She shrugged. Elvis jumped on her lap and tried to lick her face.

"You actually thought I was a killer?"

"You should have seen it from my angle. You acted suspicious, downright weird. And you seemed to have no affection for either Connie or Tony." She paused to think and shook her head, remembering the moments she'd wondered if Pete was insane. "I thought you were mentally abusive at the very least."

"I guess I'm not as good at this as I thought." He chuckled.

Nikki felt like backtracking. "Well, you had a gun. You never let them leave the house."

"How did you know I never let them leave the house?"

"I heard things...and they never came out."

He shook his head. "You are the snoopiest neighbor I've ever known." Pete chuckled as he adjusted the telescope arm.

"I never was before, but you're so secretive. It

made me want to be snoopy." She examined his profile as he scanned the skies for stars. "Even now."

He heaved a sigh and sat up.

"Private bodyguard? Police? FBI? Or CIA?" Nikki persisted.

"No. No. No and no." Pete gave Nikki a look that told her she was going too far, asking too much.

She waved a finger at him. "No, don't ask, or no, I'm not any of those? I think I might put enough together to know why you're protecting Connie."

Looking through the telescope he muttered, "At least this explains your strange behavior."

"My strange behavior?" She almost snorted. "You were the ones with the squirrel in the house that made Connie and Tony sprint to my house in the rain.

"Oh, the squirrel. Ha," he laughed. "That much I can tell you." Pete sat forward. "I saw someone in the woods and asked Connie to hide in the house while I ran out to investigate. Connie didn't stay put and while you were having tea with her and Tony inside your warm house, I was chasing some goon through your forest in the pouring rain. Someone who turned out to be on your security staff and was let go within hours, even though he was approaching your house with a Glock."

Nikki whispered. "Why did Connie come to my house?"

"She was frightened and thought if she got Tony to your house, they'd be safer if I got killed."

"And you caught Dwayne."

"He looked suspicious." Pete watched the smile erupt on her face. "It's funny that I accosted your bodyguard?"

"Well, no, but it's funny that it was you who took down Dwayne Capleoni. He's some sort of black belt phenom or something."

"He didn't have any moves that day with a gun pointed at his head."

As their eyes met, Nikki realized that Pete had kept them all safe, or thought he had. Had Dwayne been Shakespeare, Pete would've saved her life that day. And she reminded herself that this man who'd kissed her twice, once in the shower intimately, was not married. At least, not to Connie. This was proving to be a night for answers and new problems.

Pete emptied his beer bottle, stood, and asked again if she'd like anything to drink.

"No, thanks." Without thinking, her hand went to her tummy.

When he came back with another beer, Pete sat down and leaned forward, his eyes squinting in thought. "So, Nikki, if we're asking questions now…" He paused. "You are pregnant." He took a pull on his beer.

"That's not a question, and besides, what makes you think I should answer yours if you don't answer mine? You kidnapped me and are forcing me to stay on an isolated boat at least until it's light out, but you won't tell me who you are."

"Not kidnapping. You came with us after I pleaded my case. There's a huge difference. I'm a U.S. Marshal for the Justice Department." He folded his arms across his chest.

"Four months pregnant. Due at the end of March." She imitated him, folding her arms.

"Is that why you're hiding from the press?" His brow wrinkled.

"That, and the fact that they never have enough of me. I just announced my retirement from the music business. It's a big deal. Some people don't believe I'm finished." She stared at Elvis, asleep in her lap. "After all these years of me romancing the world, they don't want to lose me." She sighed. "And I understand. But I haven't got anything left to give them. It was a struggle to make it this far." Nikki hadn't realized that, until she'd said the words. "Soon they'll have to give up and let me go."

The sky had lightened enough that she could now see Pete's face clearly, the small lines fanning from his turquoise eyes.

"I read that you retired suddenly." Pete's thumb made circles on the cushion beside him.

"When I found out about the pregnancy, everything changed. It was at the end of my concert tour and the timing was right."

"To leave show business and be a mother?"

She nodded. "I want this baby more than strutting around onstage in front of thousands." She laughed lightly. "Besides, I can't go on being a rock star forever."

"Oh, I bet you could, if you wanted to."

Nikki shrugged. "I don't want to. I'm ready for motherhood without show business."

"And what about your husband? Will he quit too."

She could almost hear the wheels turning in Pete's head. "This has nothing to do with my ex-husband. He's not the father." She couldn't look him in the eyes.

The gentle lapping of the water against the boat was the only sound for an uncomfortably long time.

Nikki took a deep breath and thought about

revealing too much to someone she barely knew. "The father is no one I knew well." Saying it to Pete filled her with shame. Her breath caught in her throat. "It's hard to admit that about myself, but that fact makes it convenient." Nikki felt like she'd set something free. "I'm not going to tell the man."

"We've all made mistakes," Pete whispered.

She nodded, looking down at Elvis. "Yea, this was a whopper but with heavenly consequences." Nikki patted her tummy and a smile formed on her mouth. Pete was silent, probably feeling extremely uncomfortable. She'd just thrown a deadly snake into the room and he was trying to decide what to do with it.

She smiled at him apologetically. "Sorry, I can't imagine why I'm telling you this much."

"S'okay. I'm known for keeping secrets." He smiled.

"I suppose as a U.S. Marshal, you've kept a lot of them."

"Yup. Confessions don't scare me. I was raised a Catholic."

She laughed through the veil of tension surrounding them. "The funny thing is that I was divorced before this happened, and in spite of what Burn put me through, I was faithful to him right up until the divorce was final." Looking at Pete, she confessed, "I'm actually happy it isn't Burn's. I'd rather raise this child alone than with a father I had to apologize for all the time." She'd said enough. It was time to go to bed, before daylight ruined the moment, before she revealed any more about herself, and before she leaned in to kiss Pete Bayer. But first. "One last question."

He nodded.

What's your real name?" She knew he'd tell her now.

"Judson Peter Daniels."

"Judson," she said, before lifting Elvis from her lap.

"I go by Pete."

With the little dog in her arms, she crossed to the blackness of the hatch door.

"I'm Nicole Ann Crossland," she said, turning around to look at Pete. "But a U.S. Marshal probably knows all that."

Pete pretended to tip his hat. "It's nice to finally meet you, Nicole Ann Crossland."

****

Nikki was awake with her eyes still closed. What would she see when she opened them? Last night when she'd come into the cabin, two beds had been made from the table's bench seats. Pete must've done it when he'd gone below for a beer. Both had blankets, a pillow and a sleeping bag. She'd figured one was for her and she bedded down with Elvis, relieved to be horizontal.

She had no distinct recollection of the moments before she fell asleep. Pete might have come to bed, but she wasn't sure. Consciousness was lost as soon as her head hit the pillow. She opened her eyes to see that the second bed looked undisturbed.

It was strange to think of Pete as a U.S. Marshal when twenty-four hours before she'd wondered if he was a criminal. Everything she had thought about him was now out the window. Everything, except how he kissed. That much was Judson Peter Daniels.

An engine purred at the stern, and Nikki felt the movement of the boat, cutting through the water. Elvis sprawled at the bottom of her makeshift bed and she heard voices on deck. Sunshine poured through the windows on the starboard side. She'd woken with a feeling of freedom that she hadn't enjoyed in years. Like being on a glorious vacation. Not only was she totally protected from Shakespeare, but the press had been left in the dust.

Swinging her legs over the side of the bed, Nikki's thoughts drifted to the last few days and the whirlwind of surprises that had come her way. "Did you sleep well, Elvis?" She rubbed the little guy's tummy. He rolled over onto his back to give her easier access to his favorite scratching place. "I sleep with Elvis, don't I? Not many people can say that." There wasn't much stuff around the cabin, aside from a few books on a shelf. Was this sailboat where Pete lived when he wasn't working? He'd told her that he just bought the boat in the last few months. Maybe he hadn't moved in or maybe U.S. Marshals didn't accumulate stuff.

She raked her fingers through her hair and looked around for her bag, hoping to tame her mane with a brush before she went topside. There was a very handsome man on board who was not married to Connie after all. While brushing, she reminded herself that this was not a vacation, and contrary to her sudden lightness of spirit, this was serious. People were after Connie. And a lunatic might still be pursuing her.

Hearing a noise from the bed in the bow, Nikki peeked in to see Tony's arm wrapped around the hamster cage. Elvis obviously hadn't gotten a whiff of that thing yet.

She opened the door and sunshine poured in causing Nikki to squint at the domestic scene on deck.

Pete was at the wheel with a cup of steaming coffee in one hand. Connie was settled into a blanket on the couch cushions, talking to Pete and sipping from her own mug. A strange little pang of jealousy at the sight of them sharing a lovely moment invaded Nikki's heart.

"Good morning, Mr. and Mrs. Bayer," she said. "Tony is still sleeping."

Connie nodded. "He was so tired."

"Poor kid." Nikki meant it in many different ways, on many different levels.

"Welcome to the sunshine." Pete grinned at her. "How did you sleep?"

"Like a pregnant log." Elvis squatted and urinated at the stern. "Oh, Elvis, are you supposed to do that right there?" Resilient little Elvis, from a shelter, to hotel rooms with a rock star, to a lake house, to a sailboat. The world could learn from Elvis's ability to adapt.

Pete watched the dog finish. "That's okay. He's gotta go somewhere. I'll wash it overboard in a minute."

"Thanks." Nikki sat beside Connie. "I had a dream about you last night. Your name was Linda, I think, and you were a clothing designer."

Connie laughed. "What a stretch, especially because you've seen me wear the same clothes for weeks now."

Nikki looked at her. "Is Connie your real name?"

"Let's just say it is." Pete was quick. He stared ahead, his hand on the wheel.

She was allowed to know Pete's real name, but not Connie's.

Connie looked apologetically at Nikki, as if to say

"I'll tell you later."

"No more questions," he said. "Sorry it was so cold down there. I just turned everything on and got some heat going. Last night, I wasn't sure how the heater worked."

They were headed out from the bay. Nikki looked back to where they'd been moored. The anchored sailboats behind them looked unoccupied, with covers over the deck areas, no sign of life. Sea birds bobbed on the surface of the slight swell that rolled toward the beach. The green water was dotted with long strips of sea kelp, like cheese on French onion soup, and there was a definite briny smell to the air. It was an interesting contrast to Louisa Lake.

"I love the ocean." She breathed deeply. Maybe Pete had a fishing rod on board. But would she stay the day? Pete said he'd get her to Seattle if she wanted. Was that where they were headed? Nikki needed to decide if she was safe on this boat, with these people, or would she be better off somewhere else. "Do I smell coffee?" she asked.

"Yes, and I even have some decaf for you, mommy. Didn't you hear me twenty minutes ago, banging around in the kitchen, ten feet away from your sleeping head?" Pete smirked.

She blushed. "I guess I didn't." She had to call Quinn soon to tell her that she was on a vacation. Of sorts. With a U.S. Marshal and a fugitive and her son.

Chapter 18

Once satisfied with their new remote location, Pete turned off the engine and threw the anchor overboard. Connie and Nikki had set the dining room table for breakfast, stowing all pillows and sleeping bags on Tony's bed to wall in the hamster cage from Elvis. The mood on board was more like the prelude to a vacation brunch rather than a desperate getaway. Tony settled himself at the table and snuck a piece of bacon. Between bites, he stared at Nikki. "So, are you really Goldy?"

"And good morning to you too, Tony." Nikki laughed.

"Hi, Goooooooooldy." Tony drew out her name like it was a joke.

Nikki ruffled his hair and smiled. "Hello, Tooooooonyyyyyy." She sang to him, riffing his name into multiple notes and watched his eyes widen.

"Wow! You can even make my name sound good." He smiled at his mom.

This was not the kid from the lake. This boy seemed light-hearted and well-adjusted.

"I don't think I ate yesterday," Nikki said, sitting down.

Connie looked horrified. "And you're pregnant?"

"Pregnant, and very hungry." Nikki scooped up a pile of eggs and helped herself to toast, feeding a tiny piece of bacon to Elvis who waited at her feet.

A few bites later, she looked up to see everyone staring at her. "Okay, Bayer family. Do I leave today or what?" She took another bite of eggs. "And who made these fantastic eggs?"

"Me." Pete seemed pleased.

"I didn't know U.S. Marshals were trained in the culinary arts." She smiled warmly at Pete.

He took a piece of bacon, not meeting her eyes. "Do you want to leave us today?"

She shrugged. "Should I?"

Pete put down his bacon and sat back in his chair. "We can't keep you here against your will. Well, actually, I can, but I probably won't given who you are and that we only need a few more days of secrecy. And if anyone can understand privacy, it's probably you." He gestured to her with his open palm. "…but it's better for everyone if you remain with us."

She stopped chewing.

"Let's see how to put this?" Pete stared at the ceiling. "We'd like to invite you to stay?" He faked a smile like this was the invitation of the year, and Connie actually laughed.

She looked between the three Bayers.

Pete took another run at the explanation. "Because of the reporters at Louisa Lake, we were forced to make a quick getaway last night." Pete continued. "We had to go to plan B when the press showed up looking for you." He took a swig of his coffee.

"So you're saying…" She looked between Pete and Connie. "…that I've already put you in jeopardy by being in such close proximity to you. Now, I owe it to you to stay, because if I leave, I might be forced to tell someone where you are."

"Basically." Pete ate a forkful of eggs. "You know too much at this point for me to feel completely comfortable letting you go off on your own." He spread jam on his toast. "I doubt anyone would target you or that you'd willingly leak our location but look at your trip to town the other day. Someone photographed you. The press love you, Nikki. And now Connie tells me that you know she's a trial witness."

Nikki stopped eating. Witness? "Are we talking about the witness-protection program here?"

Pete looked at Connie. "I thought you said...?"

Connie stared at the table.

"You're in the witness-protection program and you're going to testify at a trial soon?" Nikki put down her fork.

"Shit." Pete did not look happy. "Connie?"

"I said I thought she guessed as much." Connie said.

"What's the chance of your bad guys finding us here?"

"Next to nothing." Pete was still giving Connie the stink eye.

Tony's gaze swiveled back and forth, like watching a tennis match. Poor kid had endured months of silence and now hearing this information spill out was probably thrilling.

"How can you know that?" Nikki placed her palm on her belly.

"I don't, but I'm very good at what I do, and this is considered a low-risk case. Unless someone is looking for us, and I seriously doubt that, and they know where we are out here on the ocean and are prepared to chase us in a boat, I'd say we're safe." Pete held his gaze on Nikki.

"How bad are your bad guys?" she wanted to know.

"They killed my husband," Connie whispered.

"Oh, my God, Connie!"

Pete stepped in. "The risk is when we move her to Seattle for the trial. And we have that covered. You won't be with us at that point. But don't stay out of guilt because we had to leave Louisa Lake. Only stay with us if you feel safe."

Connie jumped in. "I don't honestly think my life is in danger, or Tony's, but the DA wanted to take every precaution, before I testify. If anything, the Justice Department is being overly cautious." She smiled at Pete.

There was a feeling of respect and fondness between Pete and Connie—something she hadn't seen when she thought they were married. "How long do you need to stay hidden after the trial?"

"She can't talk about that," Pete said.

"What's your real name, Connie?"

"Nikki." Pete looked like he was chiding a bad kid. "Give it a rest."

She wiped her mouth with a napkin. "Then try this one. What's up with your laryngitis, Pete?" She stared at him.

"Vocal chord nodules." He added, "Not contagious."

"I'm well aware of vocal chord nodules and you need to stop talking to let them heal."

"Do you see me talking a lot?" He threw out his arms.

Connie chuckled sympathetically at Pete.

"What do you want to do, Nikki? Stay with us a few more days or leave and tell no one about us?" They waited for her to make a decision.

Although Connie's situation was different, both women would be starting a new life soon. Nikki had willingly chosen hers though, one she wanted desperately. Connie's life had been chosen for her and was motivated by keeping herself and her child alive. If she left and someone knew she'd been with Connie, her life might be in more jeopardy. She took a deep breath, looked at her three companions and slapped the table. "What time is lunch?"

****

He'd kidnapped a world-famous celebrity. Hell, he'd either be called up for this or commended. Nothing in-between. His punishment might depend on Nikki's view on being convinced to stay with them. The other marshals in the department would wonder if he'd kept the gorgeous rock star for reasons beyond helping her escape the press. He wondered too.

Pete pulled out the heavy nylon sails like he knew what he was doing and laid them on the sailboat's deck. Hooking up those suckers and catching some wind would be fantastic. But with the manual in one hand, he soon realized how difficult it would be to sail this boat. Especially without knowledge or crew. He closed the book *Sailing for Dummies*.

According to what the Department told him that morning, Connie wouldn't be called to testify for a few more days. He had the time to read up on sailing while they waited. And Nikki was staying. Elvis sniffed the air at the bow, keeping watch like the beast he was, making Pete wonder why he'd never used a dog before on missions. Canines had better senses than a human when it came to smelling or hearing an oncoming intruder.

Connie and Nikki talked in the stern, at the seating area, while Tony set up a board game between them. Over the last month, Connie had probably missed talking to another adult. Pete hadn't been much company, not wanting to get too close. And his vocal nodules. Many times over the last weeks, Pete had wanted to engage Tony in a game of chess or something, but stopped himself. That wasn't his job and he had to stay focused. Brandon would have been Tony's age now, but that didn't mean he had to befriend the kid. In a few days, they'd go to Seattle where Connie would become someone else's responsibility. Then she'd be gone to wherever the witness protection program sent them.

"You're doomed," Tony yelled.

"Have a heart, Tony," Nikki said.

Pete saw the Stratego game on the table. Abandoning the sails, he meandered back to watch. Nikki got along really well with Tony, and, aside from adding levity to this adventure, she was just plain fun to stare at. "You saw my flag." When she stood up to point at the Stratego board, he noticed a little baby bump that her hip-hugging pants couldn't hide. She was definitely pregnant. He'd tried to put that information away somewhere last night, but why? Embarrassment for her because of how she presented the information? She'd been embarrassed, but he reminded himself that Nikki wasn't his, just because he'd kissed her twice.

If he could take back that shower kiss he would,

simply because she'd thought he was a married man. But he'd gotten a lot of mileage out of the memory of it. The way she sighed against his cheek when he pulled back. Now he'd like to kiss her again, to see how much better it was knowing Connie wasn't his wife. Nikki's pregnancy didn't dampen his interest at all. Hell, he'd made mistakes in the past and been forgiven, even when he didn't deserve it. And he'd fathered a baby when the timing was less than perfect. The memory of that would never go away, he'd realized. It just moved aside to let new memories in. Memories that didn't involve Marnie or the baby. Or Brandon's death.

When they finally weaned Marnie off the tranquilizers, she'd wanted to get as far away as possible. "I can't stay here anymore," she'd said, and he foolishly thought she was suggesting they move to another town.

"I'll put in for a transfer."

"No, Pete. I'm leaving. Going back to New Orleans, without you." Her stoic expression frightened him.

He'd let her go. It didn't matter that what he needed the most after Brandon's death was Marnie. It didn't matter that the only family he had was his wife of two years. He'd have to cut all ties for the sake of her survival. When he found out she remarried a year later, he'd been grateful. That's when the real healing began.

Life was supposed to go on, but dating was out of the question. No woman wanted to take on a cynical U.S. Marshal and he couldn't blame them. The fear of hurting again kept him from any emotion beyond the least amount needed in the bedroom. He was better off alone.

Pete packed away the sails. He'd learn to sail another day. What was he even thinking? A new game of Stratego had been set up, and Nikki was helping Connie conquer Tony's warriors. The sound of their laughter made him smile, but he resisted the urge to join them, knowing his presence would change the dynamics. Nikki was a nice addition to their group. Before her, no one laughed. It was like she'd brought the fun with her. For a rock star, she was surprisingly personable. Not aloof, like the models and celebrities he'd been assigned to during his career as a marshal.

Pete zipped up the sail bags and considered the little dog who'd taken a shining to him. "Elvis, can you learn to sail and teach me?" The dog tilted his head as far as Pete guessed it would go, and stared. Pete laughed out loud. "Man to man, Elvis." He bent down to scratch the dog's ears. "Does your Mom think I'm a jerk, or what?" He glanced back at Nikki and realized that even her giggle sounded musical. "I think I'm growing on her, don't you?"

****

Food from a can was surprisingly tasty when you didn't have much else. Some of the canned soups Pete had stored in his sailboat cupboards were downright yummy. Just add water. Easy enough. With supplies rationed, Nikki hoped she wasn't eating more than her share. Pete had joked that Nikki would be eating them dry at this rate and if they were lucky they'd have another few hours.

"Sounds like you've been around pregnant ladies before," Nikki joked while they did dishes.

"If you're having ice cream cravings, I'm afraid you're just going to have more baked potato soup." He smiled at her.

"In my first trimester, I couldn't stand the smell of most food, especially fish, but I'm craving it now." She searched his face for a clue. He hadn't said if he'd been married, just that he and Connie weren't married. The mystery of his personal life was driving her crazy, as was the brick wall that went up anytime she asked him anything personal. "I had vocal chord nodules once." Was this a safe subject? "Chinese herbs did the trick. Saved me from surgery. You can buy the tea at health food stores. You should try it."

"I will if you'll make it for me."

"Deal." Had they just set up a date to meet after they were free from this adventure?

Nikki washed the last dish and let the water drain out of the steel sink. "Can I ask you a personal question?"

"You can ask."

"Why did you buy a sailboat if you can't sail?"

"Oh, you noticed, did you?" Pete chuckled and set down his towel, leaning against the counter and crossing his arms across his chest. "Sailing is my dream. When I got stationed on the west coast, I started looking for a boat," he smiled. "I'm going to learn to sail."

"Will you get much time out here between jobs?"

"I'm retiring after this one," he explained. "Once I learn to sail, I'm going to Mexico."

She envied his freedom waiting just on the horizon. "When my boat broke down on Louisa Lake..." Now was as good a time as any to settle this. "...did you see me out there waving?"

"I did. According to protocol, I couldn't leave

Connie."

Nikki groaned and put her hands on her hips. "Why not call someone?"

He looked apologetic. "I did call the marina, then Sandy's Bait Shop, and then the sheriff who said he'd send someone out. And he did, but you were home by then."

"Ninety minutes later."

"I had no idea that you were pregnant." He squeezed her shoulder. "Now, I feel terrible about just watching you."

"You watched me?" Nikki tried to sound shocked.

"To make sure you weren't in any jeopardy. Besides, it was only as much as you were watching me." Pete smirked.

She set her dish towel on the counter. "I was only watching you because I thought you were dangerous and couldn't figure out what your problem was."

"And now?" Pete looked sideways at her.

"And now I think you're just...slightly...strange." Nikki grinned to herself and climbed the stairs to join the others on deck.

****

The next day Tony caught a pretty good-sized ling cod with Pete's lucky pole.

"Let's fry it up for breakfast." Pete was more impressed that Tony got up early than he was by the fish. He was happy to introduce the boy to the joys of fishing at seven a.m. Pete was awake anyhow, and it was the kid's first time with a fishing pole.

"Breakfast?" Tony didn't sound convinced that the big slimy thing on the end of his line would turn into a meal.

The two women had poked their heads through the cabin door when they heard the excitement. Connie walked over to pat her son on the back and Nikki laughed, at Tony's expression. "If it's okay with you, I can cook it," Nikki said.

Tony stared at Pete who was taking the hook out of the fish's mouth. "Sure."

"Do you want me to gut it too?" Nikki came closer to examine the cod.

"I'll do it." Pete stepped in. "I know how to gut a fish." He didn't want Nikki to one-up him on his own boat, especially after the remarks she'd made about him owning a boat he couldn't sail.

Once the filets were presented to the chef, Pete watched Nikki coat them in batter she'd made from corn flakes and flour. When she picked the fried pieces out with a fork and drizzled lemon butter on top, Pete's mouth was watering. "I thought you couldn't cook."

"I can't cook many things, but I know how to fry fish. I spent my childhood summers on a lake with my grandparents and have always loved fishing." Nikki beamed at Pete, who was still studying her from his seat at the table. "My grandfather loves to fish, and it's one of the things we shared growing up. And Quinn." Nikki carried the plate of fish to the table. "Come and get it!"

The cod was melt-in-your-mouth perfect with the salty crust and a hint of lemon. Watching his breakfast companions, Pete was confounded that they were having such a good time in the midst of what was actually happening. Boat life was like that though. Living for the moment, taking pleasure in the little things—like eating fresh fish caught minutes earlier in the Pacific Ocean.

****

The third day on the boat with no name, it poured rain, trapping them in one of two shelters—the cabin below deck or under the bimini awning that covered part of the outside deck. Elvis was going crazy with a hamster sharing his quarters and had been banished to the deck if he wasn't going to play nice and leave the cage alone.

"Better put that thing out of the little guy's reach," Pete said, hanging the cage from a hook in the ceiling.

All day they played cards, read, and talked until the sky got darker and Nikki announced she would make dinner. "After all, I'm eating the most," she laughed.

"I believe in this case it's called opening cans and heating," Pete said. "Not exactly cooking." He pointed to the can opener on the counter and the display of cans they'd earlier lined up to take inventory of their food. "And if you're as good with a can opener as you are at eating" —he looked at Tony and grinned— "I'd say we can look forward to a big meal." Everyone laughed and Nikki flicked him on the leg with the damp kitchen towel.

Connie didn't appear to be jealous of the attention Nikki got from Pete. Maybe even the opposite. The two women often shared a special look when Pete was funny, cute, or flirty, and Nikki got the impression that everyone thought it was good fun.

Tony sat on his bunk with a video game while Connie read a novel from the limited stash on board. Pete was in and out of the cabin. He'd set up motion detectors on the boat and the gulls kept setting them off. "Damn gulls are as bad as the Louisa Lake squirrels."

"Did you have cameras in the trees at Louisa

Lake?" Nikki stopped opening a can, remembering her skinny-dipping.

Pete nodded. "They only worked half the time. The rest of the time the squirrels sat on them and rearranged them. That's why I kept driving in and out all day. I was adjusting the cameras." He looked at her significantly. "But in the end, those cameras saved you from drowning and from the press. And Dwayne."

"Did you ever see me skinny-dipping?" she whispered.

"Why? Did you do a lot of naked swimming?" He kept his voice low, but Connie looked up from her book.

"Not a lot." Nikki's eyes widened. "Oh, my God, did you?" she mouthed.

Pete grabbed a stack of plates to set the table. "You don't want to know."

She wasn't sure if he was teasing her, but continued to look at him. When their eyes met, his look of embarrassment mixed with a guilty grin, told all. He'd seen her swimming naked. Nikki grabbed his arms and forced him to look her in the eyes. "You saw me swimming naked?"

Tony narrated his game from the bed. "Take that, you evil sorcerer."

Pete turned his back to Connie and Tony, and whispered. "From a distance. I saw you get out of the water naked. You put on a T-shirt and walked up to your house with a towel wrapped around you, so technically" —he glanced behind him where Connie was pretending to read her book— "I saw the back side of you for four seconds, from very far away." He shrugged. "But running over to the monitor to see better made me stub my toe on the bedpost if that makes you feel better."

Nikki remembered the scream. "But you didn't see all of me?"

"No." Pete grabbed some cutlery to set on the table. "Not really."

"What?!" Nikki spun around to face him.

Pete lowered his voice and moved to within inches of her. "The first day you arrived at the lake, you were lying on the dock, topless." He grinned. "What was I supposed to do? I was surveying the area as a possible location for my job, and there in the middle of my binoculars was a world-famous rock star, topless."

"You looked?"

"Of course I looked."

"For a long time?"

"I tried not to, but Nikki, I'm only mortal." Pete obviously thought this was funny. "Don't tell me you're shy."

It was disconcerting to know that Pete had seen her breasts.

"Is dinner ready yet?" Tony asked.

Nikki took a deep breath and moved away from Pete. "Come and get it."

"Looking good, Nikki."

"Oh, stop, Pete."

"I mean the food. Dinner looks good." He smirked. "You must've been opening all day," he said loud enough for everyone to hear.

She glanced at Connie who was grinning into her novel. "I almost wore out the can opener."

Connie took a seat across from Nikki, forcing her to sit beside Pete.

"Canned spam, canned corn, canned spaghetti for Tony, canned potatoes with butter, which was not canned, and canned peaches for dessert. We've run out of milk, so we're drinking a concoction I like to call Tanglicious Cocktail." She smiled proudly.

Tony reached for the spaghetti, and everyone dug in. Having run out of the dog food smuggled from Louisa Lake, Elvis was now enjoying canned beef stew, which left him with extremely smelly gas.

"Sorry, little guy," Pete said, "but you're going to burn down the boat with those noxious fumes." He gathered Elvis in his arms and put him out on deck. Pete had fashioned a yellow lifejacket for Elvis from a child's size that he found on board. "This way, if he jumps in after a fish, we'll be able to see the yellow as he swims out to sea," he'd joked.

Nikki was grateful. "Thank you, Pete," she'd said. The effort he'd put into Elvis's safety was touching, and she'd hugged him longer than necessary, later reminding herself that she was overly emotional these days about everything.

After the canned dinner, rain pelted down on the deck and they played cards in the cabin. Elvis was allowed back in and lay down for the night on a makeshift bed under Pete's desk.

"Euchre!" Nikki hadn't played cards in such a long time. Burn had never liked games unless they involved him trying to hide a sexual liaison. Nikki laughed over her victory then stopped. A small fluttering moved in her tummy. She froze. There it was again—just a tiny indication that something was in there.

"Oh, my God! The baby is moving!" she whispered. Reaching sideways, she grabbed Pete's hand to place it on her belly. "I can feel her."

He spread his hand across Nikki's slightly rounded abdomen and waited.

"She might do it again," Nikki whispered, holding his hand in place, wanting not only for her baby to move, but for someone else to feel it. She wanted Pete to feel it.

"There. Was that it?" Pete looked up, his eyes wide.

"Yes! That was it. Did you feel it?"

"That was a definite kick, Mommy." Pete grinned at Nikki like he knew how it felt to have a life growing inside.

When Nikki looked over at Connie, she was grinning too, but not because of the baby's kick. Her happiness was focused on Pete.

Chapter 19

Later that night, Nikki and Pete stayed up late talking under the bimini tent, drinking mugs of peppermint tea. She'd napped too much during the day and still wasn't tired at midnight. They kept their voices to a whisper, even though the sounds of the rain muffled their words, even this close.

"Feeling your baby move was incredible." Pete stared off into the darkness, a wistful look on his face.

"Wasn't it?" Nikki grinned. "Have you ever felt a baby kick before?" Nikki imagined the answer was no.

Pete paused, and she knew she shouldn't have asked. The air was thick with tension.

"I have…"

Nikki held her breath.

"It's a long story."

Nikki didn't know what to say or how to change the subject.

"I was married twelve years ago. My wife got pregnant."

She braced herself. This would not be a happy story.

"….and the baby died at birth." He cleared his throat, his voice unable to hide his grief.

"I'm so sorry, Pete."

"We divorced after that." Elvis walked up to Pete, sniffed him and jumped on his lap, wet from the rain.

"Oh, Elvis, get down," Nikki said.

"He's okay." Pete positioned the dog on the blanket beside him.

"It must have been horrible."

"After nine months of waiting to meet the little guy, it was pretty bad."

"You've been through a lot." Nikki's mind was racing with all the possibilities of who Pete Daniels was. She understood that a U.S. Marshal might not fraternize freely when they were on duty, but Nikki wanted desperately to peel away more layers, see more. Even now she could feel the barrier around this man. "So tragic." After a few minutes when he didn't speak, she took the lead. "Who are you really, Pete?"

"Nobody in particular," he whispered.

"Who's in the photograph downstairs on your desk?" It was one of the only personal effects to indicate someone had claimed ownership of the nameless boat—a wedding photograph in a frame.

"My parents on their wedding day. The only picture I have of them." He looked at her, like he'd been caught.

"Are they dead?" Nikki asked.

"My dad died when I was two. Then my mother couldn't handle it. Without him, she realized she had three little kids she didn't want. When I was four, she basically gave us up, me and my older sisters. I had to go to a boy's home, and they went into a crummy foster home." He cleared his throat. "It was hard because my older sisters were my caregivers, and after that..."

"Oh, my God. Who raised you?"

"Lots of people tried. I had a big chip on my shoulders and was just lucky to grow up, considering

231

the eight foster homes I was in." He looked at her directly. "My mother never came to get us. I found my sisters when I was older." Pete rubbed his chin and looked like he was thinking about how much to tell her. "By then, they had problems of their own."

Nikki tried to hold in her tears. "Where are they now?"

"Baltimore. My sister Sherry is doing great now. She's a mother with teenage kids—nice second husband—but Beth struggles. I sent them money for years and Beth used it for drugs." He took a deep breath. "Beth and I don't speak, but Sherry keeps an eye on her. You have family?"

"Just Quinny. I was the only child of travelling antique dealers who died in Marrakesh when I was young. My grandparents raised me after that." Nikki was quiet.

"It's hard to let go of the worry for my sister, but there's only so much I can do."

"I agree. So you're retiring as soon as Connie testifies?'

Pete nodded. "I'll be done." He gestured to the gun on his hip. "After decades of being in the field, I can't just sit at a desk. I'm going to get on with my life. Something I haven't really had a chance to do yet." He smiled at Nikki and her heart twisted.

Nikki could sympathize.

"My life wasn't all bad," he said. "There've been more happy times than bad. It's just that you're asking about the bad." Pete laughed it off and turned to Nikki. "Tell me about being a rock star."

This time Nikki gave the long version, not feeling the need to keep her summary to two minutes.

Miraculously, Pete listened. When he asked about life on the road, she couldn't hold back her feelings about her marriage and the inadequacy she felt about Quinn's upbringing.

Pete moved closer when Nikki told him about the day she discovered her fifteen year old doing drugs. "The little girl I'd spent so many years protecting was snorting coke up her nose with some goddamned, fucker roadie in our bus." She shook her head. "I'd been distant because of a fan committing suicide at our concert. I was questioning my integrity, and Quinn was suffering."

She took a deep breath and told the long story of her daughter's sobriety. The conversation was so gut-wrenching that when Pete reached for her hand, she left it in his warmth.

"Life is challenging sometimes," he said rubbing the top of her hand with his thumb.

"Yes." She remembered Tony catching the fish that morning. "And goddamned amazingly wonderful sometimes."

They remained holding hands. It seemed only natural with the rain drizzling down off the awning, that they would lock eyes and feel something. Should she try to kiss him? It wouldn't be their first kiss.

"Nikki…" His face was inches away.

"Do it." She closed her eyes and let Pete come the rest of the way, like before. This time it was different. Tentative, barely brushing lips, warm breath, then it deepened ever so slightly. A careful kiss. Pete's hand cupped her face lightly. He smelled manly, salty. As he pulled back, she opened her eyes and something about his expression made her lean in to kiss him. Not lightly this time but a substantial kiss. He responded. Anything less wouldn't feel right after what they'd just learned about each other. This time Nikki tasted him, knew him briefly. He tasted like peppermint.

Pete's whiskers scratched her face. She threaded her fingers into his hair at the back of his neck.

When they pulled apart, he looked down. "You better get your sleep."

He was done. Maybe he'd only kissed her out of shared sympathy. A pity kiss. What was she thinking? She was pregnant, for goodness' sake.

A low lantern swung from the kitchen ceiling and she slipped into bed. Should she turn it off or leave it burning for Pete? Did he ever sleep? So far, she'd never seen him in that bed. Elvis had stayed on board with his new best friend.

Sometime during the night she woke to see Elvis nestled at the end of her bed. She barely made out a still form lying feet away on the other bed. Listening, the only sounds were the lapping of little waves against the bow of the sailboat and Tony's occasional cough. If they hadn't been running from people trying to kill Connie, it would've seemed like a happy little vacation group on board the nameless boat.

****

Waking up to sunshine seemed like an omen. So far, Nikki hadn't thought about when this would all end but now worried how much longer they'd have together. Even if they were only moving several miles each day to change positions, being on the ocean was glorious, and she secretly hoped that the trial would drag on or Connie wouldn't be needed after all. They'd get more supplies, head south for Mexico, and swim in the warm ocean.

After breakfast under a sunny sky, Nikki and Pete gathered all the damp towels, wet canvas covers and clothes from the previous day's rain and hung them on a makeshift clothesline to dry. The sunshine warmed their faces, and Tony made jokes about going swimming. He'd been forbidden to swim at Louisa Lake, and Nikki was sure he was just teasing Pete.

"Why not, Pete? It's hot," he said.

"That water isn't warm, or even cool. You'll freeze your little huevos off," Pete told him. "Let's catch us another one of those cod." Pete grabbed the fishing pole and beckoned Tony. "Come on, Elvis. We'll do some male bonding at the bow of the boat." Tony grabbed the tackle box as Elvis danced around at the sight of the fishing gear. He'd tasted the cod and knew fishing meant excitement and then food.

Nikki was just finishing the breakfast dishes when she heard a yell from up on deck, then a loud splash. Her immediate thought was that they hooked a seal.

"God dammit," Pete yelled. Another splash. Something or someone had fallen overboard. From the sound of things, she guessed it was Tony. She burst through the hatch.

Pete shouted from the water. "Yes, Tony, it's cold," he said.

"Here, Pete." Connie threw a life ring while Tony looked on from the railing.

Pete swam on his back to the swim ladder with Elvis in his arms. Elvis wore his yellow life jacket and was perched on Pete's tummy. "Oh, my God, Elvis." Nikki yelled. "What are you doing?"

Pete glanced up. "Elvis decided to go for a little

dip." His blue mouth barely worked.

"I'll get towels and a blanket." Connie disappeared below, while Nikki ran to the stern and leaned over the swim step with her arms extended for Elvis.

"Why did you go in after him, Pete? Elvis can swim, especially in that life jacket."

Pete grabbed the ladder at the stern, handed off the dog, and pulled himself out of the green water. "He fell off the boat. He looked like he was fighting for his life."

"That's how he swims." Nikki set Elvis on the deck, and the little guy shook off and wagged his tail like it had been a great adventure. Connie and Nikki wrapped blankets around Pete.

"I'm okay." His teeth chattered and he looked vulnerable in his wet clothes. "I was trying to get him to come to the stern, but he was heading away from the b-b-boat."

Nikki looked up to see a seal dip below the surface, forty feet off the bow, and knew what Pete hadn't seen. "You need to get those clothes off."

"If you insist, Nikki. but we hardly know each other." Through his shivering, Pete shot her a look that made her blush.

"You know what I mean, Pete. Get downstairs and take off your clothes."

"Okay, but don't be long."

Nikki slapped him on the arm, and he smiled through blue lips. Connie continued vigorously rubbing Pete's back with the towel.

"No seriously," he said, "someone is going to have to help me undress. My hands are numb." His arms hung uselessly, and Nikki remembered the day she almost drowned.

Connie backed off. "I'll go make tea. Tony, don't you fall in." Her son was back at the bow, pulling a piece of kelp off his fishing hook.

Pete turned to smirk at Nikki. "I'm not kidding, my hands won't work."

Taking a deep breath, Nikki reached up and undid his jean jacket buttons then pulled it off him.

"Faster, Nikki, I think I'm developing hypothermia from going in after your dog."

Nikki harrumphed. "He would have come back, once the seal disappeared."

"Oh, he would have come back all right. Belly up. Wait? There was a seal out there?"

She felt his icy-cold hands.

"You don't believe I'm cold?"

"Just checking." She undid his shirt snaps in one big rip.

"Oh, baby." The look on his face made her knees weak.

"Relax, cowboy. You can do your own pants." She pulled off the shirt and threw him a blanket, then rubbed his back and arms with a dry towel. Elvis pranced around the deck looking for the seal, oblivious to the cold. "Come here, Elvis. I'll do you next."

Pete grabbed Nikki's shoulders, took one look to make sure Tony wasn't watching, and kissed her. Not long and not deep but a nice kiss. His lips were soft, cold, and Nikki melted into him. A tingling down below made her deepen the kiss, but too soon Pete drew away. "That warmed me up." He kissed the tip of her nose.

"Your arms are working fine now."

"Why, yes, they are. And it's more fun kissing you as an unmarried man—" He drew back. "—and even though you probably want to now, I'll do my own pants." Pete disappeared below to change clothes while Nikki stood mesmerized on deck.

The rest of the morning passed like any other day, except the mood was slightly different. Nikki and Pete danced around each other flirting and touching each other. Connie tried to stay out of their way which was no easy task on a small sailboat. But something had changed between Nikki and Pete, and Connie knew.

That afternoon, they pulled up to small uninhabited island, no bigger than a football field. Pete set the anchor and then asked everyone if they'd like to go ashore. "Elvis can have a real pee on land," he laughed, "and Tony can run around, find sticks."

The feeling was festive as they bunched in the dinghy and motored into the only access point. As they came in to the small beach, Nikki pointed out a State Park sign. "Guests Welcome. Pack out your trash."

Walking around on land felt tippy, and Tony joked at everyone's drunk walking. Elvis took off into the trees, his tail whirling behind him like a helicopter blade. Nikki knew she didn't need to call him back. There were definite advantages to living on an island with total privacy. Maybe one day she'd buy one.

"What are you thinking with that dreamy look on your face, Nikki?" Pete stood on the beach with his hands on his hips.

It had been four hours and fifteen minutes since he'd kissed her. "I'm thinking I might buy an island." She laughed at the ridiculousness of having so much money that she could buy herself an island. "I have too much money, I guess."

Pete laughed too. "I'm sure you work very hard for your money." They'd talked the night before about Goldy's charitable foundation, and Pete had said he was impressed that a rock star would "do more than entertain the world."

"I wonder if the parks department would sell me this one."

"Oh, you'll need a bigger one for Elvis alone. And you'll have to stock it with chipmunks and bring in seals."

They laughed like they didn't have a care in the world.

****

Sitting around, eating fast food, checking the internet for news of Goldy was excruciatingly frustrating. The opportunities presented couldn't be thought of as lost though. Maybe it was time to send another letter and see if it flushed out the prey. The letters had done their job, filling Goldy with fear. It was amusing to think of the effect they had on the rock star who could have anything she wanted in the world. Anything but safety from a crazy fan. Anything but peace of mind. She'd learn her lesson.

The press had rushed her house and she'd disappeared before anyone knew what happened. But, she couldn't stay away from Quinn for long and that's when it would all go down. When Goldy came out of hiding, everything would fall into place As long as Quinn was living out in the open like this, all that was needed was time. The view outside the window promised another gray day in Seattle. A light drizzle swept against the hotel window as the man on TV touted the virtues of a juicer. After this, it would be good to leave the coast and return to normal. Or take the reward and run.

Seattle was the setting, Goldy was the prey, revenge was the motive. How perfectly sweet.

Chapter 20

That night, when Connie and Tony went to bed, Nikki snuggled under a down-filled blanket on the outside cushions. She pretended to be staring at the stars but was hoping Pete would join her. When he came out of the cabin and sat down inches away, her heart raced like a schoolgirl. Nikki loved how they'd been flirting all day, but she wasn't sure if he was just passing time.

"Tell me what you're going to do with the rest of your life, Nikki." He'd run out of Corona and was now drinking tea.

"I wish I could. With a baby on the way, it's all up for grabs."

"Music?"

"Only if it doesn't interfere with being a mother. No performing." Nikki hadn't said that out loud before. "Maybe film scores or song writing to keep my creative juices flowing but nothing with an audience. Talk led her to telling Pete about Shakespeare, the letters, other stalkers, and back to the sad story of Yellow. "She was a copycat fan. The papers said she was a pale version of her idol Goldy. The first night I met her, she wanted an autograph in cuts on her arm. She told me to cut her deep, so she could always remember this moment. She looked thrilled, crazy."

"What did you say?"

"I said, 'I can't do that, sweetie. Put away the knife. Cutting is not okay. Look, you have beautiful arms, don't hurt yourself. Let me sign your arm with a Sharpie.' But she insisted. 'No! Cut me,' she screamed at me.

When she pushed a pen knife in my hand, security escorted her off the property. I asked them to suggest she get help. It was after that she wore a gold dress, black boots, and arm cuffs, and insisted she was my daughter. I told the press that I didn't know her. They took a photo of me rolling my eyes, attached it to the headline 'Cuckoo Fan Pesters Goldy.' Another magazine published a doctored side-by-side photo of us, with captions that must've been hurtful and insulting to her.

Then a pipe bomb was found under the tour bus, she even threatened to kill Quinn, and finally, Yellow killed herself."

"I remember reading about it." Pete hung his head, listening.

"She was only seventeen, a runaway. I wrote the family a letter to express how sorry I was, but what can you say at a time like that?" She and Pete had talked so much about Goldy in the last few days, Nikki wanted to change the subject. "What about you? What are you doing after this?"

"Before I take off to Mexico, I need to learn to sail, obviously, but I also need to get back in the water." He stopped, as though wondering whether to go on. "I almost drowned last year. I haven't been able to swim, voluntarily." He chuckled. "Even after two water rescues in the last few weeks, I still hyperventilate when I think of swimming."

"How did you jump in after me?" As well as rescuing her, he was such a competent-looking man, fit and sure of his own skin.

"Instinct. I didn't think first. Today too, with Elvis."

Nikki nodded. "I can get you swimming." She was sure she could with the right tactics.

"Right after you brew me Chinese tea? Sounds like you need someone to take care of."

"You might be right." She laughed. "So many people have taken care of me over the years maybe I'm craving that now." She looked boldly at Pete. "Tell me about your marriage to Marnie."

Pete shifted in his seat. "We were married for two years when Marnie got pregnant. We were happy." He smiled, remembering. Something in the way he looked told Nikki to sit very still, not break the moment. "We saw a counselor after, but she couldn't be around me without thinking about Brandon's death. When she told me that for her to get on with her life she needed to leave, I knew it was over."

Nikki encircled him in her arms, saying nothing. She laid her head on his shoulder and tried to ignore the lump in her own throat, thinking of the couple whose hopes had died with the baby.

Pete was still. "Losing her immediately after losing the baby was the hardest part. I felt like I might get over the death of our son eventually. At least put it in the back of my heart, but to lose Marnie…It made me feel like it was my fault somehow."

"Why?"

"I don't know. It's crazy to think that way. When she first told me she was pregnant, I was upset because

I was just getting ready to go on a placement and we'd agreed to wait to have a baby. I got over it really quickly though, and then I was excited about becoming a dad. I think when she had to blame someone..."

"I'm sure that's all it was. It's a coping mechanism to find blame." She turned her head and kissed his shoulder.

Pete put his arm around her and pulled her in, kissing the top of her head. "It was so long ago, but I've never talked to anyone about it." Pete stroked Nikki's hair with his hand. "You're a good listener for someone used to the spotlight."

Nikki pulled away and smiled at him. "That's actually a beautiful compliment."

He drew her into his arms. "Ah, Nikki."

Not sure what he meant, she nestled into his chest. Staying this way, all night seemed entirely possible. She could hear him breathing. "Pete?" She nuzzled her face into his neck, rubbing her lips against his skin. No answer. "Pete?"

"Hmm?" He sounded like his eyes were closed.

"What am I going to do?" She paused. "I have a giant crush on you." Could he tell she was smiling?

Pete pulled her away, examining her face with squinted eyes. "For starters, you can applaud your good taste."

Her smile widened, her eyes fixed on his lips. Pete lowered his head and kissed her softly. "It's mutual. I like you too." He kissed her again, longer. Deeper. He whispered against her lips. "You taste good."

Nikki sighed. She loved the smell of this man, salty and rough. And the feel of his lips on hers, taking what he'd wanted for months. When things escalated quickly, she wasn't surprised. It had been building all day, all week.

Their mouths hungrily devoured each other, their hands exploring. She was surprised by Pete's intensity. He felt so different from Burn. So solid and reassuring. His hands slid under her coat and he ran one up under her sweater, in search of skin. Higher.

Nikki chuckled. "I have so many layers on….."

"Yes, you do…but I'll find what I'm looking for, don't worry," he whispered into her hair. "Ah…there you are." His warm hand found a breast. "Hmm." Pete encircled her nipple with his thumb.

"Yes…." They sank back into the couch and as Pete shifted on top of her, he fondled her breasts with his hand. Nikki could feel his hardness against her leg. Was this the first time he'd thought about her in this exact way? She sighed against his face, "I do like you," kissing him everywhere she could reach.

He pulled the blanket over them and undid her coat, then pulled up her sweater. His tongue played with her breasts while she dug her fingers into his hair and moaned. "We have to be quiet."

"Hmmm. No rock star screaming." When he slid back up, she reached between them to check his readiness. He was rock hard. "We have to slow down," he said.

"Why? I want you right now. Inside me." She looked deep into his face and he froze.

"But you're pregnant."

"I can still do this." Nikki tried to keep the momentum. She kissed his neck, his chin, his cheek, tasting his skin. She wrapped her legs around his and pushed her pelvis into his hardness.

He groaned and shifted to the side, to take the weight off her. "Wait. Hold on."

She licked his throat.

"I don't think I can do this."

"Yes, you can." She moved on top, her pelvis pressed into his groin. "Pregnant women have sex all the time."

He wasn't participating anymore. Just her. "I don't want to do anything to hurt your baby."

"Pete, the baby is the size of a blueberry and deep inside me." She reached down to rub her hand against the bulge in his pants. He wasn't rock hard anymore.

He shifted her over to the side.

"Elvis will turn away." She grabbed his sleeve to pull him to her.

"I'm trying to use a little restraint." He moved to sit up and ran his hands through his hair.

Nikki swung her legs over the side of the couch to wrap them around him, pull him back to her. "You don't have to be careful of the baby." Then it dawned on her. "Oh! You don't want to. Another man's baby and all that." She froze. "Ah. I'm not sexy."

He laughed without smiling, like he'd been holding his breath. "No, you are extremely sexy. You are the most gorgeous creature I've ever met." His looked penetrated her heart and then he turned away. "You are…" He laughed. "The most fascinating person I know, the most beautiful woman, and I want like hell to…to…do this. And being pregnant doesn't make you less desirable. Probably more." He motioned to her. "But…" He shook his head. "Nikki, I can't do this, not just because I am afraid of hurting the baby but, now that I think about it, I'm actually at work right now and

I need to stay focused."

"And you think people don't do this in the workplace?" She straddled his lap.

He laughed. "You're funny. And I'm sure they do, but I don't. Not with this job." Pete turned and hugged her to him almost crushing her in an effort to make her stop tempting him. "I want to," he whispered into her hair. "God knows I want to, but with Tony and Connie just downstairs and we have certain codes we follow and I can't do this ethically, as a U.S. Marshal. If this boat was suddenly surrounded by the men looking for Connie and I was busy with you…"

He hugged her tighter, and Nikki switched gears, knowing that it was over. For now. When he released her, she chastely kissed his forehead and climbed off his lap, falling back to the couch to arrange her sweater and zip her coat.

Pete looked at the black sky and took a deep breath. "This is my last job, and I don't want to do anything to jeopardize the mission's success, including falling for a woman I've been lusting after for months."

Nikki smiled from the couch beside him. "You have been lusting after me?"

Silence.

"That's funny, considering I was doing the same thing for you and beating myself up about you being married. I guess I should be satisfied being called a gorgeous creature and a fascinating person."

Pete ran a finger along her jawline. There was a feeling of finality to the evening. She was moments from going to bed.

"I'm impressed," she said. "You have enviable self control," she said.

He smirked and shook his finger at her. "Don't look at me like that, you brazen temptress."

In several choice moves, she could have him hard again, on top of her, sliding around under the blanket, but it wasn't necessary to make him break a code of ethics. Or to traumatize him about hurting her baby just to satisfy her need to be desirable. "Exactly when will this assignment be over?" She pretended to look at her watch.

He laughed. "I'll text you the minute I'm done."

Although she laughed, something in her worried that he wouldn't.

****

"What I'd like, right now, is a cup of coffee with a shot of Bailey's in it," she whispered to Pete over the chess board. They'd been struggling to keep their conversation low since Tony was reading his school book and easily distracted.

"Or a snifter of warm cognac." Pete captured Nikki's queen.

"Oh, damn. I was distracted by all this talk of alcohol and didn't see that."

"Don't get so distracted next time." His smile didn't say chess.

It was unfair that she had to look at him all day, knowing what she was missing. Not only was he flirting with her, but he was frustrating a pregnant woman. Wanting to frustrate *him*, she slid her foot under the coffee table and moved it up Pete's calf to his knee making little circles with her toes. "Don't *you* get distracted."

A smile teased the corners of his delicious mouth. Hopefully he was remembering their close call the night before. Lifting his free foot, he stomped on Nikki's. "No fair." He bent over the chess board to whisper to her. "Chess isn't a contact sport."

It was getting more difficult to resist grabbing him. Now that she knew what he felt like under her hands, and how his whiskers tickled her face, how his tongue searched her mouth, it was torture to hold back. She wanted more. The only relief from all this would be getting the call to court or him giving in to the temptation.

Connie screamed on deck and Pete flew out of the cabin before Nikki even looked up. She motioned for Tony to stay in his bed. Nikki peeked her head up over the lip of the door to see what was going on.

Connie said something and Pete laughed. First tentatively, then it turned into a belly chuckle. Nikki let Elvis outside and went on deck herself. At the bow, where Connie had been collecting a few pieces of laundry from the line, she saw Pete and Connie staring out at the water. Nikki couldn't see the joke but moved toward them. "Is everything okay?"

Connie turned. "A seagull swooped down and..." She could barely spit out the rest of the story. "And grabbed..."

Pete tried. "...grabbed her bra and flew away."

Nikki looked off to the bay where a seagull was sitting on a floating island of kelp and something distinctly white. "Your bra?"

Connie nodded, still laughing. "The only one I brought, unfortunately." She'd folded her arms across her ample bosom.

Pete made a surrender signal and tried to escape the girlie conversation. Passing by Nikki he whispered,

"Lend her yours, you could go without. I don't mind."

Connie stopped laughing and waited for Pete to go down below. "It's none of my business, Nikki, but I'm intrigued that Pete wants you to go without." She smiled secretly, looking out to where the seagull still sat on the bra.

Nikki couldn't think of what to say to Connie about all this. We're just flirting to fight the boredom? She didn't know what was going on either.

****

On day nine, they motored to another bay under cloudy skies, and had just set the anchor when Pete's phone rang. Minimal words were exchanged and when finished, he pulled up the anchor.

"We need to get to Seattle right away." Pete gave Tony the wheel and after pointing him in the right direction, he approached Connie. "This is it. They want your testimony this afternoon." Pete looked apologetic. "You ready?"

"I am." Connie's expression was stoic. She and Nikki had talked the day before about how she hoped after years of ignoring her husband's business activities, she could finally do some good by putting someone behind bars.

Pete ran around battening down the hatches, stopping only briefly to look at Connie with a mixture of regret and sympathy. "If you ladies pack up, Tony'll take us in the right direction."

Connie nodded at Pete. "Let's get back to the truck."

"We're not going to the truck," Pete said. "We're putting in at a dock closer to Seattle. It'll save us two hours. They need you this afternoon."

The transformation from Pete the handsome shipmate, to Pete Daniels, U.S. Marshal, was frightening. Even his face looked different, more focused. Stern. Their vacation was officially over.

There was a stillness on board, a feeling of foreboding. Strings of low clouds enveloped them like Halloween decorations hung in the sky.

"Because we're now in a rush, you're going to have to come with us, Nikki. Just until Connie is safe, and then I'll arrange to have you taken to Quinn's, or wherever you want to go, today." If this was happening too fast for Nikki, she could imagine what Connie and Tony were feeling.

When the Seattle skyline got closer, all three passengers moved below deck, as instructed, while Pete aimed for the arranged meeting place. Elvis seemed to be the only one who thought the trip was just a continuation of the fun, as he bounced around on deck in his life jacket, his little ears flapping in the breeze.

Nikki helped Connie into her brown wig then stuffed some padding into Connie's coat and pants for her disguise. "All my life I've been on a diet and now here I am trying to look fat." Neither woman laughed. Nikki couldn't. "Tony. Put on your hat now," Connie said.

The boy pulled it low over his forehead.

"Remember, my sweet boy. Stay back from me when we get out of here." Connie tried to smile at him. "You just be responsible for Hammie." She glanced at the cage in her son's arms.

Nikki felt sick. She knew that feeling of staying away from the innocents if someone was targeting her. The electrocution. Tony wasn't the target in this case.

She hoped to hell that no one was a target. She'd grown terribly fond of Connie over the last week and wasn't happy that this new friend would be taken from her now. They'd shared laughs and confidences as two women, not rock star to mobster's wife. That morning after breakfast Connie had admitted to Nikki that it wasn't until her husband opposed his business partners to remain true to his morals that they put out a hit for him and took him down.

"You don't need to explain," Nikki had said.

"I just want you to know that my Anthony wasn't a hoodlum." The look in Connie's eyes had broken Nikki's heart. "He was a good man."

"I'm sure he was, if he chose you and raised such a fine boy as Tony."

Connie leaned in to her. "I want you to know my real name."

Nikki nodded, as though this would secure them forever.

"It's Cathy Vanelli but soon it will be changed to Cate Nelson." She looked desperate for Nikki to remember that. "Tony will become Anthony Nelson." Connie nodded like this was information that would be used later for something important.

Tears welled in Connie's eyes, and Nikki embraced her. "Cate and Anthony Nelson," Nikki whispered. "I'll find you someday soon."

****

As the sailboat pulled into slip forty-three, Connie and Tony put on the bulletproof vests Pete had brought on board. "Stay below." Pete recognized the man driving the unmarked white van and spoke to him. He summoned Connie and nodded to Tony and Nikki.

"You two are next, but wait for me." Pete's face reflected his mood. All business. He put a blanket over Connie's head and they walked quickly to the van.

After locking the cabin, Pete checked the boat one last time. He'd be back within the week to move it. They hurried to the van with Tony wedged between her and Pete.

The driver nodded and, checking the rearview mirror, he did a double take when he saw Nikki. She looked down at the van floor. *Yup, I'm Goldy.*

They pulled away from the marina and made an indirect course for Seattle, along enough twisting back streets to make Tony queasy. The silence continued, the Bayer family's sailboat vacation already a memory. This was not the happy group from breakfast. Each person was now stuck in their thoughts about the worst that could happen that day.

Pete needed to keep Connie safe, Connie needed to keep Tony safe, and Tony needed to keep his mom safe. Nikki was just along for the ride. Excess baggage, she was the fifth wheel to these people who were now on overdrive.

The best thing was get out of their way as soon as she could. Once inside the courthouse, she'd get Quinn to pick her up. Subtract one from the mix. None of them had been ready for this today. She and Pete hadn't had a chance to talk about what would happen after, like when to have tea, go swimming, or continue what they'd started. At least she had Connie's name. Cathy Vanelli had the forethought to realize that when the call came, events would go down quickly and they'd be gone. It seemed trivial and selfish to Nikki, that she was worrying how she'd detach from the group at the courthouse when Connie's safety was in question.

When they pulled onto a downtown street in Seattle, Pete turned around in his seat. "When we get to the courthouse, I'll take Connie inside. Rivers, you bring Tony and Nikki."

"Sure." Rivers smelled like cinnamon gum.

Seeing the look on Tony's face, Pete softened.

"Just a precaution, sport. You know the drill. We're playing spy games to keep your mom safe. In a few minutes, we're going down a laneway and into the underground parking garage and through a tunnel under the courthouse. It's the safest way." He reached back and squeezed Tony's shoulder, but the boy ignored him, instead staring at his mother.

Elvis squirmed out of Nikki's lap and tried to get to Pete.

"Elvis." Connie grabbed his collar in time and handed him back to Nikki.

"Don't come near the front like that, Cathy," Pete warned.

He'd used her real name. This all seemed too real now. How could she abandon them in the next few minutes? She couldn't. She'd wait out the testimony with Tony. It would be cruel of her to leave the boy with a bunch of men he didn't know. If Pete accompanied Connie, Tony needed someone to hold his hand.

The van slowed and Rivers said, "Shit," under his breath. Through the tinted front window, Nikki saw news vans and cameramen infesting the sidewalk ahead.

"They must have gotten a tip she was coming in," Pete said to Rivers. "Let's see if we can enter over there." He pointed beyond the group.

"If we try to barrel through, they'll know we've got her in here," Rivers said.

The press lay in wait for Cathy Vanelli to arrive at the King County Courthouse to testify against her husband's murderer. Nikki saw the expectant faces and knew what they were thinking. They'd be desperate for a picture, unintentionally blocking access to the only safe entrance for Connie. Nikki grabbed Connie's hand.

"They're just reporters, blocking the way." Pete sounded calm but, knowing him the way she did now, she was sure he was worried. "Circle the block, Rivers. We'll get the cops to move them."

"What will they do, Mom?" Tony was on the verge of tears.

"S'okay, sweetie, don't worry." Connie glanced at Pete.

He rubbed the stubble on his chin and exhaled loudly. "They'll know it's us," he whispered, "if we move them."

Rivers turned the corner and drove the van around the block.

"Mom?" Tony was crying now.

"It's okay, sweetie, they'll find the safe way in." Connie didn't sound as confident as her words.

"Easy-Squeezie Tony," Pete said. "We just need some crowd control."

Coming around the corner, the laneway was a hundred feet away and the press was still swarming the sidewalk.

This wasn't fair.

Nikki had an idea.

Squeezing Connie's hand one last time, she turned

to face her friend. "I'll see you in there," she whispered.

Nikki flung open the side door and jumped from the van.

"No! Nikki!" Pete opened his door in a split second, grabbed the edge of Nikki's coat and as Rivers slammed on the brakes, Nikki escaped coatless.

"This'll work," she yelled back, running along the sidewalk in her sweat suit, no makeup and her hair in a dirty ponytail.

"Anyone been looking for me?" Goldy yelled, posing on the sidewalk, like she was in full Goldy costume.

"It's Cathy!" someone yelled.

She backed up to lure them away from the turnoff to the underside of the building, and as they rushed forward, she braced herself in case they knocked her over. *Go go go.* She caught a glimpse of the van that was slowly inching to the turnoff. *Get out of here.*

Nikki extended her arms to signal the press to keep their distance. "Looking for Goldy?" she asked and as she did so, something struck her chest like a rock hit her hard. She staggered back with the blow. The man directly in front of her looked terrified, and, glancing down, she saw a gun in his hand.

She touched her chest. With blood on her fingertips, her legs gave way and she sank to the sidewalk.

Chapter 21

Hell! Pete hoped Nikki knew what she was doing by jumping out of the van. The press was already flocking to her before he'd even shut the door and thrown the coat in the back. He had to leave her. His priority was Cathy Vanelli.

"God dammit, Nikki!" He hit the dashboard as they drove away.

This was her world and she was a master with the press. He told himself that, anyways. At least the distraction allowed them the break needed. It was a generous move on Nikki's part, seeing she'd been trying to avoid the press all these months. And she'd sacrificed all that to save their hides.

The alley under the courthouse was dark, and Rivers switched on the van's lights. Pete radioed for the police to find Goldy out in front. "Hey, Hitchens, can you bring her into the building?" Connie was scheduled to testify within the hour, and they had to hurry.

Once upstairs, they walked into the meeting room where the lawyer waited for Connie, then Pete joined Tony outside in the hall. "It'll be good to get a real shower tonight, huh?"

Tony nodded.

"The danger is over now." Pete ruffled Tony's shaggy black hair.

Tony didn't look convinced. Nikki would get a

smile out of him soon. Someday Tony would be able to put this nightmare behind him and have a normal childhood. He was only a kid, for Christ's sake.

Footsteps indicated someone was running down the hall, coming around the corner and Pete stood in front of Tony, instinctively. It was Hitchens, the policeman he'd asked to get Nikki outside the courthouse.

"Goldy's been shot," he whispered solemnly.

"What?" Pete's first instinct was to run.

"A shooter took her down outside. The ambulance is coming." He glanced at Tony.

"Status?" *Oh, God, please.*

"They got the shooter but...I don't know about her."

Hitchens's partner ran around the corner. "Go ahead." His nod indicated the direction they'd just come. "We'll watch the boy."

Pete hesitated. Connie was his duty. Tony too.

"I don't think she's dead yet," the partner said.

Pete had to go. Connie was in good hands.

"Go, Pete!" Tony cried.

Pete grabbed him by the shoulders. "I'll be right back."

"Just go!" Tony yelled.

The artwork on the wall rushed by him as he ran full-out, toward the front door. Once he hit the cool air, Pete took the courthouse front steps three at a time, barely touching the concrete on his way to the sidewalk where he'd last seen Nikki.

How could she be dead? He'd just seen her jump from the van. In front of him was the clumped crowd, police cars, people rushing in from every direction. Why hadn't they secured the scene?

Ambulance sirens got louder. Traffic was at a standstill. He ran closer. A crowd of incredulous bystanders silently stared at the police who surrounded something lying on the pavement.

An ambulance screamed to a halt thirty feet away, lights flashing. Squad cars moved in from every direction and a fire engine rounded the corner.

"Coming through." Pete pushed anyone out of his way, flashing his U.S. Marshal ID badge. *Don't let her be dead.*

"Give her room." Police were putting up yellow tape.

As Pete flew through to the front of the crowd, he yelled "U.S. Marshal, move aside," and luckily it worked.

Then he saw her. Her body was now on a moving gurney ahead, rushing for the nearest ambulance—her blonde hair visible, her head not under the sheet. A paramedic talked into a radio, another opened the ambulance door, and two more pushed the gurney at high speed.

She wasn't dead.

Her blonde hair fell off the bed and when the gurney turned, it looked like her eyes were open. "Nikki!" Could she hear him over the noise?

Pete tried to push forward, but was stopped by two police who didn't care that he was a U.S. Marshal. "I know her," he pleaded.

"Sorry, buddy. We got our orders."

He moved aside, watching her disappear. "U.S. Marshal!" He flashed his ID card to another police officer in front of him. "Hitchens sent me out here. I'm a friend of hers. Let me through." Only able to get forty feet from the back of the ambulance, a policeman with outstretched arms stopped him.

"I'm a friend."

"Then let the pros do their job."

Pete moved on. "How is she?" he asked a paramedic who'd just come from her side. The man shook his head.

Pete grabbed his shirt collar frantically. "What? Not good or you don't know?"

He pulled Pete's invasive hands off him. "Hey, buddy, I don't know, and it doesn't look good."

Pete turned to the ambulance which, by now, was surrounded by police. "She's not dead, right?" he asked anyone who'd look at him. "She's still alive?" He held his breath, his heart a bleeding lump in his chest.

"Still alive." A policeman shook his head. "But I don't know for how long."

They closed the doors and, on impulse, he yelled, "Nikki, hang in there!" His hands cupped his mouth. Standing on his toes, he tried to get a better view. "It's Pete, Nikki. I love you! Be strong!"

Slam. Slam.

The ambulance pulled away into the mess of people blocking the way to the hospital.

"Get out of the way. Let the ambulance through." Pete yelled, flapping his arms. Timing was essential in a gunshot wound. They'd get an IV started in the ambulance and try to stabilize her for the arrival at the ER. Pete stood rooted to the sidewalk, only feet from where Nikki lay fighting for her life. He remembered something. The baby!

They didn't know she was pregnant.

The ambulance was in the street now, the siren

engaged, lights flashing in the gloom of the dismal Seattle November afternoon. A second ambulance hadn't left yet. He cupped his hands around his mouth. "Hey, paramedic!"

A police officer tried to push him back. "Move on, now, show's over. Everybody keep moving. She's gone." People stood dumbfounded, unable to comprehend that Goldy, the famous rock star, had been shot on the sidewalk in front of them. "Break it up. Move on."

Pete needed to get closer to that ambulance. "U.S. Marshal." He flashed his badge and lunged toward the person opening the driver's side door of the ambulance.

"Hey," Pete yelled. "Paramedic!" He ducked under the yellow tape.

"Sorry, pal." Pete's ID card meant nothing to this law officer. The driver scanned the crowd.

"Hey!" Pete tried again. "Paramedic!" He waved to the man in the uniform.

Pete caught his eye. "She's pregnant!" he yelled.

The guy squinted and turned toward Pete. "What?"

"Goldy is four months pregnant." He tried to look credible by holding up his ID badge. "Trust me, she's pregnant. Let them know." He pointed in the direction of the ambulance.

The attendant walked closer, as close as he could get with the moving sea of people. "You sure?"

This time Pete didn't have to shout. "Yeah," he nodded. "The woman they just took in the ambulance, Goldy, is four months pregnant."

"Okay. Thanks." He ran back to the vehicle and Pete saw him grab the CB microphone.

"What hospital will she go to?" Pete asked the

policeman who was trying to disperse the crowd.

"Can't say."

Pete held up his ID card. "I'm a U.S. Marshal. I was protecting her." The words escaped before he thought.

"Well." The policeman looked him dead in the eyes. "You did a lousy job, buddy. She just got shot." The police moved on to yell at the press. "Keep moving. Goldy's gone."

Pete stood on the sidewalk, numb. He'd done a lousy job. Yes, he had. Although his job was to protect Connie, hadn't he taken on Nikki's welfare too when they escaped from Louisa Lake together? He was morally obligated to protect her and look what had happened.

She'd jumped out of the van and gotten shot. How did he know someone would shoot the beloved Goldy? Was it meant for Connie? He had to find out.

As Pete looked up to the buildings that surrounded the courthouse, he noticed people standing in all the windows of the skyscrapers. They'd been watching it all unfold. What they didn't know was that it was his fault.

Sure, Connie was safe, but Nikki had gotten shot and might be dying right now. She'd jumped from the van knowing she didn't look like a rock star, in a selfless act to help Connie.

The thought made Pete bite down hard on the inside of his lip, instead of swearing out loud. He had to find out what hospital they took her to and get a progress report. And Elvis. Did he go in the ambulance? He'd jumped out of the van with Nikki.

"Where'd they take Goldy?" He flashed his badge

to a police officer. The man shook his head.

"Where'd they take her?" He held up his badge to another policewoman standing by her squad car with a radio in hand.

The officer shrugged.

For the first time, Pete thought of the scum who shot her.

"The shooter?" he asked a policewoman.

"Got him." The police was distracted. "Probably thought it was Cathy Vanelli."

Pete felt like spitting. The shooter had seen a woman jump from the van with the blond ponytail and assumed it was Connie. After all, Nikki didn't exactly look classic Goldy in her sweat suit and no makeup.

Pete ran into the courthouse, through the scanner and down the halls to the secured area where Cathy Vanelli was waiting to take the stand. He had a job to finish, but his heart felt like a truck ran over it.

Tony had sunk to the floor in a ball, with his hands over his head. Hitchens looked at Pete sympathetically. "I called a counselor."

Pete nodded and slid down the wall, to sit beside Tony. "Looks like Nikki will be fine, Tony." He didn't see any reason to make the kid feel worse.

"She's okay?" Tony looked up with tear marks staining his cheeks.

Pete nodded. "She will be. They had to take her to the hospital, but it didn't look bad at all." He thought about telling a little white lie and dove in. "She said to tell you that she only hurt as bad as your last defeat in Stratego."

Tony let a little smile slip from the corners of his mouth.

Pete stood and, closing in on Hitchens, whispered, "Can you get a status for me?" Pete nodded in Tony's direction to let the officer know it wasn't to be discussed around the kid.

"I'll see what I can find out." He took off down the hall, a phone to his ear.

Pete motioned to the window in the small room, where Connie was seated at a table, dabbing at her eyes. "Did she get called yet?" he asked the partner.

"Not yet." He looked at Pete. "Why was Goldy with you guys?" Pete saw a strange look in the man's eyes. A mix between envy and curiosity.

"Long story, but she was our neighbor at the last location." Pete shrugged like it was no big deal and bent to Tony, who was staring off into space. "Hey, sport, do you want anything to eat or drink? Chips? You love chips."

Tony shook his head.

"Want a chair?" Pete touched the boy's shoulder.

Tony shook his head.

"Your Nintendo?" The bags from the truck, along with Hammie's cage had been piled on a table down the hall.

Tony just shook his head, staring at the wall across from him. Pete squeezed his shoulder. "This'll all be over soon."

"Will Goldy stay the night in the hospital?" Tony used her stage name.

"Pretty sure they'll keep her overnight, even just to have her sing." Pete smiled at Tony and pointed to the policeman who was guarding that section of the hall. "He'll let us know how she is." Even if she died, Tony need never know, seeing he was disappearing into obscurity later tonight.

Tony and the child psychologist ducked into Connie's vacated room for a chat.

Pete waited to hear something from the hospital, from Hitchens, from anyone. A raging storm whirled inside his head as he struggled to keep his emotions under control. Nikki was shot in the chest, and they were working on her at Seattle Medical Center. He didn't know much about this sort of thing but assumed that meant she'd lost the baby. A profound sadness swept over Pete. If she lived, she'd be devastated.

Pete phoned all his contacts to get any bit of information, but nothing was known about the famous rock star and the bullet she'd taken, already hours ago. The talk around the courthouse was all about the basics. Goldy was shot. What was Goldy doing at the courthouse? It felt intrusive to hear others claim a piece of her.

"I have all her CD's," someone said.

"I saw her in concert when she was here in the summer, man. She was such a hottie."

"I heard she looked pretty rough lying there on the sidewalk."

"I loved her music."

They talked like she was already dead and Pete had to bite his lips closed to prevent saying something he'd regret. What they didn't know was that the woman who got shot was Nikki Crossland, not Goldy. And he knew Nikki well. He knew stuff about her that no one else in the world knew. Now look at him. He couldn't even get through to find out if she was dead. It seemed like once he'd left Nikki's circle, others rushed in, taken over, and now he couldn't get in again.

He'd drive over to Seattle Medical and find out how she was, as soon as he could. For now though, he was still on the Vanelli case, and his first obligation was to see this through. His work as a U.S. Marshal was now measured in hours, possibly minutes. Cathy had been visibly nervous, going into the courtroom, even though every precaution had been taken to protect her before and after her testimony. She'd be fine. The courtroom was closed for her moment on the stand.

From what he could put together, the scum who shot Nikki had been standing right in front of the rock star and was nailed by the press before he'd fired another bullet. Some photographer looked sideways, saw the gun and busted his camera over the guy's head. The shooter tried to run, but he was an older guy and there hadn't even been a chase. Probably some chump who owed Cassius a favor. And, when the shooter heard he'd shot Goldy the rock star, not Cathy Vanelli, he broke out in tears and asked the police to shoot him right then and there. Supposedly his life was as good as over, having missed his target.

See how it feels to have your life over.

The shooter agreed to trade information for a lighter sentence, and Pete guessed how it would go down. They'd get incriminating evidence on Cassius or at least someone high up in exchange for the shooter getting seven years, one of it on probation. He'd be killed as soon as he got out.

If Nikki didn't make it, Pete would be begging someone to shoot him. The guilt would eat him alive, along with the knowledge that he hadn't told her how he felt. Hell, he didn't even know how much he felt for her until that morning.

"Heard anything about Goldy?" he asked Hitchens when he saw him at the coffee machine later.

"Just that she took one bullet to the shoulder."

As much as Pete didn't want her to be shot anywhere, the shoulder wasn't nearly as bad as the gut. He should know. Eight years earlier a bullet had pierced his back, narrowly missing his kidneys. It had taken almost a year to get the strength back from his gunshot wound. The effects of that accident slowed him down even now.

****

Pete was outside the closed courtroom when word came down from HQ that he'd be needed another twenty-four hours. Connie's testimony would continue tomorrow. Pete was to take her to a safe house for the night.

Dammit.

Going to the hospital was out. He'd have to get information about Nikki by phone. Feeling helpless, he pulled Officer Hitchens aside on his way out of the courthouse and pleaded his case. "Can you find out how Goldy is doing? How bad it is, and if I can talk to her?"

Hitchens nodded and said he'd see what he could do. By now, everyone suspected Pete's investment in the case.

When Pete got to the safe house, he phoned workers who'd been on shift at the Trauma Center when Goldy had been admitted to the ER. No one was talking. Where were all the nurses and hospital workers who wanted to be on TV? Surely there would be someone who'd seen her get wheeled in, knew something, and wanted air time.

Connie and Tony sat down to pizza at the dining

267

room table of the hotel suite. Pete turned on the TV to see if there was any news about Goldy. News stations often had information before anyone. Even if they were telling people to stand by, it would be better than hearing nothing.

The newspaper's headline that day had said "Goldy Shot Downtown" and stated that she was involved in the Cathy Vanelli case. They also reported that Goldy was four months pregnant as stated by a man who'd called the information to an ambulance attendant several times.

Lowering himself tentatively to sit on the edge of the couch, he scanned the stations in search of a Goldy photo.

Connie drifted over to sit down with him. "I feel terrible for Nikki. I hope Elvis is with her."

He couldn't believe with all Connie had on her mind, she included Nikki and Elvis in her thoughts.

"I'm sure he is." He patted Connie's arm absently, then noticed the police at the table watching him. Watching them. "How you doing after that ordeal in court?"

"I'm fine," she said.

A photograph of Goldy filled the TV screen and Pete turned up the volume.

"And topping the headlines tonight is the shooting of beloved rock star Goldy Burnside, in front of the King County Courthouse in Seattle, where the Tony Vanelli murder trial is taking place." The anchor woman's face was appropriately grave as she recounted the details of the shooting. The split screen showed the photo of Pete on the dock at Louisa Lake next to a Goldy publicity shot.

"Oh crap, haven't we seen that enough?" Pete groaned.

The anchor continued, "Although it isn't clear what she was doing at the courthouse, speculation is that she jumped from a van being driven by the unidentified man who was at the rock star's property only a few weeks ago. At that time, it was reported that he was a friend to the rock icon. Although we have not identified the man, we have confirmation that he is a neighbor at her summer home and, at the time the photograph was taken, he reported that Goldy was not on site. However, the allegedly married neighbor was photographed at the crime scene only minutes after the shooting, trying to get through the crowd to Goldy."

Next, they showed video footage of Pete yelling that Goldy was pregnant. The look of desperation on his face scared Pete more than the speculation he was a married neighbor. This was a side he'd never seen in himself, and he closed his eyes.

"The unidentified man is seen here, telling the paramedics that Goldy is four months pregnant. According to bystanders, he yelled it several times, trying to get the attention of the paramedic, as well as yelling to Goldy that he loved her, calling her Nikki, which is Goldy Burnside's given name."

The next tidbit turned out to be the grand finale, the piece de resistance. Someone had taken a video of Pete yelling, near the back of the ambulance. The camera zoomed in to capture him yelling. The sound was compromised but intelligible, and they'd subtitled the shouter's message.

"Nikki, hang in there! It's Pete, Nikki. I love you! Be strong!"

Chapter 22

Pete wiped his unshaven face and groaned.

Connie reached over and grabbed his hand.

"Yeah, but how is she?" he asked the television. If they hadn't reported her dead, she was probably still alive.

He switched to another channel.

"...otherwise known to the world as Goldy, the infamous rock star, was shot and injured."

Injured was good.

"It was thought the bullet was meant for Cathy Vanelli, high profile witness to the Tony Vanelli murder in Seattle, last July."

They showed a split screen of the two women in question. Anyone could see that Goldy and Cathy didn't look alike. Only the hair was similar, and the announcer said as much, going on about the shooter's identity and his association with Cassius Zetti.

"Goldy was rushed to Seattle Trauma Center where Doctor Drummond Vogan, removed a bullet from her shoulder."

When they said the word "shoulder," Pete jumped up. "Yes!" He punched the air. "Shoulder! Yes!" She hadn't been hit in the chest after all. "Whew! The shoulder is good." He turned to Connie and nodded.

"Yes, the shoulder is very good." Connie turned back to the TV.

The reporter continued. "No information is available about Goldy Burnside's condition, but we are expecting an interview with Dr. Vogan within the hour. We have no current information about the alleged pregnancy or the identity of the man in the video, last seen with Goldy Burnside at Louisa Lake in eastern Washington, where Goldy has a house. This photo was taken only weeks ago on the retired rock star's dock. At that time, Goldy issued a statement saying the man was her married neighbor. Seattle Trauma Center has taken security measures, and Goldy is under protective custody, as is usually the case in a situation like this."

The anchor went on to talk about Goldy's daughter Quinn, who attended the University of Washington, and Goldy's ex-husband Burn Burnside, who they interviewed only minutes before the broadcast. Both photos flashed on the screen. Reporters had caught Burn just outside LAX, running to catch a flight to Seattle. He stopped briefly to say that he was concerned for Goldy, but knew she was tough and would pull through. They asked him what her condition was and Burn said simply, "I'll know when I get there. Pray for her."

The newscast described Goldy's twenty-year career, Burn's career, and then reported that although no one knew what Goldy's connection was to Cathy Vanelli, it was speculated that they were friends. There was no other reason why Goldy would've jumped into the group of reporters.

Cathy rubbed her temples and turned to Pete. "I didn't figure that out until now." She sounded so weary that he put his hand on her shoulder and gave it a little squeeze. He and Cathy had come a long way and it would soon be over.

"The shoulder is fixable, Tony."

Pete tried to call the hospital again, but couldn't get through on his name or credentials. Nikki would be in recovery, doped up, unable to take his call, anyways.

He'd asked his boss and Officer Hitchens to find out something for him, but hadn't heard back from either. For a U.S. Marshal who was a master at surveillance, he felt useless.

Cathy looked at Pete. "Now you know what I've known."

Pete sat down beside her on the leather couch. "What's that?" He dropped his head to his hands.

"That you are in love with Nikki."

"Well…" What could he say? "What I said…it was…more or less said in the heat of the moment…" He snuck a look at Cathy, who was giving him a dirty look.

"Why are men so thick sometimes?" She sighed.

"Okay, I'm in love with Nikki." Pete smirked at her, then looked at Tony. "Who wouldn't love Nikki?" If he hadn't been so concerned about her life, he might have felt proud of his declaration.

"When you see her again, please tell her that I'm sorry she was shot," Cathy said.

"Of course." He leaned forward, sitting on the edge of the couch and listened to the rest of the CNN account of the afternoon's events. Nothing was said about her dog. Pete just hoped and prayed that Elvis was with her.

****

Everything was fucked. But salvageable. The thought of Goldy dying of a bullet wound was unthinkable. She needed to know why she was dying, what she did, and the only way to save two years of careful work was to act soon. In case she died. Two chances had come and gone, the second when her location at Louisa Lake was revealed. This new twist of events had to be thought of as the next opportunity. The culmination of this would happen in Seattle, not Los Angeles. That was clear. Goldy would finally pay for her selfishness. Her audacious entitlement. The wrong would be set right.

The hospital was almost within view from the hotel. How ironic. Hiding in Seattle, waiting for the moment to capture the prey and there she was cornered. Unable to run. Injured. Offered up like a Thanksgiving turkey with Seattle Medical Center as the platter. How lovely and perfect. Come to think of it, this couldn't have worked out better. The cell phone stayed charged, waiting for the call.

****

Quinn slept in a vinyl chair beside her mother. Machines beeped softly in the room as Nikki shifted her head to get a better view of her daughter. It was dark outside, and the room was dimly lit, not illuminated by the fluorescents on the ceiling. It looked like a hospital room and was probably a VIP suite. They were usually spacious and nicely decorated with more amenities for those who could afford to pay well above what insurance provided. And those who needed ultimate privacy.

Nikki tried to lift her head and a searing pain shot through her upper chest and down her arm. Her eyes widened, and she must have made a sound, because Quinn bolted upright in her chair.

"Mom?" In one quick move, Quinn was beside her

laying a hand very carefully on Nikki's thigh. "You're in the hospital."

"Hmmm." Was this a dream? A memory? At what point in her life had she dropped in, just now? What questions needed asking? She didn't try opening her mouth, in case that caused another shot of pain.

"The baby is safe." Quinn had fat tears in her eyes, ready to drop. "You were shot in the upper chest. It didn't affect Princess."

Nikki managed a smile. She'd forgotten she was pregnant. Thank God the baby was fine. She'd been at the lake. She and Quinn had gone swimming. Then Quinn left and what happened next? She'd been with Elvis. There'd been a strange family in the log house. "Elvis?"

"He's fine." Quinn said. "You need to rest Mom. They told me to call the nurse when you woke up." Quinn grabbed the button and pushed.

I was shot? "Shakespeare?"

"What?"

Oh. Quinn didn't know about him.

The nurse flew through the door like she'd been waiting. A guard stood watch outside the door. Was it Dwayne?

The nurse smiled. "Well, well, look who decided to join us." She checked the monitors. "How are you doin', Goldy?"

"Sore."

"That's to be expected. The doctor is on his way."

"How bad is it?"

"You had quite a time of it. You were shot. The bullet hit your left lung and you lost a lot of blood. The best thing you can do right now is rest, and tomorrow we'll start you eating and drinking. You've been in and out for twelve hours."

Nikki watched her daughter's face to confirm the nurse was telling the truth and there would be no hidden surprises. The baby was still there. Quinn was not a good liar, especially with her mother. "And the baby wasn't affected." Nikki reassured herself.

"He's just fine."

"He?"

"I don't know. We can ultrasound you tomorrow to see, if you want." The nurse looked flustered.

Nikki smiled to think that the baby was safe.

"The press?"

"Oh, the goddamned press can wait." Quinn snapped.

"Who shot me?"

"They got him. Some low life. It was meant for Cathy Vanelli." Quinn's lips were white.

"Who's Cathy Vanelli?"

"The woman you knew as Connie Bayer." Quinn stared at her mother's reaction.

"Connie Bayer?" Nikki whispered.

"Don't worry about that right now." Quinn's smile looked forced. "Just rest."

When Nikki woke, hours later, Quinn was still in the chair, talking on the phone.

"Phyllis, I'll talk to them later," she said. "I'll ask Mom when she wakes up what she wants me to say. Merilee's on her way to help with all this. Her plane comes in this morning." Long pause. "The trial is over and they're gone." Quinn looked like she might be beyond her capabilities. Nikki made a sound that did not exactly resemble good morning.

"Mom!" Quinn stood. "Phyllis, I'll call you back."

"Sweetie." Nikki's voice was crackly and dry.

"How are you doing? Do you want a sip of water?" Quinn held the straw to her mother's mouth.

"My head hurts." She sipped.

"Your head hit the pavement."

"Tell Phyllis to say I'm recovering, the baby is fine, and I'll offer more later."

Quinn smiled. "You must be getting better, Mom. Handling the press from your hospital bed."

A nurse entered the room silently, and began her routine of checking the machines.

"Last night, I'm sure a nurse told me that I could see the baby on ultrasound today." She knew she could get preferential treatment in a VIP suite and for once she really wanted to cash in on that privilege.

"You can. I'll get the machine in a few minutes." The nurse pushed some buttons and disappeared from the room.

"Who is Cathy?" Nikki had to ask. So many things were fuzzy.

"Cathy is the woman you knew at the lake— Connie Bayer."

That sparked a memory. Not a perfectly clear one, but something.

"Connie, Pete, and the boy Tony were renting the Dickerson's log house." Quinn waited. "Connie had to testify in a trial." Quinn searched her mother's face. "Does any of this sound familiar, Mom?"

"Kind of. They were weird." She remembered having them for dinner. "Pete was a bad husband."

"Turns out he's not anyone's husband." Quinn spat the last two words. "When they drove to the courthouse, he had you jump out of the van to distract the press while he took the others into the building. The bullet you took was meant for Cathy Vanelli."

Nikki remembered something about a sailboat and coming to Seattle.

The nurse returned and pulled back Nikki's covers to reveal her slightly rounded tummy. Nikki smiled and tried not to jiggle her aching head as the nurse rubbed the jelly on her abdomen.

"Let's take a look." The wand remained in the air as Nurse Beverly checked the dials. When the wand made contact, Nikki watched the screen, waiting.

"There's your baby."

Nikki's heart jumped for joy. With eyes fixed on the screen, she tried to make sense of what she saw. There was a fetus and in the center of it was a little hop. A jiggle. Ignoring the pain in her shoulder, she lifted her head and watched her baby's heartbeat jump. "Does she look healthy?" Nikki held her breath.

"Yes, HE does." The nurse zeroed in on the baby's legs." And this is how we know it's a boy." She aimed her pointer at a little mark on the screen.

"A boy?" Nikki looked at Quinn and smiled. "I'm having a boy?" She was touched beyond belief to be carrying a son and tears came to her eyes. Studying the screen, she watched the baby that was growing inside of her, his heart beating so quickly.

"Aren't you supposed to ask the patient if she wants to know the sex?" Quinn stared at the nurse, eyes squinted, hands on her hips.

"It's okay, Quinn, I do." Nikki grinned at her daughter to think she was getting protective, assertive.

The nurse seemed oblivious to her medical faux

pas, and Nikki was so elated to see her baby's heartbeat, she had no quibble with anyone at that moment.

"Mom, the press knows you're pregnant."

"How?" Nikki asked. "Never mind, I don't care." She stared at the screen, memorizing every aspect of her baby boy. The bullet hole in her chest would heal quickly, she'd get stronger, and then she'd give birth to a blessed little boy.

The nurse took the wand off Nikki's abdomen. "And he's right around eighteen, nineteen weeks." She turned off the machine, wiped Nikki's tummy, and replaced the gown.

Wasn't he sixteen weeks?

"Is that what you thought, Mom?" Quinn searched at her mother's face for confirmation.

"Yes, that's right."

"I'm going to call Phyllis back now." Quinn plunked down in the chair with her phone.

"I'll just rest." Nikki was confused. Sex with the movie star was not that long ago. If the fetus was eighteen weeks old, then the movie star could not be the father. Nikki closed her eyes and thought about Las Vegas, two weeks before the movie star liaison. The band had just finished back-to-back concerts in Vegas. Burn walked her to the limo. She'd asked him to ride with her to the airport so they could have a glass of champagne. Both were feeling a little happy, and a lot strange about hearing the divorce was finalized that day.

"Oh, Goldy Girl, I can't believe you divorced me." Burn thought he was joking as he pulled his new ex-wife in to an embrace.

Tears trickled down Nikki's cheeks onto Burn's leather vest. They ducked into the limo and Burn found a box of tissues to dry her tears.

"I thought you wanted this divorce." He looked confused.

"I do, but it's the end of us...and it's going to take some getting used to." Nikki blew her nose and smiled at Burn. This was the man who'd pushed her to be Goldy, the man who'd stood beside her talent for twenty years. He'd probably sacrificed his dream life of being a single rock guitarist when Nikki had insisted that if they were going to take this band to the limits, she wanted to be married to him. He'd probably seen his fantasy slipping away but knew he could figure out a way to get what he wanted and keep Nikki happy. And now, she was setting him free. Probably herself too.

Burn took her face in his hands. "I'll always love you the best, the most, and the deepest." He brushed his lips with hers.

He thought it to be true, and she kissed him back, lightly at first and then deeper, thinking that she'd never kiss these lips again. He followed her lead. It was so familiar.

Instead of pulling back, she kissed him again. When his tongue found hers, she pressed herself into him. They'd had years of making love. Limo sex was more familiar to them than conventional locations and, as Burn lifted Nikki onto his lap, he tore open her shirt and kissed along her throat and chest. Time limitations always intensified things. A private plane waited for only Goldy only a few miles down the road on the McCarron tarmac. Burn would stay in Vegas for another night, and they had to make this quick.

Two weeks later she'd gotten a light period. She hadn't thought anything of it. Stress was enough to screw up anyone's schedule. Shortly after that, she'd had sex with her movie star-crush, missing her next period and assumed that night was the conception.

The baby was Burn's. They hadn't used a condom, and Burn assured her that he always used one with everyone else. That was his idea of being loyal to her. She was not pregnant by some strange act of misplaced lust in a hotel room on tour. Strangely, she felt less sleazy and now free to lose the movie-star memory. Nikki erased the line that would have tied her forever to Roger Freemantle and smiled.

She knew how to have Burn's child. And it was a boy. The baby inside her was a sweet little boy, who'd grow up to look a little like Burn, maybe have talent playing the guitar, and possibly even have a knack for design, like Burn. She hoped he wouldn't have the propensity to cheat on his wife. Boys were influenced greatly by their fathers. Tears came to her eyes at the thought.

Quinn's voice broke through Nikki's day dream. "Hi, Dad!" Her face lit up as she talked on her phone. "Oh! Thank you, Dad! Thank you!"

What had Burn done to make Quinn so grateful? "Tell him I'm fine," she said.

"Mom says to tell you she's fine." Quinn said it like it wasn't true, and Nikki reached to take the phone.

"Hi, Burn."

"Baby, you had me scared. I was frantic when I got the news. Don't do that to me, you hear?"

Ha. This was about him. "I feel fine."

The door opened and Burn walked into her room with a trail of nurses following.

"Surprise!" Burn clicked his cell phone shut and opened his arms to Quinn.

He looked good. Like a rock star. "You didn't have to come all this way." Nikki meant it. In the last weeks, she'd trimmed her hair at the lake and even darkened it to honey blonde, had ignored her makeup bag and begun this transformation, while her ex-husband remained the same.

Burn's hair was wild, past his shoulders now, and moussed to the nth degree. He wore tight jeans, a shirt that said "Rock the Vote," and his signature leather jacket and boots. Nikki could see that he'd worn eyeliner for the hospital performance, and she almost laughed. He crossed the room to her bed, doing "the walk" for the nurses.

"Hi, baby." He'd always called her that in the tender moments. When she'd met Burn, he'd been twenty-six to her eighteen, and she'd melted into the pet name.

"Hi, Tommy." Nikki used his real name rarely, and only in private.

The three nurses pretended to be fluffing pillows, reading the chart and moving around Nikki's IV.

"How do you feel?" Burn was distracted by the nurses, his eyes darting around the room.

"Like I need more pain meds, but thankful I'm alive." Had he heard she was pregnant?

"Mom's such a trooper, Dad." Quinn snuggled into her father's side and he put his arm around her.

The shape of their eyes was similar, but that was about it.

"That guy who let her jump out of the van should be shot," Quinn said.

Nikki was surprised at her daughter's stern words. What did she mean?

Burn moved to grab Nikki's hand and Quinn intercepted.

"That's her bad side, Dad. Don't touch her."

"Oh, sorry." He glanced at the prettiest nurse who had moved to the far side of the bed to take Nikki's blood pressure. "Baby" —he looked back— "what do you want me to say to the press?"

Nothing had changed. Burn was still asking for Nikki's advice. "Just say I'm doing as well as expected. They got the bullet out, and I'll be another week in the hospital."

He looked uncomfortable and glanced sideways at the young nurse who couldn't find anything to do but fiddle with the sheet. "They're asking about your pregnancy."

Nikki shot him a look to alert him to the need for privacy. "That's all, Nancy." She waited for Nurse Nancy to get out of earshot. "Tell them it's none of their business."

Burn's eyes followed the young nurse across the room. Sensing her ex was moments from flirting, Nikki felt herself turning a corner and closing a door. She made her decision. She'd never tell him, or anyone, the truth. "Tell the press that you don't know about the pregnancy, because you are not the father."

Burn looked so relieved that Nikki almost laughed out loud. "I will." Burn leaned in. "Honey, I'm really happy for you and the guy. I was hoping you'd find someone to make you happy." Along with recently having the paternity case dropped, Burn had obviously been worrying about Nikki's pregnancy.

She smiled. Was it the painkillers that made this situation so funny, or had she really moved on? "Thanks. It's good to be happy." They grinned at each other.

Burn was overjoyed, because he was off the hook now, not the baby daddy, and because he was going to get that young nurse's phone number. After dinner, he and Nurse Nancy would fuck their brains out in his hotel suite, and the trip would be worthwhile. Nikki settled her head against the pillow and closed her eyes. The last thing she heard as she drifted off to sleep was Burn asking the nurse if she liked sushi.

Chapter 23

God dammit! Pete couldn't get in to see Nikki. After Connie finished her testimony, and the agents took the Vanellis away, he knew he had to get over to the hospital with his marshal's badge and try to find Nikki.

He stepped off the elevator and, approaching the double doors in the VIP wing, saw the usual security associated with a celebrity visit. He tried anyhow. Even his badge got him nowhere. They radioed ahead to check with someone and, in the end, Pete was not allowed in.

"Look, man, I was with her when she got shot. I've been with her for months. She will want to see me."

"Sorry, we have to clear visitors with her daughter who's in charge of this, and she said no." The guard didn't look very sorry. "They're not letting anyone in, if that makes you feel better." He motioned for him to leave.

Pete glanced through the window, across the VIP lobby and saw the burly bodyguard he'd tackled at Louisa Lake, standing outside a door with his arms folded across his chest. The fact that Pete had left Dwayne Capleoni sitting in the muddy driveway in the rain didn't bode well. Scratching his two day growth, Pete considered the situation. Should he storm these guys and make a run for Nikki?

Just then Quinn exited the hospital room, followed by Burn Burnside, the world-famous guitar player. Burn looked all Hollywood rock scene and ridiculous with his black leather and wild hair.

Through the square window in the door, Pete watched Quinn and Burn walk to a gathering of chairs at the end of the hall. He felt a pang of jealousy. Nikki wasn't even married to Burn anymore and he'd been allowed in. Pete probably knew more about Nikki and Burn's marriage than anyone, including Burn. She'd told him that she'd never felt truly loved by Burn and was trying to accept her feelings of being used by him to have the life he wanted.

"That's hard to believe that someone wouldn't cherish you," Pete had told her.

"I haven't felt wanted by a man in a long, long time," Nikki said.

Burn ran his hand through jet black hair then Pete realized that he probably looked a little rough around the edges himself. It had been a difficult few days.

"Time to move on, Marshal." The guards could see Pete was surveying the situation.

If he got himself a doctor's uniform with a clipboard, could he get past the guards? He might have to shave first. Quinn was in charge, they said. Although he'd never met her, Quinn knew who he was. Pete had been sitting beside Nikki when she called her daughter to say she'd left Louisa Lake. "I'll tell you all about it when I see you in about a week," she'd said. There'd been a pause and Nikki laughed. "No, honey, nobody is making me say this. I actually have become good friends with Connie, and we're on a boating adventure near Seattle. You can call me anytime. I'll try to keep my phone charged."

On the sailboat, he and Nikki had laughed over who Quinn thought Pete Bayer was, but now it didn't seem so funny. Had Nikki told her daughter they were friends? He pushed open the double doors again and was immediately encountered by one of the guards. "You back?"

At the end of the hall, Quinn hugged her father and, as she turned to go back into the hospital room, Pete called to her. "Quinn?" She turned around. "Quinn, it's Pete Bayer. Can I talk to you?"

The guard seemed to think this was inappropriate behavior and grabbed Pete by the shoulder to usher him forcibly out of the VIP wing.

"Here she comes," Pete pointed at Quinn who walked toward him. "Come on, man. I know her."

"What do you want?" Quinn did not look friendly.

"I want to know how your mother is doing. We're friends." He tried to appeal to her by looking defenseless.

Quinn took a wide stance that resembled a battle position, put her hands on her hips and took a deep breath. "You have no right to know that. Not that or anything else about my mother."

Where was this coming from?

"And furthermore, Mr. Bayer" —her words dripped with hatred— "return my mother's dog." She looked like this might determine his worth.

"What? You don't have Elvis?"

"No."

"Elvis jumped out of the van with her at the courthouse."

Quinn's expression changed to fear. "What?"

"You don't have him, and I don't have him."

For the first time, Quinn looked truly horrified. Her hands covered her mouth. "Oh, my God!"

As Pete reached out for her, the guard knocked him back like he was some two-bit hustler. "I'll find him, Quinn. Don't tell your Mom."

Pete didn't know how he'd do it, but now he had a mission. His little buddy was missing. "When I find him, please let me see your mom. I know she'd want that."

"She doesn't even remember who you are. And what kind of friend would lead her into a situation that puts her life at risk, while he protects his witness to look like the hero."

"I never would have—"

"Mr. Bayer, or whatever your name is..." She looked exasperated. "You are no friend of my mother's. She hasn't mentioned your name, and as long as I am in charge of this show, you will not be granted access to see her just to apologize for almost killing her." Quinn's words cut deep. "She's been shot, mistaken for your witness, and is recovering from the unfortunate bad luck of even knowing you and your....your...people."

He tried to interrupt, but Quinn was right. Nikki wouldn't be lying in that hospital bed if it wasn't for him. "I'm sorry that your mom was shot. Please at least tell her that." In the distance Burn was at the nurse's station entertaining them, waving his hands and laughing along with their nervous giggles.

"Finding Elvis is the least you could do now." Quinn turned and headed down the hall, not even glancing sideways at her father who was leaning on the counter, his face only inches from a nurse's.

He watched the teenager disappear inside the hospital room. What was going on if Nikki didn't even know who he was? Was she doing as well as he'd heard? He had to find that dog.

At the Justice Department headquarters, Pete called the police, the CIA, the FBI, everyone he knew and anyone who was at the courthouse that day, to see if they knew anything about Goldy's dog. With the phone book on his lap, he called all the animal shelters, then went online to see if there was a photo of Elvis under the pet-finder sites.

Nothing.

Next he phoned vet clinics, the SPCA, and all animal rights groups in the Seattle area. No one had seen Elvis or turned him in. From the Louisa Lake surveillance tape, he printed a photo and made a hundred copies to distribute around the downtown area. He hoped the poor little guy was still alive then, on a whim, called the city to see if anyone had found a dog body on the streets downtown. He got nothing.

After posting "lost" signs, he considered putting an ad in the paper. What should he offer as reward? Having exhausted every option he could think of, all that was left was that someone had grabbed the dog, knowing it was Goldy's.

He put an ad in the Seattle Times and on Craig's List, offering two thousand for the safe return of a small four-year-old dog that looked like the photo, answered to the dog's name—which would remain a secret—and recognized him.

Elvis had to be out there somewhere and Pete had to be the one to find him. Did Quinn think she could keep him away forever? He knew Nikki's cell phone number, the address at the lake, had her daughter's information, and with great connections in surveillance and law enforcement he'd get through eventually. But something told him that timing was absolutely essential here.

He dialed Nikki's cell number then realized Quinn would probably answer. He hung up. She'd want to know if he'd found Elvis yet. Maybe if Nikki was listening, she'd hear Quinn say "please don't call her, Mr. Bayer."

The phone went to voicemail and the sound of Nikki's words made Pete's heart jump.

"....I'll get back to you."

"Nikki, this is Pete. Please be okay." He paused, trying to figure out what he wanted to say to the woman who was now so far away from him. "I'm worried about you. If you get this, call me." He left his number. It might be weeks before she checked messages. And she might not even remember him or want to see him after this. After all, he'd left her bleeding on the sidewalk, while he took Cathy Vanelli to the courthouse.

****

The next day Pete got the call he'd been waiting for. At least one of the calls he'd been waiting for.

"I have Goldy's dog, but it's gonna cost a lot more than two thousand," the voice said.

The scum knew it was Goldy's dog. Shit. He sounded young which was good. "Name it."

"I know that dog is worth a million to Goldy."

"Ha. Ha. I doubt that." Pete was already planning how he'd catch him and throw him in the slammer.

"I'll bet he is, and I'll wait another day for you to find that out."

Maybe he wasn't a kid after all. "Hey, wait, pal." Negotiation wasn't Pete's strength, but he had enough training to know how to proceed. "It takes a day to put money together if you want cash, and I'm assuming you do." Pete wished he could trace the call but with cell phones...

"I'll call you in a few days then."

"Wait. You want money, and I'd just as soon get the dog, so let's stay on the line and do it."

"Get the money tonight then."

"I hate to burst your bubble, but no dog is worth a million. Not even to Goldy. I know that for a fact. She just adopted him. Besides, she has other dogs. Plus she's in intensive care, worried more about her health." Pete was hoping this tactic would work. "Tell you what. She might be able to put a hundred thousand together by tomorrow. You'll never get any more than that for the mutt. He's a barker and pees in the house." He waited. A hundred thousand was a nice reasonable amount. Besides, Pete didn't plan to bring any money he couldn't take back to the bank afterwards. Only the top half of the bills would be real anyhow.

"Two hundred."

Pete sighed, like he was upset about the deal. "One hundred twenty."

"One fifty. Cash in a black duffel bag."

"Hold on, kid. Send me a photo of the dog with today's paper. Make sure the date is visible."

"I'll call later with instructions."

The photo came through with Elvis standing in the middle of an unidentifiable room peeing on today's paper. This person knew what he was doing. Fuck!

****

Merilee, the blessed assistant, had arrived from L.A. and had taken over all areas where Quinn felt incapable. The two were constant presences in the hospital room, and, of course, Burn was gone. He'd flown back to LA, feeling out of place almost anywhere now, except Tinseltown. "Everyone is boring and normal here," he'd joked. She'd tried to smile. Nurse Nancy seemed particularly distracted after his departure.

Then Gateman called with bad news. "We heard from Shakespeare."

"Send it." Nikki was getting weary of the game. She opened her email.

Goldy, My Love:

I'm heartsick waiting.

Must I come to you?

I wait patiently. I listen. She speaks yet she says nothing, what of that?

Say something.

Or I shall have to come for you.

"It's his most feeble effort," Nikki said. Judging by Merilee's worried expression, her assistant wasn't as confident. "Maybe he's losing steam."

"Let me read it." Merilee moved in to analyze the letter and agreed. "I think the fascination is dying," she said.

Nikki eased back against the pillows and considered the words that made up the letter, and when Quinn walked into the room, she knew it wasn't fair to hide this stalker anymore.

"Come here, sweetie. I need to show you

something." Nikki downplayed the threat but Quinn's eyes filled with tears.

"Not because of the stalker," she said.

"What then?" Nikki asked.

"I'm thinking about your accident and how if it isn't threats on your life, then it's attempts. When will this end, Mom?"

"Soon, sweetie."

"I was in class when I got the call from the police about you being shot." She laid her head down gently on her mother's uninjured arm and sniffled. "I don't know what I'd do if I ever lost you. Daddy wouldn't be enough. I need you, Mom." Quinn cried quietly into the covers as Nikki stroked her daughter's dark hair.

No, Burn would not nearly be enough and had never been even half. Burn had always fallen painfully short as a father, and Nikki wouldn't do that to a child again.

When the nurse arrived to change her dressing, she watched the gauze unravel. Something about the sight of the white gauze made her remember a seagull sitting on something white, bobbing on the ocean's surface. It was just a brief flash. She'd been on a sailboat. Her psychiatrist said she might get her memories back this way and advised her to let them drift in on their own. And now, here they were, like scenes from a movie she'd seen last month.

She and the Bayers had been on Pete's sailboat, and when they went to Seattle, the bullet she'd taken had been meant for Connie. Dinner with the Bayers at the lake. Pete in her house, wet. Blood in the Bayers' bathroom. Tony's stitches. Hot crossed buns. Yoruba symbol. Connie's wig. The thoughts were overwhelming and soon she became weary. As she watched the outside sky darken, she couldn't help wonder what had happened to the strange Bayer family.

****

"What about this house, Mom?" Quinn asked. "It has a nice pool, overlooks the lake, and has a long driveway." She snuggled in to her mother on the hospital bed, the laptop resting against Nikki's knees.

"It's pretty, but the baby's room would be too far away from mine, honey." Finally Nikki felt well enough to think about her future. "I don't want to be sprinting down a long hall to get him."

"Mom, you know he'll be sleeping in your room until he's ten." Quinn was probably only half joking.

Now that they knew the baby's sex, the pregnancy seemed real to both Nikki and Quinn, giving way to all sorts of ideas for their future. Planning for the baby had become their new hobby, and it was impossible to hold back the excitement, knowing he was six months away from making his appearance. Names were bounced carefully between them like an egg toss at a birthday party. The prospect of raising a son made Nikki giddy, even knowing it would be a challenge without a father. She'd need to discover what little boys like to do and how they do it.

"I'm looking for a simple house for a mother and two children—four bedrooms, a big playroom, a workable kitchen and a big safe yard for a little boy to play with his trucks in the mud." The real estate agent got right on it. "This one looks nice." Nikki read the spread sheet on a rambler on the Olympic peninsula. "Dock for yacht or sailboat" it said. Nikki remembered being on the boat with the Bayers. A sailboat without a name. There had been a large bed in the bow's cabin and a seating area that turned into two beds. One for her, and one for Pete.

"Yes, it looks pretty, but maybe too far away from U Dub," she said. Nikki recalled eating at the table while the rain poured down on the deck outside, playing a board game with Tony, and laughing, doing the dishes with Pete. Had they all become friends? Were Pete and Connie married? Remembering the smell of the ocean, Nikki got a flash of another scent. Musky, spicy. Pete. She'd had a huge crush on him. Her heart flipped at the memory.

Didn't Quinn say the Bayers had Elvis? From what she could remember, her dog really liked Pete. Soon they'd bring her dog back.

****

Pete swore to himself as he approached the giant Christmas tree in the Nordstrom Center shopping mall. "Shit, we gotta be on our toes here, it's really crowded," he whispered into the microphone clipped on his inside shirt pocket.

His friend Webber, from the department, answered. "Roger that."

Pete's own photo had been given too much press lately, for him to risk recognition.

When the perp approached the intended drop-off point for the money, Pete noticed him right away. It looked like he was alone, had a nervous, hungry look in his eyes and out of his depth with this felony. It was possible that he needed money for drugs.

Webber held the black duffel bag, trying to look like a dumb roadie. With long hair and worn jeans, he could've been one of Goldy's stage crew. Pete watched the scrawny perp approach and reach for the bag.

"I'll tell you where the dog is once I count the money."

Was this kid working alone? Pete hoped so. He looked grossly inadequate but underestimating a situation too soon could be a mistake. They moved to a bench.

"Open the bag. Let's see."

Webber complied, dug through the bag to show the money was real and lifted some bills. "Don't wave it around, you dumb fuck." The kid knew that much.

"Now where's the mutt?" Webber sounded like he had a date with a six pack of Budweiser and wanted to get this chore over.

Then the perp made his first big mistake. He didn't count the money but instead, told Webber to zip up the bag. "I'll call that number in fifteen minutes to tell you."

"Oh, no, you don't." Webber put a firm hand on the duffel's handle. "Tell me now or we're done. Goldy hasn't even asked about this stupid dog."

The kid looked like he wasn't sure what to do, fidgeting, wiping his forehead, all signs that he was nervous. Pete smiled.

"Where is it? Come on, man. It's just a fucking dog."

"In a black bag at the service entrance to a restaurant around the corner."

"Which one?"

Pause. "Charlie's Grill."

"Charlie's? You mean that place with the green awning out front and the—"

"In the back alley."

Webber was buying time for Pete to get around the corner.

"You gotta come with me while I see if it's him. It could be any stray dog, and you got some big dough in there for this." Webber gestured to the duffel under his hand.

"No! I told you, behind Charlie's!"

Good, the perp was panicking. Pete was half way to the service entrance when Webber spoke. "You're not leaving here with the money until I check to see it's the right dog. You could've brought me a fuckin' dead Chihuahua. I gotta verify it's him."

There was a pause while the kid thought about what to do, then Webber said, "Tell you what. I'll let you carry your money, and when I see it's the dog, you can take off. I don't want any trouble, man. I'm just a sound guy, not some fucking criminal like you.

Pete rounded the corner and saw the black bag up against the wall, behind a trash can, near the service entrance. He prayed that Elvis was inside and breathing. As he unzipped, a snarl erupted from within. "Easy, boy, it's just me, just Pete." Elvis snapped at his hand, his teeth penetrating the flesh on Pete's palm. "Elvis." He tried to use the high voice the dog responded to the best.

It was indeed Elvis, with his camouflage collar, and his big smile. "Elvis, you okay, boy?" The little dog jumped up on Pete's knees and, clawing his way to kiss Pete's face, tried to cover him with stinky kisses.

"It's him, Webber. Affirmative."

****

An hour later, Pete was handing over a twenty-two-year-old punk to the King County Police to be booked on one charge of theft and one charge of blackmail. Even though it would have been easy to just clip this guy on the side of the head for mischief then let him go, Pete had to remember that he'd been a punk once. And punks needed the reward and punishment system. He'd let the court system figure it out.

Sitting in the truck with Elvis asleep on his lap, Pete called Nikki's cell again to tell her the good news, in case she knew that Elvis was missing.

Voicemail. "It's Pete. I've got Elvis and I'll bring him by the hospital right now." He paused. "I feel so...so...terrible about what happened to you. So did Connie." Elvis was snoring up a storm, and Pete had to speak up. "I hope you'll forgive me, but maybe not. I'm also hoping everything is fine with the baby. Every since I felt her kick, well, I feel like I know her." He stroked Elvis's head. "I hope." He chuckled. "Well, I'm doing a lot of hoping right now, so I'll just head over to the hospital and hope to see you."

Chapter 24

"I'm sorry, sir, but you cannot bring a dog into the hospital." The hospital security man stopped Pete in the first floor lobby.

"This is Goldy's dog. She's in the VIP suite." He flashed his badge, something he hadn't surrendered just yet. Everyone knew Goldy was upstairs. The guard nodded. "I need to radio ahead to check the protocol on bringing in an animal that's not a service dog."

"I'll wait."

Once upstairs, Pete put Elvis down on the linoleum and leashed him. He'd stopped at the pet store, had Elvis shampooed and while he waited, bought a leash to match his collar. He was looking fine for his reunion with Nikki and Quinn.

The guards shook their heads.

"This is Goldy's dog."

"The dog is fine but not you. Give him to us," one of them said.

Pete bent down to pick up the pug, prepared to clutch him to his chest.

"Give him up." The bigger of the two guards reached for Elvis, and the dog snarled.

Pete showed the blood-crusted bite on his own hand. "He's a biter. I better take him in."

The older guard radioed someone, and then Quinn ran down the hall, tears pooling in her eyes. "Oh, my

God, there you are, little guy." Elvis looked like he was going to burst if he didn't kiss Quinn, and Pete couldn't refuse the transfer. Hell, poor little dog had been through a long separation from the women in his life. He handed him over.

"Thank you, Mr. Bayer." Quinn let Elvis kiss her neck and laughed. "Oh, you look good for being lost."

"Pete," he said.

Quinn looked at him. "What?"

"Call me Pete."

"Oh. Where was he?"

"Some nice people took care of him." Pete handed over a bag of dog food. "Now, can I see your mother?"

"She's asleep. I'll have to call you later."

"Ah, Quinn. You're not playing games with me, are you?" He searched her face.

"No."

"Come on, Quinn. Ask your mom if she wants to see me."

"She's asleep."

Something in the way she stood and stared at him told Pete he was not going to win this. "Quinn, when your mother wakes up, please give her this and ask her to call me." He reached for his business card, but she interrupted.

"I have your number from my mother's cell."

"Are you listening to her messages?"

Quinn turned to walk down the hall then stopped. She spun around. "Thank you for finding Elvis."

There was no emotion in her voice. Dang, she was a tough nut to crack. He watched her walk away, Elvis smothering her face with kisses, and Pete felt as unloved as Elvis probably felt loved.

****

Nikki found the remote control in the folds of her thin hospital blanket and turned on the TV. Connie's photo flashed on the screen. The text under her picture said her name was "Cathy Vanelli." She turned up the volume.

"Ten-year-old son, Tony Jr., the offspring of east coast lawyer Tony Vanelli, murdered while visiting his dying mother in Seattle last summer." *Oh, God!* "Lawyer to the crime lord Cassius Zetti, Anthony Vanelli's death is thought to have been a mob hit. His wife Cathy was taken into seclusion to await her testimony."

"Mom, are you okay?" The volume woke Quinn in the chair beside her.

"I'm remembering something." Nikki squinted at the TV. She dug deep for recognition of the flashes in her mind. "Connie was a witness at her husband's murder trial and Pete's a U.S. Marshal." The whole story was unfolding in front of her like a book had fallen open to the photo pages. "Pete was protecting Connie. They were waiting for the trial to begin. She had to testify." Nikki glanced at the TV news which had moved on to another story.

The guard knocked on the door and peeked in. It was Dwayne. "Quinn, there's something out here you'll want to see."

Quinn regarded her mother with concern. "I'll be right back."

Memories flooded back to Nikki, faster than she could process. She and Connie were friends on the sailboat. But she and Pete were more than that. Secrets had been shared. She'd fallen for Pete. He wasn't married to Connie.

Quinn burst through the door with Elvis in her arms, and when the little dog saw Nikki, he let out a squeal that made Nikki laugh. "There you are, big guy. Have you been having fun without me?" She expected a visitor to follow Quinn, but the door closed behind her daughter.

"Mom, I can't put him on the bed, because he'll step all over you."

"That's fine, sweetie, just let him lick my face and I'll scratch behind his ears while you hold him." Elvis put up more of a fuss than necessary and Nikki laughed. "I missed you, little boy." She looked at Quinn. "Did the Bayers bring him?"

"No." Quinn didn't meet her mother's eyes, and when she finally put Elvis on the hospital floor and got him a bowl of water, she still looked guilty. What was going on?

Once Elvis calmed down, he curled up on the end of Nikki's bed and fell asleep while Quinn settled in to study in the chair. Nikki tried to remember the time on the sailboat with the Bayers. Elvis had gas from eating stew, and Pete put him outside for an hour. Elvis had run around on a beach somewhere, and she'd fantasized about buying an island and living there with the baby, Elvis, and Pete. Pete's lips were soft. She felt his hands on her body, his careful caress, and him saying, "Let me know if I should stop."

It had been the night before they'd left for Seattle, although neither knew they'd disembark the following day. Connie had gone to bed with Tony. The stars were out in full force, twinkly pinpricks of brilliance through a velvet sky. After looking through the telescope, brushing against one another and smiling into each other's faces, they'd zipped two sleeping bags together and lay on the outside couch to star watch. Somewhere after finding Cassiopeia, they kissed, first sweetly, then more desperately.

"Oh, Nikki, this'll ruin me," he'd whispered in her ear.

She hadn't known what he meant, but answered him by deepening the kiss. Snuggled in the sleeping bags, Pete's hands wandered under her clothes. They'd laughed about all their clothing. Still, Nikki could feel how ready he was.

"I want you to make love to me, Pete," she'd whispered.

He hesitated.

"It won't hurt the baby and you know it."

"Are you sure?" He kissed her long and deep, searching for something. Permission maybe, but not from her. From himself.

"I'm sure." The thought sent shivers through her body and had her almost climaxing before anything had happened.

She kissed that gorgeous mouth she'd been staring at all day. When he moved on top and slipped carefully into her wetness, he'd asked if that felt all right.

"Hmmm, better than all right." She couldn't help emitting a little sigh of pleasure. He'd fit inside her like it was planned, like puzzle pieces sliding perfectly together. His hard body on her, his smell, everything about being with Pete was like all her dreams merging. Going deeper with each thrust, their arousal escalated until holding back was impossible. The explosion was like shattering into thousands of glass shards, and the ecstasy took her somewhere she'd never been. Higher.

Pete smothered his face in her hair and pumped, grinding deeper and deeper until one final thrust and he shuddered against her. Nikki squeezed herself tighter. His racing heart beat against her breast, and she hugged him like she'd never let him go. They lay still, settling back to normalcy. Nikki wondered if anything would ever be normal for her after this.

"I love you, Nicole Anne," Pete said.

Having heard those words many times with Burn, Nikki kissed him and let him believe he meant it.

After he softened and pulled out, they snuggled in each other's warmth. Making love with Pete had been wildly exciting and brilliantly sweet at the same time.

"You are so...so..." He tenderly stroked her thigh.

"Sexy?"

"That too, but you are so soft, that it makes you even more sexy than you look, if that's even possible." Pete kissed her shoulder. "I've fallen in love with you, Nikki."

She wanted to cry, for many reasons. "I love that you called me Nikki, and not Goldy."

As first time lovers, they drifted in and out of sleep and each other, until the sky lightened. Then for propriety's sake, Nikki suggested they move to their own beds.

Pete chuckled in her shoulder. "Good idea. Let's just go off to bed, where we sleep inches from each other."

"Oh, you've noticed, have you?" She kissed the scar on his chin. They dressed and gathered up the rumpled sleeping bags to sneak into their respective beds quietly. "Goodnight, Pete," Nikki whispered.

"Goodnight, Nikki." He reached across the three foot expanse. She extended her hand, and was surprised when a Yoruba protection necklace passed between them.

****

The house was on five fenced acres, overlooking Lake Washington. Thanks to trees on three sides, the privacy factor was off the charts. It had more square feet than Nikki needed, but, because of its expansive yard, view of the lake, and floor plan, she would overlook the extra bedrooms and bathrooms. At least the baby's room would be next to her own, and Quinn could have her choice of rooms.

She sent Quinn and Merilee to look at the house, and three hours later they returned with a glowing report.

"It is exactly your style, Mom," Quinn had said.

Merilee was strangely quiet.

"What is it, Mer?" Nikki couldn't read her expression. Her assistant was often given to bursts of moodiness.

"I have a headache. It's a wonderful house." She turned and went back to her work at the makeshift desk she'd set up in the room's corner. Nikki knew that Merilee was still angry about being left in L.A. when she hid at the lake. Her assistant had all but begged to come with her but Nikki never even considered the intrusion. For one thing, Merilee was a bit of a stickler for details. Rules were to be followed. She was not someone you'd call good company. These were qualities that made her a great assistant but not a wonderful companion. "I sat around for months worrying about you!" she'd complained when they'd spoken of her being ignored.

"I'm sorry, Mer. Really, I am." Nikki was now over-compensating by letting Merilee take over most aspects of her life.

Thing was, she'd only signed on at the beginning of the last tour when Goldy's long-time assistant had to give up showbiz for family life, but Merilee quickly proved herself indispensable. When Goldy announced her retirement, a position was secured for Merilee with the Foundation. She'd do a fine job of keeping everyone in line over there.

"Mom. You should make an offer. It's a perfect house for parties." Quinn's eyes twinkled.

"I don't see myself throwing any parties for awhile, unless it's a baby birthday party or you're having friends over." What she could imagine was pacing the nursery floor with a teething baby, changing diapers in every room in the house, and watching her son toddle from chair to chair in the sunken family room.

"Let's offer $25,000 more than they're asking and see if they can move out this week, Merilee." She had a thought. "Quinn, what about doing the nursery in a boating theme?" Her time on the sailboat with Pete continued to creep into her mind.

"Good idea, Mom."

Unless she hadn't recalled something important, Nikki's sailboat memories were happy ones. She and Pete had become so much more than friends. Now that she realized the intensity of their relationship, she missed him. She'd gotten very used to having Pete close, teasing her, being the man in her life. *Where the hell was he?* Being heartsick over his absence was useless. She had to accept that he hadn't come to visit or called, and there was probably a reason. He was long gone. Probably in Mexico by now, like he said.

The offer on the new house was accepted and papers were signed, making Nikki the new owner of property on Lake Washington. Immediate occupancy was granted, and Merilee sent decorators over, as per Nikki's instructions. Knowing that a home waited only ten miles away did more for her state of mind than anything else had recently. Except Pete.

A few days later, Nikki and Merilee were talking about Burn's participation in the new school that the Goldy Foundation had built when Merilee's office phone rang. It was Gateman with his report. Nikki motioned for Merilee to put him on speaker.

"Nothing new?" Merilee asked.

"Nothing."

"That's good, right?" Nikki called across the room.

"Yes, sometimes things just fizzle out when the celebrity is out of the spotlight. Sometimes not. It's still an active case."

"Don't worry, Ted," Nikki said. "I'm satisfied if we never hear from him again." Truthfully, never knowing Shakespeare's identity would leave her feeling anxious, like wearing an unzipped coat in a snowstorm.

Merilee nodded at her boss and folded her arms across her chest. "Time to move on. Soon you'll be out of here and back in hiding."

Nikki didn't want to think of her new house as a hiding place. She hoped to call it a home.

The door opened, and Dr. Vogan entered with a chart in his hands.

"Gotta go, Ted. My surgeon just arrived, and I think he's going to tell me I'm ready to leave this party." According to the morning nurses, her level of boredom was a very good sign that she was on the road to recovery.

"If everything looks good tomorrow, I see no reason why you can't go home." Dr. Vogan wrote on Nikki's chart then looked up and smiled at her. "If you promise to stay away from excitement."

When the doctor left, Nikki nodded at Merilee "Did you hear that? Will the house be ready?"

Merilee nodded without looking up. "I'll make sure it is."

It would be wonderful to leave the hospital. Nikki was hungry, her appetite returning with the good news. "Can someone go get me Thai food, Mer? I'd like green curry chicken with rice."

"I'll send one of the bodyguards." Merilee said.

"Has anyone named Pete called for me?" Nikki tried to sound casual but his name caught in her throat. She held her breath, waiting for a different answer from yesterday.

"No." Merilee sounded a bit on edge and Nikki didn't blame her. Orchestrating the purchase of the house as well as everything else from a hospital room wasn't easy. Earlier she'd seen Merilee in a heated discussion with Dwayne Capleoni. When she'd asked, Merilee had simply said that he took too many breaks. "He's not a good team player." She'd sounded so stressed and Nikki made a note to not add anything more to Merilee's plate.

The door opened and Elvis burst through the room, trailing a leash behind him. "Is that my little boy?" Nikki was excited to see him run in, hear his toenails tapping across the floor. Quinn followed with an armful of textbooks.

"I didn't expect you tonight." Merilee looked annoyed at the sight of Quinn.

"You all know how much I love this place." Quinn's cheeks were still rosy from the cold November night. "Besides, I can study just as well here as at my apartment." She set four large text books on the chair and took off her rain coat.

Merilee crossed the room and approached the bed. "Actually, I have a secret." She looked at the door to make sure it was shut tight. "We're going to leave tonight." She gazed at Nikki, wide-eyed, her grin spreading across her face.

"Tonight?" Nikki was impressed with her assistant's sense of adventure. "But the doctor…?"

"He actually gave permission this afternoon. He was playing along with my surprise." Merilee looked more than pleased with herself. "After visiting hours, the shifts change and the hospital gets quiet. It'll be better to do it then, fewer people and no press." Merilee had thought this out.

Quinn grinned from the chair. "I'm in!"

"Sorry, Quinn. The fewer people, the better." Merilee looked at her sternly.

"You can wait for me at the house," Nikki said. She wouldn't overrule Merilee. Being still on pain meds, Nikki couldn't be trusted to make important decisions. Besides, Merilee looked like defiance would not be tolerated tonight.

Chapter 25

Pete paced the floor in agitated strides. Shouldn't he have heard from Quinn by now?

Maybe the problem was that she still blamed him after he'd let her mother get shot outside the courthouse. Did she even know that he didn't find out for almost ten minutes? That's why he hadn't rushed to her side. He wanted to tell Nikki that his absence had nothing to do with his duty to the Justice Department. He'd have put her safety first if he'd known she was going to be shot. No question. And if that made him a lousy marshal, then so be it.

He positioned himself in a waiting room chair to stare at the doors that led to Nikki's VIP suite.

Earlier, the guards had been annoyed to see his face again. "Scram," one of them said. That guard was off duty now and the other one had been replaced by someone who did not look like he could muscle anyone out the door. He resembled a retirement village gigolo—gold chains, skinny, and over-cologned.

With only that one weak guard on duty, Pete speculated that he could make a wild run to Nikki's room. But Dwayne Capleoni was at Nikki's door, and he might not be so lucky in taking down the big guy a second time. Dwayne would see him coming from a long way off and would be ready with his supposed black belt moves.

The clock said eleven o'clock. The hospital was quiet. At this hour there was no one but him in the waiting room. Should he spend the night staring at the doors to Nikki's private suite?

When an orderly walked through the double doors with an armload of what looked like sheets, Pete had an idea. The scrawny new guard didn't know him. Pete looked around, wondering where to get some sheets. And scrubs.

****

The older guard arrived with the Thai food and when he set the bag on her hospital tray, Nikki had a feeling that she knew him from somewhere. The look in his eyes and the way his chin stuck out reminded her of someone. She asked Merilee when he left the room. "Who was that guy, Mer? Does he look familiar to you?"

"He was on tour this year. Matt or something. From the security team." Merilee didn't look up from her desk.

"I mean before the tour."

"Dunno."

"I think I recognize him from somewhere else."

With Quinn's help, Nikki opened her take-out box of curry chicken and dug in. Quinn had insisted on staying for the excitement of sneaking out of the hospital, despite what Merilee said.

Nikki felt badly for Merilee. She was unusually jumpy and annoyed, probably from the house sale. She'd turned down food and was riddled with nerves about escaping the hospital. "It's okay, Mer. Even if someone sees us leave, they'll never follow us all the way to the house. Have Dwayne drive fast and in circles. He's good at that."

Merilee forced a smile and checked her watch.

Quinn put down her fork and settled back in the big chair. "Wake me when you leave."

The new plan involved Quinn and Elvis driving in her car.

"Close your eyes, sweetie." Elvis had fallen asleep at the foot of the bed on Nikki's legs. "Merilee, can you move Elvis for me. My feet are going to sleep."

Merilee approached the bed but instead of moving the dog, she stood staring at Nikki. "How was your chicken, Nikki?" Merilee never called her boss by that name. Always Goldy.

Nikki surveyed her assistant's expression. "You just called me Nikki." As she set the empty container on her swivel tray, Nikki felt fuzzy. She tried to remember if she'd been given a sleeping pill. The chopsticks clattered to the floor. "I feel funny, Mer. Can you ask the nurse if she gave me something?"

Merilee stared at her. "Sure." She stayed rooted, watching Nikki.

"I don't feel right."

"How unfortunate."

The last thing Nikki remembered was a strange smile on Merilee's face.

****

Dressed in green scrubs, Pete would try to get in Nikki's room, even if it was late and she was probably asleep by now. He'd bring in fresh towels. As long as Dwayne didn't recognize Pete's face from Louisa Lake, he just might make it through the door. He'd found one of those beanies from surgery and hoped it hid his look. He'd been staring at the VIP wing for hours, rehearsing what he would say to make Nikki believe he was sorry for what had happened.

When Pete opened the doors, the old guard was nowhere in sight, there was no one at the nurse's station, and Dwayne had disappeared into Nikki's room, pushing a wheelchair. This might be much easier than he thought if Dwayne wasn't at his post and Nikki was coming out in a wheelchair. She must be going somewhere tonight.

Pete's intention had been to walk straight to the room but, on closer inspection he noticed that the only nurse at the desk was unconscious. He changed his plan. Shaking her arm didn't wake her. He felt a strong pulse.

Hearing Nikki's door open, Pete careened over the counter and hid. Angry whispers came from beyond the doorway to Nikki's room. Then the chair wheeled out. The occupant was dressed in a long black coat with a hood over her head. Sunglasses covered her face and her chin bobbed on her chest. She was either asleep or pretending.

Dwayne maneuvered the chair through the doorway with the old guard. A middle-aged brunette stood behind Dwayne, saying something Pete couldn't make out. The door shut behind them, leaving the woman inside Nikki's hospital room and the gigolo guard with Dwayne outside the door.

Was Nikki in the chair or was it a double? Pete wasn't sure until they got closer and he saw Nikki's beautiful, long fingered hands. He'd know them anywhere. A foot fell off the footrest, and the old guard scooted around to reposition it. Nikki was not conscious.

Pete hadn't worn a gun and regretted that decision as Dwayne pushed the wheelchair through the double doors. The elevator would take a long time to respond. He had time to check inside the room.

The first thing he saw was Elvis asleep on an empty hospital bed. Quinn was unconscious in a chair beside the bed. He stepped forward, knowing someone else was in the room. Sensing movement to his left, he quickly spun around but something jabbed him in the neck.

"Hey!" He pulled a hypodermic out of his neck and threw the body to the floor. "What the hell?" It was a small woman, middle-aged, mousy looking. She backed up to scoot under a desk. The needle was mostly empty. He had to work fast. Before he bolted out the door he took a chance she might be on Goldy's side. "I'm a U.S. Marshal. Call the police to the main floor of the hospital."

No one remained at the elevator. Fuck! He had to get to the lobby before they got Nikki in a car. There was no way she was awake or in on this plan.

His extremities tingled as he flew down the stairs. Could he descend six flights before he passed out? Stumbling at the second floor, he grabbed his cell phone and called the last number he'd dialed. Officer Hitchens.

"It's Daniels. Dwayne Capleoni is abducting Goldy from the hospital. Get over here." He didn't wait for a reply.

Just as he crashed through to the lobby, Pete fell to the floor. His legs had lost their muscular function. His fingers too. The phone dropped on the linoleum and slid across the floor. Pete had to fight this thing. He was a big guy. He had to keep running and find Nikki before she got in a car.

They wouldn't take her out the front door. Where'd they go?

Grabbing the first person he saw, Pete tried to speak but his mouth wouldn't work. He leaned against the older woman and together they stumbled against the wall. Still upright, blackness swept in front of his eyes. "Get security. Goldy is being abducted by Dwayne," he tried to say, but his words were unrecognizable and his voice was barely audible with the damned vocal nodes blocking his volume. "Get security. Goldy."

"Help." The woman's feeble voice called as she shrugged Pete off to the floor.

****

When Pete regained consciousness, he was lying on a gurney in a busy corridor of the hospital. His vision was blurred and his head felt like it had cracked wide open to expose brain matter. Even thinking hurt. How long had he been out?

Nikki!

"Goldy was abducted!" he whispered to the next person who walked by.

The nurse turned around, startled. "It's okay. Lie down. The police are here."

He tried to sit up, but his head felt stabbed with knives. "Goldy?"

The nurse tried to reassure him. "I'll get someone to talk to you."

"Did they find Goldy?"

"I'm not sure." The woman looked down the hall to the next set of doors.

He sat up. The pain split his head. "I gotta go."

Just then, another young nurse came through the doors and ran toward them. "You'll never believe what's going on out there." She nodded down the hall. "Someone kidnapped Goldy, and the police took off after them."

The first one glanced at Pete and back. "Shhhh. He was part of it," she whispered.

"I'm a US Marshal and I'm ordering you to get the police for me," Pete said, in spite of excruciating pain.

Hitchens walked through the doors and a look of concern crossed his face when he saw Pete. "There you are."

"Goldy okay?"

"She is. It was a chase but they got her. She was drugged, like you. She's on her way back in an ambulance." Someone spoke from beyond the door. "ETA, two minutes. Vitals are normal."

"You can't stay out of trouble, can you, Daniels?" Hitchens said.

Pete tried to ease his body off the gurney. "Listen to me. I think someone else was in on it. A woman, in Goldy's hospital room. She stuck me with a needle."

Hitchens's eyes widened. "What?"

"I don't think she left with them. Caucasian, middle-aged with brown hair, glasses, dressed in black. She was in the room."

Hitchens radioed the information. "Any sign of her?"

"Negative. Besides Goldy, only two males were in the van. Both Caucasian."

Pete launched himself off the gurney and stumbled to the elevator. "602," Pete managed to whisper as the blackness overtook him again.

****

Nikki woke with a colossal headache with Elvis asleep beside her legs. She looked around the room. Papers littered the floor and the computer keyboard hung off the desk by a cord. Where was Merilee? Last thing she remembered, they were waiting to make their escape to the house. A nurse now occupied the chair where Quinn had slept. Two police officers entered the room and crossed to Merilee's desk, rifling through the papers.

"Hey." Nikki knew Merilee was very private about her stuff.

The nurse jumped up and glanced at the monitors beside the bed. "You've had quite a night," she smiled.

"Big headache." Nikki's mouth was like the Atacama Desert. "What happened?" The escape to her new house must have been postponed. But why didn't she remember?

A policewoman standing at Merilee's desk spoke into a radio. "Goldy is awake. Roger that." She crossed the room to stand at the end of the bed. Elvis didn't stir. "Good morning, ma'am," she said. "Do you remember being drugged?"

Nikki refrained from shaking her throbbing head. "No."

"You were given a non-prescribed sedative last night, loaded in a van, and taken from this hospital. We believe it was against your will."

"Merilee and I were going to the new house." Nikki tried to remember.

"Quinn was drugged as well. She's fine and on her way to see you."

"Oh, my God." Nikki leaned forward to feel the

warmth of her dog's body.

"Drugged and still sleeping it off. If you feel up to it, we'd like to ask you some questions about Dwayne Capleoni and the woman you called Merilee."

****

Nikki's assistant had double-crossed her in the worst way imaginable. Merilee was behind the Shakespeare conspiracy and orchestrated the abduction attempt with Dwayne Capleoni and a guy named Mike. And now she was on the loose. This shocking revelation left Nikki confused about why Merilee would betray her this way. And if it was true. For what reason? She hadn't been safe on tour or any time she'd been with Merilee or Dwayne. And how safe had Quinn been around Dwayne?

According to Gateman, the night before, a police officer noticed something suspicious, came in the hospital room, saw everyone asleep and got stuck with a needle. Merilee probably intended the drug for herself, to hide her involvement while a ransom was decided. Instead, she'd been seen and had to escape.

So far, the FBI team was still searching for Merilee. Her apartment in L.A. had been ransacked with no evidence of intention, but at Dwayne's place they found enough to prove that both he and Merilee conspired to abduct their boss. And that Merilee was Shakespeare.

Last night, Ted Gateman had conducted the interrogation of the two men, Dwayne and the older one, Mike, who refused to talk, so far. Luckily Mike's cell phone had enough information on it for the FBI to piece together the plan.

An apartment had been rented an hour away.

There, Goldy would wait out the time it took for ten million to clear a bank in the Cayman Islands. Merilee was to remain behind on the Goldy side, innocently aiding the negotiation. Nothing suggested that any form of torture would be connected to the abduction and when Mike was finally convinced to talk, he assured them that the Shakespeare letters were only to break down Nikki's confidence. "We never woulda done anything said in those letters. Never. She just wanted to make Goldy miserable."

Gateman looked sympathetic to Nikki's shock.

"This is like a bad dream." Nikki felt nauseous. "I trusted Merilee with my life for over a year. The letters were so venomous, so sick." It was incomprehensible how Merilee could write those things. She'd lived alongside Nikki's fear on tour. "And for what? Money? No one writes that they're going to inject cleaning fluid into the veins of their victim and stand by to watch them squirm, if they don't have a more serious motive than money." Gateman agreed and assured her they were working on it.

Dwayne claimed he was innocent, despite the evidence against him. Gateman was confident that they'd catch Merilee. And when they did, the motive would surface.

For health and safety reasons, Nikki was kept at the hospital for a few more days. Quinn recovered quickly and was more horrified that her clean record of drug use was now blemished. Thank God Merilee had chosen a sedative that hadn't hurt the baby. Nikki still wanted to believe that had been intentional.

On the morning of the third day, Nikki got the call she'd been expecting from Gateman.

"We have the suspect in custody."

"Where was she?" It was hard for Nikki to think of Mer as a criminal. That fact had not sunk in.

"SeaTac Airport. Wearing a disguise," Gateman said. "On her way to Anchorage, Alaska. Her biggest mistake was trying to leave town so soon."

"Is she remorseful?" Nikki's voice cracked.

"Only that she got caught."

Chapter 26

Nikki requested a private conversation with Merilee before the suspect was taken back to Los Angeles. While waiting for the FBI's prisoner to arrive, she reread the letters from Shakespeare and reassured herself that Merilee was some kind of a monster to torment her like this. And with two accomplices. "Why can't I place this Mike guy? I know I've seen him before.

"Mom, they're crazy. Stop trying to have it make sense." Quinn had barely left her mother's side in days.

Dressed and ready to be discharged, she sat in her hospital room waiting for Gateman to arrive with Merilee. When the door finally opened and two guards escorted the handcuffed woman into the hospital room, Nikki motioned for her to sit down across from her.

The two women stared hard at each other, the FBI agents on either side of the prisoner. Quinn and Gateman waited in the hall, undoubtedly wringing their hands.

"Merilee…" Nikki's voice was heavy with sorrow.

The woman looked down, into her wrinkly T-shirt.

"I don't know why," Nikki whispered.

Empty silence. A gull flew by the window. A siren increased in volume and stopped somewhere below the window. Finally the prisoner spoke. "You know why." The sound coming from the woman fifteen feet away was devoid of any remorse. This voice was new for Merilee and Nikki reminded herself there was no such person as Merilee.

"Do I?" Nikki leaned forward to try to make eye contact. "We were more than boss and assistant, Mer. We were friends." She paused, but the woman across from her didn't move. "Was it money? Did you need money? I would've helped."

Merilee's head snapped up, and the sparks in her eyes made Nikki lean back.

The FBI agents glanced down at their prisoner.

"I don't care about the money," she spat.

"What then? What do you care about?"

The woman hung her head, her lips tight, her face pained.

"Tell me what I ever did to you, Mer." Nikki would wait as long as she needed.

Finally Merilee took a deep breath and exhaled slowly. "You killed my daughter." Her voice was a low growl.

Nikki's breath caught in her throat. "Who was your daughter?"

"You ignored her."

Then she knew. Yellow. The runaway who'd killed herself.

"She idolized you." The woman's squinty stare was frightening.

"You were her mother?" What was Yellow's real name? Nikki searched for the name. "Kenzie." Nikki covered her mouth with her hand, holding in a sob.

Merilee's head jerked up at the sound of the name.

"Oh, my God. You are that poor girl's..." Years ago, Nikki had written the parents a letter to tell them how sorry she was for their loss. "I felt terrible about what happened."

"You didn't help her. You made a fool out of her. She loved you." A noise escaped the woman's mouth, like a cough mixed with a sob.

"She didn't come to me for help."

"She was screaming for help in everything she did." The woman's yell brought the agents closer, at the ready.

Nikki motioned for them to wait. "Merilee, you have spent a year on the road with me. You know what it's like. Fans come in all degrees. I honestly did not know how serious it was with Kenzie. I had no idea she would try to kill herself."

"She loved you. My daughter left home to be a rock star, to follow you. And you ignored her." Her eyes flashed with hatred. "And you treated her like dirt."

"I didn't know her to treat her like anything." What more could Nikki say? She'd been afraid of the girl. Searching the mother's anguished face, Nikki saw no similarities to the hard features of the fan who'd chosen to die at the Goldy concert. "Is your name Sharon?"

Merilee's weeping turned to sobs. "You wrote that terrible song about her. Like she was some evil person."

"I didn't realize she was so young, so needy. Your daughter's state of mind scared me. I asked to help her one night, but she ran away. When she put the pipe bomb under the bus, I worried she'd hurt me or any one of us. She threatened to kill Quinn." Nikki waited, took a breath and sat forward. "Your daughter was dangerous." She couldn't reason with this woman. She was a grieving mother. A grieving, crazy mother.

"What you've done is wrong. Making my life miserable over these Shakespeare letters was not fair. And carrying on for so long…" She searched the woman's face for remorse.

She whispered. "Yeah, well, I forced you to retire, didn't I? And now you can never do this to another girl." Merilee looked smug. "Forcing you out was my goal. The money was just a bonus."

"But you didn't. Pregnancy gave me the opportunity to retire, so don't fool yourself." Nikki's expression was rock hard. "Drugging me" —Nikki touched her tummy— "and your whole plan to hold me for money was so much worse than me ignoring a runaway girl who obviously had family problems or she wouldn't have followed me and then killed herself over *my* lack of attention." Nikki sat back and took a deep breath. "I hope you get good psychiatric counseling now. Writing those letters and manipulating my life was the work of a sick mind." She looked up at the FBI agents. "We're done here." Nikki stood and walked to the window, as they led the woman out of the room.

Gateman entered and stood behind the chair that had been vacated by Merilee. "Did she tell you who she is?"

Nikki nodded. "Kenzie's mother."

"We thought we'd cleared her a year ago when this all started, but she covered her tracks remarkably well. She's an educated woman, a former teacher of English literature." He ran a hand through his dark hair. "Did she tell you about Dwayne?"

Nikki shook her head.

"She pulled him into this knowing he owed the wrong guys money in Los Angeles." He waited while

Nikki assimilated the information. "Dwayne is two steps away from having his face messed up over debt, and he feared for his children who he's losing in a custody battle with his ex-wife. Mike, the older guy, is Kenzie's grandfather, Sharon 'Merilee's' father."

Nikki nodded but it didn't matter. They were terrible people for what they'd plotted and planned. She'd have to testify against them all eventually. Thinking of that reminded Nikki that she hadn't heard how Connie's trial ended. "Thanks for all the good work, Ted. It's over."

He nodded like he wouldn't spend the next few months putting this all together to make sure they went to prison.

"Did you ever hear from the Vanellis?"

Gateman shook his head.

"Connie gone into hiding now?"

"That's what the press reported. The trial ended and she left, from what I heard."

Nikki was confident that someday she could find Cate and Anthony Nelson. Somehow. And now Shakespeare had been caught, killed in some ways.

Gateman interrupted her thoughts. "There's more about their motive if you want to hear it."

Nikki sank into the chair, and waited while Gateman explained how Kenzie's family had fallen to financial ruin over the media's treatment of the girl's bizarre death. The mother eventually quit her job as an English teacher, the family restaurant had gone under, and the dad had a fatal heart attack. As Sharon's need for vengeance grew, she concocted the plan to make Goldy pay for what she'd done and rescue them from poverty. Only in the last few months had the grandfather been added to the plan when they needed a third person. Rather than see his daughter fail and go to prison, he'd relented. After all, Goldy had more than enough money to go around.

"When questioned," Gateman added, "the grandfather was remorseful. 'I didn't know about the letters until last month,' he said. 'And I'm sorry. I just thought we'd take Goldy to a house, get the money, and no one would be hurt.'" The FBI agent shook his head in disgust.

Nikki recalled photos of the grandfather in the newspaper after Kenzie's death. He'd been the family spokesperson, taking interviews at the restaurant in Nebraska. Back then, he'd been clean-shaven and plump. Now he was scrawny with haunted eyes. All along, it had been his resemblance to Yellow that made Nikki wonder where she'd seen him before.

"Merilee leaked your location to the press once Dwayne found your location. She tipped them off about Louisa Lake to try to flush you out, get you back to Seattle." Gateman used their former names. "Then when you got shot, her plan changed. She was in Seattle, waiting for you, when you summoned her."

Gateman left Seattle with the prisoners. That knowledge alone gave Nikki a sense of finality that would eventually take root. If she could only speak with Pete, say goodbye, instead of this feeling of leaving her shoes outside in the rain, she'd be closer to tying up all the loose ends from the last few months.

****

Opening the front door to her new house, Nikki held her breath. She was excited to see the home where she'd raise her son. A framed portrait of her and Quinn hung over the hall console table, and she stopped, tears dripping onto her shirt.

"It's just until we get a family picture with Junior, Mom."

As Nikki clutched the Yoruba symbol at her throat, sobs accompanied the tears.

Quinn put her arms around her mother. "Don't cry."

"Sweetie, I'm fine. It's just so pretty, and I'm grateful to have this place, especially now." She didn't want to tell her daughter that the disappointment of not hearing from Pete had suddenly overtaken her. It seemed like he'd never find her here in this new life. He'd had his chance while she was in the hospital. Every step she took away from being Goldy took her farther from him. They walked into the hallway, the heels of their boots tapping on the clay tiles.

That afternoon the rain was relentless in its pursuit of soaking the Pacific Northwest. Puddles formed all over the yard and the million-dollar view was obscured by a gray haze of cloud and rain. Nikki's first thought when she stepped into her bedroom was that the master bed was too large for one person. Thoughts of Pete, his kiss, his hands under her layers of warmth, left Nikki feeling like a hollow shell. She wished she could've seen him in this house.

Sliding her hand across the quilted coverlet, she held off tears. Her home nurse followed, pulling the suitcase to the bed. "Thanks, Bev, I'll unpack later. Right now I just want to lie down." Rain enveloped the house, the sound on the roof comforting.

"Sure thing, Ms. Crossland." Bev pulled down the covers and left the room.

****

That night, when she woke at eight, the rain still drummed rhythmically on the roof as Nikki wandered from room to room looking for her daughter. Quinn had taken up residence in a large room down the hall from her mother's, one that also overlooked the lake.

"Hello, kiddo."

Quinn was bent over her desk, studying. Surrounded by decorative surfboards, Hawaiian prints, and fake palm trees, Quinn looked happy. "You're awake." She stood to hug her mother. "Have a great nap in our new house?"

"Hmmm. So wonderful. I love the house you picked out for us." The sling on Nikki's left arm dominated her new fashion look.

"I made dinner. Are you hungry?" Quinn looked pleased with herself.

"I'll get some in a minute." Nikki stroked Quinn's forehead. So smooth and sweet. Young, innocent. "You keep studying."

Bev was sitting at the kitchen counter reading a romance novel and drinking a cup of tea when Nikki walked in. She didn't look like a former martial arts instructor, but Nikki had been delighted to hear that her nurse could throw a mean jab into someone's larynx. The memory of Merilee's betrayal was hard to forget.

"Quinn made spaghetti for an army," Bev said, sliding off the bar stool.

"Don't get up." Nikki remembered the manicotti she'd made at Louisa Lake for the Bayer family. So many memories had returned. Hopefully everything. She couldn't help but wonder how Connie and Tony Vanelli were doing and where they'd gone in the witness relocation program. Connie had passed through her life too briefly, around only long enough to teach her how to be compassionate at all costs, and then she was gone.

A thought popped into Nikki's head. Maybe Pete had gone with them to the new town, and stayed to protect them. It was possible his mission had been extended longer than planned, and he was still undercover. Her heart lifted. There were many reasons Pete might have opted out of contacting Nikki, not the least of which was her being pregnant with another man's baby. If Pete had stuck around, he'd be taking on a child, as well as all the problems of the Goldy image. She couldn't blame him for deciding against her and all the nonsense she brought to the table. All the Goldy shit. How could she disassociate herself from the celebrity she'd been for so long? Nikki still sang, had the same face as Goldy, carried all the memories of Goldy's life with her.

It was impossible to detach completely.

Nikki was Goldy.

And Goldy was Nikki.

Why had she been trying to deny it? Meshing the two was inevitable. The person who emerged would become clear in the months to come, but for now, Nikki was done trying to ignore all her years as a rock star. She'd loved Goldy for so long.

Pete had tried to tell her this when she asked him if it was Goldy he was attracted to or Nikki. "It's just you. Who you are and that's a part of both," he'd said. "Would I be crazy about Nikki if she was a secretary from Indiana? I don't know, because you're not. You're a singer from L.A. with a wicked sense of humor who's had an interesting life." They'd been snuggled into each other, talking, his hand under her shirt. A jolt of electricity shot through her at the thought of that moment on the sailboat, and she gasped out loud.

Bev looked over. "Are you in pain?" she asked.

"No. I'm just thinking about a sexy man."

Bev laughed and went back to her book.

Nikki was glad she hadn't told Quinn about her real feelings for the person who started out as the strange man in the log house, especially now when it looked like he'd dropped out of her life. Quinn would be disappointed for her mother's loss and would harbor a dislike for the man who did this to her. And Nikki had never mentioned Pete's name to Quinn without the word "weird" in the same sentence, except when she called from the sailboat to say that she was with the Bayer family. Quinn had no idea how her mother's relationship with Pete had evolved. Nor would she, now that Pete had given up on her.

Chapter 27

Where the hell was Nikki? She was damned good at this elusive act. Apparently sleeping with her and saving her life didn't grant him an audience with the rock star.

She'd left the hospital. That much he knew, but even the hospital staff seemed confused about where she went and to top off his frustration, he and Nikki had been on the same hospital floor for forty-eight hours and he hadn't even been conscious. Swear words were barely stifled when he heard that one.

After recovering from the allergic reaction to the drug he'd been stuck with, then having his vocal nodules removed when they swelled to ping-pong-ball size, he'd been told the news that Goldy had been in a room down the hall when he was recovering from surgery. And now she was gone.

Even though no one at the hospital was talking, he wasn't out of ideas. He'd start with Quinn's apartment, just in case she was still in town. Even a long shot was better than nothing.

****

Nikki needed to address the problem of the press. They were reporting untruths that were hurtful to read. They'd used Pete's picture again and assumed the baby was his. Someone had taken a photo of Pete yelling to the ambulance driver about her being four months pregnant, and they'd concluded he must be the father.

Seeing her name and photo linked to Pete in this way, left Nikki feeling wistful and she'd briefly entertained the fantasy that Pete was the father to her baby. That was dangerous territory for a fantasy because of the feelings it evoked.

If he wasn't with Connie, then Pete would be on his way to Mexico, if not already there, enjoying retirement with a fishing pole in one hand, and a Corona in the other. She hoped he took someone to teach him to sail, seeing he sucked at it.

After much thought, she phoned Phyllis to call a press conference. Nikki needed to address the baby issue and dispel rumors, even if Pete wasn't around to hear them.

****

Quinn's apartment had been vacated, but Pete found her between classes, walking from one building to another. She tried to go the other way when she saw Pete, but he ran in front and held out his hands in surrender.

"Go away," she said.

"Please, Quinn. Let me talk to your mom."

"No." She sounded appalled that he'd asked.

"She'd want to see me." He kept his distance.

"She doesn't. I asked her."

"I doubt that."

"Are you calling me a liar?" Quinn stared him down, looking so much like Nikki, he wanted to hug her.

"Not exactly. I'm sure you're trying to protect your mother."

"Something you didn't do." Quinn looked

triumphant that she'd hit him where it hurt. "Excuse me. I have a class I don't want to miss."

"Just ask her if she wants to talk to me."

Quinn passed him and he spun around.

"Quinlan Marie, named after your great-aunt, your Poppi's sister. Just ask her, okay?"

Quinn's step slowed.

"Ask your mother how I know you like homemade rhubarb pie at Katie's house, and how I know you and your mom had pedicures in Seattle, Sunset Peachilicious, and that you laughed about that silly name. How I know that your mother has such guilt about being a crappy mother that she ate fish when you were at the lake so she wouldn't disappoint you, even though she threw up after."

Quinn stood still.

"Ask her, Quinn." He watched her walk to the next building and disappear, never turning around.

****

When Quinn arrived home that night, Nikki saw she'd had a rough day at school. Dark circles had taken up temporary residence under her eyes. Exams were taking their toll.

"Were you studying late last night?" Nikki brushed a strand of hair back from her daughter's face.

"Not really." Quinn flashed a fake smile that Nikki recognized only too well from her own publicity shots.

"Nice smile, Goldy," Nikki said to make Quinn laugh. "I called a press conference tomorrow."

"What for?"

"To set the record straight. They know I'm pregnant, they want to hear it from me, and I want to tell them it's none of their business who the father is."

332

Nikki could see Nurse Bev's head turn away with the last statement. She stood immediately and left the room. A good sign in an employee.

Quinn frowned. "You're not going to tell them, are you?"

"No. But I am going to deny the rumor that it's Pete."

"Wait, they're saying your baby is the U.S. Marshal's?"

Nikki nodded. "Where have you been? It's all over the news."

"Studying."

"It's because of that picture of him on my dock. Remember they thought he was my new boyfriend? And then he told the ambulance driver that I'm pregnant, something I will be forever grateful for, even though it must have been embarrassing for him." Nikki adjusted her sling and winced. "I can't believe you haven't heard this?"

Quinn shook her head. "No."

"But you know all that he did for me."

"What did he do for you, besides abduct you and get you shot?"

Nikki stared at her daughter in disbelief. She rarely saw Quinn like this. She was almost resentful of Pete. "He did no such thing, Quinn. I went willingly with them to the sailboat and stayed with them because I chose to help."

Quinn looked confused. "I thought he made you stay."

"I didn't want to leave. I stayed to keep Connie safe. To help."

"Including jumping out of the van to take a bullet

for her?" Quinn's eyes searched her mother's.

"I never thought there would be an assassin waiting to shoot Connie. I thought it was just a group of reporters. And I know how to handle reporters." She looked Quinn purposefully in the eyes. "Pete had no idea that I planned to jump out to distract the press. When I opened the door, he grabbed me by the arm so fast, I barely had time to shrug out of my coat which, by the way, was his because it was warmer than the one I'd run away in. Pete is a sweet guy." She emphasized this last part.

"Wasn't it planned?"

Nikki's eyes flew open. "No. Pete would never let me do that. I wanted to buy time for everyone to get to safety. How would I know there'd be a hit man who didn't know his subject well enough?" She paused. "I'm sure Pete was horrified when he heard I'd been shot. I still don't know if he got in trouble with the Justice Department." Saying his name out loud validated his existence, and she needed to take a deep breath to continue. "We became really good friends and promised…to meet up after all this, but he must have left town or he's busy or something." She didn't want her daughter to know she'd been dumped, especially with the current look of horror on Quinn's face.

"Oh, Mom." Quinn's voice sounded very far off.

"Now don't feel sorry for me because I never heard from him again." Nikki changed the subject. "Hey, guess what? Phyllis is flying in for the press conference."

****

Pete was pretty sure Nikki was back in L.A. now that the stalker had been caught. Who wouldn't want sunshine and palm trees at this point? Hell, he did. Only trouble was, it would be hard to enjoy his new freedom unless he set things right with Nikki. An apology was in order—from him. If he sent a fan letter, would it reach her? Probably not. As long as Quinn was still at the U, Nikki would come back. Plus, he had to learn to sail, spend some time in the shallow end of a pool, apologize for taking advantage of a rock star in a vulnerable time. Too many stones unturned.

Judson Peter Daniels had a nine a.m. appointment with the debriefing team and a counselor at the Justice Department. His goal at that meeting was to hide how distracted he'd been by Nikki on this last case. In the department they'd been taught to not blame themselves for matters that weren't under their ability to change, but he could've held back with Nikki. Thing was, he only felt mildly guilty about all the flirting. And when she'd jumped from the van, he'd followed protocol. That much he knew.

On his way to the appointment, his cell phone rang and Pete answered before checking the number. "Hello."

"Pete Daniels?"

"Yes."

"It's Quinn Burnside. I made a terrible mistake."

****

Phyllis had flown in, the night before. A limo delivered her to Nikki's house bright and early, and the women sat in the family room overlooking the lake, working on Nikki's statement to the press that would take place in two hours. Words like "appreciate my privacy" and "discretion" floated in the air between them.

Wearing a black Chanel dress with a sling that Bev made out of a scarf, Nikki hoped to show the press her physical departure from Goldy. A hairdresser had come the day before to recolor her hair light brown and cut it in a fashionable bob. She was determined to convince the press to set her free. At least, to let their obsession die. Today she would answer most of their questions and then call an end to the nonsense.

Nikki stepped into the limo first and waited with Phyllis while Quinn finished a phone call on the walkway. Finally the sun had come out and a beautiful November day had emerged. "Is that my cell phone?" she called to Quinn. "I've been looking for that." Nikki held out her good hand as Quinn entered the limo.

"Yes, sorry. I forgot I had it. I bet you need it now that life is beginning again."

"That's fine." Nikki already knew that Pete never called. She'd asked every day in the hospital. Where the hell was he? Someone had to know. If nothing else, when this press conference was over and Phyllis flew back to L.A., Nikki would go to the dock where they'd left Pete's sailboat. If the boat was still there, she'd leave him a note. If it was gone, she'd drive to Shelton to find the cove where it had been moored. If he hadn't left for Mexico, she'd get on that nameless sailboat with a sack full of groceries and wait until he showed up. At the very least, closure was needed.

Chapter 28

Quinn had called Pete to say that he could see Nikki later, after her press conference. He didn't know if he could trust Quinn to orchestrate a meeting and, after getting details of the press conference from a reporter friend, he changed his morning plan. He had to forget his debriefing and get over to the Westin Hotel. After leaving his apologies with a secretary at the Justice Department, he ran to the curb to hail a taxi. In two minutes Goldy's press conference would begin. There was a good chance he'd miss it, even if he got there immediately. But he was gonna try.

If the U.S. Marshal badge didn't get him in the door, he'd pretend to be a reporter. How hard would it be to get into a press conference as a reporter?

No taxis. Shit. He hailed a police cruiser. After flashing his badge and explaining he needed a fast ride to the Westin, they'd smirked. "Oh yeah, we heard about you and Goldy." Even though he'd put on a Seahawks cap to hide his identity, the morning paper had a photo of him with the caption "Baby Daddy?" The cops stared at him strangely. Nikki was right. Fame had a price.

He showed his marshal ID at the Westin ballroom doorway and was admitted to the back of the packed room. Even though it was after nine, the room was still buzzing in anticipation. Just knowing Nikki was in the building, settled his nerves in one way and jangled them in another.

He walked up the aisle but was muscled out of the way by a burly man with arms as thick as tree trunks.

"I'm a friend of Goldy's," Pete said.

"Sure. We all are, pal."

Pete was ushered to the back of the room, and, sitting down amongst the crowd, he told himself to be thankful he was even here. He needed to hear Nikki's voice, to know she was fine, to see that she was alive, and hear from her lips that the baby was fine.

A middle-aged, gray-haired woman in large black glasses walked onto the stage and positioned herself behind the cluster of microphones at the podium. The room quieted.

"Good morning, Seattle." She looked comfortable behind a microphone. Good thing, because a hundred press members in attendance waited to hear from Goldy, including those representing European publications.

"In a moment, Goldy will come out to read a prepared statement," the woman said. "After that, she will answer only a few questions." She scanned the sea of faces. "I'm going to ask you to be kind. Remember, she's been through a lot lately and is still weak from the gunshot wound." She smiled at the familiar reporters, waved here and there, and continued. "Although I offered to issue Goldy's statement on her behalf just now, she insisted on doing this in person, and taking questions at the end. Goldy is a real trooper, a consummate lady and I want you to treat her as such."

There was a collective murmur from the press.

"Goldy is not allowed to answer questions about

the investigation, which is still underway. You know what I'm talking about." She looked sternly over the heads of the front rows to the back of the room. "And to enforce that, we have Sergeant Hitchens of the Seattle Sheriff's Department." Pete knew at that moment, he'd get to talk to Goldy today. Hitchens was his advocate.

The abduction attempt was top secret, he'd been told. Hospital staff had been sworn to secrecy so the press knew only about the Vanelli case, not about Shakespeare. That was FBI territory.

Hitchens approached the podium. "Because of the ongoing investigation, Goldy will not answer any questions about the shooting that occurred in front of the King County courthouse on November 12th. Nor will she take questions about the shooter or the case connected with that incident. Thank you." He backed away from the microphone, folded his hands in front and with that gesture, the curtains were pulled back at the side of the stage.

Out walked Goldy—international rock diva and superstar.

Pete's heart pounded against his chest at the sight of her. She looked like Nikki. Her hair was shorter, darker, and in this monstrous room, she looked very small. Almost frail. The crowd buzzed. Quinn was at her side, along with a nurse. Hundreds, possibly thousands of photos were taken in the time it took Nikki to walk to the podium, the room abuzz with the energy of getting the shot that would sell.

Nikki stood behind the microphones and smiled. The loose dress didn't show a baby bump and Pete hoped to God it was still under there. He found himself holding his breath. *Dear God, don't let this be an announcement about losing the baby.* His heart stopped.

"Hello, everyone. How are you?" Nikki's voice was soft and sweet and so familiar to Pete, that he felt tears at the back of his eyes. She sounded like she was addressing long lost friends, beloved, cherished people she'd lost touch with. She waved the fingers of her right hand at reporters in the front and cleared her throat. "I've missed you, but I needed downtime." She smiled at them. "And now, look how happy we are to see each other." As she flirted with the crowd, Pete's heart melted. Was this the same woman he'd been intimate with only weeks before?

Nikki flashed a big smile and proceeded. "Do you like my hair?" She flipped it with her good hand and smiled broadly at the crowd. She was a master at handling the press, and Pete wished he could run to her and kiss her for being so brave.

She waited for the room to fall silent. "I don't look very Goldy-ish, and there's a reason for that. Firstly, let me announce to you that I am doing well, my gunshot wound is healing and will be a distant memory, soon enough."

The group erupted in applause and Goldy waited again for the noise to die down. "And I want to confirm that I'm having a baby in the spring." She nodded, looking very proud of herself.

Pete heaved a sigh of relief and joined in the applause.

"The baby is doing well, and I couldn't be more thrilled about the addition to my little family." She cleared her throat. "On a more serious note, you have to admit that I have been very open to sharing myself with all of you over the last twenty years. I have granted interviews even when I was exhausted, answered questions when it was inconvenient, and have included you in every aspect of my life. You've watched Quinny grow up, followed me through my marriage and divorce, and been included in everything. And I have benefitted from your involvement. Don't get me wrong. It's been a beautiful love affair."

Chuckles and murmurs spread through the room.

"Up to this point." She paused. "I have loved this life as Goldy and how you've helped me achieve this life, but I'm sorry to announce today that this is where our love affair ends. I'm breaking up with you and you have to move on."

The words troubled Pete, but then he remembered she was talking to the press, not him.

"I look forward to being a mother again, with privacy this time." She looked over at Quinn standing at stage left. "And I will not be doing anything in show business that you will need to report anytime soon, aside from a short birth announcement in February."

Wasn't the due date March?

"I plan to be the most boring person in history, so you will have no reason to follow me." She laughed. "In the past, I've made good press, but that's all going to change. I know this game well. I will not be your story from now on." She looked sternly at the crowd.

Nikki paused briefly and scanned her audience. "When I was shot—" She fought to keep her voice even. "—it was the press who saved my life. That day, wonderful people set down their cameras and surrounded me in a protective circle. My guardian angel, Gerard Thomas of the Seattle Times, risked his life to shield me after the first shot." She looked sideways and took a tissue from the podium. "In his words, he 'asked for guidance to save my life.' Several of you, and you know who you are, took down the shooter at risk to your own lives…" She took a moment to compose herself. "…and for that I will always be grateful." Nikki dabbed at her eyes. "I want to thank the press for saving my life, for giving me back this life, for saving my baby." The applause was deafening. Nikki waited and blew her nose. When the noise died to a hush, she named names and asked that the people who'd helped her that day stand up to enjoy their moment of fame. They did.

"And lastly I want to thank you for giving me the greatest gift of all…the privacy I need now to have a normal life." She backed away from the microphone to let the older lady in glasses step in front of the microphones.

"Goldy will now take only a few questions."

Nikki pointed to someone in the second row, who waved frantically. "Jim."

"What about the man on your dock, Goldy? Can you tell us who he is?" Although a pin didn't drop, you could've heard it.

She looked over at Sergeant Hitchens and a man in a suit, who was probably her lawyer standing off to the side of the stage. Both shook their heads. She continued. "Jim asked about the man on my dock, photographed a month ago." She cleared her throat and adjusted her sling. "He was a neighbor and a friend of mine. The day that photo was taken, he was attempting to get rid of photographers for me."

"A boyfriend?" The reporter looked desperate.

Nikki didn't miss a beat. "Next question." She

pointed to someone standing halfway back, at the side of the room.

"Does this pregnancy change any terms in your divorce, and will Burn be joining you and the baby in Seattle?"

Nikki looked calm. "No and no."

Someone shouted out, "Is Burn the father?"

"I didn't call on you," she chided with a smile.

Nikki pointed to another reporter in the middle of the room.

"Will you remain in Washington State or raise the baby in Los Angeles?"

"I haven't decided yet. Probably not L.A. For the time being, I'm here with Quinny."

The publicist leaned into the group of microphones. "Last question."

Pete threw his arm into the air, waved it madly, and stepped into the aisle to be seen, knowing this was his chance. He wasn't sure if she'd be glad to see him, but he had to try.

Nikki's gaze stopped when she saw him waving from the aisle. The expression on her face was one of disbelief, causing people to turn around. As he moved cautiously up the aisle, two security guards descended on him, and she shook her head at them. "It's okay." Nikki pointed to Pete. "The handsome man in the aisle."

Pete stepped forward. "Firstly, let me say that pending motherhood suits you, Ms. Crossland."

"Thank you." A smile spread across Nikki's face.

Phyllis looked annoyed.

"Next, may I ask if part of your glow has anything to do with being in love?"

Nikki put out her good arm to stop Phyllis from cutting him off. Photographers had pulled out their cameras and were madly taking pictures of Pete walking up the aisle. He pulled his baseball hat further down his forehead.

"Good question," Nikki answered. "May I ask you, Mr..."

"Daniels." Pete stopped and cocked his head.

"Mr. Daniels...do you believe that absence makes the heart grow fonder?"

Ha! "I don't know what to believe anymore." The room was silent. "I'm afraid, Ms. Crossland, that absence has recently made my heart break." Camera flashes went off on both sides of the aisle, as Pete continued a slow walk to the stage. "In my case, anyhow."

"Why broken?" She looked puzzled.

"The absence wasn't my choice."

Nikki smiled sympathetically, and leaned on the podium. "I've heard the heart mends remarkably well."

Pete was close enough to see that Nikki wore the Yoruba necklace. "My heart is making a miraculous recovery, right now, in fact." He took another few steps.

Nikki laughed out loud. "Where was this heart, these last weeks?"

"It was here." Pete put his hand on his chest. "It wasn't for lack of trying to get through." He held out his arms in surrender. The room was deafeningly silent as Pete approached the stage. "Will you mend my broken heart, Nikki?"

"You know I will." Nikki's smile lit up her face.

Pete jumped up onto the platform, removed his hat,

and took her in his arms.

"I love you, Pete. I didn't say that before, but I love you."

Even though he wanted to hug her tight, he was careful of her left shoulder and whispered into her hair. "I love you, Nikki, and I love your baby, and I'm so happy that you're both alive."

He pulled back to look into her eyes.

Tears filled Nikki's eyes. "I've been heartbroken, waiting for you," she admitted.

"I'm here, now. And not going away. Ever." He kissed her cheek tenderly. "I have a name for the boat."

She searched his face. "What is it?"

"Forever."

She closed her eyes and smiled sweetly. "I like the sound of that."

"I'm never letting you out of my sight again." With one finger under Nikki's chin, he tipped her head up to brush her lips with his, in only the hint of a kiss. It was a kiss to suggest what might come later. A kiss that the press couldn't see because Nikki Crossland had turned her back to them.

Nikki Crossland's Hot Crossed Buns

2 ¼-oz envelopes of dry active yeast
1/2 cup warm water (100-105 degrees)
1 cup warm milk
1/2 cup soft butter
1/2 cup sugar
1/2 tsp salt
3 large eggs
1 1/2 tsp vanilla extract
5 cups all-purpose flour
1 1/2 tsp ground cinnamon
1 cup raisins

Combine yeast and water in bowl, let stand 5 minutes. Add milk and next 5 ingredients. Beat at medium until blended. Combine flour and cinnamon, add to mix, beat 2 minutes. Stir in raisins. Place in greased bowl, cover with damp towel. Let rise for 2 hours. Punch down. Rise another 30 minutes.

On floured board, roll to 1/2 inch thick. Cut into two inch circles and let buns rise in rectangular pan for 45 minutes.

Bake at 350 for 20 minutes until browned. Cool and *glaze in the shape of a thick X.

*Glaze- 1 cup of powdered sugar, 1 1/2 T milk, 1/2 tsp vanilla, whisk together until smooth

When finished, package in a pretty basket and wander innocently next door to see if the handsome neighbor is hungry.

A word about the author...

Once a rock singer herself, Kim traded her microphone and sparkly costumes years ago, for a jean jacket and motherhood in the Seattle area. Kim lives overlooking a lake with her hubby, Roland, her two kids, Jack and Ila, and two extremely disobedient dogs where the Pacific Coast rainy days leave lots of time to daydream and plot books.

Thank you for purchasing
this publication of The Wild Rose Press, Inc.
For other wonderful stories of romance,
please visit our on-line bookstore at
www.thewildrosepress.com.

For questions or more information
contact us at
info@thewildrosepress.com.

The Wild Rose Press, Inc.
www.thewildrosepress.com

To visit with authors of
The Wild Rose Press, Inc.
join our yahoo loop at
http://groups.yahoo.com/group/thewildrosepress/